STORM
ROSE

ALSO BY CORINA BOMANN

The Moonlit Garden

STORM ROSE

CORINA BOMANN

Translated *by* Alison Layland

Text copyright © 2015 Corina Bomann and Ullstein Buchverlag GmbH
Translation copyright © 2016 Alison Layland

Previously published as *Die Stürmrose* by Ullstein Buchverlag GmbH in Germany in 2015. Translated from German by Alison Layland. First published in English by AmazonCrossing in 2016.

Published by AmazonCrossing, Seattle

www.apub.com

Amazon, the Amazon logo, and AmazonCrossing are trademarks of Amazon.com, Inc., or its affiliates.

ISBN-13: 9781503936010
ISBN-10: 1503936015

Cover design by M. S. Corley

Printed in the United States of America

Prologue

The woman had made herself comfortable in the battered old armchair by the window. A green head scarf covered her shorn hair, and her skinny body was almost swamped by a beige linen dress. Next to her, on a small table, was a cassette recorder. As she had not said anything for a while, she reached out a hand and switched off the softly humming machine.

I can hardly believe that a cassette recorder has become a relic from days gone by, she thought. In the old days, young people would have done anything to get hold of one—stood in line for hours, begged relatives in the West, bribed shopkeepers—battling against a shortage that was now impossible to imagine.

Now everyone had an MP3 player or a cell phone to play music. The shops were full of them. The woman was not enamored with this ever-more-rapidly developing technology—she preferred the more old-fashioned ways, especially when it related to something as important as this matter that had burned into her soul for years. These modern devices could also record speech, true, but how did you pass it on? Simply e-mail it? She thought that was horribly impersonal. In the old days, people would give their boyfriend or girlfriend a mixtape, carefully recorded from the radio, as a token of affection. Now they simply e-mailed a playlist. Everything had changed.

So she was all the more amazed that they had still been able to get her a cassette recorder. A friend had placed it on the table on one of his visits.

"What do you want with that?" he had asked.

"To leave behind something for posterity," she had replied with a smile, as her friend hadn't known the full truth of her situation.

As the years passed, her world had grown small; all that was left to her now was to wait. To wait for the right moment, the right day, for letters, for visits. It had taken an incredibly long time before she received that all-important letter. But it had come, and had triggered a chain of events that had now reached their climax.

She opened up the cassette deck and took the cassette out. In fact, what she had created there was also a kind of mixtape. The mixtape of a life. She hadn't told all, just the parts that mattered. A person had to have a secret or two to take to the grave with them.

She let her gaze roam over the table before coming to rest on the stack of papers that lay on the small chest of drawers. The notes had helped her get her thoughts in order, and she had composed a letter that now lay on the pile, addressed and stamped. She needed only to put it in the mail.

Then the waiting would begin again. She still had time. Not much, but with a little luck it would be enough to explain the things that had happened so long ago. Bring the truth out into the light. Finally put an end to something she had drawn out for far too long.

Part 1
Annabel

1

The first time I went to look around the house, I was captivated. Elderberry bushes and brambles lined the front yard, and climbing roses sent tendrils curling up toward the veranda and the decorative wooden gable.

Over the past three months, I had envisioned what it would be like to move in here, to go for walks along the beach, collecting shells with my daughter, free from the baggage of the recent catastrophic years and a past that I had suppressed out of fear.

Now the time had come. The lease was signed, and the owners were waiting for me. I was as excited as I had been on my first date.

"Mommy, are we there yet?" came a small voice from the backseat. Leonie, my little angel, had spent most of the journey asleep—we had set off at the crack of dawn. Now she stretched with a yawn.

"Yes, darling, we're here," I replied as I withdrew the ignition key. The Volvo's engine ticked gently beneath the hood. Although the car had more than fifteen years on it, the journey from Bremen to Binz had gone off without a hitch.

After my marriage had failed, I had bought the car mainly because it was reliable and had the capacity to carry a lot. Jan would have shaken his head. But I no longer cared about his opinion. I tried to leave that behind me, as I had left all the other material things behind in Bremen.

I got out and released the catch on Leonie's car seat.

"Look, this is our new house. Hasn't it got a lovely big yard to play in?"

Leonie's eyes widened in amazement, and she nodded.

Separated from the driveway by a white picket fence, the yard was a miniature paradise that would be the envy of any gardening magazine. There was a variety of native shrubs and borders planted in a way that looked almost haphazard. Paths wound between dense rosebushes, past a small herb garden.

I still couldn't grasp why the Balders wanted to leave this house and move south.

"Will Papa visit us here, too?"

Leonie's question jerked me abruptly from my gardening dreams. Some things were impossible to escape.

My daughter missed her father badly. Again and again she expressed her hope of a visit from him—and again and again it broke my heart to have to lie to her by promising he would come. But what else could I do? Tell her that although her father paid child support, he wasn't interested in seeing her?

The monthly payment into my account was the only sign of life from him since our divorce had been finalized in court. That was a year ago. Since then he had not once called to ask about Leonie. Not even on her birthday. He had set up the support payments, and to him that meant the matter was closed.

"He might visit us," I replied, suppressing my bitter feelings and hoping that Leonie would accept my smile. My daughter pushed past me and jumped out of the car.

I turned to see the landlord coming toward us.

August Balder was once the captain of a merchant vessel, but had been retired for ten years now. With his checked shirt worn over corduroy pants, he looked more like a gardener than a sailor.

Fortunately, the interior of the house was not particularly nautical either. I liked the simple style and was glad they were leaving the furniture. I had also lived in furnished accommodations in Bremen, after moving out of Jan's house, so it wasn't a problem. The things I had kept filled only a couple of moving boxes, which had been sent on ahead with a shipping company and which the Balders had kindly agreed to hold for me.

"Ah, here come the two lassies!" he called out as he opened the yard gate.

"Hello, Herr Balder," I called and waved. I took Leonie's hand and led her over to him.

"Did you have a good journey?"

Balder held out his hand for me to shake.

"Yes, it went very well," I replied. "Even the Rügen Causeway was free of traffic for once."

"You made good time." He looked at his watch. "The rush-hour traffic has been over for two hours. You must have set off in the middle of the night!"

"Not quite, but it was rather early in the morning." I had to admit that I was feeling a little woolly, and no wonder after almost six hours on the road, thanks to a traffic jam in Hamburg. It was eleven o'clock now, and I could easily have gone back to bed.

Herr Balder seemed to read my thoughts.

"Well, you can get some rest soon. My wife and I will be setting off for Hamburg in a bit. We're flying to Fuerteventura from there."

"How lovely. But won't you miss home?" However much I loved going on vacation, making a new life in the Canaries or some other islands in the tropics was something I couldn't begin to imagine.

"We'll see. One thing's for sure, with my rheumatism I certainly won't miss the cold. You needn't fear we'll be back to drive you out of your home. And who knows, perhaps you'll decide to buy it at some stage."

"Perhaps," I replied diplomatically. However lovely it was here, ownership always meant more responsibility, and right then my life seemed a bit too unstable for that. What if I came to realize that I didn't like it here after all? And in any case, a large mortgage was out of the question.

"You just take your time, Frau Hansen. We're in no hurry. But if we did sell it, we'd like it to be to you!"

"Thank you; I appreciate the thought."

Balder bent down to Leonie. "Well now, young lady. I don't believe we've met."

My daughter, who was chewing on a lock of her curly red hair, pressed herself more closely up against my leg without flinching from the man's gaze. A shy smile stole across her face. She clearly liked the old sea dog, but was reluctant to let him know.

"What's your name?" Balder asked.

"Leonie," she replied.

Balder laughed. "Leonie, is it? Did you know your name comes from 'lion'?"

My daughter's eyes opened wide, and she shook her head. She had never asked about the meaning of her name—there had always been plenty of other more interesting things to concern her.

By knowing about her name, he had won her over.

"I can tell you a thing or two about lions," he continued. "I've been to Africa and I saw some there."

"August, aren't you going to invite the girls in?" Lucia Balder looked at him reproachfully from the doorway. Her leg was still in a brace from when she fell down the small wooden steps that led from the property down to the beach. Not because the wood was rotten—she had merely tripped.

I had seen the steps myself and did think they were quite steep; it was possibly the only fault I could find with the house. I'd have to find a way of preventing Leonie from climbing down there alone.

"We're on our way!" Herr Balder called back.

As we entered the house, we were greeted by the smell of coffee, bread rolls, and cake. I hadn't anticipated this—I'd merely expected them to hand over the keys and go.

"Hello, Frau Balder." I shook hands with the lady of the house, as she still was. Her temporary disability had not held her back from her baking, which gave the kitchen a lovely homey feel. "How are you?"

"Getting better every day," she replied, indicating her leg. "I've got a walking cast now, so fortunately it won't affect our travel plans. It's hard to make plans, isn't it? You arrange everything so carefully and something always crops up to get in your way."

She was right there, and usually the thing that cropped up was so serious that it ruined the whole plan. I could have written a book about it.

"Well, you've always got me." August glanced at his wife as he served the coffee. "If need be I'd have carried you on and off the plane myself."

"I'm sure you would, but I prefer to stand on my own two feet. Fortunately, our doctor has an acquaintance on Fuerteventura who can take care of me until I can walk properly again. And the flight isn't a particularly long one. But enough of that." She turned to me. "You haven't introduced me to the young lady here. She's obviously your daughter; that's plain to see."

Leonie had a little of her father in her, but in general people noticed only her green eyes and red hair, both of which she'd inherited from me. She possibly had the shape of my nose, too, but I wasn't totally sure of that.

"This is Leonie," I said.

"What a lovely name," Frau Balder replied, reaching out a hand to my daughter. "And what a pretty girl. When she grows up I'm sure you'll have no trouble finding a nice young man for her."

"I'd rather leave that to her, as she's the one who'll have to live with him. I don't mind who it is as long as he makes her happy."

Leonie nuzzled her cheek up to my hand like a cat. Fortunately, she was too young to catch the edge that lay beneath the lighthearted banter about young men. My parents had liked Jan, and where had that led? Fair enough, they hadn't actually done any matchmaking for me, but they could have been a little more perceptive and critical.

"I'm sure any future husband will appreciate your sentiments," Herr Balder interjected. "But do sit down. You set off so early, and I'm sure you need a bite to eat."

Half an hour later, we had eaten our fill and the Balders were ready to go.

"I hope you don't mind us leaving a few of our books behind for you," Herr Balder said as he pressed the key into my hand. All the important details had been discussed—I knew how the heating worked, as well as where the shutoff valve and circuit breaker were.

"No, that's no problem at all," I replied.

"If there's anything you don't want, feel free to give it away," Frau Balder added. "Everything we need is ready and waiting for us in our new house."

She smiled as she spoke. I could understand how much she was looking forward to her new start.

We shook hands; the time had come. My heart was suddenly in my mouth. The last time I had experienced such joyful excitement was when the Balders accepted me as their tenant.

"And remember, whatever we dream about on the first night in our new house will come true," Frau Balder said playfully as she reached for her crutches.

"I thought that referred to a new bed," I replied.

"No, it works for new houses, too," she said with a wink. She turned and allowed her husband to help her into the car.

From the doorway I watched Herr Balder load the final suitcase into the trunk and get in. The engine sprang to life, and a moment later the Mercedes rolled away. The space beneath the carport was now home to my Volvo.

After the Balders left, peace and quiet settled on the house. The wind rustled in the trees, and sparrows hopped around the sunny courtyard.

Leonie was still lost in the pages of the lion book that Herr Balder had given her. I watched her, smiling, then walked through each of the rooms in turn.

The bedroom had the best view of the wild yard. A huge dog rose was full of buds about to bloom and fill the air with their sweet scent. A little farther beyond was a hedge of white burnet roses that lined a narrow path, which led to a small patio with pretty white yard furniture surrounded by a green labyrinth.

Turning back to the room, I saw that the mattress and bed frame appeared brand-new—a double bed, much too big for me. Back in Bremen I'd felt lost in my marriage bed from the time that Jan began to work "overtime." Overtime with his colleagues, overtime with women he met at some trade show or other. By the end I no longer remembered how it felt to share a bed with another person.

The bedroom looked out over woods that embraced the yard protectively, while blocking the view out over the water. The sea could be seen only from the attic.

Passing by the two other rooms, one of which I would have to alter a little for Leonie, I climbed the stairs to the attic.

The room had been made habitable and decorated but had never really been used for anything. Perhaps the Balders had kept it free in case their son ever needed to move in.

I stood in the middle of the room, which was divided into equal rectangles by bare wooden pillars, and in my mind's eye saw the office I intended to set up in there. In one corner there would also be a small "office" for Leonie whenever she wasn't at her nursery school. She liked it when I sat her down at a table and we pretended she had her own office. She'd sit there for hours—just like I did when I was working on an assignment—drawing horses and princesses.

I was particularly pleased that there was room for a full-size drawing board, something I had not had in my little office in Bremen.

In my imagination, I arranged the furniture in this huge space and saw myself holding a small opening party for my clients. Sure, the journey to Rügen would be quite a long way for some of them, but perhaps I could entice them with the prospect of the sea. I already had the perfect place for a sideboard, and over there, from where I could see out over the trees to the surf-capped waves, would be my desk . . .

Paradise, I thought once again. *It really is paradise here.* And I was sure that everything would be different from now on. Everything would be better.

2

"What do you think—where should I hang this poster?"

Leonie chewed on her index finger as she always did when she was thinking hard. At five years old she already had very firm ideas about how her room should look, so I left it to her to decide what should go where on her walls. Even if that meant it would take a while.

Leonie stared at one wall after the other. The furniture in the room wasn't particularly colorful, as the Balders had used it as a guest room. I would be able to cheer it up a bit with her princess sheets, her snuggly throw, and her soft toys—and of course with her posters, on which a succession of pink princesses, elves, and unicorns romped playfully. Anything else would have to be picked up from Binz's town center, which lay spread out below our house's elevated position.

"There!" my little princess finally decided, indicating the wall above the bed.

"Nice choice," I replied and hung it up.

I had just fixed the last strip of adhesive tape in place when my cell phone rang. I picked it up from the table and saw the number of a new client whom I'd begun to canvass while I was packing to move. My chances weren't particularly good, as my competitors included three large, well-regarded advertising agencies. Nevertheless, the call quickened my pulse, since I was sure he wouldn't have bothered calling to turn me down.

"Annabel Hansen."

"Hartmann from the Seaview," the caller announced, and it occurred to me that his name would be fitting for an aristocrat. But of course, Joachim Hartmann wasn't nobility.

"Hello, Herr Hartmann, it's good to hear from you," I replied, then fell into an expectant silence. *Come on,* my inner voice cried out, *let the cat out of the bag!*

"Hello, Frau Hansen. Have you arrived safely in Binz?"

"Yes, thank you. We've been unpacking since this morning."

I glanced over at Leonie, who was busy arranging her little figurines on the windowsill.

"I'm glad to hear it. Would you possibly have time to come by tomorrow? We'd like to talk to you about the new project."

"Does that mean you're accepting my quote?"

I was astonished. It took a great effort not to shout out for joy. My first assignment in my new house! I was sure it was going to bring me luck.

"Yes, we're giving you the job—of all the proposals we received, we liked yours the best. I'd like to discuss a few details with you tomorrow before I go away. That would give you enough time for the campaign."

"Tomorrow suits me fine," I replied quickly, although I had no idea where I was going to leave Leonie. The nursery school only had a place free starting Monday, and tomorrow was Friday. Perhaps she wouldn't mind a little trip to town.

"Would you have anything against me bringing my daughter along? She can't go to nursery school until Monday."

"No problem," Hartmann replied. "Would eleven o'clock be OK?"

"Yes, excellent!"

I smiled to myself. The new house really did seem to be bringing me luck.

I hung up feeling like I was floating on a cloud. I had set my heart on being given the advertising campaign contract for the Seaview Hotel in Sassnitz. It wasn't only that Joachim Hartmann paid well, but the location of the hotel was unique. It occupied a magnificent position above the harbor of Sassnitz, a prime location for watching the ships come and go. There was even said to be a submarine there. I wasn't sure whether Leonie would be interested in it, but I usually found it easy to excite her enthusiasm.

Joachim Hartmann had built up his own hotel chain over the years, and the Seaview was known to be his favorite. He had employed a famous interior designer to redecorate the rooms—all that was needed now was a suitable advertising campaign to let visitors know that a stay in the hotel would be like no other in the area.

"Mommy, Mommy!" came a sudden excited cry from the kitchen. During the telephone conversation, I hadn't noticed Leonie slip out of the room.

I jumped in alarm, as I always did when she called to me from somewhere she hadn't been last time I looked. I knew I was being silly, but I was always afraid that something could have happened to her.

My heart thumping, I dashed into the kitchen.

Leonie had hitched up the flowery skirt of her dress and was pointing at a cat that had ventured through the open door. The gray-striped animal took fright as I watched and it shrank back, all the while staring at me with yellow-green eyes.

Had the Balders left their pet behind?

"Look at the kitty!" Leonie cried out in delight. "Can we keep her?"

The words were hardly out of her mouth when the cat took its opportunity to escape, its sleek body vanishing at lightning speed out through the door.

"Kitty!" Leonie called and ran after it without a moment's hesitation.

"Leonie!" I called, dashing out after my daughter.

As we came out into the courtyard, the cat was of course nowhere to be seen.

"Where's she gone?" Leonie asked, searching the bushes with her eyes.

"She's bound to appear again sometime," I said. Although I had not grown up in the countryside, I knew that cats kept turning up in certain places—especially when they had no reason to be there. "Come on, let's go back in and finish your room. Maybe she'll come back then."

***

Although the day had gone perfectly, I was unable to get to sleep. As I listened to the wind that had come up during the evening and was now buffeting the trees, I couldn't help thinking what Frau Balder had said before she left, that whatever you dreamed on the first night would come true.

I wasn't superstitious, and if it were true, I would have been a streetcar driver by now, since that was what I'd dreamed about when Jan and I moved into our first apartment together.

Still, I was worried that something negative could slip into my dreams. Something I didn't want to come true. I wanted nothing to take away my hopes for a new start.

My eyelids grew as heavy as lead, and it was impossible to hold out against my fears any longer. I found myself back in a kitchen. A very old-fashioned kitchen, rather a small one. An apartment building in the eighties, as I saw from a glance at the calendar on the wall: September 17, 1985. Tea towels were hanging on a clothesline. The ones at the back, which were already dry, looked as stiff as cardboard. Something was clattering in the kitchen, and sounds from a TV drifted through from the living room. I heard a nasal male voice reading the news.

I was sitting at a table. The blue polka-dot tablecloth was a little frayed at the corners, the pattern was broken in places by small cuts.

Every so often the bread knife in my mother's hand would slip from the cutting board, so that every few months we had to go to the store to look for a new oilcloth. They could be difficult to find, especially when the shops had been empty of goods for some time and even the tablecloths with hideous patterns had already been sold.

I suddenly became aware that I was about to paint a picture. There was a paint box in front of me, with most of the colors almost used up. The water I used to clean the black bristles of my worn-out paintbrush was a strange muddy color—no wonder, as I had used nearly all the colors. I always did that when I was painting—I made sure that my pictures contained every color.

Yes, *I*. This was me almost thirty years ago. A girl with red hair and freckles, not much older than my daughter was now.

I was so absorbed in my painting that I didn't notice my mother coming in through the kitchen door.

"Bella, time to finish your painting. It's nearly time for your bed-time cartoon."

"Just a little more," I begged, without looking up from my picture.

"You can finish tomorrow," my mother said and began to put away my painting things.

I looked longingly at the paint box and the water glass, then picked up my picture.

"You'd be better off leaving it there. The paint's not dry yet," my mother said, but I didn't want to let go of it. It was my masterpiece, the best I had ever painted—I was convinced of it. Mom finally gave in and let me take it with me into the living room, where she maneuvered me into an armchair covered in rough fabric.

Sometimes, when we were playing, it was my throne, even if the armrest on the left was rather scratched.

I snuggled up in the armchair with my picture and felt my body grow heavy. My eyes fell shut. There was going to be a Fuchs and Elster story on the Sandman program, but I couldn't stay awake. The

Sandman theme began, and at that very moment my eyes went fuzzy. Then everything went dark.

When I woke again, a blue light was flashing in my eyes. Everything was dark except for that light. It conjured up regular second-long flashes of people and vehicles from the darkness. I heard voices, but they came from far off. I couldn't grasp what was happening, so I closed my eyes and hoped I'd soon go back to sleep so I could dream something else. Something nice . . . Because I was convinced that the vehicles and the blue light were only part of a dream—or the flashing police lights from the TV crime series Mom sometimes liked to watch . . .

At that moment, I surfaced. My sweat-soaked nightgown clung to my body, and my heart was racing. I heard the murmuring of the wind and the rustling of the trees. In the distance the sea surged against the shore. Although I knew where I was, and that what I had seen was far back in the past, it took me a while to shake off the images.

The dream was one I knew well. Years had gone by since I'd last experienced it, but now it was back and brought with it the same sense of panic I always felt when it descended on me.

When I was a child, I dreamed of that evening almost all the time— that last evening with my mother. I couldn't remember much about it, but those last moments together with her were burned into my mind, together with the date. All attempts from outside to erase what had happened had failed. From time to time it resurfaced and reminded me that behind the facade of adult Annabel, who had everything under control, there was a little Annabel who didn't know why she'd been abandoned by her mother. Little Annabel, who constantly had it drummed into her that she'd been abandoned by her mother, until eventually she believed it.

And what did the adult Annabel think about it? I had long since stopped thinking about whether my mother had really left me or whether it was all a lie peddled by the Party officials.

But why had I not thought about it since the Iron Curtain came down? And why was I doing so now?

I stared at the ceiling, my heart beating wildly. The last time my heart had raced like this was a while ago, too. A friend had advised me that when something like this happened, I should open the windows and throw off the bedclothes. But I needed more than that.

My heart still thumping, I tiptoed across the landing. It was stupid, but at that moment I knew I would be able to sleep only if I found it. The picture.

Over the years it had always traveled with me, tucked away in a folder. No one other than me knew about it. Wherever I went, I always had it with me, hidden away. And I'd never found the courage to throw it away. It was the only testimony to my old life.

I entered the living room and with uncanny certainty found the box in which I'd stowed it. I couldn't have said which box held my red dress or the alarm clock with the cat's ears—but I knew exactly where I'd put the picture. Weak at the knees and with shaking hands, I pulled out the box and opened it.

First I had to rummage through a lot of other things—scarves, little bags of bobby pins, a box of old stamps I'd used to decorate greeting cards. At the bottom were a few old samples of my work. And then I found it.

The folder that I kept the picture in was as old as I was. I knew that because someone had written the date of my birth on the faded cardboard. I had no idea what the original purpose of the folder had been, but in the appropriate space was the name *Silvia Thalheim*. It had been rubbed out, or at least someone had tried to erase it. The black of the pencil lines was gone, but the impression remained. It would probably still be there until the day the folder was thrown away.

A shudder ran down my spine as I pushed back the elastic cords from the corners of the folder and opened it. All it contained was this one picture. A faded image of a girl in front of a windmill. The girl was standing in a meadow full of flowers, holding a balloon in her hand. Her body was a simple, red-painted triangle, and her hair was as yellow as the oversized sun hovering over the sails of the windmill. I had painted this picture on the evening before everything changed. I ran trembling fingers over the windmill, but snatched my hand away as a flake of paint peeled away from the paper.

This was the last picture I had painted in our kitchen, the last picture my mother had seen before she vanished from my life, leaving a deep rift inside me.

"Mommy!" I heard a voice calling from the landing. "Mommy, where are you?"

I snapped into the here and now. Leonie was awake. I quickly stuffed the drawing back into the box and stood.

"I'm here, darling," I called as I left the room. My daughter looked at me wide-eyed.

"What were you doing there?" she asked, hugging her pink cuddly rabbit tight.

"I couldn't sleep, so I was looking through the things in that box."

"What were you looking for?" Although she was only five, I was never able to fool her; she always saw right through me.

"Nothing in particular," I replied, gathering her up into my arms. "I just wanted to make sure I hadn't forgotten anything."

I hated lying to my daughter, but I didn't want to tell her anything about the picture. Not yet, at least. The time would come, and yet . . . What should I tell her? What had happened back then had vanished into mist. I had suppressed it so successfully that I no longer knew myself exactly what had happened. And I was on my guard against stirring it up.

"Do you want to come into my bed?" I asked Leonie, hoping to distract her from her questions.

"Oh yes!" she cried in delight.

My plan worked. I carried her to the bed that was far too big for me, with its fresh sheets, and sang her a lullaby. And I held her in my arms as her eyes fell closed and her breathing became steady and deep.

3

Having Leonie with me comforted me a little. Her warmth gave me security and a future and a counterbalance to the things that sometimes caught up with me in the night.

Yet I couldn't get back to sleep. The dream images persisted stubbornly in my mind. I usually managed to suppress them quickly and make a smooth transition to the business of the day, but this time things were different. I listened to the wind, my daughter's breathing, the beating of my heart. The voices of the past whispered to me insistently.

If everything had happened differently back then, would I be here? If my mother had stayed, would I still be living in Leipzig? Would I perhaps have trodden a completely different path from the one I had?

And what if she had suddenly returned for me? Would I have been able to—or wanted to—leave the Hansens?

I was happy with my lot—but nevertheless I sometimes felt a nagging doubt and experienced the old inner conflict. Perhaps it could all have turned out much better if there had not been that rift in my life. I breathed deeply and tried to bring the chaos to order, to concentrate on the here and now.

I liked to think of the new start ahead of me; I liked this house. And I loved my daughter more than anything. What had happened with my mother was a long time ago, I told myself, eager to concentrate on the mountain of wishes and desires that I had set aside in the past, especially during the previous year.

I wanted to have a close relationship with a man again—sexually, yes, but not only that. I wanted a partner to take me by the hand, to comfort me when things went wrong, to share in my joy when things went well, and to help me whenever I felt out of my depth.

But at that moment, the certainty that I couldn't simply shake everything off nagged at me more than ever before. I had to concede that I lacked the courage to come to grips with what had happened on September 17, 1985. There had been many attempts to explain; people had tried to influence me in various ways until I no longer knew the difference between right and wrong. I would have been able to put it all behind me a long time ago, had I been able to find out what actually happened. But the fear and disappointment lurked deep in my bones. Far too deep, even now.

I brooded for a long time until I became aware of a sound. The sound of the morning sea. I heard its murmur like the longing calls of a lover. It warmed my heart to see the sun rise over the water, not least because it was something I'd rarely had the opportunity to watch.

When we were on vacation, Jan's presence had often prevented me from doing so, or we had slept late, so late that when we rose the beach was already full of people. And in Hamburg, when I had driven early to school, the sunrise over the Alster hadn't interested me.

But now I was overcome by an irrepressible urge to see the sea in the early morning light. I looked at Leonie, who had snuggled up beside me like a sleepy kitten. Her fingers twitched a little, as if she were grasping at something in a dream. I carefully eased her away from me and gently tucked the covers around her. I'd be back by the time she woke.

Once out of bed, I tied my hair back and slipped into my tracksuit. It had been a while since I'd gone jogging, but the thought of running along the beach here, feeling the wind in my hair and lungs, seemed wonderful to me now.

Before slipping out of the bedroom, I stole a final glance at Leonie. She stirred and snuggled down deeper into the blankets, apparently unaware of my absence. I used to worry whenever I left her alone in the bedroom, but now I knew better. If Leonie awoke and I wasn't there, she'd know I was somewhere in the house. I'd never leave her. The very thought of it was enough to break my heart, and I hoped she knew it.

As I stepped out of the front door, I was greeted by the dawn chorus, with the soft accompaniment of the sea. There was still a dark blue hint of night, but the morning light spread over the water from the east, heralding the new day.

The air was still cool and carried the pleasant smell of seaweed. This was such a departure from waking up to traffic noise from the streets or the clattering of the garbage collectors who didn't care that people might have been working late and had no reason to be jumping out of bed at six in the morning.

I stood for several minutes on the driveway and looked around, scarcely able to believe that we were here at last. *My paradise.* That was exactly what it would become, even though the shadows of the past—and the dreams they lingered in—still would not leave me alone.

I finally tore myself away from the view of the trees and made my way through the yard. Dew soaked my ankles and drove from my bones the heaviness that I always felt when I hadn't had enough sleep in the night.

I walked past the roses, their blooms still half-closed and glittering with dewdrops. I couldn't help thinking of bygone days and my parents' yard—I called them "my parents" because, after all, ever since that fateful night they had been the only ones there for me.

Back then I had read a fairy tale about a princess who wanted a crown made from dewdrops. I knew that was impossible, but for a while I was obsessed with having a yard where the dew glittered like diamonds. Whenever we were in the cottage on the edge of the city, I would water a section of the yard and wait for the evening sun to sink to the right place. Then I would sit in the wet grass and watch the droplets begin to glisten. They would do that here, too, and as soon as I could, I'd show Leonie my palace of dewdrops.

I left the abundant, sweet-scented roses behind and headed for the little gate, nestled among the bushes, that led to the beach. I had always been rather cautious of steps, and so I made my way slowly and carefully downward. The thick foliage eventually closed in over me, bringing the night back for a moment. But then the rocky beach lay spread out before me, greeting me with a rosy dawn glow behind the chalk rocks.

Moved by the view, I paused for a moment and looked out over the water, the waves breaking onto the beach in a rhythmic song.

Apart from a few seagulls swimming lazily on the water, I was completely alone. The rocky beach stretched away to my right, while to my left I could make out the town with its beach bars, hotels, and guesthouses along the boardwalk. The lights along the pier, where the tour boats were moored, grew gradually fainter. It wouldn't be long before the breaking dawn sent them to their daily rest.

Although the beach boardwalk looked very enticing, I chose the shingle beach. I began jogging slowly, knowing I was unfit, which my lungs confirmed after just a few minutes. But before long it began to feel better, and I found my rhythm.

At first I still had sand beneath my feet, but the farther I ran, the rockier the ground became, until I could see large rocks sticking up through the sand before me. Some of them were half-submerged in the water and sported thick growths of seaweed, and many were thickly encrusted with salt and sand at their bases.

I paused briefly, then wove my way between them for a while, before sitting down on a rock and looking out to sea. The wind dried the beads of sweat on my brow. In the distance, enshrouded in mist, a freight ship made its way toward Sassnitz, its white superstructure gleaming in the sun.

There had been times when I would have yearned to board a boat and sail far away from it all, escape from all my cares. But even though some of my cares still haunted me, I didn't feel such a yearning that morning.

I turned aside and noticed something on the rocks. At first I thought someone had lost a pair of pink swimming trunks. As I climbed down from the rock and moved closer, I saw that it was a bunch of pink wild roses. The flowers were still fairly fresh—they couldn't have been here for long.

Who had placed them there? And why? Was someone setting the scene for a romantic marriage proposal? This thought gave me a pang, but only a slight one. A few months ago the very idea would have brought me to tears.

After I found out that my husband hadn't really been my husband for quite some time, my world had collapsed. I couldn't bear to see other people's happiness. Wherever I went with Leonie, I couldn't escape the sight of couples in love. I envied others their happiness and hated myself for it.

I looked at the roses for a while and touched them carefully. The leaves were cool and soft as silk, and they gave off an enchantingly sweet scent. These were the same kind of wild rose that I had in my yard. They probably grew in profusion all around.

Should I wait to see if anyone came? No, I still didn't want to look on the happiness of another couple. It was their life, and I should concentrate on my own.

4

Sassnitz was bustling with activity. An invasion of motor homes and trailers snaked through the old town. As I searched for the turn that led to the Seaview Hotel, I encountered at least fifteen of them—the camping season was clearly under way.

After getting well and truly lost, I stopped in a no-waiting zone to search for directions on my cell phone. It wasn't very professional, but I hadn't considered the possibility that Sassnitz would have secret routes that confounded even a GPS.

"Are we there yet?" Leonie asked. She was restless. In truth, I was, too, because it was now ten to eleven and time was running out. I had to find the hotel.

"Not yet, darling—soon," I replied absently.

After another tour around the block, I finally saw the entrance to the small street and turned off. The rest was child's play. At the end of the steep, rather narrow street, I saw it.

Magnificent though it had looked on the Internet, in reality it was truly imposing. I parked my car in the only vacant space in the visitors' lot and got out. Holding Leonie by the hand, I strode along the paved path to the entrance, where a man in red livery was standing. He gave us a friendly greeting and held open the large glass door, with "Hotel Seaview" etched in gold on the glass panels.

It wasn't only the doorman who gave me the feeling of having been whisked back to the nineteenth century. The interior of the hotel's foyer was in the Art Nouveau style. Solid, cozy-looking leather armchairs invited guests to sit awhile, and the reception desk appeared not to have changed since the hotel was built. The wood, inlaid with beautiful marquetry, had been painstakingly restored. Even the key rack was original.

"What can I do for you?" the woman at the reception desk asked. Her suit was also red, but in no way old-fashioned.

"I have an appointment with Herr Hartmann at eleven." I looked at the antique grandfather clock behind the reception desk. Three minutes past. Damn!

"One moment; I'll call him," the woman said with a smile as she reached for her telephone.

As she called her boss, I looked at Leonie. She was entranced by the sight of the old furniture and the chandelier that hung above our heads like a glittering, oversize bunch of grapes.

"Can we have one of those?" she asked, unable to take her eyes away.

"No, no, darling. I'm afraid our house is too small."

"Can't you get smaller ones?" she insisted. Before I could reply, the receptionist turned back to me.

"Herr Hartmann's waiting for you in his office on the second floor. Just take the elevator and then follow the corridor to the end."

I thanked her and led Leonie to the elevator. An elderly couple was just getting out. The woman had a pale pink tint to her hair, and she beamed at the sight of Leonie.

"What a lovely little girl!" she cried in delight. I had no time to lose in polite small talk, but thanked her with a friendly smile and disappeared into the elevator.

I glanced nervously in the ornate, gilt-framed mirror. I always felt like a stranger in my blue suit, on my way to meet a client.

But it wasn't a bad feeling—I was showing the world that I wasn't some failed wife who didn't know where to pick up the pieces of her life. I was a businesswoman who knew just what she was doing—one who could play the part well, even if it was sometimes only a front.

The door opened with a quiet ping, and cool air flowed against my face. Either the air-conditioning was turned up a little high or there was a draft here. But I was sure we'd make it to the end of the corridor without catching a cold.

I knocked, and a woman's voice told me to enter.

The woman behind the desk was wearing a pink blouse over a black skirt, and her dark hair was tied back neatly. She gave us a questioning look.

"Good morning. I'm Annabel Hansen."

"The advertising expert," she said before I could continue, a businesslike smile on her face. "Could you please wait a moment?"

The secretary vanished through an ancient-looking double door, leaving it ajar. I stroked Leonie's hair and glanced outside. What a wonderful view of the harbor!

"Mommy, when can we go and explore the town?" asked Leonie, for whom the view was of little interest.

"Later," I promised. "I have to talk to the hotel's owner now, then we can go have an ice cream."

Leonie's eyes lit up. She loved ice cream more than anything else, and it was the best way to curb her impatience.

"Here you are." I got out a picture book with an illustration of a mermaid whose scales glittered green and blue. "Look what the little mermaid's up to."

Leonie smiled at me mischievously. "But the story always turns out the same."

She was five years old, and I could no longer lead her to believe that the story in a book would turn out differently.

"Well, maybe it does. But perhaps the pictures will make you think of a new story. Just because you've finished a book doesn't mean the story has to come to an end."

"An intriguing thought," a man's voice behind me said.

I started. I hadn't heard him come in. As I turned, I saw a tall blond man in his early fifties. His face was narrow and striking, and his slim body was clothed in a dark blue pin-striped suit. The color of his tie matched the handkerchief in his breast pocket perfectly, setting off sparkling blue eyes.

"Joachim Hartmann," he said, reaching out a hand to shake mine. His fingernails were perfectly manicured. I felt almost embarrassed to offer him my hand because it had been a long time since I'd seen the inside of a nail salon, and my nail polish bottles contained nothing but solidified residues.

"Annabel Hansen." I straightened my back and returned his handshake firmly and self-confidently. He probably didn't even notice my short nails. In any case, I was here to work with him, not to impress him with my appearance. "I'm very pleased to meet you, Herr Hartmann."

"The pleasure's all mine." His voice sounded richer than it had on the phone. "I take it this is your daughter?"

"Yes, this is Leonie."

As I spoke her name, a brief smile flashed across her face. Until that moment her eyes had been fixed on the man in front of us. Perhaps she'd make a good detective one day; in any case, she was a keen observer of people. And she knew in a flash who she liked and who she didn't. I could tell from the way she gnawed at her index finger that she was a little skeptical about Hartmann.

"Hello, Leonie," he said, offering her his hand. He seemed not to mind that her right hand was wet with saliva where she'd been nibbling on her finger. Leonie hesitated a moment, but as I'd taught her to shake people's hands when they offered, she placed hers in his.

"Hello," she said shyly.

"A very polite young lady," Hartmann said, giving me a bright smile. "And she looks every bit her mommy's girl."

It would have served no purpose—and been totally out of place—to tell him how much she took after her father. I always kept my professional and private lives strictly separate; it was only when I had to take Leonie with me to a business appointment because the nursery school was closed or the babysitter wasn't free that the two halves of my life coincided briefly.

"Now, please come into my office. You're welcome to bring your daughter in. There's a little table at the side for her."

The table wasn't designed for a child, but fortunately Leonie was big enough to sit at it.

"Here are some crayons for you," I said, getting them out of my purse, which served as a survival bag for any occasion. It contained a book for me, in case I had to wait anywhere, and for Leonie, a set of crayons, a coloring book, and a little sketchbook in case she lost interest in coloring the princesses' clothes. "You sit here quietly. It won't take long."

Leonie nodded obediently before settling down to her task.

Now I had the chance to admire the decor and furniture of Hartmann's office. It was surprisingly modern, in contrast to the lovingly restored antique stucco ceilings. The location of the heavy desk had been well chosen. From here, Joachim Hartmann was not only able to command the whole room and, when the door was open, the anteroom, but if ever he grew tired or bored of his work, he could also look out at the view from the window.

"Please take a seat," he said. I was surprised that he didn't indicate the chair in front of the desk, but the leather chairs arranged by the window. "Stefanie's just bringing us coffee."

The secretary appeared shortly after we'd settled down in the comfortable armchairs. And it was not any old coffee, but a latte macchiato as good as any that a professional barista could have served.

Hold it right there, I told myself. *This hotel's bound to have a barista; the secretary's hardly likely to have made the coffee herself.*

She closed the door discreetly behind her and left us to our negotiations.

"Now, as I said on the phone," Hartmann began as he smudged the cocoa leaf design on his milk foam with a long spoon, "of all the campaigns submitted to us, I liked yours the best. I can only hope that you never enter the hotel trade, at least not around here, or you'll be the ruin of me."

He laughed—a little forced, as he presumably knew I'd never be opening a hotel. It was true that I'd thought about a café, but to date my advertising agency work had kept me from it.

"Don't worry, my profession is advertising. And I hope I'm good at it."

"You're perfect."

Hartmann looked at me. It was not the look of someone who had just awarded a contract, but someone who wanted to get to know the other person better. I found it quite bewildering. Since Jan, it was rare that a man had looked at me in that way. And I had never responded to such a look in the expected manner. That was no different now, although Hartmann was extremely attractive. But he was probably only seeking confirmation of his own desirability— surely someone like him wasn't interested in a divorced woman with a daughter.

I switched to full-on professional mode and began to reiterate my ideas to him before providing him with specific examples of possible advertising campaigns. He listened to me attentively, and that penetrating look gradually faded.

As I spoke, I kept glancing over at Leonie out of the corner of my eye, but she was immersed in coloring something or other with a bright pink crayon.

When I'd finished my descriptions, Hartmann smiled.

"The best choice I could have made," he said again, and pressed my hand in a sign of affirmation.

"What are you doing this weekend?" he asked me.

I almost choked on the remains of my coffee. In my description of myself I had stated that I was divorced, but why did that lead him to assume I was interested in him?

Nevertheless, I had to take care, since until the contract was signed, he could withdraw his approval at any time. Was he that kind of man? Had he perhaps only chosen me because he believed he could involve me in an affair?

I smiled to conceal my uncertainty and replied, "My parents are coming to visit this weekend. They want to have a look at our new house."

It was a whopping lie, but better that than getting involved in something I had no interest in.

"Oh," he said. He'd clearly taken it for granted that I wouldn't have anything planned. I gave him a searching look. Would this affect my work? If so, it would be better if he reconsidered his position. I might be young and divorced, but that didn't mean I wanted to get involved with my clients. My expression must have betrayed my thoughts, as he looked a little embarrassed.

"OK, well, another time maybe," he said as if to himself.

"Thank you very much for the coffee and the instructions. You won't regret awarding me the contract," I said quickly, ignoring his remark. There wasn't going to be "another time." If the years spent with Jan had taught me anything, it was that it was wise not to get involved with successful, easily bored businessmen.

As I turned to go, I looked once more through the window at the marvelous view over the harbor. A ship slid lazily by; fishing boats swayed on the water. The submarine lay at the dock like a big black cigar.

And then I saw it. For a moment I stood, transfixed. All of a sudden I heard a voice in the back of my mind, whispering that I had to get closer to it. I had to see it.

"Are you all right?" Joachim Hartmann asked, following my gaze and noticing me tense up.

"Yes, of course," I replied quickly as I busied myself gathering up Leonie's crayons. "Something just occurred to me."

I smiled and took my leave.

"Where are we going now, Mommy?" Leonie asked. She was really a bit too heavy by now to be carried, but in order to make a quicker exit, I had swiftly gathered her up and was now hurrying down the steep street to the harbor. A few cars drove past us, some of them with their engines protesting loudly. There was no sidewalk where we could take refuge, so I kept as tightly as I could to the right-hand side.

Once at the harbor I set Leonie down. Only then did I realize that I hadn't answered my daughter's question.

"I just want to have a little look around the harbor," I said, taking her hand firmly in mine.

"Are we going to the submarine?" she asked, looking at the black steel giant hulking out of the water. We had talked about it on our way into town.

"No, to another boat. You'll see!"

The harbor was bustling with fishing boats. Some of their crews were unloading crates of fish, while others were checking the equipment. A man on a tour boat was sweeping the top deck, while its nearby sister ship was preparing to let on board the rather sparse group of tourists who were waiting on the jetty.

Between them was moored the boat that had caught my eye from Hartmann's office. As I approached I could think of nothing but how perfect it had looked. I knew that anyone else would have thought me mad, including the sailors who watched me leading my daughter over the wooden landing stage to its mooring.

My "dream boat" was an ancient fishing cutter that looked as though it hadn't caught anything for years. Someone had removed most of the fishing tackle and erected a spacious passenger cabin to the fore of the wheelhouse.

The blue paint of the hull, which was slender for a fishing cutter, was beginning to flake, as was the white of the superstructure. Patches of rust showed here and there, but didn't detract at all from the striking impression of the vessel. As far as I could make out, the rigging was still intact, and the floor also looked sound.

The prow was emblazoned with the weathered name: *Storm Rose.*

I was hypnotized.

The boat had clearly seen better days, but despite the patches of rust and other signs of decay, I was fascinated. Who in the world would convert a fishing cutter to a passenger craft? No home port was shown on the prow, so I looked at the stern, where I found that the original port had been painted over. In its place read "Timmendorfer Strand." I narrowed my eyes and thought I could make out the traces of another name beneath it.

"What are you staring at, Mommy? You look funny."

"I want to find out where this boat comes from," I replied, gripping her hand tighter. I didn't want her to slip away from me.

"Doesn't it say?" my daughter asked. She couldn't read yet, but I had taught her a few letters, including her own name, which she always added in capital letters to her drawings.

"Yes, it's there, but I think it's painted over another name."

I made out an *H* and an *A*. The previous name was short, so it could only mean that the *Storm Rose*'s former home port was Hamburg.

Cogs immediately started to turn in my head. Would there be some documents about the boat in Hamburg? Could I find out why it had been sold? Why it had been converted?

Why did I want to know? I couldn't explain, but the urge was insistent. It was probably because I'd grown up in a family of shipbuilders.

"Can I help you?" I heard a man's voice behind me. It was similar to Joachim Hartmann's, and for a moment I thought he must have watched me from the window and come after me. But as I turned, I found myself looking into the face of a bearded man in a woolen cap and workman's overalls. His bright eyes were regarding me quizzically.

"Um . . . I was just looking at this boat. It's . . . it's quite old."

The man nodded. "Yes, it is. But I'm afraid you can't go on."

Had I looked as though I was about to step aboard? Probably, as I'd been looking at it so intently my eyes had practically peeled the paint away.

"No, I was only looking . . ." I gnawed my lip. Why not ask? It looked like the man worked here, so maybe he knew something.

"Do you have any idea who the boat belongs to? It looks rather the worse for wear . . ."

He shrugged. "No idea. But I've heard it's for sale. It probably belongs to some guy from the West."

After more than twenty years of German unification, "from the West" sounded rather strange, at least to my ears. But it seemed that for some people the border still existed in some form.

I merely nodded in reply. If the boat was to be sold, it would have to be renovated, or else it would be practically unsellable.

"Mind your little girl doesn't get too close to the edge," said the man.

"Don't worry," I replied, instinctively drawing Leonie a little closer. "We'll be leaving soon, anyway."

Since the man was still regarding me intently, I asked him one last question before we left.

"Do you know where I can find out who's selling the cutter?"

"There's bound to be something on the Internet. Just go to the harbor website; there's a classified ads page."

I thanked him and walked off down the dock with Leonie. I realized we were being watched.

A man in a brown peacoat was sitting on one of the artificial rock walls that encircled and sheltered the harbor. I couldn't make out his features clearly from afar, but he had designer stubble, and his dark brown curly hair was sticking out at all angles as though he had just gotten out of bed.

He noticed me looking at him and turned away, as though he had an all-consuming interest in the submarine on the other side of the harbor. *Caught you, my friend,* I thought to myself with a smile. Could he be the owner, keeping an eye on his boat? I couldn't tell from that distance. But I had no desire to approach him and ask him why he was so interested in us, so I kept walking.

There's bound to be something on the Internet. The harbor worker's words went around and around in my mind.

I'd look it up as soon as we got home.

I wandered around the town with Leonie, and we had the promised ice cream in a café called the Lighthouse. Still, I couldn't get the boat out of my mind.

The cutter was for sale. It got me dreaming. What could you do with a boat like that? A floating café, perhaps?

And oh, what stories the details I'd noticed on the boat must conceal! Given its age, it must have seen so many rough sailors—and even rougher seas.

If I'd guessed its age correctly, it must have been around in the Second World War. A story like that would certainly make good publicity!

5

Back at the house that evening, Leonie's spirits plummeted. It had been happening occasionally for about a year, and worried me every time. Normally my little angel was cheerful and carefree, but suddenly a cloud would fall over her spirit and cause her to sit listlessly in a corner, staring into space.

We had been spared this for two months, as Leonie had been as excited as I was about the new house. Perhaps she had even hoped the move would bring her father back to live with us.

Leonie's mood swings had been appearing since the day I had to tell her that her daddy no longer wanted to live with us. She hadn't cried, but withdrew into her own world. Sometimes these phases lasted so long that I feared she would sink into depression. I had read somewhere that this could happen even to very young children, although it was rare.

The pediatrician said that the separation from my husband had traumatized her. It had added considerably to my anger toward Jan. His selfishness was traumatizing our child—the worst possible thing he could do. It incensed me all the more since I knew how it felt when a parent suddenly vanished. Leonie's situation was different—unlike me, she still had her mother, but as she was used to being with both her parents, she must have been just as hurt as I was when I lost my birth mother. I had never known my birth father; Elfie, who eventually just became my mother, had just said that he died before I was born. What you never have, you never really miss, although as a child I'd sometimes wondered if it might all have turned out differently if he'd been there.

Leonie, on the other hand, knew her father and missed him. Sometimes I wished she would realize how mean her father's behavior had been and that he didn't deserve the love she felt for him. But she did love him and dreamed of the day when we would get back together and everything would be how it used to be. She couldn't know that Jan's love for me had already ceased to exist by the time she was born.

"What's the matter, sweetie?" I asked, but she only stared at the doll in her hand, whose tiara had slipped down over its tousled hair.

"Are you sad?" I asked, although I knew perfectly well what was wrong.

"Shall I look for the kitty-cat? Perhaps we can entice her in with some milk?"

It went against the grain to get involved with a strange cat, but I was sure it wouldn't appear in any case.

Leonie shook her head. I sighed deeply. It was no good ignoring the obvious. I had no idea what parental counselors would advise in these circumstances, but it seemed to be the best thing for me to talk to her. Maybe it was the only way to bring her out from behind her wall.

"You're missing Daddy, aren't you?"

Leonie nodded. I drew her into my arms and was relieved when she let me. She snuggled up to me, and I buried my face in her hair.

"I know you miss him very much," I heard myself saying, my voice sounding like my adoptive mother's shortly after I'd been taken to the Hansens. *I know you miss her,* she'd said, *but things are as they are, and you'll have a good life with us.*

Leonie knew she had a good life with me, and after all, I was her mother. There was only one remedy for her sadness—her father's attention. But how could I get that?

For a while I weighed the words in my head, unable to speak them out loud. It broke my heart to see Leonie so sad, but I couldn't bring myself to make a promise I couldn't keep—one I didn't want to keep.

I breathed deeply.

"Would you like me to call him and ask if he'll come to visit?"

I could already imagine her being even more depressed when Jan told me in his arrogant tone of voice that he had a lot to do and no time for a trip to the Baltic. I could equally well imagine myself feeling so pissed at hearing him that I'd have to go back down the steps to the beach and yell out the rage from inside me.

I'd hardly spoken the words I didn't want to speak when my little ray of sunshine turned to me.

"Oh yes!" Leonie cried, hope lighting up her eyes. It was clear that she really had believed a new house would change everything. That it would have the power to undo everything that had happened.

"OK," I said and kissed the top of her head. "I'll call him."

"Now?"

I should have known. Leonie always wanted the important things immediately.

I wasn't ready to hear Jan's voice, and I was even less ready to talk to him, to have an actual conversation—the first one since we'd seen each other for the last time in court. But what else could I do? Leonie was my daughter, and I'd do anything to see her smile again. The only concern was whether Jan would play along. It wasn't the first time I'd tried to reach him.

As the phone rang, my heart thumped in my throat. What should I say if he actually picked up? Simply tell him we'd moved? Or add that Leonie was missing him and it would make her happy to see him again?

He was sure to reply that he had no time and would call back some other time. And that return call would never come.

After the third ring, the voice mail cut in. On hearing Jan's voice asking the caller to leave a message, I hung up. My heart was still racing, this time with anger. I hadn't heard his voice for so long that I'd forgotten how slick and smooth it sounded. I used to find it sexy, but now I could no longer bear the sickly way he stretched out the vowels.

But this wasn't about me. It was about Leonie, who loved her father's voice and longed to hear it. And who was probably smart enough to wonder why her daddy no longer wanted to see her.

I tried again, only to get the same outcome: Jan didn't answer. I hung up with a sigh and returned to Leonie. She had calmed down a little and was sitting with her dolls on the bed. When she heard me enter the bedroom, her curly head shot up.

"So? Is he coming?"

"He couldn't get to the phone; he must be working," I replied. And like I had before, I found myself making excuses for him to our daughter. "I'll try him again later."

I could have left him a message.

Leonie nodded, trying to be brave, but she couldn't hold out for long. After only a single breath, a tear welled up and fell on her doll's face. I rushed over to her.

"Hey, sweetie, you mustn't do that," I said. "Otherwise your doll's going to think it's raining outside. What would you say if a big fat raindrop fell on your cheek?"

Without answering, Leonie snuggled up to me so that her trickle of tears fell lightly on my T-shirt. I wrapped my arms around her and vowed to leave Jan a voice mail once I had calmed down, once I was able to speak to him as coolly and professionally as if he were a client.

***

Leonie was peacefully asleep now, but I lay awake for a long while and thought about my childhood—about what I knew and what I didn't.

I had suffered loss, too. I had been sad, too. I remembered well the attic of the children's home in Leipzig where I'd lived before the Hansens adopted me. There had been a skylight in the room. I'd opened it as wide as the safety chain would allow. From my place by the window, I'd looked down onto the street in the hope that someone would appear and tell me it had all been a mistake. I'd hoped my mother would come. But none of the people who walked past the house were coming for me. The familiar figure of my mother faded as time went by, until I could no longer recall what she looked like. Even if she'd walked past the home, I wouldn't have recognized her.

As the thoughts died away, I noticed that my cheeks were wet. I was crying! I hadn't done that for so long. And it was the last thing I needed. I turned over in my bed toward the window, through which the darkness was full of murmurs. I concentrated on the sound of the sea, and finally saw something else in my mind's eye: the blue and white cutter.

Storm Rose was a wonderful name for a boat. Beauty and strength in one. It was a shame that it was rotting away in the harbor under the threat of the scrapyard. Couldn't anything be done about it?

I had inherited the love of boats from my father, or rather my adoptive father. He worked at the Volkswerft in Stralsund, back in East Germany, and later at Nikolai & Jensen in Hamburg. Whenever I went to meet him after work, I'd been fascinated by the huge vessels lying in the dry docks. For a while I'd wanted to become a shipbuilder myself, but my father had dissuaded me. His words wouldn't necessarily have stopped me, but at some stage I'd come to realize myself that it wasn't the career for me. I settled into my role of helping companies by providing them with good publicity, yet this dream had stayed with me, the dream of a white boat on which I would sail away from all my problems.

And that boat was now lying in Sassnitz harbor as if it had been waiting for me all along. The harbor worker had said it was for sale. Was fate giving me a sign?

This thought struck me so hard that I sat up in bed.

What if I were to buy this boat? What if I created something meaningful out of it—a tour boat or a café? Yes, a café seemed good to me. Not just any old café where you sat eating strawberry cake during a trip along the coast—my boat café would be something special. With exhibitions, concerts, readings, and small-scale drama productions. The idea was probably a little crazy, especially in current times, but were these not the times we had feverishly looked forward to more than twenty years ago? Times in which we could make dreams come true, whatever the actual outcome?

I reached for my cell phone and entered a search for the *Storm Rose*. How expensive could a rusty old boat be? Surely it wouldn't cost too much. Of course, the restoration would gobble up enormous amounts, but it wasn't as if I didn't know how to market my finished product. After all, I was an advertising expert!

A range of boats from the surrounding area were up for sale on the harbor's website. There was no vendor's name, but I saw a contact number. The picture of the cutter must have been retouched, as it looked far better than it had in the harbor, but that didn't prevent me from saving the number.

I looked at the alarm clock by my bed. A quarter past three. I was so excited by the idea of owning the *Storm Rose* that I felt like calling immediately, but I held back. If it was a private number, they'd be alarmed and think me a madwoman, and if it was the number of a company or an agency, there'd be no one in the office in any case.

Wide-awake now, I got up quietly and went into the living room, which was still filled with unpacked boxes. Leonie was sleeping deeply; the crying had tired her out. Anger against Jan flared up briefly, but I suppressed it. I wouldn't let him spoil our lives here!

I began cleaning up quietly. My hands mechanically sorted through all kinds of things in drawers and on cabinet shelves. When I came to the folder I'd looked at briefly the previous day, my vigor was suddenly extinguished. I stared at the cover for a moment, but didn't have the courage to bring out the picture of the windmill. Something lay heavy in my breast, and once again I thought I heard my mother's voice. It was strange that these feelings, which I thought I'd long since shaken off, had suddenly returned with such intensity.

I stowed the folder away in the bottom drawer of the living room cabinet and sat down on the sofa. I didn't switch a light on; I didn't need it. I stared into the darkness for several minutes, listening to the house creaking and breathing. Was it missing its former owners?

As I sat in the blackness, I felt myself calming. Of course everything couldn't suddenly be all right overnight. Especially not where Jan was concerned. Could Leonie ever forget what had happened? I wondered, and thought I could hear a small voice in the back of my mind countering my thought with a question of its own: *Have* you *forgotten everything that happened in your own childhood?*

I knew the answer only too well. And all of a sudden they were back, those images from the past. But this time I didn't run away from them as I always had before by distracting myself with activity.

I let them flow.

6

Annabel

"Annabel!" The caregiver's voice drifted up the stairs, but I didn't want to reply.

I had been here for three months, in the home where they brought me after my mother disappeared. It was an old three-story house with yellowish-white wallpaper. The wallpaper was the same throughout—in the hallway, the bedrooms, and the kitchen. It was even in the closet. But I didn't care. In any case, my favorite place was the attic, where you weren't supposed to go—but since I'd discovered that the door to the stairs was never locked, I kept going back there.

Today, too, I was sitting there, clutching the picture of the windmill I'd painted at home. As if it could help me to summon my mom back to me. I liked my playmates as little as they did me. I didn't want to be here. Once I had tried to slip out through the door and run home. I was rewarded by a resounding slap from one of the caregivers at the house.

The attic was the only place where I could be alone. The only place where I could hope that my mom would come. I didn't dare switch the light on, but in spite of the darkness and the strange boxes in the attic, I wasn't afraid. Monsters in the dark just couldn't compare.

I had a good view of the street from the window. Cars roared past the home, pedestrians carried their shopping bags, and in the afternoons a few children played outside. Sometimes I saw the home's head warden out there, or other children, running errands for her or coming back from school. It was winter, and the city looked particularly gray and bleak. It got dark quickly. Overnight the roofs had received a sprinkling of snow. The sky, which appeared to hang low over the city, was leaden.

"Annabel, where are you?"

I didn't reply. I knew there would be trouble if they found me up here. But I didn't want to move from the attic window. I was convinced that Mom would come to get me one day. After all, I was still in Leipzig. She knew her way around here. In the early weeks I'd still believed that every time they called me it was to tell me my mom had come for me. Time and again I was disappointed.

I sat there for as long as I could, looking out and waiting. I imagined my mother wandering through the city, searching for me, asking people if they'd seen me, showing them my photo. Mom had lots of lovely photos of me and her, the latest ones taken when we had spent a few days on the Baltic coast. Often we were unable to take a vacation, but last summer we had simply gone.

Why had I been brought here, anyway? I still didn't really understand. But I clearly saw in my mind's eye the events after I awoke in the police car.

A woman had gotten into the car with me. A policeman sat in the front. I still clutched my picture, the windmill I'd painted the evening before.

"Where's Mom?" I asked, grasping the paper like a lifeline.

"Your mom's no longer there," she said kindly. "We're taking you to a children's home now."

"But where's Mom?"

Tears sprang to my eyes. Had something happened to her? Death was still an abstract concept to me; I had no idea what exactly it was about, but I knew people died and were no longer there. The woman next to me, who smelled kind of funny and whose face looked strange, told me that my mom had gone away.

"But she's not dead, is she?" I asked, panic-stricken, as I looked desperately for a way to open the car door. I was terribly afraid, especially since the woman hesitated like all adults did when you asked them a question they couldn't answer.

They took me to a strange house with rooms that smelled of cabbage and gravy. This was the children's home? I'd never been in a home of any kind, and my fear grew even more. I began to cry again. The woman was unable to console me. My arms ached from hugging the picture to myself so hard.

It was only when two men in brown suits entered the room that I fell silent. Not because they comforted me, but because I was so afraid of them that I had to stop crying. One of them sat down behind the desk, laying a mustard-yellow folder down in front of him. In my fear I had scarcely noticed two more women entering the room.

"So you are Annabel Thalheim," the man said after opening the file. I nodded, terrified.

"I'm sure you're not happy that we had to drag you from your bed like this. But we had no other choice."

I looked down at myself and only then realized I was still wearing my pajamas. I felt my cheeks flush with embarrassment.

"Your mother has betrayed the German Democratic Republic! And for that reason we're taking you to be looked after by people who can bring you up to be a better person."

I stared at him in shock. I had no idea what he meant.

"I want my mom," I sobbed.

"Didn't you hear me? She's no longer here! She's gone over to the West. You'll be living here from now on."

His severe expression did nothing to calm me. My tears fell harder.

"Comrade Paulus, please go easy on the child," said a woman's voice, softer than anything I'd heard. She laid her hands gently on my shoulders. "Everything's still so new for her. She should have a chance to get used to things, and then you can talk to her."

I didn't like the woman who tried to console me—she smelled so strange and felt so cold—but I had no choice. Terrified, I clung to her like a rock. At least she had silenced that nasty man.

"Very well. Take her upstairs. We'll talk to her later."

"Come with me," the woman said in a friendly voice. "We'll go find the others now. You'll have lots of new friends here, and we'll take good care of you."

"Will Mommy come back?" I asked. I had no interest at all in any new friends. I already had plenty of friends in my nursery school.

"Maybe," she replied. "But for now you need to get some sleep. We'll talk some more in the morning."

At the time I didn't realize how lucky I had been. I could just as easily have been sent to a juvenile workhouse. Even six-year-olds sometimes ended up in those places. But I only found that out much later. The woman, who wanted me to call her Aunt Margot, took me to the bedroom I was to share with twelve other children. I was extremely afraid. Of course the others were awake and looking around, their whispering hanging in the air like the buzzing of insects. Everything had been prepared, including a freshly made-up bed, as if she'd known that my mother would run away in the night.

"Do you want to put the picture away?" The woman reached out her hand to me. I shook my head. "But it'll get all creased if you take it to bed with you! I'll put it somewhere safe for you."

What reason did I have to trust her? Perhaps the picture would be gone by the morning, as quickly as my mother had disappeared. But at last I gave it to her.

"I'll take good care of it," she promised.

Fear and worry gripped me again as I lay down on the bed. It was hard and uncomfortable, and gave no more comfort than a hammock.

The woman didn't explain to the others who I was—that would probably come tomorrow. Instead, she ordered them to settle down and turned off the light.

I stared into the darkness, alone. The other children carried on whispering secretively for a while, then silence fell all around me. None of the children came up to me; not even the one in the bed next to me asked who I was. But at that moment I didn't care. Although I was very frightened, I was eventually overcome by weariness and sank into a deep, dreamless sleep. *Maybe everything will be all right in the morning* was the only thought I had.

But of course it wasn't all right when I awoke. Only my picture, which was, in fact, still there. The next morning, I met the other caregivers who worked there. I didn't listen to their friendly questions and words, but pestered them over and over again, asking when my mom would come back. It was probably only to get some peace from me that they said she would be back sometime, but not right away. So I'd be staying here for the time being, and I could play with the other children.

I didn't want to play with the others; I was burning with fear and questions, racked by fear that my mom had abandoned me. Maybe something had happened to her. What or who had Mom betrayed? And why had the man in the brown suit been so angry? I hadn't done anything to him!

In the meantime, they had at least brought a few things from my house—clothes and my folder of pictures. The things smelled so strongly of home that part of me was thrilled to have them, even though I was torn apart by my longing for my mom and my former life.

A few days later the men returned to the home. They weren't any gentler than before when they spoke to me, but I'd come to realize that I made them even angrier when I cried. So I let them talk, nodded or shook my head, and gave them as many answers as I could. Most of the time I didn't even understand the questions.

Words such as "defection," "antisocial," "non-Socialist foreign country," "enemy of the state" swirled around me, but meant nothing.

The men eventually gave up, and Aunt Margot brought me back to the other children, who were playing in the yard. I didn't join in, but sat on a bench to one side, trying to make sense of what had happened.

"Annabel?"

The mental images vanished in a flash as footsteps banged up the stairs. I started. The caregiver who had been looking for me must have realized where to find me. I briefly wondered whether to hide, but she was there before I could run off. The first thing I saw was her back-combed red-brown hair, quickly followed by her angry face.

"Here you are!" she snarled. A few seconds later her fingers had closed around my wrist like an iron claw. She dragged me down the stairs without caring whether my feet touched the steps or not. She didn't let go until she had pulled me into the kitchen.

"What on earth were you doing up there?" the woman we called Aunt Elke said in her grating voice, giving me a shake. "We thought something had happened to you. You can go to bed without supper for that!"

At least she didn't hit me, although in the hours that followed I almost wished she had. The telling-off and missing supper weren't enough. I also had to go to bed earlier than all the others. And of course I had to tell them why I was being punished. The caregivers encouraged the others to laugh at me for my behavior. That hurt more than any blow would have done.

While the others were still up in the common room watching TV, I lay in bed, the caregiver's instructions to think about what I had done ringing in my ears. But what had I done? I'd been waiting for Mom, That was all!

Yes, of course I knew she was supposed to have gone over to the West, and that this wasn't right. But perhaps she'd change her mind.

The next day I stayed away from the attic, although I still took every opportunity to try and look out the windows. The caregivers kept a watchful eye on me, and the whole time I felt that one of them was nearby, checking I didn't disappear upstairs. They were obviously afraid I would run away again.

After a while this fuss died down, but the constant urge to go up to the attic and be alone was still there. I retreated into my fantasy world and imagined a hundred different ways in which my mother would come and take me away. Perhaps she would take me with her to the West, although I didn't really know where that was.

Despair sometimes gained the upper hand, and I would cry for hours. No one was able to console me. The other children withdrew from me; I must have seemed weird to them. The caregivers tried to cheer me up with cups of cocoa, but how was that supposed to take the place of my mom?

It was particularly bad over Christmas. All the others in my group looked forward to it, but all I could think about was Mom. Where was she now? Why had she still not come to take me away from there? I stared despondently at the wall, while the other kids chattered away cheerfully. Why weren't they sad? Hadn't they ever had any parents? I never had the courage to ask them.

I didn't talk to the other children much at all. Most of them ignored me; the rest were hostile. I didn't have a single friend, probably because I made no attempt to approach the others. I was waiting for the only person who had ever meant anything to me—my mother. I even went as far as secretly asking Santa to send my mom back to me for Christmas. I didn't want anything else that year.

I would have loved to write it on my wish list, too, but I didn't dare. The caregivers collected our wish lists, and if they'd seen that I was asking Santa for my mom, they would probably have made the others laugh at me again.

They'd done it several times before. I felt like hitting every one of those laughing faces, but I didn't dare. I would probably have been punished even harder if I had. So whenever Aunt Elke or Aunt Sabine incited the others to laugh at me, I tried to close my ears. After a while I got so good at it that I could transport myself back to our house in those moments. The laughter, which I still heard, of course, was transformed into my mother's laugh as she danced cheerfully with me around the apartment.

Since I didn't want presents in any case, I wasn't disappointed when I hardly received any. All I got was a little pack of plastic beads and a small doll with matted hair. The older children were given rulers, pencils, and drawing pads.

While we sang Christmas carols together, my eyes wandered again and again to the window, through the curtains to the outside. My biggest wish wasn't granted. My mom didn't appear. I was utterly disappointed in Santa and didn't want the other gifts he had given me. That very night I tore out the doll's hair and then hid it among my things.

The following months passed without much happening. The only thing that caused me trouble was when one of the caregivers found the doll among my things. I was punished harshly for my treatment of such a valuable gift, but I simply let it wash over me. It seemed I had succeeded in building up my armor. I no longer cared about the laughter of the other children. When the caregivers told me to do something, I did it.

I grew to love the story hour in the evenings, when one of the caregivers would read from the book of fairy tales that was locked away in a cabinet the rest of the time. The fairy tale that fascinated me the most was "Cinderella." Her mother had gone, too, as had her father, and she was left to her stepmother and two stepsisters. Her life wasn't good; she had to work hard, but one day a pair of doves gave her pretty clothes and made it possible for her to go to a beautiful ball and meet the prince.

For weeks after I heard the story, I went regularly into the yard, to a tree where a pair of city doves were nesting, and whispered my wishes to them. I didn't want them to shower me with gold and silver, but to bring my mom back to me. I didn't mind it when my wish wasn't immediately granted. I knew my wish was much bigger than Cinderella's, so it would take them a bit longer.

At least I could still go to my old kindergarten and keep my playmates from before. But I didn't tell any of them what had happened with my mom. I had no idea whether their parents knew about it and told their children not to ask me. In any case, there seemed to be some tacit agreement between the caregivers in the home and the nursery school teachers that there should be no talk of the whereabouts of my mother. If anyone's parents came to talk during the activity sessions, I remained silent, and the nursery teachers said nothing to me, either. I could feel the pity in their eyes all too clearly, but it faded when the time came to go home.

The summer arrived, and I was almost ready to start school when Aunt Margot appeared at the nursery school one day. The appearance of the home's head warden there on a normal morning could mean many things. But it must have to do with me, as I was the only child from the home there.

I immediately felt a thousand butterflies fluttering in my stomach. What if Mom had turned up at the home? What if she'd found me and was now forcing the warden to give her daughter back? All of a sudden I was so excited that I forgot to wash out my brush that was still full of red paint.

"Hey, watch it!" cried out the boy next to me as a glob of red paint from my brush dripped into the blue in the paint box. We were supposed to be painting farmers at work, and I had just painted a big red tractor. And now this! I stared, horrified, at the paint. The boy next to me was a little sneak. He jumped straight up and ran to the nursery teacher.

"Frau Meier, Frau Meier, Annabel made the paint all mucky with her brush."

I looked at him angrily. Such a fuss about some paint! But I knew I'd be punished for it—at the very least I'd have to go and stand in the corner. Or, like in the home, I'd be laughed at for my bad behavior. I took a tissue out of my pocket and tried to save the ruined paint.

At that moment the warden appeared. I was sure I was about to be told off about the paint. I looked down at the dirty tissue in my hands; another thing for Aunt Margot to give me a tongue-lashing about. But the telling-off didn't happen, at least not yet.

"Annabel, will you please come with me."

I trotted behind the warden fearfully. Aunt Margot told me to fetch my bag, then she took me by the hand and led me out of the nursery school. We went back to the home, where she took me to her office.

I was sure the telling-off about the paint would come now. I was already steeling myself, trying to dream myself back into the apartment with Mom. I was also harboring a tiny hope that she would be standing on the other side of the door. All the way there I hadn't dared to ask about her, but perhaps my wish was about to be granted now.

The door opened. Mom wasn't waiting there. A man and a woman were sitting in the office. The man had dark hair and sideburns, and the woman had her hair tied back with an elastic band, which made her look young.

"This is Annabel," said the head warden. Since I had arrived, I had lost my surname; I was merely Annabel now. Even to people from the outside, who perhaps knew full well that I'd once had a mother.

"Annabel, this is Elfie and Martin Hansen. They've come from Stralsund to take you back with them."

Take me with them? I was too shocked to notice the friendly way they were both smiling at me.

"But why?" I asked. "Why do they want to take me with them?"

I involuntarily gripped the warden's hand tighter. If they took me with them, Mom wouldn't know where to find me!

"You'll go live with them. They'll be your new mom and dad."

"But I have a mom!" I burst out. I didn't have a dad, of course, as he'd died. But I'd never missed him; my mom was all I needed.

And now these strangers had come and wanted to be my new parents?

"I don't need a new mom and dad!" I broke away defiantly and ran to the door. Aunt Margot caught me easily.

"Please excuse us. The child . . . still hasn't quite gotten over it," she said to the strangers, then dragged me out into the corridor.

"Now you listen to me!" she hissed at me. "Your mother isn't coming back! She went to the West and left you here. You don't matter to her at all."

I stared at her in horror. Tears sprang to my eyes. That wasn't true. She hadn't left me behind! She'd never do anything like that!

"Those people in there want you to be their daughter. You should be grateful to them. They'll look after you, unlike your mother. She's never coming back, there's no point waiting for her! So you'll behave yourself when we go back in. Do you understand?"

I was choking on fear and anger. My mother had left me on my own here? I couldn't believe it. But on the other hand, almost a year had gone by and I was still here. Could it be true that I didn't matter to her?

I nodded numbly and allowed myself to be led back into the office.

I didn't take in anything that was discussed, but at the end of the conversation between Aunt Margot and the Hansens, it was decided that I would be going with them. To Stralsund.

All through the night before I left, I stared at the bedroom ceiling. Everyone around me was asleep, but I couldn't sleep, as I kept thinking that I'd be leaving the home in the morning. That I'd be going to Stralsund. Stralsund! Where was that, anyway?

All it meant to me was that my mother would never find out that I'd been taken away from here. When she came to look for me, she wouldn't find me! But what if Aunt Margot was right, and she didn't care at all? I wanted so much not to believe that, but it was true that she hadn't appeared in all that time. Suddenly I began to feel a fervent hatred for "the West," where she'd gone without taking me.

When the Hansens picked me up the next morning for my "probationary period," as Aunt Margot called it, I plucked up my courage and picked up my child's suitcase, in which I'd packed my windmill picture among my things, and left the bedroom.

If my mom really loved me, I told myself, she would find me in Stralsund. To make sure, I whispered to the doves in the tree to tell my mom where I was, as I still believed in fairy tales.

The woman was very friendly and also very pretty, and the man who was to be my new—no, my first—dad smiled at me.

"So, Annabel, are you looking forward to seeing the sea?" he asked. "When we get home I'll show you some really big ships. You'll be amazed!"

I was actually interested in the big ships. Perhaps my mom would come to me on one of them!

We got into the yellow Wartburg that was parked outside the home. Then we set off. I turned back one last time toward the home—not to wave at the kids who were standing by the fence, but to silently beg the doves to remember my wish.

7

Although it was still a little early to be making a call on a Saturday morning, I dialed the number for the *Storm Rose* with a thumping heart.

I had assumed I'd get an answering machine, but after the third ring a woman's voice answered. She told me her husband wasn't there and asked me to try again later. I hung up and began to bite my thumbnail in agitation. The coffee machine bubbled behind me, radiating a scent that filled the kitchen and stirred my thoughts.

My cell phone suddenly buzzed. Was the man back already? I quickly pulled the phone from my pocket. No, it was my father's number.

"Hey, good to hear from your voice!" he said. "We thought you must have lost your way between Bremen and Rügen."

"No, Dad, don't worry. We arrived safely and we're settling in nicely."

He didn't need to say anything; the brief pause he left hanging told me I should have been in touch. Since I was eighteen I'd lived alone, organized my own life, made my own decisions. My parents got involved only if I asked them to. But they expected one thing from me—that I keep in touch and reassure them that all was well with me and Leonie.

"So, do you like it there?"

"Oh yes, very much!" I replied. I'd been raving about this house ever since the first time I'd seen it. I'd seen the real estate agent's ad in the newspaper purely by chance, and the idea of moving to my old homeland had appealed to me immediately.

Skeptic that he was, my father held back from sharing my enthusiasm until I'd lived in this town for a while and really gotten to know it.

"Leonie's room has a lovely view of a wonderful wild rosebush. And I can look out to sea from my office window."

"And at the ships," my father added. "You see some going past, don't you?"

"Dad, you know Binz well," I reproached him. We hadn't been here often—only once, to be precise, shortly before we moved to Hamburg. But he'd spent most of his life in the Mecklenburg region. "Sassnitz is really close by, so you see all kinds of boats here, from ships to trawlers."

My father laughed. "I was only teasing."

I wondered whether this would be a good moment to broach the subject of the cutter, but my father got in before me.

"Is your little angel awake yet?" he asked.

"No, she's still sleeping peacefully." I glanced toward her bedroom door, which was slightly ajar. Morning light streamed out onto the landing, but no sound came from the room.

"How's she taking the move?"

"Very well, I think. She's got other things on her mind." I almost regretted saying that, as my father would inevitably ask more.

"She still hasn't gotten over Jan, has she?"

"She probably never will," I replied, a hint of anger troubling me again. How was a child supposed to get over the sudden disappearance of a parent? One who no longer seemed to care about them . . .

My stomach cramped. All of a sudden the smell of the freshly brewed coffee seemed unbearable. We were silent for a moment on the phone. My father said nothing because he expected me to say something more, to offer a solution. And I said nothing because I didn't want to. I couldn't change the fact that Jan wasn't interested in his daughter and didn't care that she longed to see him.

"Perhaps you should call him," he ventured after a while.

My parents had been desperately unhappy when Jan and I split up, but they had neither tried to dissuade me nor made any attempt to influence Jan.

"I tried yesterday, as it happens. But he wasn't there. You know how hard it is to get hold of him."

Even when we still had a marriage of sorts, I had only been able to get him to the phone with difficulty, because he was always busy with some meeting or business appointment. And texting him fared no better—he simply ignored anything he didn't consider important for as long as he could.

"Hmm," my father said, like he always did when he couldn't think how to reply. Or rather, when he wanted to spare my feelings by not speaking his thoughts out loud. He believed the best thing would be to take Jan and beat it into him that he really ought to be there for the child he had fathered. If he ever said anything like that, I got terribly agitated even though I knew my father would never resort to physical violence.

"Ah well, I have some good news for you, too," I said, eager to change the subject.

"And that is?" I could hear my father suppressing his anger about Jan.

"I've found a boat in Sassnitz harbor. It's called the *Storm Rose*. It's an old fishing cutter that's been converted to a tour boat. Can you believe it?"

"You've found a boat?" He could have been asking me if I'd seen a Martian in the front yard. "What do you mean, you've found a boat? Were you looking for one?"

"No, not really. I just saw it when I was visiting a client. I looked out his office window and there it was." Silence. My father was surprised. "Hello? Dad? Are you still there?"

"Of course. I'm just wondering how you come to be taking an interest in a boat."

In truth, I couldn't really explain it myself. It was just my dream to find freedom by sailing off in a boat.

"Love at first sight, I suppose," I replied. "Imagine all the things you could do with a boat like that."

"Oh, I know full well what you can do with a boat like that. But does this mean . . . you want to buy it?"

"I don't know," I replied. "Maybe. I could give myself a second string to my bow by opening a floating café. Or some sort of cultural center. Something they don't have in this area yet."

"You do realize a lot of people don't know what to make of culture," my father pointed out.

"But it's different when they're on vacation. And I'm sure the locals aren't all ignoramuses. After all, we weren't when we were still living in Stralsund."

"Those were different times. No cell phones or constantly chattering TVs."

"I think there are still plenty of people who can tear themselves away from those." I took a deep breath. "So, what do you think? Would it be something for me?"

"Hm. A boat like that means responsibility, you know. And it'll be expensive. You need your money to get your new life going. On the other hand, I'm always in favor of people taking the chance to make their dreams come true. Especially my daughter. But you should be absolutely clear why you want it and what you intend to do with it. Anyway, you know you've got someone here who knows his way around boats and is always ready to help you if you want."

"And who would that be?" I laughed, knowing full well that my father would give me his blessing whatever mischief I got into.

My father snorted, but his smile could be heard in his voice as he said, "Go for it, lass, and keep your chin up."

"You can depend on that."

After finishing my call with my father, I tried the boat owner's number again, hoping he'd be there by now. It rang only three times before someone picked up. This time it was a man's voice.

"Ruhnau."

I started. The voice was deep and a little curt. He sounded like an old sea dog, probably surprised that a woman was interested in his boat.

"Hello, my name is Annabel Hansen, and I saw on the Internet that you're selling the *Storm Rose*, the boat that's in Sassnitz harbor."

"That's right. The viewing's on Monday morning, if you'd like to come." Viewing? Like for an apartment? It meant I wasn't the only one interested in the boat.

I wanted to ask how many other people would be coming, but stopped myself.

"What time?" I asked instead.

"Ten o'clock," the man replied.

Clearly not one for conversation. I made a note and thanked him before hanging up. I looked at the piece of paper. Monday. I had the whole weekend to consider what it was I wanted—and whether the boat would give me the freedom my heart desired.

8

On Monday morning I was sitting on a bench with a mug of coffee in my hand, watching the Sassnitz harbor come to life. Cars trickled one by one into the large parking lot, and men in blue overalls and work boots got out. Crates of fish were stacked outside one of the warehouses, waiting to be loaded onto ships. One of the dockside buildings was being renovated by a team of builders. In the distance I could hear the rumble of cranes unloading a freighter.

The small shopping center near the dock was still closed. The shops sold souvenirs and clothes, mostly swimwear and warm, waterproof gear for colder days. Perhaps I'd take Leonie there soon.

Her first day at nursery school had gone more smoothly than I'd hoped. My daughter was quite reserved by nature, especially around strangers. But as we were standing outside the door of the Starfish Nursery School in Binz, a few children had waved to her from the windows, and while I was still talking to the nursery teacher, a little girl appeared and took Leonie by the hand. They vanished into the playroom, and although I felt a slight pang, I was pleased that she had been given such a welcome. Who knew—maybe a real friendship was forming there. I really hoped that Leonie would find some friends to distract her from worrying about her father.

I looked up as a man walked past me. He was wearing a corduroy jacket and a blue sailor's cap. His footsteps were heavy, and his hands thrust deep into his jacket pockets. He was carrying a black folder under his arm. I was sure this must be the owner of the boat. His gait was that of someone who wanted to be rid of a heavy burden. Perhaps this was my chance?

I could have hurried up behind him, but I decided to wait and continue drinking my coffee. If I showed too great an interest, it would only drive the price up. In any case, there was still a good hour to go.

Over the weekend I had followed my father's advice and given serious thought to my possible purchase of the boat. Of course it would mean taking on a lot of work, and the financial outlay wouldn't be small. But as I went through all the eventualities, it became clear to me how much I longed to be taking on something new. Something that had nothing to do with my old life in Bremen.

When I woke up that morning, I knew that I wanted to view the *Storm Rose*. And keeping myself busy like that might stop me from brooding about my birth mother again. Now I was here.

Half an hour later my coffee cup was in the trash, and the first of the other interested viewers was strolling up. A man in corduroy pants and Wellington boots, who I guessed was around fifty and clearly knowledgeable about boats. A somewhat younger man in a denim jacket and blue work pants. Another in rubber boots and an oilskin jacket, and a surfer dude who looked bored by the whole thing. Two more men in checked shirts and jackets, who looked almost like twins. No women. And no one seemed to be expecting me to join them.

Although my heart was in my mouth, I stood and walked along the jetty. How would someone go about buying a boat? I'd heard friends saying that when looking around houses, some people tried to butter up the landlord or vendor with smooth talk. Myself, I'd never needed to present myself as the perfect tenant. I'd always gotten my apartments more or less by luck and chance. And now here I was, without the slightest experience in sucking up to people.

Two of my competitors were deep in conversation, which they cut off as I approached. The others all looked at me, too. Only the surfer boy was checking his cell phone, apparently unaware of my arrival. I greeted them all, hands shoved into my pockets. I felt uncomfortable. From their expressions, the men were clearly wondering what I was doing there. I tried to ignore it by looking at the name painted on the hull of the boat and concentrating on the algae staining the peeling paint.

The two men finally resumed their conversation, and the others took no notice of me. I raised my eyes, but the owner, or the person selling on his behalf, was nowhere to be seen. Was he waiting for some more people to arrive?

I looked aside. A man was striding purposefully toward the boat. He was wearing a suit, as though he was a banker on his way to a business lunch, although he wasn't wearing a tie. He wore his clothes like a suit of armor.

As he came nearer, I saw above the rather formal clothes a friendly angular face with designer stubble, framed by brown curls. Even from a distance I could see his eyes shone. This was by far the most attractive man on the dock. And I recognized him from somewhere. Yes, this was the man I'd seen when I'd been by the *Storm Rose* with Leonie! He'd been wearing a harbor worker's clothes then, so what was he doing in a suit now?

He looked me up and down briefly, without a hint of recognition. He was probably just wondering what I, a woman, was doing here, before going over to join the others. I stared at him for a moment, but he took no notice of me. The viewing of a boat wasn't the typical dating scene, and from the look of him, he was surely married or in a long-term relationship.

I looked away and saw a man in a blue corduroy jacket take up a position at the front. He glanced at his watch. I had been so preoccupied by watching the man in the suit that I hadn't noticed him appear. He cleared his throat and said, "I assume we're all here."

As no one agreed or disagreed, he began.

"I'm Heinz Ruhnau, the boat's owner. For now, at least." He held out his left hand at arm's length, holding the folder he had been carrying under his arm. "I'm delighted to see you all here to view this wonderful vessel. The *Storm Rose* was built in 1940 in Hamburg, initially as a fishing cutter. Then the fishing equipment was removed and it was used during the war for fishing of a different kind—as a minesweeper. After the war it was converted to a tour boat and brought to Timmendorfer Strand."

The man tripped out the facts totally dispassionately, but in my mind's eye I saw the boat being launched for the first time with all the hopes that accompanied it. How, instead of bringing in nets full of fish, it then searched for mines, perhaps getting damaged along the way and experiencing the bombing of Hamburg. And how the war had come to an end and it had been given a peaceful purpose . . .

"I was intending to restore the boat myself, but unfortunately my wife has fallen ill and we need the money to make some changes to the house." He sighed deeply, and I sensed that he didn't find it easy to part with his boat. Fate could be a real bastard.

"But I hope it will now find a good owner in one of you, someone who'll bring it back to its former glory."

He then began to show us around the fore and aft decks, the wheelhouse, the engine room, and the passenger cabin.

"The boat is twenty-four meters long and six wide; it has a two-hundred-and-twenty-horsepower engine which, once repaired, will give a speed of nine knots. You can find further technical details on the flyer I'll give you when we're back outside," Ruhnau continued. I would have expected some questions, but the men seemed a little stunned. And with good reason—time had really taken its toll. I could just imagine my father's sigh if he had been there. Many of the ropes were damaged, the floor of the engine room was awash with oil stains, and the engine itself painted a sorry picture. The paint was completely gone from the passenger cabin. Every surface was peeling and flaking.

"Please take your time to look around," the owner said once his tour was complete. "I'll be outside if you have any questions or want to know the purchase price."

With that he withdrew. I looked around at the others. What was the procedure for buying a boat? Although my father worked at a shipyard and I had grown up with boats, I didn't know much about what to look for. So I followed those who looked most like they knew what they were doing and took some photos with my cell phone to show my father, a specialist I trusted.

With my layman's eye I saw only two things. First, it would be very expensive to restore it all. Seats, paint, windows, floor—everything would need replacing from scratch, and I heard some disparaging comments from the self-professed experts about the engine and the rigging. Second, I knew that once the boat was restored it would be wonderful—and that it was far from being a candidate for the ships' graveyard, as I'd heard one of my competitors muttering when we left the engine room. Fortunately, this man soon disappeared, and most of them followed suit. Some signaled their withdrawal immediately; others looked more indecisive.

I let them all go before me, as I wanted to take in the boat's atmosphere alone. The good-looking man in the suit had also gone out, so I stood in the middle of the passenger cabin, ignoring the mishmash of strange smells that had penetrated the boards over time, and looked around.

The remains of an old advertising poster for lemonade clung to the wall. The seat upholstery was of a rough orange-striped fabric. Something had been scratched onto the surface of one of the tables. I saw a heart with an arrow, the names "Susi + Peter," an anchor, and an illegible scrawl.

What had this boat seen? What had she experienced during the war? What had happened to the people who sailed on her? There must be some stories. Taken together, all these things would make a fantastic backdrop, which could be used to excellent effect for marketing.

When I, too, finally left the boat, I saw the man in the suit. Apart from the owner, he and I were the only ones still there. Didn't any of the others want the boat? The man in the suit saw me and came over.

"Well, what do you think?"

I looked at him in surprise.

"It's a lovely boat."

"So you want to buy it?" He tilted his head a little as if trying to read my thoughts.

"It depends on the price. But if that's right, why not?"

I squared my shoulders. This guy might be good-looking, but his questions made him seem a little less likeable.

"Why do you want the boat?" the stranger asked, his hands thrust deep in his pockets. He clearly didn't intend for anyone else to snatch the boat away from under his nose.

I could have retorted that it had nothing to do with him, but my instincts told me that it was better to talk to him calmly and professionally.

"I'd like to turn it into a café," I told him, but soon regretted it.

"Why don't you open one on dry land?" he asked scornfully.

His words infuriated me. Who did he think he was? My business adviser?

"There are plenty of cafés on land. It would make no business sense at all to open up another here."

I looked at him challengingly.

"There are hordes of day-trip boats floating around the harbor. With restaurant service."

The way he said it made these boats sound like old tubs stinking of rancid fat and cabbage, whose passengers frequently offered up their meals back to Neptune because of the rough rides the flimsy craft gave them as they tossed about on the waves. Many years ago my parents had taken me out on a tour like that, and I had only my strong stomach to thank for the fact that I hadn't been leaning over the railings alongside the rest of the day-trippers.

"Believe me, that's not what I have in mind at all," I replied. "I'm not interested in cruising up and down the cliffs while feeding people eggs and chips. I want this boat to be all about culture. Proper culture, and a complete absence of stories about the pirate Störtebeker."

That legend had stuck in my memory because it had been told at precisely the moment when people had run out, clutching their stomachs.

"Those stories are very popular around here."

"But there comes a time for change."

I folded my arms. It annoyed me that I was getting drawn into this conversation and had revealed more than I'd had a chance to think out for myself.

"So what do you want the boat for?" I fired back.

"That's my business. Nothing to do with anyone else," he replied with a smug smile.

At that moment I felt like slapping that self-satisfied smile off his face, but that was when the owner appeared.

"I see you're still here, at least," he observed.

"Yes, and it looks like we don't intend to leave until you've told us the price," my competitor replied, looking at me.

I tried not to show how annoyed I was that he had pumped me for so much information.

"The starting price for the boat is twenty thousand," the owner said almost casually, pressing the information sheets into our hands. "But please feel free to offer more if you like."

I felt as though someone had pulled the boards out from beneath my feet. Twenty thousand! OK, the boat was something special, but it was in dreadful condition, and if I were honest, I'd had no more than ten thousand in mind. That would still have been rather steep, but plenty of junk mail arrived every day offering loans for that kind of amount. I struggled to regain my composure, and finally managed to get ahold of myself. No way would I let the guy next to me see that I couldn't afford it. He merely accepted the price with a casual nod. I was sure he would have done the same if the amount had been even higher.

"If either of you decides to buy the boat, can you please call me by the end of the week? The highest amount offered by Friday will get it."

The highest offer? Did he have other potential buyers up his sleeve? Would there be other viewings? I went hot with panic.

"OK," the man in the suit said, shaking the owner's hand cheerfully. "I'll definitely be in touch."

He gave me a brief glance then moved away. I was left standing there as if someone had dumped a bucket of cold water over me.

"Is there anything else?" the owner asked, probably hoping I'd now give up and leave. He clearly liked the man in the suit much better.

"No," I began hesitantly. "I . . . I'd just like to know the time I have to call by to make sure . . . to make sure my offer stands a chance of being accepted."

Hot flushes were running up and down my spine. My adversary had appeared so nonchalant that he couldn't be half as interested in the cutter as I was.

"You can reach me till six p.m. I've got to go out after that. If you call me by then and your offer is higher than the gentleman's, you can collect the boat the following Monday."

He took his leave with a nod and trudged off down the boardwalk. I watched him for a moment and then turned to the *Storm Rose*. I would love to have thought something like *Don't worry, old girl, you'll be mine soon.* But I couldn't make such a promise.

***

When I got home, I settled down in the living room, where a few boxes were still waiting to be unpacked. My laptop was on the coffee table, and I sank down into the sofa. It wasn't the best posture for my back, but I'd order some office furniture tomorrow. I would have loved to bring the furniture from Bremen with me, but it had belonged to the landlord. I hadn't wanted to gather any baggage around me after Jan left, as though I'd known that I wasn't going to stay.

During the hours that followed, I mulled over the campaign for the hotel. The foundation was already in place; I just needed to refine the details. I tried to focus, but the *Storm Rose* kept returning to plague my thoughts.

At first glance, twenty thousand euros wasn't a huge sum for a boat of that size, but it was far too much for a single mother, one who would have to invest at least as much in the restoration and conversion work. I was well provided for by Jan's child support money, and Hartmann would give me a nice amount for the advertising campaign, but that was money I needed to live on until I netted the next big job. I had to pay the rent, electricity and water bills, and taxes and nursery school fees—not to mention groceries and anything else that cropped up. I couldn't come up with the purchase price without taking a risk.

And then there was my adversary. This time he hadn't looked like a scruffy sailor, but someone who could easily lay his hands on the money. Was he perhaps a scrap dealer, who would rip the cutter apart for profit? He hadn't looked the type to do anything sensible with the boat, but rather someone who would see to it that a gem like the *Storm Rose* would end up in an anonymous ships' graveyard—or at least those parts that couldn't be sold—to be hacked apart by hydraulic machinery.

The buzzing of my cell phone brought me back to my senses. The display showed Hartmann's number.

"Hansen," I said.

"It's lovely to hear your voice again. Hartmann here," my employer said in honeyed tones. He was clearly in an excellent mood.

"The pleasure's all mine," I replied, not entirely truthfully, but with a smile to ensure I came across cheerfully enough. "What can I do for you?"

I thought nothing would have surprised me, but Hartmann said, "You'll be bowled over! We've found an album of historical photos!" He sounded like an archaeology professor who had just discovered the all-important final pottery shard. "Why don't you come by and we can look at them together?" The suggestion *This evening?* hung almost audibly in the air.

I could almost hear myself saying he'd be welcome to send the album over to me, but at the same time I was aware that he was my only client. Asking him to send it over wouldn't give him grounds to cancel the job, but it would sound really impolite.

"I'd love to," I replied. "I take Leonie to nursery at nine. How does ten o'clock tomorrow morning sound?"

I heard Hartmann leafing through his diary. "Would two in the afternoon suit you?"

"Of course," I replied. That gave me a ready excuse to leave by four at the latest in order to pick up Leonie.

"Agreed," he said. "See you tomorrow at two!"

He hung up, and I breathed deeply. I desperately needed more clients, to provide security for us and for my business. And I needed money for my boat. I had to start looking for some new clients.

***

"How did you like the nursery, sweetie?" I asked as I helped my daughter into her coat. A few other children were still there, playing with building blocks. Leonie looked as though she'd really wanted to stay a while longer.

"Awesome!" she said. "I played with Janine and Peter and Claudia."

Three new playmates! Who would have thought it?

I smiled at the teacher, who was just coming through the door. Nicole was the very image of a nursery school teacher—tall, a little plump, with curly hair and freckles. The kind of woman every five-year-old would want as an aunt.

"Hello, Frau Hansen," she said and turned to give Leonie a big smile. "Well, that was your first day!"

"It looks like it's gone really well!"

"Um, could we perhaps talk alone for a moment?" Nicole asked suddenly. I was totally unprepared for that and looked at her in surprise. What could she want to talk to me about?

"Yes, of course."

I looked at Leonie. "I'll be right back."

She nodded seriously and played with her shoelaces, undoing the bows and retying them.

I accompanied the nursery school teacher into the group playroom, where two boys were playing at car crashes, shrieking loudly.

"Is there something wrong?"

The teacher gnawed her bottom lip. She clearly didn't know how to begin.

A fist-sized stone lay in the pit of my stomach. I suppressed the feeling of déjà vu that rose up in me, as I'd had to face conversations like this with the teacher in Bremen quite often.

"Yes, everything's fine," Nicole eventually said. "But Leonie . . . during question time she . . . reacted a little sensitively."

I raised my eyebrows. "To what?"

"Well . . ." Nicole's cheeks flamed red. "It was about her father . . . We always get together in the mornings and talk about what we did on the weekend. As Leonie's new, it was natural that we wanted to find out a bit about her. And when we got to talking about her father . . ."

A chill crept down my spine. "I told you that my husband and I are divorced," I said, willing myself to stay calm. Surely Leonie hadn't been teased because her father no longer lived with us?

"Yes, you did, and I tried to tread as cautiously as possible around the subject . . . but then one of the children asked about him and why he isn't there anymore." She lowered her head in embarrassment. "And then Leonie burst into tears."

I turned to look at my daughter, who was sitting quietly on a bench tugging at the zipper of her shoulder bag.

"Was it one of her playmates?"

Nicole shook her head. "No, another girl. Leonie refused to play with her for the rest of the day. I just wanted to know . . . how we should deal with it," she said.

I stared at her as if she'd just spoken to me in Greek. "I beg your pardon?"

"What should we do if it happens again?" she asked, now a bit more sure of herself. "She cried so badly we were hardly able to console her."

"Well, it's barely been a year since we split up. She's still missing her father."

"She told us her daddy doesn't love her and doesn't want to see her."

I inhaled sharply. Not that our family business had anything to do with this teacher, but I understood that she was worried when my daughter had cried so bitterly and then explained it by coming out with the truth.

"Her father hasn't been in touch with us for quite some time," I explained, suppressing the emotions I always felt when forced to apologize for Jan's behavior.

"Is everything all right with him?"

"Yes, I think so. I can't be sure, but he continues to pay child support regularly."

"Doesn't he make use of his custody arrangements?"

I glanced over at Leonie again, glad that she was far enough away not to hear us. I nevertheless lowered my voice.

"No, he doesn't. It's no surprise, though. He even made it clear to the divorce court judge that he wanted only to support us financially. And he does that well, at least. The money comes regularly and on time." I paused, then heard myself saying something I'd never told any other teacher or babysitter. "It's just sad that no amount of money can alleviate his daughter's longing to see him. I keep trying to get ahold of him, but what can I do if he won't answer his phone? He doesn't respond to my messages. Well, if it was something urgent I'm sure he'd call back, but I'm afraid he doesn't consider the fact that his daughter wants to see him to be an urgent enough matter."

The teacher's expression suddenly changed.

"Men," she hissed, so quietly that I wondered if I'd been meant to hear. Then she added, "That's OK. I know now, and I'll make every effort to make sure the subject isn't raised again."

It sounded almost as though Leonie would be given special treatment from that moment on. She couldn't be the only child here with divorced parents, could she?

"That's very kind of you, but I doubt you'll manage it. The children who've heard about it today might talk about it at home, then hear something from their parents, and repeat it here. And children talk among themselves outside the group sessions. Please just be kind if anyone says anything to her, and try to comfort her. I know you've got a lot to do, but that's all I ask."

The teacher nodded. "Of course."

"And if you have any serious problems just call me. I'll come and collect Leonie if necessary. But I think she'll be fine. She's already told me about her new friends."

The teacher was smiling again now, clearly relieved, or so it seemed to me.

I said good-bye to her and went over to Leonie.

"Would you like a pizza?" I asked, and she beamed at me. If the teacher hadn't told me about her crying, I wouldn't have guessed.

"Oh yes!" she cried out and threw her arms around my neck.

"And then I'll tell you about the boat I went to look at today." Leonie's eyes widened.

"What kind of boat? The one we saw a few days ago?"

"Yes, that one. And perhaps you'll be able to sail on it soon! Come on, I'll show you some photos." Perhaps the *Storm Rose* would cheer her up a little. Perhaps it would also be the thing that would finally enable us to put our problems behind us.

9

I stood on a blue-lit station platform, an old-fashioned suitcase by my side, waiting for a train. It was late, but unlike the other passengers, I didn't go for a coffee, preferring merely to wait.

A figure suddenly appeared on the opposite platform. I could make out only that it was a woman. And suddenly I knew it was my mother looking across at me. I tried to wave to her, but I couldn't raise my arm because the heavy, bulky suitcase was chained to my wrist. I wanted to go to her, but a train passed by, blocking my way. By the time it had gone, my mother had disappeared. She had obviously not recognized me.

I came to as a melody penetrated my hazy dream. For a few seconds I had no idea where I was. As I became aware of a flickering light in the darkened living room, I realized that I was in our new home—and the late film had obviously not been as exciting as I had hoped. The last few lines of the credits rolled across the screen.

In a daze I rose from the armchair, felt around for the remote, and switched the TV off. I put out the light and hauled myself off to the bedroom. On the way I looked in on Leonie for a final time. My little princess was sleeping deeply, her pink cuddly rabbit lying across her stomach.

She hadn't told me what happened at nursery school. Instead she had been enthusiastic about hatching plans for the boat. And since she was a child who wouldn't even think of holding back on her dreams, she also talked about using the boat to travel to her father and bring him back.

She had been so happy that I promised her we'd try—even though I didn't know if I would get the boat, and I certainly had no desire to sail after Jan.

A few minutes later, with the cool pajama fabric warming up against my skin, I realized that my body didn't need any more sleep for the moment. The dream images resurfaced. My mother on the opposite station platform and my desperate attempt to reach her. The heavy weight on my wrist holding me back. Thinking about it gave me a bitter feeling in my stomach.

I knew that weight inside me all too well, but if I were able to shed it, would that be enough to find my mother? Would she recognize me?

It was madness, I told myself. Just a crazy notion. Like the dreams I used to have. This was merely a variation of them. Although I kept my eyes shut, tried to suppress the stupid dream and listen to the soughing of the wind, I awoke fully. A few minutes later I got up again. The red light on my alarm clock showed 3:28. Something was drawing me, an inexplicable force like the moon affecting the tides. I slipped into my tracksuit and left the house.

On the beach the silver strip of the new day on the horizon lit my way. The wind was cool but soft, and the roaring of the waves sounded subdued. I was clearly the only living soul out on the beach at that time. The windows of the hotel were almost all in darkness, one or two still lit up and looking lost in the night. The lights of the pier were like a beacon in the darkness.

I sat down on a rock and drew my knees to my chest. I had no desire to paddle in the icy water. I was buzzing inside as if I had drunk ten cups of coffee. I tried to imagine my boat anchored at the pier to pick up passengers. The interior was full of the scent of warm crumble-topped tarts, chocolate cake, and coffee, and a guitarist was playing songs of heartbreak, while in the background a nervous writer was working on his manuscript.

Would anything come of it? I really wanted that boat. But where would I get the money for it? I didn't have the security for a large loan. At that moment I wasn't even sure if I'd manage to raise ten thousand euros.

I couldn't ask my parents; they needed their money for themselves, especially now that my father was semiretired, since the shipyards were reducing their capacity. My mother didn't earn much from her secretary's job.

Jan was a possibility, but one I dismissed before I could even think about it. It was embarrassing enough that my number would have shown on his cell phone. He had probably deleted my message immediately.

Apart from them, all that remained were the banks, which brought me back full circle. I was racking my brains so much that I didn't notice that I wasn't entirely alone on the beach. Only once the footsteps were almost upon me did the image of the boat fade, returning me to reality. I spun around in surprise as a shadowy figure went past. As far as I could see, it was a man, but there was not enough light for me to make out his features in the darkness. Pebbles crunched beneath his shoes, and I caught a whiff of aftershave. What was he doing here so early in the morning?

For a moment I was seized by fear, stories of women being mugged and raped racing through my head. But the man didn't seem to have noticed me; he didn't pause but walked by without so much as a greeting.

As I watched him disappear into the darkness, I was gripped by curiosity. Why on earth was he here? Was he on his way to some kind of early shift? Or was he on the way home from work? Was he up to some kind of shady business? I was briefly tempted to follow him, but decided against it. I wouldn't want anyone creeping after me, especially not if I had come here to think. So I turned back to the sea, ignoring the stranger. I stuck to my own thoughts, he to his.

With the sun peeping up from behind the chalk rocks, I made my way back. I didn't go directly home, but searched for the rock on which I'd seen the bunch of roses. I expected to see the leaves withered, but the flowers looked as though they had been freshly picked—there were even drops of dew glittering on the pale pink petals. I gazed at them like a miracle, then looked around. The ghostly stranger had disappeared, but I was sure it was he who had placed the flowers here. But why? Was it a romantic gesture for someone who came by here every morning? Or was it a gesture of sadness and remembrance?

A seagull flew overhead with a screech, bringing a legend to mind. The souls of drowned sailors were supposed to return in the form of seagulls. Was someone bringing flowers for them? I stayed for a while by the memorial, then shook off my thoughts and looked at my watch. Ten to five. I had more than enough time to prepare breakfast before waking Leonie.

***

"Are you ready for a new day's adventures at nursery school?" I asked my daughter as I got her pink pinafore dress from the closet.

"Yes!" she cried out in delight, to my great relief.

Her new friends were waiting for her when we arrived, and they dragged her off to join them almost before she had time to take off her jacket. I drove from the nursery school straight to Sassnitz. I arrived much too early, so I didn't park up at the hotel, but down by the harbor. Once again I was drawn to the *Storm Rose*.

It was still moored there, unchanged, and I was unable to tell whether an offer had been submitted or whether any new interested parties had emerged. I took out my cell phone and called my father.

This was when he usually paused for breakfast, so he was bound to have a few minutes to spare. He picked up after just one ring.

"Is everything OK?" he asked, since we usually spoke on the phone only in the middle of the day.

"Yes, couldn't be better," I replied, and heard him heave a sigh of relief. "I wanted to tell you the latest about the boat. And that Leonie's already found three friends at nursery school."

"That's wonderful!" he replied. "At least the news about Leonie. I always knew she was a bright girl." He paused briefly, then added more seriously, "So what about the boat? I hope it hasn't sunk yet."

"No, it's still here. But unfortunately the price is rather steep. The owner's asking twenty thousand euros."

My father whistled through his teeth. "You could almost afford a little yacht with that." And then he asked the question I'd been fearing. "What condition is it in?"

I knew it would do no good to try to conceal anything. My father would hear that something was amiss.

"It's quite run-down inside. It was once used as a day-trip boat, but that was a long time ago. The owner says it hasn't been used since German reunification and it had been lying abandoned in the marina at Timmendorfer Strand. He bought it to renovate it, but his wife fell ill, and now he needs the money to fit out the house for her."

Silence on the other end of the line. I knew what was going through my father's mind. No single mother should saddle herself with a boat like that.

But I had fallen in love with it. Father had always maintained that boats had souls. I didn't know if that was true, but the *Storm Rose* had the most beautiful aura of any boat I had ever seen.

"You want it, don't you?" My father tore me from my thoughts.

"Yes, I want it. I have no idea how I'm going to raise the money to buy it, or how I'm going to afford the restoration, but I know I've got to have that boat."

Father sighed.

"I'd be happy to chip in, but as you know . . ."

"I wouldn't hear of it," I interrupted. "You need your money for yourselves. This is my responsibility."

"Well, I wasn't actually going to offer you money," Father replied, and I could practically see him smiling, the lines at the corners of his eyes deepening. "But your father happens to be a shipbuilder, with friends who could help you to restore the boat. It'll mean lots of persuasion on my part, and you'll have to provide more than a few crates of beer, but if you trust my abilities . . ."

"I certainly do," I replied quickly, as I knew Martin Hansen wouldn't make an offer like that twice. "But . . . will you have time?"

"Of course. However, the boat would have to be towed to Hamburg, as I can't keep driving to Sassnitz. But I could ask Uwe. He has a friend with a tug in port."

I couldn't imagine it all happening totally free of charge, but my father's words were like chocolate after a stressful day, and my mood was suddenly much brighter. *I can do it,* I told myself. *I will do it.*

"Thank you. It'd be really kind." I realized how emotional I sounded. I hadn't even sounded like that when I was a child and got the toy I'd set my heart on.

"Anything for you, honey," he replied. "But now I've got to get back to work. We'll talk about it later—after you've robbed a bank for the purchase price."

As I hung up, I sensed a broad grin on my face. My father hadn't tried to persuade me against it; at least that was something.

The time came for my appointment with Hartmann. He was waiting for me with freshly brewed coffee and a thick leather-bound photo album.

"Please take a seat, Frau Hansen," he said, indicating the chairs.

My suit was a little tighter than it had been when I bought it six months ago, and I opened a button on the jacket, beneath which I was wearing a high-necked white blouse, before taking my seat.

"I'm pleased you have the time to see me. This find has really floored me."

He served the coffee, then handed me the album. As I opened it, I could see that it really was a fantastic find. Nothing was as good for publicity as an interesting history.

Watched by Herr Hartmann, I leafed through the life story of the hotel. I saw the first team of staff with their boss, a man with a Kaiser Wilhelm beard, a stand-up collar, and a watch chain adorning his coat. The maids were wearing long white dresses and starched caps, the male servants were in plus fours, and the bellhops looked terribly stiff in their liveries.

As I looked at the picture, I thought again of the *Storm Rose*. Were there any photos of its first crew? I would love to have seen the sailors and their captain. Sometime, perhaps . . .

"It's really fascinating, isn't it?" Hartmann asked, but I scarcely heard him, as I had come to the pictures from during the war. On some of the photos, the swastika had been scratched away from the flags that had been hung to adorn the building for some occasion. The staff consisted almost entirely of women, and the owner of the hotel was in uniform. A little further on I saw severe damage to the masonry, and refugees housed in the hotel.

"The pictures would make great material for a brochure," I said. "Especially the photos of the front of the hotel."

I was particularly drawn by a photo from the 1980s. It looked as though the only people in it were construction workers, but I could have sworn that one of them was a spitting image of the man in the suit from yesterday's viewing. Of course it couldn't be him—or if it was, he must be hiding a fountain of youth in his cellar. But it could be his father.

"Ah, I find this picture particularly interesting," said Hartmann, interrupting my thoughts. "It shows the renovations during the Communist period. Over the course of the renovations we decided to remove the tiled plinth and return the building to the way it was before the Second World War."

It wasn't until then that I noticed the ugly tiles that had been added in an attempt to make the hotel look more modern. I was young before reunification, but I could still remember tiles like those on other buildings, sometimes even the high-rise blocks. I was glad that it had been restored to its original condition—and that Hartmann hadn't noticed that my interest was not entirely focused on the building.

"Could I perhaps take copies of some of these pictures?" I asked after taking another look at the construction workers.

It was unlikely that I would ever meet the stranger again, and if I did we were bound to have some serious arguments about the boat. Or I would see him going aboard while I stood on the dock for lack of money, watching my dream sail away from me.

"Of course!" Hartmann replied immediately. "Just tell me which ones you need and I'll send the copies over to you. Are you going to put a brochure together?"

"A brochure containing historical information for your guests," I confirmed. "I saw something like that once in a castle hotel in Austria and I thought it was very interesting. Unfortunately, they only had a copy to borrow, and you had to hand it back in. For your hotel I recommend a copy for every room. I even know where you could have them printed inexpensively."

Hartmann waved me away. "Money's no object."

At that moment I wished I could say the same. I selected fifteen pictures from the album and asked Hartmann to have a new photo taken of himself together with his present-day staff—if possible in the same place as that first picture from the last century. I then said good-bye.

Once outside, I looked at my watch. A little after three. We had taken only an hour. That gave me the opportunity to look at the *Storm Rose* again.

This time I didn't take a seat near its mooring but went over to the large stone wall that had been raised around the harbor, so high that its shadow stretched a long way across the walkway. I sat down on one of the broad stones and looked at the houses that rose up beyond the harbor. I also had a view of the *Storm Rose*, of course, and of the Seaview Hotel. Should I suggest to Hartmann that he buy the boat, as a floating extension of his hotel? He certainly had enough money, and he was bound to like the idea of setting up a café in it. But that was not what I wanted. I didn't want to see the boat in anyone else's hands; I wanted to fix it up myself, and maybe even run the café. And Leonie had been thrilled by the idea of sailing in a boat.

"You again?" asked a man's voice behind me. As I turned, I recognized the man in the suit. Except that now he wasn't wearing a suit, but jeans and a light blue shirt that set off his eyes to great effect.

"I could say the same of you!" I replied, my defenses immediately up. I tried to convince myself that he was here purely by chance. He certainly wouldn't be here to bother the boat's owner at all hours of the day. I immediately saw the photos in my mind's eye. Yes, the man from the 1980s looked startlingly like him. A pity I didn't have the photo with me . . .

"It's a small world, isn't it?" He smiled broadly and sat down on a nearby rock. "I don't think I introduced myself properly. Christian Merten."

He offered his hand, and I stared at him for a moment, as if I were worried his handshake would give me an electric shock, before shaking hands as confidently as I could.

"Annabel Hansen."

"My goodness!" he exclaimed. "You have the handshake of someone who moves a thousand crates of fish around every day."

"Who knows, perhaps that's what I do."

His eyes fell to my hands. "No, you don't. Which makes me wonder what brings you to the harbor."

I leaned my head on one side. I was only too well aware how he'd wound me up the previous day.

"I told you far too much about myself last time. I'm afraid I might do the same again unless you tell me first what you're doing here."

It occurred to me that we were eyeing one another like two cats who were unsure which was going to lash out at the other first. Merten smiled, then turned his gaze to the boat. *Aha, caught!*

"She's beautiful, isn't she?"

I followed his gaze. The *Storm Rose* was rocking gently up and down as a tour boat chugged past.

"Yes, she is. And if you're going to start trying to talk me out of buying her, I'm leaving."

"No, don't go," he said quickly. "I'm sorry I was pumping you for information like that yesterday. It's just . . . I don't want that boat to fall into the wrong hands."

I raised my eyebrows. "Really. Why? Do you have some kind of personal connection with her?"

His expression closed off momentarily. "I do, actually, but I'd be grateful if you didn't ask me any more about it."

Wasn't it a good connection? It made me curious, but I decided not to insist. Not yet, at least.

"Do you come here often?" I asked instead.

He was gazing a little distractedly at the boat and at first seemed not to have heard me, but then he turned and met my eyes.

"When I'm on a break, yes. I like coming here. A harbor's a place full of opportunities, don't you think?"

"To be honest, I hadn't really thought about it. I just like looking at the boats. Out there on the waves . . ." I broke off as I felt I was about to open up too much. I didn't want to do that. This man was a stranger and an adversary. Perhaps he was trying another way of kicking me out of the race, once he had seen that he couldn't simply talk me out of it.

"How would you like to go for dinner tomorrow?" he asked suddenly.

"Why?" I burst out. An invitation like that was the last thing I'd expected to hear from him. And the last thing I wanted.

"You'll see," he replied mysteriously.

"You want to check out the competition, don't you?" I said. "Have you made dates with all the others?"

An involuntary smile rose up in me, as I imagined what it would be like to see him meeting the surfer boy or the older man who had been complaining about the boat's engine.

"No, only with you," he replied sincerely. "But of all those who were there, you seem to be the only one apart from myself who's really interested in the boat. I'd safely wager that the others won't be in touch by Friday."

"How do you know that?"

"You're here, aren't you? And the others aren't. They saw the old tub and decided that it's worthless. A day later you're sitting here on the dock looking at the boat, even though I'm sure you have better things to be doing. That's a sure sign to me."

He was right. And I was slightly embarrassed that I was so transparent. He shoved a hand into his pocket and took out a map.

"This restaurant, here, is very good, so I've heard. And I really would like to talk to you about the boat."

The certainty with which he gave me the map unnerved me.

"I have a little girl," I told him, my voice serious. Even if I agreed to an evening out, I'd need to find a babysitter.

"So you're the woman with the child I saw recently by the *Storm Rose*?" he asked. I knew from his expression that he remembered me as well as I did him.

"Yes, probably," I replied. "But what I meant was that I can't go out for an evening just like that."

"Why not? Your husband can look after her, and you can make sure you give her a good-night kiss before you leave."

"There is no husband," I heard myself saying before I realized the ingenious ruse he'd used to find out my marital situation. But it was too late to take it back or conceal anything, so I continued, "We moved here only very recently, and I don't know a soul I'd trust to babysit."

"Where do you live?"

Another personal question, I noted, my instincts warning me against answering. But then I did, despite myself.

"Binz. And I doubt that—"

"A friend of mine works in Binz, in one of the beach hotels," he interrupted. "She has a sixteen-year-old daughter who often babysits for people."

I didn't feel at all comfortable with the thought of leaving Leonie alone with a completely unknown teenage girl. I didn't feel comfortable with the whole situation.

"If you like, I can send Lisa over to see you tomorrow. You could get to know her and see whether your daughter takes to her. And possibly agree on payment terms."

He sounded so confident that he appeared to think it the simplest thing in the world. But I was inwardly rebelling against the idea. Not that I hadn't used babysitters in Bremen. It was usually neighbors' daughters who had looked after Leonie if ever I had an appointment and couldn't take her with me. But I knew those girls—and they hadn't been recommended to me by a complete stranger who was competing with me over the purchase of a boat. A stranger whose reasons for making such an offer were a mystery to me. I hesitated over my reply.

"Don't worry, Lisa's a lovely girl and very responsible. And I won't keep you out too late. I only want us to find a solution for the boat. And that doesn't mean me trying to get you out of the running, if that's what you're thinking. I've got something else in mind."

The way he looked at me as he said it made my resistance begin to crumble. This wasn't the look of a man who wanted something from me—it was the look of a man who needed help. Was that really the case? Was he also short of money for the boat and believed I had a money tree growing in my yard?

"When can Lisa call to see me?" I heard myself asking before common sense could take over.

"I'll ask her later, when I get home."

"Do you live in Binz?"

"Yes, but I'll tell you the rest if you agree. So?"

"Provided my daughter doesn't dislike your friend's daughter . . ."

He nodded, and a smile stole across his face.

"OK. So, you only have to tell me how I can get hold of you—and of course, give me your address, so Lisa can find you."

Back in my car, the doubts came flooding back. What had gotten into me? I'd given a complete stranger my cell phone number and my address! That wasn't the kind of thing I usually did. But I'd never been in a situation like this one before. I wanted to see this project through. Definitely. Because I felt it would do me good, and because I could perhaps put off having to face up to my past for a while. It would be a good idea to meet up with Merten and at least listen to what he had to say.

***

On the way home from the nursery, Leonie chattered away excitedly about her new friends and the fact that one of them had a pony.

"Can I have a pony too?" she asked.

"No, darling, I'm afraid not," I replied, thinking to myself that maybe she would be getting a boat instead. "Our yard may be big, but it's not suitable for a pony."

"We could ride him along the beach," Leonie replied. She'd clearly been thinking about it.

"But he'd have to climb down the steps, and he might break a leg."

Leonie considered this for a while, and I was worried it might make her sad again. But then she asked suddenly, "Have you bought our boat yet?"

"No, not yet. But I'm going to be meeting someone about it soon, and perhaps I'll be able to buy it then."

"Ponies aren't allowed on boats, are they?"

I had to smile. "They might be allowed, but they can't. It would make them seasick."

"Seasick? What kind of an illness is that?"

"When being on board a boat makes you feel bad."

"That's not nice," she said. "OK then, we won't buy a pony. A boat's much better anyway."

She turned to her coloring book that I kept in the car for her. My daughter was right—a boat was much better. Now all I needed was to get it.

Back home, Leonie rushed happily into her bedroom while I took the mail from the mailbox. There wasn't much. A letter from my tax adviser and a questionnaire from the insurance company to brighten up my evening. And an advertising flyer from a fashion boutique in Binz. Frau Balder had obviously been a customer there, since it had her name on it.

My cell phone rang, and I answered without looking at the name. I assumed it was Christian Merten telling me whether the babysitter could come.

When I heard the caller's voice, I froze.

Jan.

"You've called me twice. What's up?" he asked in a businesslike tone, as though he wasn't talking to his ex-wife but to some subordinate who'd had the audacity to drag him out of a meeting.

At first I didn't know what to say. I hadn't imagined that he would call back.

"Hello?" he said into the ether when I failed to reply. Perhaps the best thing would have been to hang up. But I remembered the tears Leonie had shed over him. I'd promised her I'd talk to him.

"I only wanted to tell you that I've moved," I said finally. "And that Leonie's missing you."

"Ah. Then you'd better give my secretary your address, so I can get hold of you if need be."

What about Leonie? He was obviously pretending not to have heard that bit. I tried again, swallowing down the bile that rose to my throat—I hated asking him for anything.

"Leonie's missing you. And she's asking if you'll be coming to visit."

Silence. Clearly Jan believed he'd misheard. Now I was the one who was close to asking if he was still on the line.

But then he said, "You're joking, aren't you? You call me several times when there's nothing wrong, and then you ask if I want to visit my daughter?"

"She's five, and I'm sorry to say she can't yet call you herself," I replied stubbornly. I hated it when he spoke to me in that tone of voice. I'd heard it often enough.

"And because she's five she doesn't understand that I don't have time to drop everything just to come for a visit." He sniffed irritably. He'd soon be pawing the ground like a bull ready to attack. "That's your job," he continued. "We've discussed it. You take care of the child, and I support you both financially. We agreed that we didn't want joint custody arrangements."

"I know that," I replied. "And personally I see no reason to change it. But Leonie's missing you. I can't do anything about that."

That sniff again. I was ready to believe he'd simply hang up. But Jan wasn't like that. He met all difficulties head-on until he'd won.

"Then take her to the zoo. Do something. Go on a trip. If you can't afford it, tell my secretary and I'll transfer the money over to you. Now please spare me any more calls unless it's about something important."

He yelled the last words into the phone. I said nothing, trying to let them roll over me. I failed. Every word hit its mark, and I was unable to respond for sheer rage and disappointment.

"I'm sorry, I have an appointment," he said, a little more calmly. "Call me if there's anything important. And remember to leave me your address."

He hung up. I heard a brief beep, and then the connection was lost. Blood rushed through my ears, and something crumpled deep inside me, like a photo in a merciless hand.

Why couldn't we talk reasonably to one another? There had been a time, once, when we understood each other well. At the beginning of our relationship, he had been attentive and loving, and had given me the feeling that I was the most beautiful, most important woman in the world. But then he had turned to his career, and his work became more important than I was. And eventually so did the other women who naturally chased after such a successful man.

Jan had forgotten all the promises we made when we were first in love. I might have forgiven him for putting me second to his career, but not for his infidelities . . . and certainly not for his indifference toward our daughter.

Tears were suddenly running down my cheeks. I knew he was an idiot, and I could have predicted how he would react to Leonie's request. And yet I cried as I had in the old days, when I discovered that the reason for his absences from our life together was an affair.

"Why are you crying, Mommy?"

Leonie came padding into the kitchen. She must have heard my sobs. She cuddled up to me and curled her arms around my leg. Should I tell her that her father had just yelled at me because I'd told him he should talk to her? If to no one else, then to her. I put the phone down on the table and took her in my arms.

"I'm just a bit sad," I replied, burying my face in her curls. It was impossible for me to be brave at that moment, as I knew that I was unable to fulfill my daughter's greatest wish.

The cell phone rang again. At first I wanted to ignore it, but then I remembered Christian Merten and the babysitter.

"Is that Daddy?" Leonie's eyes shone like they did at Christmas. I swallowed my anger toward Jan and answered.

"Christian Merten here. I hope I'm not disturbing you." I raised my chin. Damn it, I was all tearful and now I had to talk to him!

"No, no, it's good to hear from you."

A sob escaped my throat. How embarrassing!

"Oh, what have I done to deserve this honor?" he replied, then turned serious. "Is everything all right?"

"Yes, I . . . I've just been chopping onions," I fibbed. He didn't need to know why I was crying. I tilted my chin again and asked, "Have you spoken to your friend's daughter?"

"Yes, and she has time to come and introduce herself to you later. About six o'clock this evening. Is that convenient for you?"

"Yes, yes, I think so," I replied, thinking in the back of my mind that we ought to invite her to eat with us if she was making the effort to come and visit.

"Good. She's looking forward to the chance to earn a bit more pocket money. So you still agree to our arrangement?"

"Provided I think she's a suitable babysitter, yes." I wiped my face. "Thank you very much for asking her."

"I'm glad to help. And I'm sure Lisa will be suitable. So, till tomorrow. I'm looking forward to our conversation."

"Me too. Speak to you later."

I hung up and rubbed my eyes. I found it hard to swallow Jan's dismissive attitude, but I tried to suppress all thoughts of him. The girl would be showing up here in two hours, and I wanted to have something to eat on the table by then—and also to make sure that Lisa wouldn't get a hint of anything wrong.

***

"Ba-by-sit-ter." Leonie divided the word into syllables and paused between each as though she wanted to test out the sound of each. "Why is it called that?" she asked.

I opened the oven and took out the pizza I'd hastily conjured up. It was Leonie's favorite, and I hoped Lisa had nothing against it.

"That's what you call someone who looks after children."

I'd told Leonie she would be having a babysitter the following evening. She'd had one occasionally before, but had never taken an interest in the word. Now that she was five, she wanted an answer to everything. It drove me to distraction sometimes. Who, apart from a five-year-old, would want to know the background of a word like that?

"But I'm not a baby anymore!" she protested.

"I know, but that's what it's called. I can't do anything about it. Ouch!" I quickly pulled my hand away from the baking pan and blew on my index finger where I'd touched the hot metal.

Since Jan's phone call I'd been all over the place. I couldn't tell Leonie about it; it would only have made her unhappy again. And I didn't have time for a long conversation with my mother.

"Have you hurt yourself?" Leonie asked with concern as I held my burned finger under the faucet.

"Only a little."

"There's someone in our yard," Leonie suddenly called out. I hurried over to her. Someone was indeed there, someone in jeans and a light-colored T-shirt. She was coming up the steps from the beach. It must be Lisa.

"That's our visitor," I said as I headed outside.

Why had she come up the steps? Was it a shortcut? Did people around here know about the steps? Of course they did, and if not, they were easy enough to find. When the beach was busy, I would have to watch out that no one strayed over our land.

"Wait here; I'll just go and meet her."

As I reached the yard gate, Lisa was already approaching between the rosebushes.

"Those steps are rather steep," she said with a smile and held out her hand for me to shake. "Hi, I'm Lisa."

I looked at her. A typical sixteen-year-old with long blond hair and freckles. No doubt a few of the island's boys had their eyes on her. I couldn't help suddenly seeing myself in her. A young woman full of hopes, dreams, and even ambitions, waiting to find the love of her life, only to fall for the wrong one, maybe. But maybe not. They weren't all like me.

"Hello, Lisa, I'm Annabel Hansen," I said, shaking her hand. "I hope you like pizza."

She nodded and followed me into the house. Leonie was waiting for us in the kitchen. This was the moment of truth. As we entered, she stared wide-eyed at her potential babysitter.

"Hi, I'm Lisa," our guest said, introducing herself easily as though she looked after other people's children every day. "What's your name?"

My daughter stared at her for a moment longer before replying. "I'm Leonie. Are you my babysitter?"

Lisa looked at me hesitantly. "Yes, if your mom agrees."

"Do *you* know why a babysitter's called that?"

"Well, perhaps it was because in the old days a babysitter used to sit on the edge of a child's bed and watch over them?"

"But I'm not a baby anymore!" Leonie protested.

Lisa nodded with a smile. "Well, in that case I'll be a playmate for you. Or a friend, if you like."

"That's good," Leonie said, visibly relieved. "You're my friend."

I went over to the table, smiling, to serve up the pizza. If the conversation with Merten went half as well as the meeting between Lisa and my daughter, I would be satisfied.

10

Before I went into the restaurant Merten had chosen for us, I called Lisa on my cell phone. Merten had been right—the girl, who told me she wanted to be a nurse, really did seem reliable and was very likeable.

"Yes, hello?" Lisa said after the second ring. That was good; she was on the ball.

"Hello, this is Annabel Hansen. I just wanted to check that everything was OK."

If I could have seen her, I wouldn't have been surprised to find her rolling her eyes in irritation.

"Couldn't be better, Frau Hansen," she replied. "I'm trying to teach Leonie how to play Ludo. I think she'll be thrashing me soon."

I was surprised that young people still knew the old board games; I thought it sounded really nice.

"That's great. You can get back to your game. I'll let you know when I'm heading home."

"OK," Lisa replied cheerfully, Leonie squealing with delight and excitement behind her. Incredible.

I said good-bye and retuned my phone to my purse as I glanced in through the large tinted window of the entrance door. I had chosen a simple beige dress with a waterfall skirt—not too dressy but elegant enough not to look out of place in a nice restaurant. I was possibly a little overdressed, but I was happy to take that risk.

Once inside, I was greeted by a waiter in a pin-striped vest. I told him my name and said I was here to meet Herr Merten. He led me to a table where my adversary was waiting for me. He was wearing a light blue jacket and had given his beard a trim.

"You're here!" he called out, and shook my hand as the waiter withdrew. "I hope you don't find the nautical atmosphere here too off-putting."

The impression the place had given me from the outside was confirmed by its interior decor. Of course it looked substantially more upmarket than some harbor tavern, but it nevertheless seemed like the place hardened sea captains would come to for a schnapps or two after a successful voyage.

"I've got nothing against a nautical atmosphere," I replied as I placed my purse on the spare seat by my side. "Otherwise I wouldn't be buying a boat."

I noticed he was looking me up and down. Normally I wouldn't be bothered by men's glances. On the contrary, since Jan's interest in me had waned I had actually sought them out as a kind of affirmation. But I found Merten's scrutiny perplexing and hurried to sit down.

I half expected him to make some remark such as *Nice dress* or *You're looking great*, but fortunately he refrained.

Instead he asked, "Are you from the coastal region? You have quite a marked North German accent."

"I'm from Bremen," I replied. "Before that I lived in Hamburg. And before that in Stralsund." I had no idea why I added that. I'd been approaching my teens when we moved away from Stralsund and was very excited to be moving to West Germany.

"So you were born in the East?" He grinned.

"Yes, I lived there for eleven years. Is that a problem?"

The last sentence came out more harshly than I intended. Perhaps it was because in Hamburg I'd quickly learned that once the euphoria surrounding reunification had died down, people tended to associate coming from the East with being antisocial.

"No, not at all. I'm interested in people's roots, that's all. I was born in the East myself, and after living in various places in between, I'm back here again."

"Really? So you're a bit like me."

As I spoke I felt a spark of sympathy light up inside me. Perhaps he was actually really nice and had the best intentions with this meeting.

"Why did you come back here?" Fortunately, Merten's further questioning was interrupted by the waiter arriving with the menus. They were presented in huge covers, and the prices after the descriptions were rather extravagant. But it wouldn't be good to appear miserly in front of a man you were competing with for a boat.

"Well?" he asked.

I breathed deeply. "Well, if you ask me, the scampi in sage butter looks good. Unless you know of a reason not to have them."

He grinned at me, and I realized he didn't want to know what I was having to eat—I hadn't answered his previous question.

"Oh," I said and felt myself blushing. I set the menu to one side. "I . . . we needed a change. I've been divorced for a year and I thought it would be a good idea to make a new start."

"Here?" Merten raised his eyebrows doubtfully.

"I liked the house. And the terms are very good. I can live anywhere with my job; my work isn't tied to any particular place."

"Are you an artist?"

"No, an advertising executive. I'm building up my own advertising agency. And I've already found my first clients here."

I wasn't about to reveal that it was actually only one client. He nodded, but said nothing.

"What about you?" I asked, as I felt I was beginning to have revealed enough with nothing in return.

"I'm a management consultant."

Now he was the one to set his menu aside. I glanced at his hands. They were neatly manicured, and I saw he had no rings on his fingers, not even the faded trace of a wedding ring. They could indeed be the hands of a management consultant. The suit fit the bill. My spirits sank. Management consultants earned good money; he must be well-off. Provided he wasn't kidding me. He seemed to be able to tell what I was thinking.

"You don't have enough money," he said bluntly. For a moment I felt as though I were sitting opposite Jan again, listening to him listing all my shortcomings as if to confirm to himself that there were better women out there.

I searched desperately for a suitable reply, and when I failed, I felt like grabbing my purse and running out of the restaurant. But I stayed where I was, held in place by the look in his eyes.

"It's true, isn't it?" he asked.

I would like to have snapped that he was wrong.

"What about you?" I countered. I didn't need to add anything; he knew what I meant. "Do you have enough money?"

"Of course," he said, leaning back. At that moment the waiter appeared with a bottle of wine. As I watched him fill my glass, I suddenly found my mind was empty. If Merten had enough money for the boat and knew I wasn't a competitor, why was he meeting me? To confirm his suspicions? He could just as well have put in an offer and knocked me out of the race. Despite my bitter disappointment, I couldn't bring myself to give up on the meal. It wasn't the right moment to sulk like a little child, but I nevertheless said nothing when the waiter asked for our order.

"You wanted the scampi, didn't you?" Merten asked. I nodded. And regretted it, as it meant I'd have to stay even though my instincts urged me to flee.

The waiter noted our order and vanished without me noticing what Merten had chosen.

"So why am I here?" I asked, trying to hold back the tears that threatened to well up.

"Because you have an idea," he replied. "You know what you want to do with the boat."

I looked at him in surprise.

"Don't you know what you want with it?" I sniffed scornfully, with half an eye on my purse. It would probably be better if I vanished then and there before I made a complete fool of myself. What did it matter if I didn't get the boat? I had my daughter, I had a commission for work, I was living in a nice house, which might not belong to me, but that wasn't everything. Why on earth did I want more than what I already had?

The answer rang out in the back of my mind. Because you're always searching for something. Searching for happiness, for a life that's like you imagine it should be.

"To be honest, I don't have any plans for the boat. I just want to have it, for personal reasons. But then there you were before me, telling me with your eyes shining that you wanted to turn it into a café, and I liked the idea. Especially for this boat."

I would have loved to know what he would have done if I hadn't appeared.

"You could take over the idea," I replied coolly, as I still didn't know why he wanted to talk to me. "Why don't you just turn it into a café?"

"I'm not the kind of man who steals other people's ideas," he replied, giving me a penetrating look. "I'm just a man who knows when it's a good idea to find a business partner. You've told me you know something about publicity. There you are—I have no idea about that."

"So how do you keep your business afloat?" I asked in amazement.

"By knowing people. And knowing all about business." He said it drily, without a trace of humor.

The waiter appeared with our plates. The scampi smelled delicious, but I wasn't hungry. Merten's offer should have filled me with delight, if it weren't for the heavy stone in my stomach. Merten folded his arms on the table and leaned forward slightly. The steam from the potatoes next to his fish wafted against his chin.

"Listen, I know you have no reason to trust me. But believe me, I'm very interested in working with you." He took a drink of his wine as though his mouth was dry. "I can assure you that I'd never take advantage of the fact that your stake wasn't as high as mine. While we're talking about bald figures, how much could you afford to pay without ruining yourself?"

I thought about it. I had thirty thousand euros put away, but on the other hand I had only one client, who wouldn't pay me until the campaign was under way. Unless I found new clients, I would be back to living off my savings for a while. Rent, nursery, food, and if Leonie continued to grow as she was doing, I'd also have to pay for a few new clothes. Of course, I was getting child support for Leonie, which was generous enough and could support us both if necessary. I had calculated that I could survive on twenty-four thousand euros a year.

"I could come up with eight to ten thousand."

"That would only pay half the purchase price," Merten said. "There'll be the repairs on top of that."

"I'm working," I replied, hoping I would land some more clients soon. "And perhaps something else could be arranged."

I was thinking of my father and his offer to help repair the boat. Of course that would also involve costs, but I was bound to get mates' rates.

"OK. Then it sounds like I'd be landing myself a good partner. But you ought to eat now. Cold food doesn't taste half so good."

***

The night air was warm around us, full of the smells from the nearby bars and restaurants. I sensed that the weather was about to change, that summer was on its way. Perhaps we'd have a warm June.

The scampi tasted wonderful, but it lay a little heavy on my stomach, probably because I was still looking for the catch in Merten's offer. I had hinted at it several times, but he had insisted there was no catch. If I refused, he would simply snap up the boat himself.

He accompanied me out to my car. His own was also parked in the lot.

"Which one's yours?" he asked, dashing my hope of finding out something about him. He wasn't even revealing his car to me.

We wandered over to my Volvo, and I could tell that Merten considered it fit only for scrap. He was probably wondering how I could ever presume to be buying a boat if I couldn't even stretch to a newer car.

"It gets me from A to B," I said apologetically as I unlocked it. The car didn't even have power locks. "It's reliable and always passes its safety inspection. As long as it keeps doing that I won't be looking for another."

"Do you have a soft spot for the old clunker?" he asked, a little scornfully.

"I've gotten used to it. Maybe I prefer old things to new ones. They already have a story to tell, while new things still need to earn theirs." From the way he looked at me, I thought it was best to turn back to business. It was the safest topic of conversation when you were standing in a parking lot with a man you hardly knew who had made you a business proposition. "Thank you for the offer concerning the *Storm Rose*. I . . ."

Merten raised a hand. "Please don't feel you have to decide on the spot. Drive home, think about it, and let me know. This project is only going to grow, and if you agree to get involved there'll be no going back, so you need to be certain. I'm not a man to go back on my word, and I really hope you're the kind of woman who can see that."

I certainly wasn't the kind of woman to shrink from something, but at that moment I was much too thrown by the offer to simply jump in and assure him that I was also on board and intended to stay there. A boat! I'd always wanted a boat. But I'd wanted to have it for myself. What if I couldn't be an equal partner? Perhaps Merten would change his mind when he realized I couldn't keep up with him financially.

"Here, you'll need this." He handed me his business card.

It was very plain, but the lettering was elegant. Merten radiated professionalism, even with his business cards.

"I'll be in touch tomorrow morning," I promised, then paused, unsure of how to say good-bye. I thought a hug would be too much, although deep down I was dying to throw my arms around his neck. I offered him my hand to shake—formal, but not unreasonable.

"I look forward to hearing from you," he said, his look suggesting he already knew what my answer would be.

11

I arrived home hot all over and trembling with excitement. I was still trying to comprehend what had happened. Was I really going to get that boat?

I got out of the car and looked at the only window where a light was still showing. It was flickering; Lisa was watching TV. I had called before heading home, and Leonie was already asleep. I was amazed that my daughter had obediently gotten ready for bed at Lisa's request. The babysitters in Bremen had often given in, and I would find Leonie sitting in a corner, playing, completely overtired and waiting for her mother to take her to bed.

When I entered, I was met by low voices. Some film. As I put my keys down on the telephone table, I heard it being interrupted by a commercial break. A moment later Lisa appeared in the doorway.

"Ah, you're back. Everything's fine with Leonie; I've just been up to check on her."

"Did she give you any trouble?" I asked.

"No, we played some games and she did a drawing. A cat."

So she hadn't forgotten our visitor.

"I took a soda from the fridge," Lisa continued, although I'd told her she could help herself to anything she wanted. "And thanks for the sandwich. It was lovely."

"No, thank *you*," I replied, getting the agreed payment from my wallet. "It would be great if you could help me out again if I need it."

It was her turn to smile. "I'd love to come back here again. Leonie's a fantastic little girl and the house is awesome."

I was sure that no sooner had she gotten Leonie into bed than she would have taken the opportunity to have a look around. But I didn't mind that. The furniture was long since in place; only the attic was still empty. Had she perhaps sat by the window and looked out to sea? It didn't matter if she had. I wished her good night and warned her to take care on the steps.

Once she'd gone, I slipped into Leonie's room. My little princess hadn't put away her toys, so I had to take care not to trip over her building blocks. But she was sleeping deeply and peacefully, her pink bunny in her arms. I cleared the bricks away from beside her bed as quietly as I could; I didn't want her hurting herself if she got up in the night. Then I bent over the bed and gave her a light kiss on her brow. I was sure she'd be delighted by the news I had.

Then I sat down at the kitchen table. Lisa was a very organized girl; she'd put away the glasses and plates in the dishwasher and wiped the table.

I felt slightly embarrassed that I'd called Merten's honest intentions into question. He might be a bit strange, but his suggestions had been good ones. Lisa had been worth every euro, and the partnership sounded wonderful. Even if I still didn't know what I had done to deserve it.

My own boat. Not entirely my own, but all the same. And I wouldn't have to sacrifice all my savings to get it.

I took out my cell phone. *Take your time to think about it,* he'd said. But what was there to think about? I was sure that in a few months' time I would still think it was better to go into partnership with him than to watch as the *Storm Rose* was snatched out from under my nose.

I looked to see if there were any messages and found an e-mail from Hartmann, telling me that the photos were on their way and wishing me a good evening.

Then I took out Merten's business card. His office was on Goethestrasse, here in Binz. Alongside his office details was his cell phone number. Would he be back home yet, or had he gone to a bar to treat himself to a drink? Was he negotiating with some other potential purchaser I knew nothing about? No, I was sure he wouldn't be. Not if my instincts were right about him.

Since I didn't want to disturb him in private—although there had been no ring on his finger, it was still possible that he had returned home to the arms of a woman—I simply sent a text telling him that I definitely wanted to accept the deal and looked forward to bringing the *Storm Rose* back onto the water.

***

I had forgotten to switch my phone to silent, and a sound from my phone awakened me from a dream in which I was a surgeon experimenting on an animal painted on paper. I looked at the ceiling, illuminated by the morning light, and heard the first notes of the dawn chorus. The sea was murmuring in the background. I rolled over with a sigh and reached out for the cause of my disturbance.

A message had arrived. The number was vaguely familiar. I opened the message and saw that Merten had written back. At 4:15 in the morning! Hadn't he gotten home until then? Or had he already been asleep when I sent him the text, and was perhaps an early riser?

```
I'm delighted you accept. We can talk more
about it on Friday. I'll call Ruhnau.
All the best, Christian
```

Christian. He'd signed off with his first name.

Sleep was well beyond my grasp by now, but because the sound of the sea was louder and the morning light turning a leaden gray, I decided against a morning walk and turned over in bed. I stared at the first drops of rain pattering against the windowpanes and thought of the man who had walked past me in the darkness a few days ago. Suddenly I was filled with an urge to see the roses on the rock. But I could do that later. First I had to wait a while and then see to the most important thing on my mind—phoning my parents.

"My goodness, it's five o'clock in the morning!" my father grumbled as he answered the phone.

I was aware that I'd torn him from his sleep, but I knew he'd never hold it against me. Especially not with the news I had for him.

"I'm getting the boat!" I said quickly, before he could ask if anything was wrong.

"Have you won the lottery?" I heard him yawning.

"What's the matter?" my mother asked in the background.

"It's Annabel," my father told her. "She's the owner of a boat now."

"What?" She sounded more horrified than anything. She was probably sitting up in bed, trying to shake off sleep and find out if her husband was kidding her.

"You're serious, aren't you?" my father asked.

"Of course," I replied. "I've gotten together with the other interested party. We're buying the boat together."

"Well, there's a piece of news!" My father was wide-awake by now, as he always was where boats were concerned. "Congratulations!"

"Thank you. Of course we still have to discuss exactly how it's going to work. To be honest I have no idea. But we're going to get it, and then . . ."

My father was listening intently, and I knew what he was waiting for.

"Well, I'd be really grateful if your offer still stands."

"Which offer?" He played dumb, but I knew it was only one of his little games.

"Dad, you know perfectly well what I'm talking about," I replied, feigning reproach and making him laugh.

"Of course I do," he said. "You know, I always love to hear you calling me 'Dad' in that tone of voice. You hardly ever call me that anymore."

I could have reminded him that I was grown up now, a mother myself and divorced. My days as a sweet little girl were long past. But I knew that meant nothing to my father. His father had always been known as Dad, whatever age his family.

"But, seriously now," he said when he realized I didn't have a ready answer. "Of course my offer still stands. When can I come and look at the old tub?"

"Well, I've got to buy it first."

My father thought briefly, then said, "Sounds like a good prospect, anyway."

"The boat?"

His reply stunned me: "No, I mean your new partner."

"It's not that kind of partnership," I replied, nonplussed. "We're each paying our share for the boat, and we're in the process of working out how to market it."

My father sniffed. "Market it?"

"Yes. A boat like that can't be kept for pleasure. I intend to turn it into a floating café. One where readings and even small-scale concerts are held. Not afternoon coffee for seniors with a bit of entertainment, but events that'll include young people, all happening as the boat sails out onto the open sea."

It sounded wonderful to my own ears, and in my mind's eye I could see the boat riding the waves on a beautiful sunny day. I refused to think about how different it could be when the weather was stormy.

"What does your partner think about it?"

Dad probably couldn't imagine a man getting anything out of coffee, cakes, and the arts, unless he were gay.

"He likes the idea. That's why he's offered me the partnership."

I could practically see my father filing away this potential new man in my life under the reference "Not an Item." He thought for a while, then said, "OK. Let me know when you're ready to begin and when I can come to see it."

"You can come here anytime," I replied. "I'm sure you both want to visit Leonie and me, don't you?"

"You think so?" His sense of humor had returned. I smiled. I could still sense a little resistance in him; he believed a stranger involved in a project was a risk factor. But by the time he met Merten, I would have prepared them for each other.

"Yes, you do. Because you want to see the house and Leonie. And me."

"Of course we do," he agreed quickly, eager to leave me in no doubt that we were important to him. "So, just tell me when we can come. I'll get Mom in the car and we'll be on our way."

"Give them both my love," my mother called from behind him before presumably vanishing into the bathroom.

"Did you hear that? Mom sends her love," he said.

"Give her ours back and kiss her for us."

"I will. See you soon, Anni!"

I hung up. Anni. His special name for me. He rarely used it, mainly when he was feeling proud of me for some reason. And suddenly I heard his words echoing in my mind: *I always love to hear you calling me Dad in that tone of voice.*

I knew exactly why he liked it so much when I called him Dad. It had taken a while for me to accept him as my father, as my dad. Our relationship had been difficult at first, but at some stage common sense had gotten the upper hand with me. There was no point putting up barriers against people who were absolutely determined to save you and make you into a good person.

I gave in, enjoyed his attention, and took my own advice. And my mother had become my mother and my father, my father. I buried what had gone before and looked to the future.

As I was doing now. I wouldn't let myself get dragged down into the past. I had the boat. And I would somehow find my way with Merten, even though he was so goddamned secretive it made me want to hit him.

12

Friday finally arrived, and with it my imminent ownership, or half share, of the *Storm Rose*. As it had soon become clear that no other potential purchaser for the boat had emerged to compete with our offer, we had arranged an appointment with Herr Ruhnau to sign the contract.

"Can we sail on the boat today?" Leonie asked excitedly as I lifted her from her car seat. She had really wanted to come with me, but I'd managed to persuade her that it would take too long and would be too boring for her to wait until all the paperwork was done.

"No, the boat's not fit to sail yet. It's old and needs to be cleaned up first. And then we have to see whether the engine's still working."

"If it's not working, will Grandpa come to make it better?"

My father hadn't missed an opportunity to tell Leonie about his profession. When she was only three, he had taken her with him to the shipyard, where she had been the darling of all his coworkers. The men had showered her with candy and chocolate bars, some of them even raiding their lunchboxes to give the little princess a treat.

"Yes, Grandpa's going to make the engine better," I replied.

"Will I get chocolate again?"

She obviously hadn't forgotten her day at the shipyard.

"Of course you will!"

I led her to the nursery school door, from which we could hear the noise of children playing.

Half an hour later I was on my way to Sassnitz harbor. Leonie was bound to be the star of the show when she told them in the morning assembly that her mother was going to buy a boat. I hadn't told her yet that buying the boat involved a business partner. That was something for later. First I wanted to go to the *Storm Rose*.

As I drove onto the Sassnitz harbor parking lot, the clouds parted and flooded the surface of the water with sunlight. The black submarine lay like a rock in the glittering waves. A few tourists were making their way to the tour boats or disappearing into the little shopping center. I walked up to the dock.

Merten was already there, wearing his peacoat again. He only needed a sailor's cap to make him look like a real ship's captain. It occurred to me that we would also need someone to steer the boat, let alone crew and staff for the café. Did Merten have a license? I could easily believe it.

He greeted me with a smile, a cheerful "Good morning!" and a handshake that would have earned the respect of any wrestler.

"Was your journey OK?"

"Yes, the traffic wasn't too bad."

"I'm glad you've told me that. If Herr Ruhnau blames the traffic we'll know he's making it up."

"Why, is he late already?"

I looked at my watch. Ten to ten. We were supposed to be meeting at ten.

"No, it was a joke," Merten replied.

Christian. Christian Merten. I thought back to the text, but as long as he didn't tell me formally to use his first name, I wouldn't use it.

"You know how it is," he said. "Someone arrives late and blames it on the traffic. Since you can't usually prove it, you accept the excuse, but in fact people are usually late because they can't tear themselves away from their morning paper, because they've overslept, or because they'd like another slice of toast."

"That's a fine way to talk about your clients," I replied. "You've obviously experienced it firsthand."

"Yes, and to be honest it's an excuse I've used often enough myself. And not without success—that is, no one's caught me yet." He paused a moment as if thinking about something, before adding, "I'd better not try it with you from now on, hm?"

I waved him away. "I always prefer to hear the truth. You can happily tell me if an article, a slice of toast, or ten minutes' more sleep keep you from being on time."

Or a woman, I added in my mind.

"I still haven't asked you what your wife thinks of you buying the boat with me," I suddenly heard myself saying, kicking myself the next moment for making such a blunt observation. God, what had gotten into me? Such a remark was out of place. And was none of my business. The way he'd kept himself to himself until then meant I didn't really expect a reply. But he gave me one.

"I'm in the happy situation of being able to make my business decisions as I want to. Just like you are."

Did I hear a hint of annoyance? Well, his answer could mean anything. That he had a wife who didn't get involved in his business, or a girlfriend who wasn't yet his wife, or perhaps he was even single. It was irrelevant to our agreement. I looked at my watch in embarrassment. It was ten o'clock precisely. And I'd managed to create an uncomfortable silence between us.

I desperately tried to think of how to save the situation. This was supposed to be a good day—the first day in the new life of the *Storm Rose*. I was about to venture to make a comment about the weather when a dark blue VW Polo tore past.

"There he is," Merten said, pointing to the car. It had passed us so quickly that I hadn't seen the driver. Herr Ruhnau turned off the engine and hurried over to us.

"Good morning!" he called while still a long way off. He was carrying the obligatory briefcase under his arm. My heart began to thump.
The moment had arrived—provided Merten hadn't reconsidered
because of my stupid question.

"I'm sorry I'm late. The traffic!" The boat owner shook our hands.
"Let's get down to business!"

Merten gave me a conspiratorial glance, together with a grin that
suggested he hadn't taken offense at my veiled question about his marital
status. I returned his smile, fighting hard not to laugh at Ruhnau's excuse.

The paperwork was finished an hour later, making us the official
owners of the *Storm Rose*. Merten handed over the down payment of
ten thousand euros in cash; I was to transfer my share within two weeks.

"I hope you enjoy owning her and she does well for you," Ruhnau
said as he got ready to leave.

I bit back on the remark that it would be quite a while before the
Storm Rose had any chance of doing anything, but we thanked him
politely and took possession of both the briefcase and the responsibility.
Herr Ruhnau gazed into space, visibly relieved. No trace of regret. It
was a millstone from around his neck, and things would soon be more
convenient for Frau Ruhnau around the house.

We stayed for a while on board the boat, like people who pause
for a moment in an apartment for which they've just been given the
key. Merten strode across the passenger cabin as if he were looking for
something. He stopped on the port side and looked at the flagpole.

"Well?" I asked. "What do you think?"

He didn't react, but continued to stare to the aft of the boat. His
expression was distant, almost blank, as though a cloud had covered
the sun. I found it very strange, and didn't say anything more. I waited
for a few moments, and when it still seemed as though he wasn't going
to speak, I turned and walked past a rather threadbare life preserver to
the wheelhouse.

The smell inside was similar to a filling station—diesel and old oil. The steering wheel was wooden and looked worn. The instruments were concealed beneath a layer of dust. Herr Ruhnau had clearly realized that he would never be able to make this boat seaworthy. I laid my hand on the wheel, and although I had no idea how to drive a boat, I imagined maneuvering it out of the harbor. Leonie would be thrilled if her mother became a sea captain.

"There you are." Merten's voice penetrated my daydream. "It looks as though you're about to start her up."

How did you start up a boat? That was a question Leonie could well ask—and probably would as soon as she got the chance.

"I don't have my captain's certificate," I replied, letting go of the wheel. I could see that the dark shadow had left his face. And that he was standing so close to me that I could smell his aftershave. As there was no other way out, I stepped slightly to one side and turned back to the wheel. "How about you? Can you sail a boat?"

"I have a license for motorboats," he replied. "It's valid for rowboats and sailboats too. But I've got no experience with anything as big as this." He'd be amazed at what my father called *big*. "But you're right, you need to get a permit," he continued. "Don't worry, by the time this boat's ready to sail I'll hopefully have obtained one. Or maybe have found someone who does have one."

We stood for a while longer in the wheelhouse, then stepped back outside. Merten avoided looking toward the back of the boat.

"Well, we ought to get to work," he said enthusiastically. "We need a plan of attack for the repairs, reconstruction, and marketing."

I liked that he didn't want to waste any time. And my mouth ran away with me before my brain was in gear. "Why don't you come by my place tomorrow and we can discuss our plan of attack over a coffee."

Merten gave me a broad smile. "OK, what about three o'clock?"

"Perfect," I replied as I shook his hand.

13

"When's the man coming, Mommy?" Leonie asked as she brought me the baking book I'd found on the bookshelves the day before. The recipes sounded rustic enough to appeal to someone who had grown up by the sea. I didn't have to, but for some reason I wanted to convince Merten that my taste in baking was suited to the boat.

"In two hours," I replied as I took the book from her. Normally she would have had a nap at midday, but she was in such high spirits that it would have been pointless to put her to bed.

"What do you want to talk to him about?"

"About the boat. We need to have it repaired so it will go again."

"Oh, great!" Leonie cried out. She sat down at the table, her eyes gleaming with anticipation. She loved helping me bake, and it occurred to me that we hadn't done it for a long while.

"Does the boat need new sails?" Leonie asked as she clamped her hands around the edge of the table and briefly chewed on the table-cloth. She was still short enough to be able to do that, but soon the table would be too small and she would no longer like the taste of the oilcloth. I removed the corner of the cloth from her mouth.

"The boat's going to be given a new engine, but it doesn't have sails."

"But it's got the thingy for sails," Leonie said.

"You mean a mast?" I was amazed that she'd noticed. It wasn't actually a mast but the remains of the fishing tackle that had been left on board for some reason.

Leonie nodded and started gnawing the tablecloth again. Perhaps I should use a fabric tablecloth; she didn't like those. But an oilcloth was better for baking since it was easy to clean, and it reminded me of my childhood. There had always been an oilcloth on the table back home.

"That wasn't a mast," I told her. "That's where the nets used to be fixed. Our boat will have an engine."

"Does the engine use gas?"

"Diesel."

Leonie repeated the word over and over as though sucking on a piece of candy to find out whether or not she liked the taste.

"How far can you go in it?" she asked then. I prepared myself for a long question-and-answer session about boats while I weighed out the ingredients for the cake and added them to the mixing bowl.

"Oh, quite a way," I replied.

The next question followed immediately.

"All the way to America?"

"No, but perhaps to Hamburg."

"To see Grandpa?"

"Yes, to see Grandpa." I realized too late that we were approaching dangerous ground. If we could take the boat to see Grandpa, then why not to see Daddy?

"When the diesel's all gone, do you have to take it to a gas station?" Leonie asked after a brief pause to think.

I breathed a sigh of gratitude. It was too early for pure relief, but if I came up with a good answer now, that would keep her mind off it.

"I'd have to go to a port, yes," I replied. "That's where you fill up boats. Like you take a car to the gas station, yet completely different."

I could see my daughter's imagination running wild, visualizing what a gas station for boats looked like and how it worked.

"Why don't you draw me a gas station for boats?" I asked as I could feel her fidgety creativity growing, the urge to give a form to her thoughts.

"What about the cake?"

"I can manage by myself. You can stay in the kitchen to draw if you like."

Leonie leapt up happily and ran out of the room. She was soon back with her crayons and sketchbook. The fact that she had picked out her best crayons told me the project was really important to her.

"I'm going to draw the boat," she announced. "And the gas station at the port."

I smiled. "You do that, darling. And when the cake's ready you can try it first."

I turned back to my baking ingredients, but when I looked up, I saw myself in the little girl arranging her sketchbook and crayons at the end of the table before sitting down on her chair. Back in the days before I had been awoken by the blue light and the voice telling me that I had lost my mother, my real mother, forever. A shudder ran down my spine, and I forced myself to shake off the mental image.

As the time drew near, I sat with Leonie by the kitchen window and felt almost as excited as I had before my first date with Jan. I hoped Merten would arrive a little early so that I could finally release the tension building up inside me. But he kept us waiting.

I couldn't help remembering what he'd said about excuses. Would he claim he'd been held up by traffic? Or that a client had kept him?

The hand on the kitchen clock moved to three o'clock as I heard an engine rumbling outside the gate. There he was!

Who else would it be? The mailman had already come by—he always hurried to get finished on Saturdays—and still hadn't brought me the photos from Hartmann, which meant I wouldn't be able to show Merten the picture of the construction worker who looked so incredibly like him.

"Well, let's go and greet our guest!"

Leonie followed me outside to see Merten cruising into the driveway on a motorcycle. That was unexpected. Had he also come to our meeting on this bike? An Indian. Made in 1950. Heavy, shiny, loud. And on top of that, rare and expensive. I'd seen a bike like that once at a car show I attended when I was organizing the publicity campaign for a motorcycle manufacturer. That was where I'd first come across the Indian. Or rather, several of them. Vintage models and replicas. I found them fascinating. Deep down I'd wanted to take over all the advertising for the company, but they had their own in-house specialist.

My impressions of this motorcycle had stayed with me, though—I could pick one out from among thousands. I would never in my life have imagined I would see a machine like that here. And now there it was, with the cloud of dust thrown up by its wheels slowly settling around it.

The thundering roar of the engine subsided. Merten fumbled with his helmet and took it off, then turned to us, his admiring audience.

"I hope I'm not late," he said. "The traffic was dreadful. I've never seen so many motor homes in all my life."

"The second wave," I replied. "I got caught in the first last week. The season is officially open."

"I can believe it." He dismounted his machine with all the elegance of a men's cologne ad, put his helmet down, and pulled off his gloves. He didn't look as though he had come from his house in Binz, but from farther away. Where had he been?

I shook his hand, and he asked, "Who's this young lady?"

Leonie made no move to get any closer, but she didn't cling to me nervously, which was a good sign. She looked at Merten as though he were a knight in shining armor from one of her fairy tales. With an Indian for a steed. Not bad.

"This is my daughter, Leonie."

"Leonie," he said. "That's a lovely name." That caused her to run over to me and press herself up against me. She wasn't looking at me, but giving Merten a winning little girl's smile. So she saw him as a knight, or even a prince.

"Have I said something wrong?" Merten asked.

"No, you've hit the mark," I replied. "She's just a little shy right now."

Leonie chewed on her finger as if she were only three, then smiled at Merten again. She obviously really liked him.

"I'm Christian," he told her and offered her his hand.

Leonie shook it, and I noticed with some surprise that he didn't mind that her hand was soaked in slobber. He shook it gently, and I noticed from the corner of my eye that he didn't even wipe it afterward.

"Come in. We've been baking."

I led our guest indoors and showed him where to hang his jacket. A warm scent of leather permeated the hallway. Would it be appropriate to show him around? It was so long since I'd had anyone come to see me at home that I hardly knew anymore.

I decided not to scare him off and led him straight to the kitchen, where we had set the table. Some people received visitors in their living room, but we had always eaten all our meals in the kitchen.

Merten settled himself on the bench and put an envelope down next to his plate. I switched on the coffee machine. Leonie sat down in her usual place, swinging her legs, still watching our visitor as though he had magically appeared from a fairy tale.

"So, these are the documents from the initial survey. Photos and such. I took the liberty of arranging it yesterday—an acquaintance of mine happened to be free and I admit I'd already aroused his curiosity about the boat beforehand."

I hadn't known anything about it, but it was fair enough. And it clearly indicated that Merten had always been serious about getting the boat.

"Well, have we bought ourselves a bottomless pit?"

Now that we had actually bought it, I found that hopes and doubts came over me in waves. What if we couldn't handle it? What if it was a success?

"Of course we'll have to pour plenty of money into it, but my friend was surprised to find it wasn't as run-down as I'd feared. We'll only be able to see for certain once it's in dry dock."

That was my cue.

"I've been talking to my father. He'd be prepared to undertake some of the restoration work. That is, if it's OK with you."

Merten looked at me for a while, as if trying to penetrate my thoughts.

"Your father knows about boats?"

"He's a shipbuilder in Hamburg. Didn't I mention it?"

"No."

A fleeting look crossed his face but was gone before I could grasp it.

"I called him before it was even certain that I'd be getting the boat. He immediately offered to help work on it. But if he did, the *Storm Rose* would have to be towed to Hamburg."

"What would that cost?"

"It would certainly be less than if we paid for it to go to a shipyard. My father and his friends would also be prepared to work on it on weekends—none of it should be a problem."

Merten smiled to himself.

"What?" I asked.

"Nothing. I'm just telling myself what a lucky man I am. Approaching you was definitely the right decision."

Now it was my turn to smile. I poured the coffee. The business of the repairs more or less dealt with, we used the time to figure out ideas for what could be done with the *Storm Rose*.

"We could set up more benches and tables on the upper deck, for those who like to be outdoors," I suggested. "And rig up lights for evening events."

"But we won't be able to do anything like that when the weather's bad, or it could end in disaster," Merten replied playfully.

"Anyway, I think all of our events should be based in the harbor," I said. "A little trip first, then the culture. Otherwise customers and artists alike might get seasick."

"And that would be a waste of the lovely cakes."

"Hey, do you know how a boat's filled up with fuel?" Leonie burst in suddenly, grabbing his arm. I was a little embarrassed, but his expression was perfect.

"Um . . . you put diesel in the tank?"

Leonie wasn't satisfied with that reply. She jumped up from her seat and ran into her room, where she must have taken her drawing.

"Here," she said as she held it out to him. "I've drawn a filling station for boats."

I had expected Merten to look confused or dismissive, but his expression suddenly softened and his eyes seemed to be gazing somewhere into the distant past. Had he drawn boats when he was little? Or perhaps he had a child who did? Again I realized that I knew practically nothing about him. He might not wear a wedding ring, but that didn't necessarily mean he didn't have a son or a daughter.

In my eyes his reaction to Leonie's drawing was too emotional for someone who had no connection with children.

"That's very good." As he praised her, he stroked her hair so gently that she hardly felt his touch.

"Have you been down to the rocks?" Merten asked. Leonie shook her head.

"No, never!"

"Oh, you've got to make up for that!" he replied. "Sometimes, if you go down to the sea very early in the morning, you might see mermaids there. They look out to sea, waiting for the ships. And when the sun rises they go back down into the sea, otherwise they're turned to foam on the waves."

Leonie looked at him wide-eyed, her mouth hanging open. Of course she knew about mermaids; Ariel was one of her favorite princesses.

"Is that really true?" she asked.

"Of course," Merten replied. "But they're very shy and have very good ears. If they hear someone coming near they jump quickly back into the water and swim away."

Leonie let this new information sink in.

"Mommy, can we go down to the rocks?" she asked then, and I recognized her tone of voice that meant *right now!*

"Yes, Frau Hansen, how about a little constitutional?"

"OK, we can go for a stroll," I replied.

I was rarely able to resist Leonie's demands. And perhaps it would be good for her to see how steep the steps were. It would make it easier for me to warn her of the dangers.

A few minutes later we were walking past the rosebushes to the yard gate. I took Leonie into my arms as a safety precaution, since she was still too small to climb the steps.

On the beach there were several people out walking their dogs. The sky had become overcast and lay gray and heavy over the water, which reflected the color of the clouds. We passed the dog walkers and reached the shore, where surf-capped waves washed around rocks and stones. The wind had grown fresh and tugged at my hair. I wished I'd worn a cardigan.

"Are you cold?" Merten asked.

Before I could reply, I had his leather jacket around my shoulders. The passersby must have taken us for a couple, but I didn't mind.

Leonie was peering intently at the rocks, her eyes narrowed as she gazed into the distance. She was probably wondering how big mermaids were, and whether they might actually appear even though the beach was full of people and dogs.

"Can we go and have a look over there?" she asked suddenly, as though something had caught her attention.

"Of course," I said and noticed that Merten was smiling as he watched us.

All of a sudden I wondered how I looked to him. Was I maybe too obsessed with Leonie? Too preoccupied? Or, even worse, did I remind him of his own mother? I would probably never find out.

On the way we talked about the company we would have to establish to make money from the boat after its restoration. We discussed marketing plans and finances. About banks and other sources that could help us, as we would be a new business and possibly eligible for start-up grants.

Then we arrived at the rocks. The mermaid rocks, as Merten called them.

"Is this where the mermaids are supposed to sit?" Leonie asked, placing her hand on one of the large chunks of rock green with seaweed. It was as though she wanted to feel the warmth of where the mermaids had been—or perhaps even the coldness. After all, they were hybrids of people and fish. Would they be cool or warm?

As I thought about it, I noticed another rock. One I had walked past a few times before. The roses on it were a little withered, but I could clearly see that they had been replaced. I was about to mention it to Merten when I saw that he was staring out to sea, where a ferry was heading off in the direction of Sweden. What was going through his mind? Was he dreaming of freedom? Or something else? Just like I did . . .

"So your father's willing to help us?" he asked as though he'd been thinking of nothing other than the *Storm Rose*. But I couldn't shake off the feeling that his mind had been somewhere else entirely.

"He hasn't changed his mind."

He smiled confidently. "We can do it. The *Storm Rose* will be moored in the harbor, ready to go, by next year at the latest." He pointed to the pier, a narrow white strip above the gray-green expanse of the sea.

***

Merten stayed until the evening and entertained Leonie with a whole series of stories about mermaids, pirates, and princes of the high seas. He was a born storyteller, and I was amazed at how quickly Leonie had warmed to him. He told her to call him Uncle Christian, and she even gave him her crayons to draw with.

"You'd have made a great nursery teacher," I said as he was putting his leather jacket back on before leaving.

"Maybe," he replied with a shrug. "Maybe not. I always think of it like this: just as I don't like all adults, I don't like all children. I'm indifferent to most of them, but some of them I find simply charming."

"Well, I'm glad that Leonie belongs to the latter category."

"She really is a bright little girl. It must be difficult for her to be apart from her father."

His words shot through me like an arrow. I stiffened momentarily. Leonie had been happy all day, with no hint of sadness about her father.

"Believe me, I know what it's like," he said after regarding me briefly. "My mother died young, and I had only my father."

He paused briefly, maybe to hide something he was reluctant to say out loud. That brief moment of opening up caught me unaware, so that I didn't question him further.

Merten shook my hand. "Thank you very much. It's been a lovely day and I hope we can do it again soon."

"I'll call my father tomorrow and ask when he can come to look at the boat. I'd love you two to meet each other."

"I wouldn't miss it for the world. After all you and your daughter have told me about him, he must be a special man. I want to meet him at the first possible opportunity."

"He'd like it, too. Have a safe journey home!"

He nodded, put on his helmet, and got onto the bike. The Indian's engine noise drowned out all other sounds and continued to ring in my ears long after Merten had vanished.

Part 2

The Boat

14

After spending all Sunday trying to get ahold of my father, who was probably out in the yard with my mother, I finally managed to speak to him in the evening. We arranged for him to come the following weekend; all the while Leonie danced exuberantly around the living room, claiming to be a mermaid.

Her interest in marine gas stations had waned; in its place she had taken to asking me constantly if we could go out very early in the morning to watch the mermaids.

"But you heard what Herr Merten said—their hearing is excellent and they'd have vanished before we got anywhere near them."

"We could slip silently down the steps," Leonie countered.

Although I was pleased to see her cheerful again, carefree and without a thought of her father, I was worried about her interest in those steep steps. Was I fussing too much? Clucking like a mother hen?

"We can do it sometime," I said, fully aware that to a child the forbidden fruit became all the more enticing the more it was prohibited. "But you'd have to get up really early in the morning."

I knew that once Leonie was asleep, she hated getting up earlier than usual.

So, next Saturday, I said to myself as I sat for a while by the window that evening, looking at the place where the Indian had stood the day before. The tire tracks could still be seen, and I had a kind of warm, pleasant feeling to know that I would be seeing Christian Merten more often from now on.

I found myself back on the *Storm Rose* on the following Wednesday. Before my father and mother arrived to look at my new acquisition, I wanted to clean it up a little. It didn't matter about the dirt accumulated in the corners, as the boat was going to be completely overhauled, but it made me feel better to create a sense of order about the place.

The boat rocked gently up and down on the waves of the harbor. Despite the dull sky, a few passengers were gathering around the tour boats, but I could tell from the faces of the crews standing on the dock that they'd been hoping for more customers.

One of the sailors looked across at me with an angry expression. Did he believe our boat would be competition? The *Storm Rose* certainly didn't look like a likely candidate for that. I ignored him and carried my cleaning equipment on board. I would save scrubbing the decks for later, once the interior was looking as presentable as possible.

I began with the wheelhouse, most of which was thick with dust. A number of spiders had made themselves at home across the ceiling. I hadn't noticed them on my first visit, nor the second, but now I gazed at their life's work—thick, gray, and full of hatched eggs. I was sure they must have spread over the whole boat, and felt fortunate that I wasn't afraid of spiders. The webs were soon removed, but since I didn't find the spiders themselves, they would probably be replaced before long. But it would do for the trip to Hamburg at least.

Once finished with the ceiling, I turned to the floor, which presented quite a challenge, with its thick covering of dirt. But I managed to clear the worst of it. Once I had cleaned the windows, the passenger cabin was well on the way. I then turned my attention to the paneled walls. At one point I pressed too hard with the cloth and suddenly found a piece of paneling in my hand.

"Shit," I swore and tried to fit the panel back in place. Then I noticed there was something tucked away beneath it. Although folded down impossibly small, this piece of paper was undoubtedly the reason for the panel refusing to go back into place. I pulled it out with a sigh. I unfolded the piece of paper and saw that it was an envelope. There was no address on it, and it had probably been pushed between the panel and the wall to seal a draft.

But then I realized that it contained something. I opened the envelope carefully and pulled out a page covered in hurried handwriting. The ink had faded to light brown, and a few letters and words were illegible from damp stains.

13 May 1976

Dear Bob,
I have no idea how to begin. There's probably no rational explanation for what I'm doing. For so many months we've been preparing to come together, dreaming of escape, of Route 66. You've made it clear to me that on the other side of the walls that close me in there's another life, full of freedom and unlimited opportunities. You've captured my heart, loved me, and done everything to bring me here, out on the ocean, at the point between East and West.

But now I'm overcome by doubt. Should I really go? I could jump overboard, but now it's nighttime and an attempt to swim to shore would certainly end in death. And you know that I love life. And I love you and couldn't inflict the pain of that loss on you. So I'll go to the captain.

Palatin is a very kindly man, if a little taciturn, as coast dwellers often are, but you'll know all that if you've spoken to him. Somehow I feel as though I could tell him everything, and I wonder what he would say if I told him about my dilemma.

But I won't do it, don't worry, since our story is ours alone.

I'll always remember how I met you that time in Hungary, how I couldn't forget you, how I did everything possible to stay in touch with you.

Now I'm sitting here on this boat, after all that we've been through, and suddenly I realize that it's not right. I can't just come to you. Crazy, isn't it?

One thing is certain, I'm not going to alight from this boat as you expected and hoped.

I have no idea how you will react to what I intend to do. Perhaps you'll appear at my house and curse me to hell. Or perhaps you'll simply suffer in silence. The choices are all yours. Choices for which I envy you. But they are choices I have to forgo in order to follow my heart where it really wants to go. I hope you can understand.

Love, Lea

I lowered the letter. I found it painful to have read it, while at the same time wondering who this Lea was. And what she was seeking on board the boat. I scanned the words again, and given the date, there was only one conclusion to draw.

The girl, or young woman, had been trying to defect from East Germany! The realization hit me like a physical blow.

Just as my mother had fled the country. The thought resounded through my mind. So much for the idea that the boat would distract me . . .

A bitter feeling welled up inside me, but fortunately I soon got a grip on my emotions. My mother may have fled, true, but that was my own story. Lea's story was a different one and had nothing to do with my own personal disappointments. All of a sudden the wall panel was forgotten. I sat down on one of the benches and stared at the envelope. There was no address on it. Was the letter supposed to have been sent? Or had it simply been hidden here?

An incredible possibility opened up before me. An advertiser's dream. Of course I could be getting ahead of myself, but what if this boat had not only been a fishing cutter, minesweeper, and tour boat, but also a refugee boat?

I took a deep breath and looked at the letter again. A woman writing about escape. Or a decision not to escape. The ship's documents showed that it had been lying in Timmendorfer Strand until German reunification. In the harbor at West Timmendorfer Strand, not far from Poel Island. A boat from the West that may have brought defectors over. We couldn't have hoped for a better story.

I immediately took my cell phone and dialed Merten's number. But it went to voice mail. He was probably out somewhere or with a customer. I didn't want to try his office; he might have been discussing something important and didn't need me interrupting to yell out: *Our boat could have been used to help refugees during the Cold War!*

It was hardly a trivial piece of information, but I certainly wouldn't like it if someone told me something like that in the middle of a formal business meeting. I left him a brief text.

```
Found something interesting on the Storm
Rose. Please get in touch when you get
a chance.
```

I put the phone back in my pocket. A refugee boat. I could hardly believe it. I could see the headlines in the local papers when our boat was relaunched. This boat brought hundreds of people to freedom! A knock on the window tore me from my thoughts. I looked over and jumped as I saw the face of a stranger. He was wearing blue overalls; he probably worked at the harbor. I rose and went out.

"What are you doing here, young lady?" he asked indignantly. "You can't simply go aboard that boat!"

Now I knew why the tour-boat man's expression had appeared so angry.

"I think I can," I replied with a friendly smile. "I'm the co-owner of this boat. Annabel Hansen." I offered my hand for him to shake, and he looked at me as though I were an apparition. "We bought the boat only this past weekend, so word might not have gotten around yet. My partner is Christian Merten; he's from Binz."

Still no answer. Didn't he believe me? If I were someone who wanted to take unauthorized possession of a boat, I'd hardly be giving him our names, would I?

Once the information had taken time to penetrate his synapses, he came around.

"Albrecht Pohl," he said, finally shaking my hand a little tentatively.

"Pleased to meet you. Do you work at the harbor or are you with one of the boats?"

The man looked at me in confusion. He had clearly thought I'd take my opportunity to make myself scarce.

"I'm on board the *Nansen*," he said, and, realizing that I had no idea which boat the *Nansen* was, he waved an arm toward the other side of the harbor. "Sorry, I really thought you had no right to be here."

"That old superstition about women on board ship?" I replied with a wink. "I can safely say I've been on board a few boats in my time and they haven't sunk because of me."

I earned myself a blank look. Either he hadn't understood the joke or sailors no longer believed that a woman on board brought bad luck.

"OK." Pohl scratched the back of his head. "I'll be on my way. If you like, I'll keep an eye on the boat every now and then for you. I used to do that for the previous owner. We're in port most of the time; we don't get much of a catch these days, so we usually see anything that's going on."

"Thank you, that would be very kind," I said, fully aware that he would soon be making inquiries around the harbor to check that I really was entitled to be here.

Once I had finished my cleaning, I got back into my car. My cell phone rang. I grabbed it from my pocket, caught a glimpse of the name Merten, and answered.

"What's your exciting news?" my business partner asked. I could hear loud traffic noise behind him.

"I've found something," I replied and was about to add that we could talk about it later if it wasn't convenient. But since he had called me, he must have time, so I said, "I wanted to get the boat spruced up a little—I assume you got my e-mail?"

"Yes, I did. And I'm really looking forward to meeting your father on Saturday. I was going to write back later. I'm on my way to the station right now."

"Hamburg?" I asked.

"Hanover. I met a customer here and I'm now going on to Berlin. If I ever get to the station."

"What's holding you up?"

"The Great Pedestrian Crossing Conspiracy. All the lights are obviously conspiring against me and staying red for ridiculous lengths of time whenever I appear."

I grinned so broadly that the corners of my mouth ached.

"So, what have you found?" he asked.

"A letter."

"A letter?" he echoed. "And?"

"It was folded up and tucked away behind a panel on the wall that came loose as I was cleaning. Yet another thing that needs repairing."

"Not the end of the world. Tell me more about the letter."

"At first I thought it had been put there by chance, a piece of paper used to plug a gap." *Come on, get to the point,* I told myself, *he's on the way to the station.* "Anyway, it's a letter from a woman who was clearly escaping to the West on the boat, or at least trying to."

I paused, waiting for his reaction. Silence. Only the hum of the traffic indicated that Merten was still on the line. Was he having to fight his way through a crowd of pedestrians?

"Hello?" I said after a few moments. Perhaps he'd dropped his phone, or . . .

"Yes, I'm still here. Sorry, I'm just crossing the road."

"Did you hear what I said about the letter?"

"Yes, I did. Very interesting."

Nothing more? I was already envisioning the range of marketing possibilities offered by a letter like that. But he was taking the information as though I'd told him that I'd found a layer of blue beneath the white paint. Maybe he really was having to concentrate on the traffic.

"Well, I think it's amazing! It gives our boat a story. To be honest, I'd never have thought our boat could have been used to transport escapees. Of course, I'll have to do some research, but if it turns out that the letter is more than just any old piece of paper . . ."

I still couldn't sense any enthusiasm on his part. What was the matter? His silence was putting a damper on my excitement.

"Um . . . of course we don't have to tell anyone about the boat's past, but I think it would be a great way of getting some publicity. I bet there isn't another tour boat in Sassnitz that has a history like I think the *Storm Rose* has. But if you've got something against the idea . . ."

"I don't have anything against it," he replied. His voice sounded different. Softer, with a certain tone that I couldn't quite catch because of the traffic noise. "You're right, it's wonderful."

"Do you want me to scan the letter and e-mail it to you, or would you like to wait and see it for yourself on Saturday?"

"I'd like to look at it for myself," he replied, adding, "I'll be quite tied up in Berlin and probably wouldn't get around to it. And a scan doesn't come across too well on a cell phone."

"Oh," I said, quickly adding, "Yes, you're right, these things are really difficult to read on a phone screen."

As if he'd be on a business trip without taking his laptop with him, I thought, but quickly pushed the thought aside. He was under no obligation to look at anything immediately, however exciting I might find it. I'd put the letter in a plastic sleeve and would try to find out by Saturday who this Lea might have been.

"Listen, I'm at the station now." Merten's voice pulled me back to the present. As if to confirm his statement, I heard the distinctive *bing-bong* and a muffled voice announcing the arrival of a train.

"OK, see you Saturday," I replied, trying not to sound too disappointed.

I was being silly. Merten had things to do; his thoughts could be full of plans for changing the fortunes of some company or other. And there I was with a trivial letter. After all, what would I have said if he'd interrupted a meeting I had with a client to tell me something of the kind? It had been good enough of him to call me back.

"Have a good trip," I said before hanging up.

15

In the evening I sat for hours at the kitchen table, the letter in front of me and a notepad and pens within reach. Lea's words played on my mind as I sought to make a connection between her story and mine. I had put strong barriers up against letting everything come back to the surface, and finally decided to get all thoughts of Lea off my chest by writing them down, so I could keep the two things separate.

"Are you going to draw something?" Leonie asked.

She was sitting at the other end of the table, starting another mermaid picture. Apart from finding new inspiration in her fairy tale books, she had been euphoric when I picked her up from the nursery. As I had imagined, she was the star of the group because of her news about the boat. Many children now wanted to be her best friend in the hope that it would get them a ride on board. My daughter had naturally made the most of the opportunity and kept them hoping. I would never have believed it of her. She'd obviously inherited her father's business brain, which even I couldn't deny was excellent.

"No, I'm just writing down a few thoughts," I told her, looking at the few lines I'd set down on paper. They were only key points that I'd distilled from the letter. A man called Bob. A captain called Palatin.

Escape across the Baltic. Lea, the name of the woman. Timmendorfer Strand, the boat's home port.

It all sounded like an exciting story, but told me little about the writer. I looked at the letter again. Beautiful, neat handwriting. Traces of the typical letters taught in schools throughout East Germany could be made out clearly. The woman must still have been young. I tried to visualize her. Lea—it sounded almost elfin; maybe she was red haired, a gentle person who had found the love of her life. A good-looking, muscular man, perhaps even an American on vacation behind the Iron Curtain. She had wanted to leave the East for him . . . And then reconsidered, for whatever reason.

The phone burst into my reverie. Not my cell phone, but the landline. The only ones who had my number were my parents. I jumped up, ran into the hall, and picked up.

"Hello?"

"Hello, my love; it's Mom here." My mother usually left phone calls to my father because she had a thousand and one things to do. The fact that she was calling now, and unexpectedly at that, caused a sudden concern. Had something happened?

"I hope everything's OK with you," I said.

"Of course, why wouldn't it be? I do like to make the occasional telephone call, you know. I hope I'm not disturbing you."

"No, of course not. So, how's everything? Are you ready for your visit to our humble Baltic abode?"

"Humble abode?" my mother retorted. "In that case the photos must have shown a completely different house. The one I saw wasn't humble. Are you going to tell me you've found dry rot in there?"

"No, everything's great. And I admit, it's hardly a humble abode and it's in great condition."

"Unlike your boat, I take it."

"There's nothing that can't be fixed. At least I hope not. Dad will be delighted; it's just the kind of boat he likes best. Not an oversophisticated freighter, but no rowboat either." To my father, anything less than thirty feet in length was a rowboat.

"Your father sends his love and asked me to tell you that he's arranged for the boat to be picked up. He's convinced his boss to let you rent the empty hangar. Of course it'll cost you, but if your business partner is as well-off as it sounds, that should be fine."

"Not to worry; he keeps saying that the cost isn't a problem. I wish I could say the same myself."

I could imagine all my mother's possible replies. From *People who don't have any spare cash shouldn't buy boats* to *Maybe you should threaten Jan that you'll come and visit him—I'm sure he'll pay any amount to keep you away.* But she didn't give voice to any of them since she knew that I didn't want Jan to have anything to do with my new life. And it wasn't like her to reproach me. She believed that families should stick together, however crazy their members.

"It'll work out, and your father's gotten his friends really excited about your cutter. Was it really a minesweeper?"

"Yes, that's what it says in the documents." Should I drop my bombshell now? With her love of history, my mother would certainly have something to say about it. "And I've just discovered something today that will bowl you over."

"Out with it!"

I told my mother about my find. "Just imagine, our boat was probably used to transport escapees from East Germany—isn't that incredible?"

There was silence at the other end of the line.

"Hello, Mom? Are you still with me, or did I send you to sleep with my tale?"

"No, no, I'm still here."

"So what do you have to say about it?"

"Well, yes, it's an old letter. It must be a valuable document."

"And?"

"And your boat was used to transport escapees." She made it sound as though it were nothing special.

"But don't you think it's amazing? I've found the starting point for a possible publicity campaign. And apart from that, I've just gotten a client with a beautiful hotel who also wants me to bring some history into his advertising . . ."

Why did I feel as though I were talking to the wall?

"I'm sure you'll be able to make something wonderful out of it," my mother replied. No further questions about the letter or whether it was possible to find out who the woman was.

"Could you put Leonie on for me?" she asked after a moment.

I'd been brooding and forgotten to respond to her last remark. I suddenly felt heavy as a stone inside. This was the second time I'd told someone about my escapee's letter, and neither my business partner nor my mother seemed to find it at all exciting.

Sure, the word *escapee* would trigger memories in my mother; perhaps she even hoped I'd forgotten all that had happened in the past. Under the East German regime, she had been fiercely opposed to those who tried to defect from the Republic, as she believed that you could only make life better there by staying. But this had nothing to do with my birth mother. It was merely a letter written by a young woman—and after all, it had been twenty years since the Wall came down. Surely it was possible to turn a blind eye to it by now, especially since the story would make really good publicity for our boat.

"OK," I said eventually, as I had no desire to discuss all that. I hadn't seen my mother for quite a while and didn't want to pick a fight about the past. "Leonie, Grandma wants to speak to you!"

The chair scraped along the floor, and a moment later she was there. I handed her the receiver, which she held in both hands, crying out "Grandmaaaaa!"

I left Leonie telling my mother all about the nursery school and went back to the kitchen. My eyes fell on the letter. No one else had seen it. Was that why? Was I a step ahead of the others and that was why I couldn't understand how they weren't as overjoyed as I was? I stroked my finger over the crumpled page and wondered about getting a frame for it.

When I returned to the hall, Leonie was still in the middle of her story.

"A man came to our house and told me all about mermaids," she said, her eyes shining. "They sit down by the water just in front of our house, but when people come near they swim away."

I didn't hear my mother's reply, but I was sure she'd soon be raining questions down on me.

"I really want to see one, but Mom says I'm not allowed to go down the steps. They're steep and I could fall."

I was glad my daughter had taken my ban to heart, even though it made the steps that much more enticing to her. I continued to watch her for a while, until my mother must have asked her to put me back on. Leonie said good-bye and blew a big kiss before handing me the receiver.

"A man, huh?" my mother said playfully. Her voice was back to normal. Not that it hadn't been before, but when I mentioned the letter, she had briefly sounded as though a shadow had fallen over her. "So why haven't you told me about the new man in your life?"

"Mom," I said, drawing out the syllable. "That man's only my business partner. He was here last week to discuss a few things with me. Repairs, marketing plan, and the like."

"Oh." My mother didn't sound convinced. "You haven't told me—or your father—a thing about him. Apart from the fact that he has money and he's bought the boat with you."

"What else was I supposed to tell you?" After all, I hadn't given them a detailed description of Herr Hartmann from the Seaview Hotel. But then he wasn't the "man" who had come to our house. My mother was always interested in any men who entered my life. Although "men in my life" was rather an exaggeration, as prior to Jan I had only had one relationship, which hadn't lasted long and hadn't meant much to me. And after Jan I hadn't even been on a date.

"Well, what he looks like, for instance," my mother replied, clearly eager for some exciting gossip. "Is he attractive? Your age?"

"No, Mom," I replied. A year had passed since my divorce, and during that time I hadn't been out with a single man. Not for personal reasons. I was fine with that; I had Leonie and my small advertising agency to keep me occupied, and now the house here and half a boat that needed fixing up. The last thing that had crossed my mind was to look for a new partner. "He's three times my age and has a hump like the Hunchback of Notre Dame."

"Oh, really," she said. "So that means he's really good-looking. Otherwise you wouldn't be inventing such tall tales to try and stop me from pairing you off."

My mother knew me too well.

"You don't need to pair me off with him. I'm OK as I am. And yes, he's good-looking and I think he's a few years older than I am. He has a motorcycle and has really won Leonie over." I paused and heard my mother holding her breath in anticipation. "But all those qualities make it more than likely that he's already spoken for. It looks like he's not married, but that doesn't mean anything. And you never know, it could be possible that I'm not his type."

"Well, that's a lot of information about a man you say you're not interested in."

"I never said that."

"So you *are* interested in him?"

I rolled my eyes. "Mom . . ."

"No harm in asking. You're still young and you're pretty. It would be a waste if you didn't find a man."

"If the opportunity arises I'm sure I won't say no," I replied, a little irritated, although I wasn't sure why. My mother meant well. No one wanted to see their child alone forever. "But I've only just arrived here and so much has happened that I haven't had a chance to think about it." I paused and then added in a more conciliatory voice, "You'll get to meet him this weekend anyway. Then you can see if he's suitable for us. But for God's sake don't drop any hints or try to get him to go out with me."

My mother hesitated before replying. I knew her well enough to know that she would try. Fortunately, my father would also be there, and the men would probably be more interested in the boat.

"OK, I promise," she said at last. "So, see you this weekend. Give Leonie a kiss for me, will you?"

"Of course. See you Saturday!"

I hung up and looked into the kitchen, where Leonie was back in her seat, drawing. I wasn't alone. And I wasn't lonely. But my mother's words echoed in my thoughts. Perhaps it would be a good thing for Leonie to have a new father figure. One who cared about her even though she wasn't his own flesh and blood. One who wouldn't let her down. And it would also be good for me to be close to a man after all this time, one whom I could love with all the pent-up longing in my heart. One who would be there for me and hold me.

16

My work progressed slowly as I waited for Saturday to arrive. I had sent Hartmann my first draft of the publicity brochure and was waiting for his response, although the auto-reply from his e-mail address indicated that he was away on business until the following week.

That left me with enough time to think of the elfin Lea and her American boyfriend. Admittedly, most of my musing slipped into the territory of the soaps, but I told myself that TV dramas were notorious for exaggerating reality rather than departing from it altogether.

"Leonie, have you cleaned your room?" I asked as I folded up the last few moving boxes. Saturday had finally come, and we were adding the finishing touches before my parents arrived. I had stowed everything away in the cabinets and was amazed at how good the living room was looking.

"I'm working on it!" Leonie called from her room.

Since yesterday Leonie had been going wild at the prospect of her grandparents' visit. She hadn't seen my father and mother for a few months and missed them as much as she did her father. We had been cooking and baking to make sure there was enough to eat. If I knew my mother, she'd turn up with the biggest pickled-herring-and-potato salad in the land, with a cake in hand, too—enough to feed half of Binz. I really hoped that Merten wouldn't be alarmed by it all.

After quickly checking Leonie's room, and finding that it did actually look quite a bit cleaner, I went to get the mail. The furniture company from whom I'd ordered a desk and some shelves for my office wrote to inform me that they would be delivering during the coming week. I hugged the card to my chest. I was looking forward to getting the furniture so my office would finally become a real office.

As I turned to go back indoors, I heard the rumbling of engine noise behind me. I turned and recognized the car right away.

"Leonie, Grandma and Grandpa are here!" I called.

"Hooray!" came the cry from indoors.

Moments later my daughter came rushing out. My father parked his Golf neatly in front of the gate and switched off the engine. Leonie ran up to the car before either of the doors had opened. I followed her, smiling; it was lovely to see my parents again.

"That traffic was crazy!" my father muttered as he opened the door and got out. Leonie fell on him immediately, leaving him with no choice but to gather up the little whirlwind in his arms and let her shower him with kisses.

"Hello, Mom," I said, giving her a big hug. She looked well and relaxed, in a flowing blue dress patterned with white flowers, her salt-and-pepper hair neatly tied in a bun. She smelled of vanilla cookies— she had probably been baking since the crack of dawn, and she also loved vanilla-scented perfumes. During the East German years it had been difficult to find a perfume she liked, and now, with the vast range available, she found it hard to choose which one she liked best.

"Hello, darling," she replied, planting a kiss on my cheek. Then she gave me a playful tickle, feeling my ribs. I recoiled, giggling.

"You've gotten thinner," she said reproachfully. "You mustn't forget to eat."

"Don't worry, I'm eating. We're eating." I pointed at Leonie, who was still clinging to her grandfather. "Leonie will confirm it. We even have cake every now and then."

My mother didn't look convinced.

"I know what it's like when you're on your own. You think it's not worth cooking a proper meal. But that's a mistake."

"I know," I replied obediently. "I'm hardly anorexic, though."

It was simply that when I was immersed in a job, I sometimes forgot the passage of time—and that included eating. And when I had been in the depths of the divorce, I had sometimes lost my appetite, feeling as I did that my stomach was full of stones.

"I promise I'll eat everything you put out in front of me today. There's a wonderful smell coming from inside your car." I had seen a number of Tupperware containers in the backseat, alongside a certain something wrapped in a large dishcloth. It looked like a cake box.

"In that case we'd better have a little digest if ready for afterward—as usual, your mother's cooked enough to feed an army," my father chipped in. He passed Leonie to my mother and kissed me on the cheek.

"You want to make a good impression on the co-investor in your boat, don't you?" my mother said.

"Herr Merten is one man, not ten," my father countered. He knew full well that making a good impression on a man had little to do with the amount of food he was served. "But let's not argue about our guest's appetite. Come on, show us around the house and yard. We need to take our minds off our rather eventful journey."

"OK. Let's get everything inside, then I'll give you the grand tour."

***

"You've got everything nicely in order," my father said as he sat down on the kitchen bench. Over the previous half hour, he'd seen everything—the rooms, the outside of the house, the yard, and the dangerous steps. Leonie had wasted no time in telling him that he had to take care on them in case he should fall. I was proud of my little girl. "It's a shame you can't buy the house. You'd have it for life then," he continued.

"Who knows where her life is going to take her?" my mother replied. "She's bound to marry again at some stage, and her future husband may already have a lovely house."

"Mom," I protested weakly. "I couldn't buy the house, anyway. Half a boat, perhaps, but not a house. The prices on the coast are comparable to those in Hamburg, and the bargains all come with a catch."

"The way you said that, it's as though you've ruled out the possibility of ever meeting another man."

"I'm not ruling anything out," I said. "But we've got to get settled in here first, Leonie and I. Then we'll see what happens."

The thundering of the Indian rolling onto the drive saved me from having to continue.

"Is that him?" my mother asked, hurrying to the kitchen window and craning her neck.

"I think so." I felt my pulse quickening. They were about to meet him. And he would see us, my family and me. What would he think about the cake? The vast array of Tupperware? Was he the kind of man for whom these things mattered? And why was I even thinking about it?

Merten parked his Indian next to my father's car, hung his helmet on the handlebar, and walked up to the front door.

My mother was so excited, I thought she was about to sprint over to open it, but my father's look, accompanied with a slight shake of the head, held her back.

Merten rang the bell, and I went to the door.

"I have to warn you," I said as I opened up, "my mother seems to think you're my potential future husband. Expect to be both interrogated and fattened up."

"What?" Merten turned pale, then blushed.

"Don't worry," I said. "Only joking. But the bit about the interrogation and fattening up still stands."

"I guess that puts my mind at rest."

I led him into the living room and introduced him. My mother's eyes lit up on seeing him. She was probably already imagining what our children would look like.

"Uncle Christian!" Leonie cried out and rushed over to him, greeting him almost as enthusiastically as she had my father.

I saw my mother raise her eyebrows. A smile crossed her face as she saw Merten ruffle Leonie's hair and promise her to tell her a new mermaid story.

"These are my parents," I said. "Elfie and Martin Hansen. And this is Christian Merten, the other shareholder in the *Storm Rose*."

"I'm pleased to meet you," Merten said, shaking their hands in turn. "I've heard a lot about you."

That was a slight exaggeration, but my parents were flattered.

"The pleasure's all ours," my mother assured him.

"It's nice to meet someone who shares our passion for boats," my father added. "There aren't many of us around these days."

That was also an exaggeration, but in turn it flattered Christian. I immediately felt that he and my father would get along well.

"I hope you're feeling hungry," my mother said, bringing our guest back down to earth. "I've brought a few things. Do you like potato salad?"

Merten grinned. "I love it."

As we devoured my mother's potato salad, she tried to get as much out of Merten as possible, but he managed to dodge her questioning without appearing the slightest bit disagreeable. My father, on the other hand, almost overwhelmed him with tales from his life and work. And with praise for his motorcycle. I realized where I had gotten my own garrulousness from.

Later, once we had eaten our fill, Leonie showed off her latest pictures and earned herself plenty of praise before disappearing into her room with my parents so they could see her posters. Although he had held his own admirably, Merten now looked a little relieved.

"Wears you out, doesn't it?" I said as I began to clear away the plates. "I'm sorry, my parents are always like this when they meet someone new."

"Your parents are very nice. You've inherited a lot from them."

"Well, it's nurture rather than nature," I replied without thinking. "Actually, they . . ." *Shit,* I realized I'd said too much once again. "They adopted me."

Merten's eyebrows shot up in surprise.

"You're adopted? Well, well, I could have sworn that you take after your father."

He'd noticed, too.

"Many people think so. And I'm glad about it."

I could have told him that I had never known my biological father and hardly remembered my birth mother, but I managed to pull myself together in time. We were silent for a moment, then a sudden draft caught the card from the furniture company, which I'd put down on the windowsill after our little guided tour of the house. Before I could react, he'd picked it up and turned it over.

"You've ordered some furniture?" Merten asked.

I took the card from him, a little embarrassed.

"Yes, for the office upstairs."

"Do you need some help to put it together?"

I thought about the last time I'd tried to assemble a desk. The kit had been pure hell, with screws missing and mismatched holes predrilled in the wrong places. I'd succeeded in making a piece of furniture from it, but afterward I'd felt as though I'd been run over by a steamroller. A little help wouldn't be a bad thing, but in my mind's eye, I saw the way my mother would rejoice when I told her he'd helped me.

"Are you offering to help me?" I asked in surprise.

"Only if you'd like me to."

"Yes, I'd like that," I replied. Once again I felt that warm feeling of pleasure that had washed over me when he visited us for the first time. "If it's no trouble."

"Not at all. I like working with my hands. Well, I should say it's in my blood—my father was a construction worker."

His remark shot through me. I remembered the man in the photo who bore such an uncanny resemblance to Merten. Perhaps it was mere coincidence, but possibly . . . If Merten was originally from this area, why shouldn't his father have been involved in the construction or reno‐vation of buildings around here? I bit my lip, and suddenly had an idea.

"Wait here a moment," I said.

"What for? Are you about to go and get your toolbox?"

"No, something else." I slipped into the living room. Leonie was still keeping my parents busy, so we had a few more moments. I went to the pile of material for the Seaview Hotel and pulled out the envelope containing the photos. I took it to him.

"Here, have a look at this," I said. Merten looked at me in amaze‐ment. "If your father was a construction worker, you might like to see this."

I rummaged among the pictures of the hotel and its staff, and found the photo I was looking for. Only then did it occur to me that it was out of place in the collection. Hartmann must have wondered what I wanted it for.

"I'm doing a publicity campaign for the Seaview Hotel. When I was looking at the photos for it I noticed a man who's a spitting image of you." I passed him my find enthusiastically. "Do you happen to recognize this man?"

Merten looked at the picture and froze. I couldn't read his expression.

"That . . . that's my father." The words finally passed slowly over his lips. Then he turned away, but not fast enough. I clearly saw tears in the corners of his eyes.

"I'm sorry, I . . ."

The words stuck in my throat. He raised his chin and got ahold of himself.

"It's not your fault," he said in a husky voice. "It's just that I haven't seen a picture of him for so long. He's been dead for a long time. Life . . . life got to be too much for him."

Awkwardly, I took the photo back and shoved it into the envelope. I shouldn't have shown it to him. But how was I to know that it would affect him like that?

"I'm really sorry."

I was full of questions, but I didn't ask them. If Merten wanted to tell me, he would.

"Oh, here you are!" My mother peeped into the room as if she'd caught us kissing and cuddling. But she soon saw that neither of us was in the best mood.

"I . . . I was just showing something to Herr Merten," I felt compelled to explain.

I waved the envelope in the air and slipped past my parents into the living room. My heart racing, feeling completely unsettled, I pushed the envelope away beneath the other papers and took a moment to calm myself before returning to them.

That was the second time he'd reacted strangely. Once to the letter, which I still didn't understand, and now to the photo, which I understood completely. Time healed, but couldn't erase all pain. I remembered him telling me he had lost his mother at an early age, and then his father had died when he was barely an adult.

I remembered the helplessness I felt when I realized that my mother had gone. But fortunately I had other trustworthy people who had stepped in to take her place. People who were still with me and who were right now beginning a conversation with my guest that would probably allow him to forget for a moment what had happened.

***

"Mommy, where are you?" Leonie's voice echoed through the corridors of my mind.

I'd been staring out the window into the courtyard, gazing at the tall trees that surrounded our house like watchmen.

"Grandpa wants to go to the boat!" she added.

"I'll be right there!" I replied, tearing myself away from the window.

The harbor was very busy that afternoon, and we were lucky to find a parking space. We finally managed to park the Volvo and the Indian a long way back from the seafront.

Merten had wanted to make his own way, which I could well understand. He would want to be alone and reflect after unexpectedly seeing his father again. Nothing helped more than driving, as I well knew.

Once in Sassnitz he seemed to be back to his old self. He hid his feelings so well that I couldn't make out the slightest trace of anger or sadness on his face.

"Come on!" Leonie tugged my sleeve impatiently. The others had already gone a ways ahead. My mother and father had obviously taken a liking to Merten. She was mothering him as if he were her long-lost son.

We wound our way through the groups of tourists heading for the tour boats, earning ourselves curious glances from those standing nearby as we went out onto the jetty and walked up to the cutter. I recalled the overeager sailor from the *Nansen* and grinned.

"You've got yourselves a beauty here!" my father said, his eyes shining. He seemed not to have noticed the patches of rust, the peeling paint, the barnacle-encrusted hull, and the damage to the superstructure. "I can hardly believe she's so well-preserved after all these years.

I've seen newer cutters in the scrapyard and thought, *what a shame.* But this one's going to last another hundred years easily, if she's well looked after."

I tried to imagine how things would be a hundred years from now. Would Leonie's grandchildren be sailing on this boat? Or would her children have sold it after I died and they were unable to keep it? I found no answers and knew only too well that I couldn't expect my grandchildren, if I had any, to share my dream. But I hoped they would.

"Just wait until you've seen inside, especially the engine room," I replied, as I knew my father was particularly critical when it came to boats' engines.

The two men vanished into the engine room. I had planned ahead and brought a couple of towels, since I was sure my father would emerge with his hands covered in oil.

Meanwhile, my mother and I went with Leonie into the passenger compartment. I felt a little uncertain. Since her strange reaction to the letter I hadn't brought it up again, but my gaze fell immediately on the panel that I hadn't been able to fix back in place. I had stowed the letter in a plastic sleeve and made a copy for Merten. I should have given it to him that morning, but something had held me back until just before we left. And then I'd made that misjudgment with the photo. I should have shown him the valuable historical document instead.

"This boat reminds me of the sixties somehow," my mother said as she sat down undaunted on one of the stained benches. No cleaner in the world would be able to remove those patches. New upholstery was a must—another job I had to take care of.

"It's strange how some things weren't so different."

"Between West and East, you mean?"

My mother nodded. "There comes a time when everything gets old and doesn't look any better than the things we had to put up with for years."

That was true. All things grew shabby over time, the only problem in former East Germany being that some shabby things were never replaced.

"So this is where you found that letter?" my mother asked out of the blue, her arm around Leonie, who was now tired and snuggling up to her. Normally it would be time for her midday nap.

My mother's question surprised me. I hadn't expected her to raise it with me again. I pointed to the missing cladding panel.

"Over there. It was behind that."

"What did it say?"

"That the writer was in the process of reconsidering her defection. Of course I don't know the background, but she's apologizing to a man for her change of heart."

My mother looked out the window to the nearby boats. "She must have done it, though, if she left the letter here."

"You think so? She could have given it to the captain. Maybe he didn't pass it on because he didn't want to disappoint the recipient. Or the man didn't come to get it."

"But why would it have ended up hidden like that?"

"Perhaps the panel came loose and the captain simply used the letter as a wedge."

My mother stared ahead of her in silence for a moment. A thought occurred to me.

"Say, Mom, would you ever have left? If the Wall hadn't come down and things had gotten worse? If things got too difficult to bear?"

My mother shook her head. "No, probably not. It takes a lot of courage to leave behind everything you love. Or a lot of indifference."

It took a moment for me to grasp what she meant by that. My mouth suddenly turned dry. My birth mother had left me behind. I was sure that she had been indifferent to me. It was true—Elfie Hansen would probably never have done it. Before either of us could say anything else, the men entered the room.

"So?" I asked.

I had a sinking feeling when I saw their worried expressions.

"The engine's had it. I tried to start it up, but nothing doing. We'll have to tow the boat to Hamburg," my father said.

I looked at Merten. His face was dark, confirming my worries.

"Can we manage that?" I asked, silently figuring out the money it would swallow up.

"Sure," my father said after exchanging a conspiratorial look with Merten. "I can ask Uwe if he can come to tow the *Storm Rose* away. His boat's much bigger."

Uwe Norden was a fisherman, the owner of two huge trawlers and a barge. He and my father had become friends shortly after we'd moved to Hamburg. At first they had hated one another, each full of prejudice about people from the other side of the Iron Curtain. But somehow they'd come together and were now like brothers.

Transporting it wouldn't be a problem, but we now had a much bigger one.

"How much do you think a new engine will cost?" I asked.

My father scratched his head. "Well, that's the question. We need one that will fit into the engine room, and if I'm honest, that's quite small for a boat like this. In any case a new engine will be ridiculously expensive. But with a spot of luck we should be able to find a second-hand one."

"For the bargain price of . . . ?"

I could tell that they had already discussed the cost, as they both looked rather awkward.

"Between twenty and fifty thousand, all in. You ought to get a reconditioned one, if you don't want to heap a whole load of problems on your backs forever and a day."

"On top of all the other expenses . . ." I muttered, more to myself than the others. "Can't anything be done with the one that's there?"

My father shook his head. "I'm afraid not. There's so much wrong with it that it would cost you double that to have it reconditioned."

I took a deep breath. It all sounded anything other than good. And the way Christian was looking, it would overreach even his finances.

"Where would we find a suitable engine? The Internet? Classified ads?"

"You should try everything. And I'll ask around. Perhaps one of the scrap dealers will get something in before long. If we find a good engine, it'll be no problem to install it."

And if we didn't? I didn't ask that one out loud, as I didn't want to lose heart before we had even tried.

"Chin up! We'll get it worked out, won't we?"

He looked across at Merten, who concealed his worries behind a smile.

"Sure we will. There's no such word as *can't*."

"Of course there isn't," I replied, mustering my fighting spirit and hoping that no one could see the worry on my face.

My business partner finally took his leave, turning down the invitation to have dinner with us. My mother was sad about that and, to be honest, so was I, since I feared that his sudden departure had something to do with me and the photo of his father. I returned to the house with my parents and Leonie. We sat talking in the kitchen for quite a while. It was a cozy evening that reminded me of the old days.

I had intended to show them the letter, but since I knew that my father had no time for those who left East Germany, either, I let it go. At least I had managed to give Merten his copy of the letter so he could take a look at it.

Once my parents had disappeared into the living room with its sofa bed, I sat in front of my bedroom window, looking out into the night. I had anticipated that there would be costs, major costs, but getting a new engine was an enormous challenge. And Merten's expression at the news unsettled me. He surely wouldn't be able to afford all the expense himself, and as for me, I certainly didn't have enough money.

My cell phone suddenly buzzed nearby. It could only be one person, as any of the others who might have been calling were sleeping peacefully in the next room.

I'm sorry I acted so strangely. I'll tell
you everything one day. But at the moment
the Storm Rose comes first, OK? Thank you
for the letter. It's wonderful.

I studied the message for a while, nodded to myself, then wrote back with trembling fingers:

OK.

Another message soon followed:

And my offer to help install the furniture
still stands. Just say the word. Good
night!

17

The boat was picked up at 6:00 a.m. the following Wednesday. As agreed, Merten was there. When the *Storm Rose* had been hooked up to the tow rope, he sent me a short video with the note:

She's off!

It was a wonderful moment when our boat was towed out of the harbor. If everything went according to plan, she'd be returning under her own steam.

Later that afternoon, as I was waiting for my office furniture, whiling away the time by toying with the Seaview brochure, my father called.

"Hi, Dad, how's everything?" I asked.

Something was roaring and beeping behind him. It sounded like a garbage truck, but since he was at the shipyard, it must have been a crane's warning bell.

"How's my little girl?" he said in reply, as if I were still ten.

"As you can imagine," I replied. "Has the *Storm Rose* arrived yet?"

"She's just come in. If you can believe the captain of the tug, the old girl behaved herself well."

"No wonder. Without the engine there wouldn't have been any resistance."

"You're right there. I just wanted to ask when you want to come and have a look at her. I've persuaded the foreman to let us put her into dry dock this evening. The surveyor happens to be coming tomorrow, so he can have a look at our old girl while he's here. Then we can put a cost estimate together."

Cost estimate? That sounded unsettling, somehow. I envisioned a stream of zeros stretching into infinity.

"How does Friday sound? Three in the afternoon, perhaps?" I asked after a quick look at my calendar. I could keep Leonie home from the nursery and set off early so as to avoid the weekend traffic. And my mother would be thrilled if we stayed until Sunday.

"Friday is excellent," my father replied. "But you know that means you'll have to spend the night with us."

I grinned. "We have no problem with that. Leonie was really sad when you left."

"So, we'll look forward to seeing you. I'll tell your mother so she can get to work on the guest room right away."

"You do that. Give her my love!" I blew a kiss to the phone and hung up.

Cost estimate. The moment of truth would soon be here. Would we be able to repair the *Storm Rose*, or would my—no, our—wonderful dream burst like a bubble?

"Mom, there's a big car in the yard!" Leonie's voice drove my thoughts aside.

The doorbell rang a few moments later. At last!

"We've brought some furniture for you," one of the deliverymen said. In their gray T-shirts and blue overalls, he and his colleague looked more like plumbers. "Where do you want us to take it?"

"Upstairs, please." I indicated the way.

They looked at one another, nodded, and a moment later the first man appeared with a huge package. I was amazed to see him carrying it on his narrow back.

"Just put it down wherever you like; there's nothing else in that room yet," I called after him. His colleague followed shortly afterward with a similarly large load on his shoulders. I watched him go, then went to get my wallet. Once they were both gone, I'd call Merten.

***

"Friday? As soon as that?" he said, a little surprised.

He was away again, but this time I caught him on his cell phone right away. I figured that he might already have had plans for the weekend, and wanted to let him know in plenty of time that I was about to wreck them.

"Yes, Friday. Provided you don't have anything else going on."

"I don't," he said easily.

"You could come with us if you like," I suggested, a little rashly as I wasn't sure if that was what he wanted.

"Thank you, that's very kind, but I've got an appointment on Friday morning."

"We don't have to be there until three o'clock," I replied. "If that's too early for you I could always call and put it back a little."

"No need for that; I can manage it. So, see you Friday?"

"See you Friday," I replied and hung up, feeling a little let down.

On Thursday night I was extremely agitated. I tried to make myself sleep, but that ominous cost estimate kept appearing before my mind's eye, plaguing me with horrific visions of tens of thousands of euros that I didn't have and couldn't imagine ever seeing in my account.

When the alarm finally moved to seven thirty, letting me know with a soft beeping that the night was over, I felt as though I'd taken a dose of stimulants. I woke my daughter, or rather I got her into a state where I could dress her and carry her out of the room.

We didn't have to set off so early, but the journey to Hamburg gave me the chance to make a slight detour to Timmendorfer Strand. The idea had come to me when the cost estimate had finally retreated from the forefront of my mind, allowing my attention to wander back to the letter. Maybe I would find my first hint of Lea there.

I strapped Leonie into her car seat, packed some necessities and our travel bags into the trunk, and set off. Binz was deserted. As I was heading toward the autobahn, I passed an old American school bus parked opposite a hotel. It was probably used for tours around the island.

As I drove along the autobahn, I remembered the last time I had been in Timmendorfer Strand. That had been over five years ago. Jan and I had made up after a series of difficulties, and he had decided to spend a bit more time with me.

I didn't know yet, but I was already pregnant with Leonie. We had been trying to have a baby for some time. After feeling nauseated at the smell of a plate of mussels, and realizing when we returned home that these attacks occurred even without shellfish, it became clear that the makeup sex had left behind more than the short-lived increased attentions of my husband.

Jan had been delighted when I told him I was expecting a baby. At last we would be a real family, and I convinced myself that things had only been so bad between us because of our childlessness.

I was mistaken.

After Leonie was born, things rapidly declined between us once again, and I had to concede that a child was no cure for an ailing relationship. In her first few months, Leonie had been very restless and cried a lot. Jan went to work early in the mornings, so I was the one who had to get up in the night, give her a bottle, and calm her. It was not long before Jan began to feel neglected and he became indifferent toward me. He threw himself into his work, started a fling with a new employee, and allowed himself to be flattered by the attention that I, exhausted after a day with the baby, was unable to give.

At first it made me sad, but I had Leonie now. She was my anchor whenever the sea of lovelessness threatened to engulf me. For my part, I began to ignore Jan, and that was fine for a while—until he told me he could no longer live with me. That had been a good two years ago.

But my memories of the vacation in Timmendorfer Strand were good. At the time I would never have dreamed that I would return here to research the history of a boat that I co-owned.

The sun rose, radiant, over the Baltic as I finally steered my Volvo off the autobahn. After a short drive, we saw the sign welcoming us to the resort. Leonie was awake in her car seat by now. When she saw the beach, she probably didn't realize that we wouldn't be staying long.

I was less interested in the promenade this time, but drove to the suburb of Niendorf, where there had once been a harbor and a small shipyard. If the documents were telling the truth, the *Storm Rose* must have been brought here for refitting after the war. Perhaps there was still someone here who had worked on her, and who had known Captain Palatin. Someone who could confirm that the boat had been used to transport East German refugees. Maybe Palatin even lived here himself?

Since I didn't have a surname for either Lea or Bob, Palatin was my biggest hope of making any kind of discovery. I hadn't found his name in the phone book, but that didn't necessarily mean anything. He might have moved away or had an unlisted number.

Here in Niendorf there might be someone who had some information about the captain and his boat. The *Storm Rose* could have been refitted at the Evers shipyard, which was now a marina, but was bound to have some old documents still. And if they didn't, there might be people around who could tell me something.

The sailboats rocked lethargically at their moorings around the harbor. A few people were getting their craft ready to sail, pulling on windbreakers and loading boxes on board. I tried to imagine the *Storm*

Rose here. She would have looked huge beside these sailboats, like an elephant among a herd of gazelle. But those had been different times.

I left Leonie safely in the car with her crayons, the window rolled down a little, and went over to the boats. After wandering around the harbor for a while, I finally met a man who looked as though he worked there. He was standing with a bucket of water in front of an advertising sign, which he was clearly about to clean.

"Excuse me," I said, earning myself a look of irritation. "I don't want to keep you from your work, but I'd just like to ask if you know someone called Captain Palatin. And whether there's anyone here who worked at the Evers shipyard." The man looked at me as though I'd asked him about a shortcut to Mars.

"Are you from the press?" Did that make any difference?

"No, I've just bought a boat that used to be based at Timmendorfer Strand."

The man raised his eyebrows. He clearly thought I was among those who moored their sailboats here. I wanted to dispel that impression right away.

"It's an old fishing cutter. The *Storm Rose*."

The man before me seemed old enough to remember the boat.

"Someone from the East bought that," he said. "It's a while ago, a few years after reunification."

"Yes, and now the boat belongs to me," I said, noticing that his reference to "from the East" was said in a slightly disparaging tone. "It's had quite a colorful history, and now I'm looking for people who may know something about it."

"All the former shipyard people are long gone," he said. "And Georg Palatin hasn't lived around here for a while."

"Where did he move to?" I asked. I knew that even if someone seemed mistrustful, it was still possible to draw information out of them.

"To Timmendorfer Strand," the man replied. Before I could question his sanity, I realized that we were in Niendorf here, and although the place was a district of Timmendorfer Strand, it had preserved its own identity—at least in the hearts and minds of some of its inhabitants.

"You don't have an address, do you?" I asked, figuring that he would now send me over to one of the buildings. He studied me for a few moments, then told me the address.

"Oh, thank you so much!" I said in surprise.

"I've no idea whether he's still there, but he'll be the one who knows most about the old tub."

He turned back to his work. I glanced once again over the sailboats and yachts before making my way back to the car to drive to the address he'd given me.

Georg Palatin lived on the edge of Timmendorfer Strand, in a nice area that would have looked good on any postcard. I decided to leave Leonie in the car for a few minutes and then go back to get her if Palatin happened to be in.

My heart thumping, I approached the little house. It was incredible to think that this was the home of the captain who had tried to help a woman to escape to the West—or had even done so. I wasn't sure what the truth was, but the fact that the letter had been hidden behind a cladding panel in the passenger compartment was perhaps an indication that she had gone through with it.

I looked at the flower beds and the lawn that needed mowing. I saw a wreath of dried ears of corn and artificial poppies hanging on the door. A completely normal house, in which a hero might possibly live. A hero who had preferred to stay in the shadows, it seemed.

"Hello?" a woman's voice croaked. I stopped. As there was no one around except me, I turned. Standing by the neighboring fence was a woman in overalls and rubber gloves, holding a bunch of carrots she had just pulled from the soil.

"There's no one in," she told me, adding, "I hope you're not trying to sell something."

I raised my eyebrows.

"No. I was just paying Captain Palatin a visit," I replied. "I've bought a boat, the *Storm Rose*."

The woman regarded me blankly. She clearly didn't know what I was talking about. Had Palatin moved here after his active days at sea? It was entirely possible when I thought about what the man at the harbor had said.

"When will Herr Palatin be back?" I asked, aware of the neighbor's suspicion. "I swear to you, I'm really not here to sell anything," I added to reassure her. "I simply want to talk to Herr Palatin about the boat."

No reaction. Was she hard of hearing, perhaps?

"It's a lovely boat," I added.

"The Palatins are on vacation." A younger woman approached, clearly the daughter of the elderly lady with the carrots. "They set off only yesterday; you're really unlucky to miss them."

I was indeed; I had so hoped that the captain would be able to tell me who had written the letter. Of course, it was entirely possible that he had no idea. Maybe he had simply taken on board a group of nameless refugees and delivered them to their destination—not because he had no interest in their names, but to protect himself from the inquisitive questions of the Stasi.

"I just wanted to talk to Herr Palatin about his boat," I repeated to the younger woman. "I've bought it and would love to know something about its history."

"Oh, he'll be able to tell you a thing or two," the woman replied. "He was at sea for a good sixty years. Whenever we get together he always has lots of stories."

That was good. Very good. Even if I didn't track down this Lea, I would at least learn something about the boat. And about how her captain came to be transporting defectors from East Germany.

"Do you perhaps have a telephone number I could reach him at?" I asked, without really believing she would give it to me. After all, I was a stranger, and as I knew from my own experience, people in the north didn't always react well to questions like that. "Or could I leave you mine?"

I took out my business card. I had quickly printed some off on my computer a few days ago. The woman nodded and took the card.

"So, you've bought a boat, have you?"

I nodded. It would probably become the next big topic of conversation for the street's gossips.

"Well, I hope you always have fair weather and a following wind!" said the neighbor as she waved good-bye. I thanked her and waved back.

When I returned, Leonie had drawn a big fleet of ships—a whole harbor full. From a distance, it looked like the one in Niendorf.

"Did you see the captain?" she asked.

"No, he's on vacation," I replied as I slipped in behind the steering wheel.

"He must be sailing around on a boat," Leonie said. She began to draw a fat yellowish-green sun in the sky.

18

I had always been fascinated by shipyards—the huge cranes, the extensive docks, ships' hulls large and small lying in dry dock. As a child, after I had been accepted by my adoptive family, during the school vacations I was sometimes sent to the shipyard in Stralsund with my father's lunch, which he occasionally forgot. When I moved to Binz, as I drove over the Rügen Causeway I had glanced over at the distinctive big blue hangar of Stralsund shipyard and was immediately transported back to my childhood.

The shipyard in Hamburg also triggered good memories in me. I had visited my father here sometimes and watched how a ship came together. They had constructed the really big vessels here—in the past at least, as orders for such ships had gown rare in recent times.

My father was waiting for me at the entrance to the works, which was guarded by a gatekeeper. This was Kalle Blom, one of the few employees who had been kept on.

"Good morning, Herr Blom," I called over and waved. Although I had known him for many years, I had never dared to call him Kalle as other people did, even though he would insist on it.

"I don't believe it—the little Hansen lass!" he shouted out. "And the even littler Hansen lass!" He got up from his chair in the gatehouse to have a look at Leonie, whom he obviously recognized.

"My, my, you've grown, girl!"

Leonie looked at the man in amazement, then tightened her hand around mine. The last time she had been here, she had still been too small to remember him.

"Yes, they all grow up," my father said. He greeted us with a kiss, then scooped Leonie up into his arms. She let him with a whoop of joy.

"Well, my love, did you have a good journey?"

"The Volvo can still manage it," I replied with a smile.

"Who knows for how long. As a future boat owner, perhaps you should get yourself a new car."

"Maybe being a boat owner means I can't afford a new car," I replied. "Have you gotten the *Storm Rose* into dock yet?"

My father nodded. "We have indeed. There's not a lot to do around here at the moment. A few yachts and motorboats, a new fishing cutter. The age of the big ships is long gone."

"Don't say that. The time for a revival can come around for anything."

I knew perfectly well that my father was right, but I also knew how much he hoped that the times would improve. And maybe his wish would come true, and the time would come when the really big tankers would be launched down the slipways once again.

"Where's your business partner?" he asked, looking around. "I thought he was coming with you."

"He had an appointment today," I said. "And he probably wants to impress your workmates with his Indian."

"He's bound to make an impression with that bike." My father looked over toward the work sheds, and I could sense he was itching to get over there. "Does he know he needs to check in with the gatekeeper?"

"He'll soon find out. I really have no idea when he'll be arriving, so we can happily go on ahead."

My father led us to Hangar 5, the doors of which stood wide open. It was a space used for smaller boats—if a fishing cutter like the *Storm Rose* could be called small. She was now lying in dry dock and looked even bigger than she had in the harbor. The damage, however, was much more visible.

"She's a magnificent lady, isn't she?" my father asked, indicating the cutter. "And she'll be even more magnificent when we've finished with her."

"So she can still be saved."

"Of course! And don't worry about the engine; I've already started putting feelers out. By the time we've gotten the hull shipshape we're sure to have found something suitable."

"There you are!" someone called out behind us. I turned and saw Merten coming through the door. His leather jacket was open, and beneath it was a gray T-shirt with a large black anchor print. I thought about how he must have caused a real stir at the shipyard gates with his Indian.

"The gatekeeper said you were here." He shook our hands in turn, including Leonie, who was thrilled to see her "Uncle Christian."

"It's good to see you," my father said. "And I'm looking forward to hearing what you've got to say about the way our old girl's coming along."

"The pleasure's all mine," he replied, giving me a radiant smile. His gaze rested on me as my father began to tell us about the work that was being planned for the boat. It sounded overwhelming to me, as though they were trying to revive a total complete wreck.

Merten nodded at each of the items, his face betraying nothing. After looking a little perplexed that day he first heard that the engine needed replacing, he seemed to have gotten his reactions well under control.

"It all sounds much worse than it is," my father concluded, tucking his clipboard under his arm.

"How long will you need?" Merten asked, still as cool as if he had a goose laying golden eggs in his cellar.

"I figure we can do it by October. Of course that means the tourist season will be over, but it won't be too late for events in the harbor."

Merten looked at me.

"That's true. As long as the weather's warm enough we can start holding events," I agreed. "And the boat has a heating system, so we can get it all cozy inside. The only thing we won't be able to do then is go out on the open sea."

"You're the expert where events are concerned," Merten replied with a smile.

"So, if you agree I'll get a cost estimate over to you. We won't be charging labor for the hours my friends and I spend on her on the weekends, so you'll have to pay only for the materials. But we'll need to get professionals in for some things."

"You're professionals, too," I reminded him, but I knew what he meant. This job wouldn't get done on just a few hours' work on weekends.

"True, but you want this boat soon, not in a couple of years' time. She won't be able to stay in dry dock for that long, either—the costs would be enormous."

"Here you are!" Dad's coworker, Helmut Siewert, strode in through the door. "Martin, you're needed."

My father excused himself and disappeared, while we stayed behind with the *Storm Rose*.

"It sounds like an enormous challenge, doesn't it?" Merten asked without taking his eyes off the boat. "But you must have taken all that into account—didn't you?"

"If I'm honest, no. When she was in the water she looked quite a bit better, and I can't help thinking that old Ruhnau ripped us off. But we've got her now and we're not going to give in."

"We're certainly not."

I looked at his profile, and noticed that his beard was a little more pronounced than the last time we met. Was he growing it? With the warmth and the scent he emanated, I felt like moving a little closer to him, but I stayed where I was and glanced instead at Leonie, who was beginning to look rather bored.

"Well, I think we're real business partners now," Merten said suddenly, finally turning his eyes away from the boat's hull.

I found his remark rather strange. We had been partners ever since I'd accepted his offer and we'd signed the purchase agreement together.

"And as business partners it would perhaps be more appropriate to be on first-name terms. Or do you have any objection?"

I stared at him in surprise. Another bolt from the blue. You usually got more informal over a glass of wine.

"No, not at all. I've nothing against it," I replied, offering him my hand. "Annabel."

"Christian," Merten replied as he shook it. "What would you say to drinking to that at a nice restaurant this evening?"

"I'm afraid my mother's going to be monopolizing me tonight." I saw disappointment cross his face. I thought about how nice it would be to go out with him again. "But . . . well, I could ask my mother to babysit Leonie, and we could get together for a glass or two."

"Really?" he asked as if worried I might change my mind again.

"Really. Actually, my mother would be delighted to have her granddaughter to herself for a while."

"That's great. So, eight o'clock? I'll pick you up."

"On the bike? Have you brought a second helmet?"

"I do have a car as well. And as it happens, that's what I've come here in."

I smiled. "OK. Eight o'clock it is, then."

Before I could ask him where he was going to spend the night, my father reappeared.

"These young ones," he muttered. "They can't do anything for themselves."

"You mean us?" I joked.

"No, the guys at Dock One. You just begin to think they've learned all they need to know, and then you find they have to consult the experts for every little detail." He went on, losing me in the technicalities, but soon got himself under control. "But never mind. I've discovered something else about this boat that could interest you."

He strode off. I threw Christian a questioning glance before hurrying after my father.

"What is it?" I asked when I'd caught up with him.

"There—do you see those roughly patched-up areas?"

He pointed, and I saw what he meant. From a distance they looked like irregular patches of rust—nothing particularly noteworthy. My father took out his cell phone, fiddled with it for a moment, then held it under my nose.

"This is what they look like from the inside."

I couldn't make heads or tails of the photo, but Christian, peering over my shoulder, said, "Bullet holes."

I looked at him in amazement. "Are you sure?"

He nodded. "Yes, totally sure. I saw their like when I was in the army."

"The boy's right," my father confirmed. "They're bullet holes. Someone's fired at this boat."

"Well, it has been used as a minesweeper, so it's highly possible that it's been shot at."

I did wonder why the holes hadn't been repaired when it was remodeled, but it sounded like a plausible explanation to me. Christian and my father looked at each other. I suddenly had the feeling that they could communicate telepathically.

"No, these shots don't date from the war," Christian said. "I bet they were caused by the National People's Army."

"You're saying the NPA fired at this boat?"

My father's next words made me think he'd read the thought that sprang into my mind.

"Your mother told me about the letter. The boat may well have come under fire, since it entered East German waters. And someone wanted to leave a message for posterity to show that it happened."

Could that be Palatin? Had he wanted the boat's history to be uncovered?

"Are you sure?" I asked, turning to look at Christian. He looked as though he'd turned to stone, his eyes glued to the hull. It was like that first time we'd been alone on the boat together.

"I can't think of any other explanation," my father said. "The former owner of the boat was West German; he could easily have had these bullet holes repaired, but he simply mended it himself with these makeshift patches. It's not particularly noticeable from the outside, but he knew that if someone ever gave this boat a complete overhaul, they'd see it."

"And possibly ask questions," Christian added a little absently.

My heart was thumping in my throat. I imagined the captain's desperate attempt to bring the writer of the letter into West German waters. Could the woman have been shot? Was that why he'd hidden the letter behind the cladding—so that it would be found one day? My hands went cold. So cold that Leonie noticed.

"What's the matter, Mom?" she asked worriedly.

"Nothing," I replied. "I just find this story so exciting."

"Think about whether you want to leave the holes as they are or have them repaired," my father said pragmatically. "If you manage to find out what happened back then, it'd be great if you had the evidence, wouldn't it?"

"Yes, that'd be good. What do you think?"

Christian didn't react at first, but eventually he broke out of his reverie. "Yes, it'd be good. We'll consider it. This evening."

He smiled, but it didn't reach his eyes. What was the matter with him? After we left the dock, my father took his leave from us for a while.

"I still have a bit of work to do, but if you want, you can go home now." He turned to Christian. "You're welcome to go, too. My wife would be delighted."

"Thank you, but I've booked a hotel room. I'm meeting a business colleague tomorrow, so this trip has fit in well with my plans."

"Whatever works for you." He shook his hand, gave Leonie and me a kiss on our cheeks, and went off across the shipyard.

I felt a bit self-conscious with Christian. He'd suggested we should be more informal with one another, but I still felt I needed to be careful not to scare him off.

"So, I'll see you this evening," he said as we arrived at the shipyard gate. He shook my hand and hurried off. I hung back for a while, and noticed the gatekeeper's broad grin.

"Seems like a nice young man," Herr Blom remarked. Of course he would know from my father that I was divorced, and presumably men were not so different from women when it came to pairing off a recently divorced acquaintance.

"Yes, he is," I replied, although I had no desire to discuss my relationships with Herr Blom. "Have a nice weekend, Herr Blom. I'm sure I'll see you again soon."

"I hope so!" he replied.

I couldn't tell from his voice whether or not he was disappointed by my evasion.

By the time we reached the parking lot, Christian was nowhere to be seen. Damn, I hadn't given him the address! I felt myself blush, quickly took out my cell phone, and saw that a text had already arrived.

```
If I'm to keep my promise, I'll need the
address to pick you up.
```

I tapped in my reply with a grin, then strapped Leonie in her car seat and drove toward the Altona district of Hamburg.

The three-story apartment building on Abbestrasse had recently been modernized. My parents had moved here after my father had been made redundant from the Volkswerft. Stralsund may have been my hometown, but I felt just as at home in Altona.

By the time we moved, we had become a proper family; I had accepted the Hansens as my parents, and the adventure of the West lay ahead of me. I was fourteen, my head full of music and fashion, and I thought Hamburg was the most wonderful city in the world. I had lived here for the rest of my school days and while I was in college. It was only after I met Jan that I moved away.

Whenever I returned, I felt as though my life with Jan had never happened, as though I had never been away. I wondered whether Leonie would remember our house in Binz as well when she came to visit with her own children.

Our steps echoed dully as we climbed the stairs, the sisal matting on the stairs muffling the sound of our feet. The interior of the building had also been substantially renovated. One thing that was the same was the neighbor's cats that roamed unchecked throughout the building and watched every new arrival with curiosity. Of course Leonie was delighted by them.

"That cat looks like our kitty," she said, and I could only agree. The brown-striped tame tiger did indeed look just like our furry occasional visitor. Fortunately, Leonie's excited anticipation at seeing her grandmother was greater than her love for anything with a fur coat. My mother opened the door with a broad smile. I hugged her while Leonie snuggled up to her legs.

"It's so lovely to see you. Have you been to look at the boat yet?"

"We have," I replied as I removed my cardigan.

The apartment smelled of freshly baked cake.

"Well, what do you think? Your father's talked of nothing else since Wednesday. That boat really has him under its spell."

I wondered if he'd also told my mother about the bullet holes.

"The *Storm Rose* seems to have that effect on anyone who goes near her," I replied as Leonie hurried through to the living room with little shrieks of delight.

"How about Herr Merten? Is he coming too?"

"No, he's checking into his hotel right now."

"Hotel? But he could have stayed here."

"That would be a bit much, don't you think? Not for you; I know how much you like having visitors, but he can be a bit . . ."

"Reserved. I know. But you could at least have asked him."

"Next time, maybe," I replied as I followed my mother into the living room.

19

Two hours later I was standing nervously in front of the mirror over the kitchen sink. My parents did have a well-lit bathroom, but ever since my early club-going days, this had always been the place where I got myself ready. It was especially good since I didn't have far to go to get a soda from the fridge. As I had suspected, my mother was ecstatic when I told her about the invitation—because of both Leonie and Christian.

"So you're on a first-name basis," she said with a wink, as if I'd confessed to having performed a striptease in front of him.

"Yes, we are. Business partners sometimes use first names, you know."

"But not only business partners."

"Mom, I know perfectly well what you're hinting at. But I still don't know for sure whether there's anyone else on the scene."

"Well, ask him."

"I have, and things got really embarrassing."

"Did he refuse to answer?"

I sighed. "No, I went about it the wrong way and he must have misunderstood my question."

My mother, who was sitting at the kitchen table with a small glass of red wine, giggled. "You're in advertising and you can't find the right words! I've never heard anything like it."

"There's a difference between using words professionally and trying to avoid embarrassment when talking to someone else."

"Someone you like."

"Yes, I admit it. I like him. And I'm sure we'll have a lovely evening, and I'm grateful to you for looking after Leonie."

"Anytime—it's my pleasure! But of course you know that."

I applied some eyeliner and gave my handiwork a critical appraisal.

"In any case you must be thinking this Christian might make a nice man for you. If I were you I'd make it my business to find out this evening if he's spoken for."

Fortunately I was saved by the doorbell.

"Got to go," I said, gave Leonie a big kiss, and grabbed my bag. The flowery dress I was wearing wasn't particularly dressy, but I was sure that Christian wouldn't be wearing a suit.

"Have fun!" my mother called after me. I couldn't help hearing her inevitable undertone.

I'd been half-expecting to see a Ferrari parked outside, but my business partner drove a perfectly ordinary VW, not even one of the bigger models. It made him seem even nicer.

As I got into Christian's car, I knew my mother would be standing at the upstairs window as she had when I was sixteen. Although I secretly wished he would at least kiss me on the cheek, I was actually relieved when he merely held the door open for me before getting in himself.

I fastened my seat belt and laid my hand on my purse, where I also had Lea's letter. Over afternoon coffee with my mother I hadn't had a chance to think much about the bullet holes. I was now really eager to know what Christian thought about them.

We drove into the center of Hamburg, where Christian parked his car in a multilevel garage. The restaurant he took me to was tasteful but fortunately not one of those temples of fashion.

"Is this one of your regular places?" I asked after a waiter had led us to a table.

The evening was warm enough for the patio doors to be open, and a mild breeze blew gently around us.

"I come here now and again, when I'm in Hamburg."

"On business or privately?" I asked, trying to discover whether this restaurant was the place he came for romantic evenings. It gave me a small pang of jealousy to think that he might sit here every now and then with a pretty woman, be it friend or business associate.

"Both," he replied as the waiter handed us the wine list. "Do you trust me or do you have your own ideas?"

"What about?" I asked, confused until I realized he was talking about the wine. "Ah. If you're here often I'll leave it to you to choose the wine."

I covered up my embarrassment by getting out the plastic sleeve containing the letter. The old paper lent me a little security. It was stupid to feel so unsure of myself in Christian's presence. That was probably all due to my mother, since she clearly saw me walking down the aisle with Christian, while I still saw him as a business partner and friend.

"I wonder what we should do with this," I said, sliding the letter across the table. Christian had only seen a copy before now. He reached for it, and his fingers lightly brushed my hand. The touch went through me like a tiny electric shock. Was I certain that he was only my business partner? Perhaps I really did want more, and my mother had only said out loud what she had seen inside me and I was refusing to admit.

Christian picked up the letter in its sleeve and read it. Several times, it seemed, although he had seen it before. Was he trying to read something between the lines?

"It's a lovely letter," he said finally. "Beautifully written. Although the recipient won't have been happy."

"That is, if he received it," I said. "As it was hidden behind the wall cladding, I assume that he didn't."

"Or maybe this Lea started again and wrote another. The letter looks rather crumpled."

"It was stuffed behind a panel. Perhaps she had to hide it away quickly."

"It still raises the question of why." Christian laid the letter back on the table.

"Exactly. Why?" I agreed. "Maybe they came under fire. I think that's entirely possible after what we found today."

"Do you think the boat was seized by the border guards?"

"I don't know. Why not?"

He shook his head. "I don't think so. They might have shot at the boat, but they didn't catch it. Otherwise it would have been in the East long before 1997."

It hadn't been there before, according to the documents, where we had seen no remarks by the Stasi. The East German authorities would certainly have impounded the boat, annotated the documents with all kinds of remarks, and sent it back out only after reunification. If at all.

"There might not be any direct connection between the shooting and the letter," Christian continued. "If the captain often transported defectors it could have happened on a different trip."

"We'll have to wait until we can ask the captain."

I regretted not having met Palatin.

"If he's still alive," Christian said.

"He is." I took a piece of bread from the basket. Our conversation was briefly interrupted by the waiter bringing our wine.

"The captain's still alive? How do you know?"

"I went to his house today. I stopped at the Timmendorfer Strand harbor and someone gave me his address. Unfortunately he's on vacation at the moment. But I gave his neighbor my phone number and asked her to tell him I'd called."

Christian gave me a broad smile. "I knew you were a woman of action."

"I'm just so interested in what happened back then. And the bullet holes have made me all the more eager to know what happened to Lea. And of course to our boat." After a brief pause, I added, "And that's precisely why I'm glad you're my business partner."

Christian picked up his wineglass and proposed a toast. "To us and the *Storm Rose!*"

"To us and the *Storm Rose*," I replied. I took a drink, confirming that it had also been an excellent idea to let him choose the wine.

My cell phone suddenly began to buzz in my bag. I tried to resist the urge to see who it was, but it could be my mother calling about Leonie, so I excused myself and took it out.

"Anything important?"

I shook my head. "No. An unknown number." I put it back in my purse. Who could it have been? Hartmann, perhaps? "Funny."

"Maybe it was a spam call. Those people have every reason not to let you know the number they're calling from."

"True. But it's strange all the same."

I shook my head and tried to forget about the call. But I couldn't. Christian seemed to notice I had something on my mind.

"If it's important they'll call back, I'm sure," he said. "And if it's a spam call and they try again I'll have the waiter bring me a whistle. Just give me the sign and we'll have them unable to put a receiver to their ear for a while."

He grinned, and I couldn't help laughing out loud.

After dinner we strolled for a while by the Alster. I hadn't realized just how many lights there were in Hamburg at night. They were reflected in the broad band of the river, which had drawn a good number of people out to walk along its bank on that mild evening.

"I envy you for having spent a good part of your youth here," Christian said. He sounded thoughtful. "As a teenager I would have loved to have lived in Hamburg."

"Is that because of the Reeperbahn nightlife?"

"No, because of the city itself. I love Hamburg. And I haven't been here often enough."

It occurred to me that I had no idea where he'd grown up. I had already told him that my parents had moved here after reunification.

"Where are you from originally? From Rügen?"

Christian stared at the path ahead of us for a moment, then turned to look at me. "Originally. Later we went to Oldenburg."

I assumed that was after reunification. "So we're practically fellow countrymen."

"Apart from the fact that you're a woman."

He smiled, his gaze not moving from my face.

"I'm sorry if I stirred up some unpleasant memories when I showed you that picture of your father," I said.

"There's nothing for you to apologize for," he replied. "My strange reaction had nothing to do with you or the photo. It's just . . . my father had to suffer a lot of crap. Crap that I unfortunately experienced with him. I've always wished that life had been a bit kinder to him."

What did all that have to do with Seaview Hotel? I got the feeling that there was somehow a connection. But I didn't want to spoil our lovely evening with more questions.

"So, what do you intend to do about the woman who wrote the letter?" he asked eventually. "Apart from grilling poor Captain Palatin."

"Well, provided she's still living, I'll try to track Lea down. Palatin may be able to tell us what he knows about her escape, but only she knows what her personal motivation was."

"What if she has an everyday surname like Müller?" he said. "You could do with a bit of help. Get the TV involved."

"You're joking!" Telling a TV reporter was the last thing I had in mind. "Would you like a complete stranger to appear on one of those crazy shows and expose your story? Perhaps there's a good reason why the letter shouldn't be made public."

"Then perhaps you should drop it and not go in search of her. Let the story be."

Christian gave me a searching look.

"I can't do that. I want to know what happened. If I find the woman and she tells me it's her own business and I should keep out of it, then that's fine, but giving up before I've started just isn't my style."

As we passed a closed newspaper kiosk, it gave me an idea.

"What if I take out an ad asking for anyone who left East Germany on the *Storm Rose* to get in touch? Perhaps she'd be among them!"

"That might not be a bad idea. That would also be a way of finding out whether the captain ever carried any more refugees on board. In case he can't remember or didn't ask their names. That's possible, for security reasons."

As he spoke, I imagined a whole list of people unfolding before me. That would be amazing! Of course we would have to be careful if we were to use it as publicity—if I were in a situation like that, I wouldn't want someone exploiting my fate. But even so, it would be interesting to know the stories that had played out on the *Storm Rose*.

"OK, I'll put out a call as soon as I get back home."

I grinned at Christian, but noticed he was gazing out across the water.

"Is everything OK?" I asked.

He nodded absently.

"Yes, yes, I'm OK. I was just thinking."

"What about?"

He shook his head. "It's not important. I think we ought to be getting back. I've got a fairly early start in the morning, and you . . ."

"We're staying at my parents' tomorrow," I replied, trying not to let my disappointment show. Whenever it felt we were about to get a little closer to one another, he sank into his thoughts and blocked me out. Why?

We returned to the parking lot in silence and got into his car. All the words I wanted to say to him, all the questions I wanted to ask, were welling up inside me. I didn't dare speak them out loud, because I was afraid of either running into a wall of silence or making him sad.

As we drove toward Altona, I watched the street scenes that passed before us. So many people and lights. So many unknown lives playing out. Who could say what stories were hidden out there? Perhaps at that very moment we were driving past people who had risked everything twenty-five years ago to reach freedom. Or perhaps there were people who were still suffering from the change.

We finally reached my parents' house. The silence was weighing heavily on me, but I forced a smile and said, "It was a lovely evening, thank you."

"I thank *you*," he replied, looking at me.

I returned his gaze and felt strange. Confused. A moment like this would have been the right time for a kiss, but I was unsure what to do. After our conversation by the Alster had taken such a strange turn, I didn't dare get too close to him. It was the right decision, as he didn't seem interested.

"So . . . we'll see each other in Binz, shall we?" I asked as he leaned back.

A brief smile crossed his face. "We'll see each other in Binz."

I smiled back and got out of the car. At the front door I turned and watched him drive down the street. Deep inside I sensed the empty echo of a missed opportunity.

20

During the journey back to Binz, Leonie slept peacefully in her car seat. It was Sunday evening, and the autobahn was full of traffic. We found ourselves in a traffic jam on several occasions, but by the time the sun was sinking below the trees, I was driving up the narrow lane to our house. A few people were out walking along the side of the road, but I hardly noticed them. I was exhausted after the weekend and had hardly slept a wink.

For one thing, my meeting with Christian was haunting me, and the costs of the repairs to the boat were another worry. How much would I be able to contribute? I didn't want Christian to bear the whole financial burden. I hoped that one day he wouldn't come to regret taking me on board.

The more I thought about it, the stranger his behavior seemed. On the one hand, he was friendly and wanted to be on a first-name basis; he suggested ways for me to track down the defectors and seemed committed. And yet his mood would suddenly veer; he would fall into silence, block me out, and I didn't know how to react. I found him a huge puzzle.

I pushed my thoughts of Christian to one side. The next day was going to be tiring; I was going to present Hartmann with the campaign package for his hotel, and really hoped he would accept it. In addition, over the last few days I had been constantly looking for new assignments. I had discovered some promising possibilities.

I drove the Volvo into the carport and woke Leonie.

"Are we home?" she asked sleepily, stretching as she spoke.

"Yes, we're here. If you like, I'll make us something to eat and then you can go to bed."

"OK." She looked tired. I carried her into the house and took her to her room, then brought in the suitcase. In it was the envelope containing the cost estimate. My father had given it to me on Saturday, but I hadn't found the courage to open it. Christian had been given the same letter, but we had until Monday or Tuesday to worry about the numbers.

After getting everything from the car, I went into the kitchen and found some leftovers in the fridge to make a passable dinner. I still had a few things to prepare for the publicity campaign, so I switched on the coffee machine. A little extra-strong coffee should get me going again.

As I listened to the machine's bubbling, I set the table and happened to glance out the kitchen window. I stopped short. Had I really seen someone, or was I just imagining it? I turned slowly, wondering if I was hallucinating after the long drive.

But what I saw was no apparition. I couldn't believe it. Outside, by the gate, was my ex-husband, Jan.

"It can't be true," I muttered, still unable to move.

Jan was standing by the fence, clearly unsure what to do. He was wearing a light sport coat, a white shirt, and jeans; and the sea breeze was ruffling his hair—the dream of many a woman in Bremen. In fact, the dream of any woman who didn't know him, who saw in him the chance of a happy life.

"Leonie!" I called, without stirring myself to go to the door. I kept an eye on Jan, who was still unsure whether to come in.

"What is it?" my daughter asked as she appeared at the kitchen door.

"Come and look who's here."

Totally unsuspecting, she went over to the kitchen window.

"Daddy!" She shot past me like a bolt of lightning and rushed out to her father.

I felt a knot inside. All that love for a man who, only a few days ago, had scolded me for calling, insisting that we should leave him in peace. Now he was standing there in the yard, and my little princess was flying out to meet him.

I finally succeeded in shaking myself from my immobility. I pushed myself away from the door frame and approached him. He'd lifted Leonie into his arms, like he used to do shortly after she was born, when our relationship had settled back into some semblance of normalcy and he wanted to play the proud father.

"Hello, Jan," I said. I could have sounded a bit more friendly, but my voice refused to obey. What was he thinking, turning up here without letting me know first? But when I saw the happiness lighting up Leonie's eyes, I didn't dare question him.

"Annabel," he replied, and then I saw something new in him—uncertainty. Jan was never uncertain; he came, saw, and conquered. He was a winner. And he simply pushed aside anything that got in the way of him winning. But now he was here, just a few days after that spiteful conversation.

"I'm sorry to show up out of the blue," he said, lowering Leonie down from his arms. She stayed by him, looking up at him as though he were a beacon in the dark. At that moment I wished he hadn't changed his mind. "I was here this morning, but you weren't in. And I tried to call you on your cell phone the day before . . ."

I remembered the call from the unknown number. Since when had Jan done that kind of thing? Was he in trouble?

"We were in Hamburg," I replied. I spoke stiffly, since it was no business of his where I was. "What are you doing here? Have you finally decided to visit Leonie?"

I still couldn't believe he was really here. Maybe I would soon wake up and find I was still in Hamburg.

"I have to talk to you," he said in earnest. That was also something new. A few days ago it would have been the last thing he wanted. What could be so important that he came here in person? Everything in me rebelled against letting him into the house. But then again, I had called him and asked him to come. And now he was here.

"Let's go inside," I said and turned.

Leonie followed me, holding her father's hand. I didn't look back at him, but could imagine what was going through his mind. He was probably studying the house right now, figuring out what it cost and how I was paying for it. I'd be damned if I'd tell him I was only renting it. Leonie steered him into the kitchen. Dinner wasn't yet ready; all I had to offer right then was coffee.

Jan stared at me. Something flickered in his eyes that I'd never seen before.

"I got your address from my secretary and, well, when I couldn't get hold of you, I just wanted to come and see your house."

Who are you and what have you done with the real Jan? I almost asked. The man I had last seen in the divorce court wasn't someone who would simply come by to find out how his ex-wife and daughter, whom he saw only as an item of monthly expenditure, were doing.

That man had a full schedule, lived to the principle of strict time management, and needed an attractive woman by his side who would be the envy of all his business associates. The man sitting here next to his daughter, whose tiredness had evaporated and was beaming at me in delight as though I were responsible for the reunion, was his doppelgänger.

"It's nice here," he began. "Peaceful. Since you weren't here I took the opportunity to have a look around the area. You don't have many neighbors."

"A cat comes to visit every now and then. That's enough. And the town isn't far."

He took it in with a nod. Again I wondered what was wrong. Was he up to something?

"How do you manage with Leonie? You must be working?"

Alarm bells suddenly began to ring in my mind. Was all this about proving what a bad mother I was? That would really take the cake! Had he decided to interfere in my life—probably with his mother egging him on?

"Just tell me what you want," I said, trying to bring him to the point. Two years ago I would have been delighted to get so much attention from him. But now he was like a foreign body that didn't belong here.

"I have to talk to you," he replied, looking at Leonie. "Alone."

I nodded.

"Leonie, can you leave us for a while?" I asked, stroking her hair.

"Yes, of course," she said, looking at me to check that it was OK. I nodded and followed her to the kitchen door. Once she'd disappeared into her room, I pulled the door shut and returned to the table. I sat down opposite Jan. My stomach was churning.

Jan tugged nervously at the sleeves of his jacket. That, too, wasn't typical of him. He was never unsure of himself, not even when he had proposed marriage.

"I know our last telephone call didn't go well," he finally began.

"You think so?" I folded my arms. "At least you called back. That's more than I could realistically have expected. And as you can see, I obeyed your instructions and gave your secretary my address. And far more importantly, I led my daughter to believe that the only reason her father doesn't want to see her or talk to her is because he has a lot to do. All things considered, I've been a very obliging ex, don't you think?"

My words felt vitriolic, but I couldn't help myself. He raised his head and looked at me. I waited for some kind of denial, perhaps even for a reason to throw him out of my house, but he didn't give me either.

"I went to see the doctor two days ago," he said quietly, and hesitated.

"Well?" I prompted.

"I have testicular cancer."

The words hit me like a wall of ice-cold water. Over recent months I'd sometimes caught myself wishing that something awful would happen to him. A hump on his back. A horn growing from his brow. A failure to get it up. But it had never included anything as serious as this.

"You can't mean it!" I burst out. I didn't know what else to say.

"The doctor says it can be treated and the prognosis is good," he continued. "But it's highly likely that the intervention will result in infertility."

For heaven's sake, this was just what I'd been looking forward to discussing after all the hours of traffic jams and freeway driving. Of course I was shocked by the diagnosis, but if it was curable, did he really have to come all the way here and talk to me about it? He could have phoned or sent an e-mail . . .

Get a grip, I told myself. *Calm down. The guy has cancer, isn't that bad enough for you? However big an asshole he may be, he doesn't deserve this.*

"I'm sorry to hear it," I said stiffly. "But aren't there things that can be done . . . Couldn't you have your sperm frozen . . . ?"

His eyes met mine and stilled me to silence. I had absolutely no idea what else to say. Or how I was meant to feel. Jan had been my husband for almost eight years. And a good husband for three of them.

And he was still a part of my life to an extent—Leonie meant I still had a tie with him, like it or not.

"I wanted to ask you if you'd share custody of Leonie with me," he continued. "After all, she'll be my only child, and . . ."

He broke off as he heard my deep sigh. I was mentally reliving the scene in front of the divorce court judge. Hearing Jan's callousness as the judge read out his statement that he renounced any active custody entitlement and was satisfied with the child support payments. He had given no indication that he cared for Leonie in the slightest.

And now he wanted to share the custody arrangements. That meant he'd have Leonie on weekends or during the vacations. It meant that, if he became seriously ill, she'd be fully aware of his suffering. It meant that, if he recovered, she would see his succession of partners and wonder what kind of a person he really was.

"I know I'm asking a lot after all that's happened," he went on. "And you'd be perfectly entitled to say I've blown my chance. But I'm asking you to consider it."

I still couldn't say a word. My thoughts were swirling around wildly in my head. Jan wasn't a man who took no for an answer. Maybe he'd file a renewed court application for custody, which would mean dragging back into the open everything I'd tried to leave behind. I'd have no other option but to respond by washing all his dirty laundry in public again. All the women, the neglect, his meager involvement in Leonie's upbringing.

And then there were Leonie's feelings to consider. She so wanted her daddy to be a part of her life again. Could I deny her that wish just because our marriage had failed?

I had a huge stone in my belly. My mouth had gone dry, and my hands were shaking slightly. I almost felt as though I were having a panic attack. Everything had been going so well, and my biggest concern had been the boat. Now Jan was back on the scene. I suddenly wished I'd never called him.

I had to get up and walk around before I burst. Jan followed me with his eyes as I paced back and forth in the kitchen. I pressed my ice-cold hands to my cheeks and hoped for some rescue, but none came.

"You're angry, aren't you?" he said.

His words brought me to a halt. The stone in my belly weighed ever heavier. I shook my head.

"I don't know what to think. We haven't seen each other for a whole year. For a whole year you've avoided any contact with Leonie. And now you're sitting there telling me that you're ill and that means you want to share custody." I looked into his eyes. Mine were burning, and my pulse was hammering in my ears. "Tell me, would you ever have thought to be concerned for Leonie if you hadn't been given that dreadful diagnosis?"

He pressed his lips together. No, then. As I would have expected.

"Annabel, please understand. What's gone on between us—"

"I understand full well what happened between us," I interrupted. "You're right, things couldn't have gone on as they were. And I don't mourn for it. But what am I supposed to make of your request when a few days ago you were dismissing me on the phone, telling me to give our address to your secretary and not to bother you again? I really do feel sorry for you; it's a lousy diagnosis and I hope you come out of it OK. But if that happens, if you get your head back above water, will this still be what you'll want? Will you care for Leonie because she's your daughter, or will you just drop her again?"

My voice caught in my throat, leaving me unable to draw breath. My heart was racing. Here it was again, the old rage. I was amazed at myself, the fact that I was able to bring it out into the open. Jan said nothing, merely stared at me wide-eyed. I picked up my glass of water and gulped down the contents. And with each swallow, I wished he would disappear, simply disappear.

It took a few moments, during which Jan was mercifully silent, for me to emerge from my frenzy.

"I'm sorry to have spoken so plainly. But it's been building up inside me for a long time. If you have the slightest speck of understanding for me you'll agree that I can't just come running, overflowing with joy, and grant your every wish."

"I was fully aware of that when I decided to visit you," he said, looking down at the oilcloth. "But please have some understanding for my situation."

"I do," I replied, wondering if he had actually thought about it for longer than a minute or whether it was merely a gut reaction. "But I have to protect my child. I know from experience what it's like to feel left in the lurch—no, abandoned—by a parent. Leonie's already suffering because you never get in touch with her. I don't want to risk the prospect of you dropping her again as soon as you've recovered."

"So what can I do?" he asked.

Of course. He, the man of action, believed that a solution for everything could be found just by snapping his fingers.

"I don't know. First of all, I have to digest all this news I've suddenly been given. And then I'll think about it. It's not as though I've banished you from Leonie's life. After all, I was the one who called you. And I wasn't the one who stood up in court and asked that you only pay child support. If you remember, I was in favor of sharing the custody arrangements. But no, you didn't want that, because your lovers would have taken to their heels if they saw a child playing in your living room."

"Annabel!" Now there was a hint of a threat in his voice. I didn't care; I was only speaking the truth.

"I'm sorry." I relented, raising my hands dismissively. "What you do with other women has nothing to do with me. I just wanted to say that you cut yourself off from Leonie of your own free will and that I actually wanted it to have been different."

"Does that mean you'll consider it?"

"It means I'll think about it, yes. Your diagnosis should have nothing to do with it. In sickness or in health, you'll always be her father.

We've come to the current arrangement and no one can accuse you of not paying up. But I need to be sure that you intend to take on an active role as father, come what may. And that you're able to do it, because believe me, it's not always a picnic in the park. It changes your whole life. And we have to see what it will mean for Leonie—after all, we now live hundreds of miles apart, and it wouldn't be good for her to be traveling all the time."

At this point he could have promised the sun, moon, and stars, but he was wise enough not to do so. Instead he rose heavily from his chair. He actually looked healthy enough, but I knew that appearances could be deceptive.

"Then I'd better leave you to yourself."

"Yes. But go and say good-bye to Leonie."

He nodded, looking rather disappointed. Had he really believed I'd agree on the spot? A year ago I might have, but something had changed in me. If Jan wanted to take an active part in caring for Leonie, he had to prove that was what he wanted.

I followed him from the kitchen into Leonie's room. Of course, my little princess was sad, but Jan was clever enough to promise her he'd call soon. Whether he really would was another matter, but Leonie was satisfied for the moment.

"Are you going straight back?" I asked as I went with him to the door.

"No, I checked into a hotel when I saw you were away. I'm leaving tomorrow."

He looked at me, his expression completely closed. I knew that look only too well, and it didn't bode well at all.

"Take care, Annabel."

"You too."

He turned and walked to the yard gate. I watched him for a moment, then closed the door and leaned against it. My cheeks were glowing. However deeply I breathed in and out, I couldn't relieve the pressure inside.

"Mommy, I'm hungry," Leonie said, having followed me into the hallway.

Of course, we were going to eat after we came home. It was getting dark. I sighed again, then switched back into mother mode. I'd have plenty of time later to reflect.

"OK, what would you like?" I asked, lifting her into my arms.

"Cheese on toast!" she said excitedly as I carried her into the kitchen. I was glad that she didn't ask why her father hadn't stayed to eat with us.

21

Leonie had hardly fallen asleep, a peaceful smile on her face, when I left the house and walked down to the beach. The wind was milder, and the waves murmured sleepily. The last hints of daylight glowed on the horizon.

Distant laughter drifted toward me. A fire was flickering somewhere among the dunes; a few young people must have settled down for the evening there. I saw two lights in the distance, which looked like beach bars.

It occurred to me that since I'd moved here I hadn't thought of my own pleasure—not since my divorce from Jan, in fact, or even before that. I'd always been there for Leonie, and gladly so. And now I had enough goals in view on which to build my future. But pleasure, thinking only of myself, like having a few drinks at a beach bar or simply going dancing, was something I hadn't indulged in.

Unlike Jan. He'd always lived life in the fast lane—worked hard, played hard. Leonie and I had recently been pushed to the edges of his life. Now, under the threat of illness and treatment, he wanted to share with me the role I had taken on alone. I wasn't sure whether he had really thought it through. Maybe it had been an impulsive decision.

Maybe the diagnosis had given him a real shock. Maybe his mother had also been whispering in his ear. His mother, who had never really liked me, and who was also conspicuous by her absence from Leonie's life.

I briefly toyed with the idea of going past the young people's campfire to one of the beach bars and getting well and truly drunk. But I settled for simply walking along the beach. I needed peace and quiet, not a diversion. There was enough confusion in my head.

In the fading twilight I reached the mermaid rocks. Thinking of Christian and the stories he had told Leonie made me smile again.

I didn't see any mermaids here, but I knew exactly where I was. The white roses on the rock had dried up—it looked as though they hadn't been replaced for a while. What was the matter? Had the bringer of the flowers lost interest, or had he fallen ill? I reached out a hand to the blooms, which disintegrated at my touch.

I felt the wind in my hair and the moisture in the air. I gradually found peace, my thoughts about Jan retreating a little, as I sat on a nearby rock. A moment later I heard footsteps approaching. I thought it must be one of the young people. Perhaps he or she needed to get away from the others for a while, to find a place to be alone. I didn't turn, but a moment later sensed a presence behind me. The footsteps halted.

Whoever was standing there clearly hadn't expected to find me here. I waited a moment for them to leave, but they stayed put. I finally turned to see who was there, and froze.

In the fading twilight I recognized Christian Merten. He had a fresh bunch of roses in his hand. The wind carried the scent of the flowers to my nostrils. Beneath the seaweed-heavy sea air it was a gentler scent, but I caught it clearly. Christian looked surprised. I couldn't blame him. So was I.

I thought back to my previous encounter with the mysterious figure who had laid the roses down here. Never in my life would I have thought it could be Christian.

"Hi," he said.

Our eyes met for a moment, then he looked down awkwardly at the roses. I'd obviously discovered his secret. I didn't really know what to say.

"Hi," I replied.

He hesitated, then appeared to give himself a shake and went up to the rock. He took the old bouquet down and laid the new one in its place, then he came to sit next to me.

I was bewildered, wondering what he was mourning with the roses. A past love? Was that why he was so reserved?

"You come here often, don't you?" he began at last, without looking at me. Was he annoyed that I'd seen him? Or did he fear my questions?

"Yes. Whenever I need to think," I said. "I usually come very early in the morning or late in the evening, but today . . ."

Could I tell him about Jan? About his diagnosis and his request? I hesitated—hadn't I always told him too much?

"My ex-husband appeared today, just after we arrived home," I began. "It was totally unexpected."

"What did he want?"

I took a deep breath. "The doctor told him . . . that he has cancer. And now he wants to be involved in caring for Leonie again."

Christian said nothing. I could understand that; it had been quite a blow for me.

"What are you going to do now?"

"I don't know." I looked down at my shoes, which I could only make out faintly. A little farther away the young people continued their partying. "On the one hand, Leonie misses her father. She wants to have him back with her, or at least have him visit her, enjoy his attention. After the divorce I was disappointed that he didn't want to care for her, but now . . ."

"Now it's no longer what you want."

"Well, yes, it is, but . . . if he did I'd have to be in contact with him again. And I'm afraid it would all come to the surface again, all the crap I went through with him."

The fact that I'd cried my eyes out after the recent telephone conversation with him was all the evidence I needed.

Christian thought for a while, then said, "You have to ask yourself whether you're prepared to associate with him for the benefit of your daughter."

"It's not as straightforward as that. Jan could quite easily claim that he's entitled to share the custody arrangements with me. And Leonie so wants to have her daddy back. I'd go along with it for her. And yet I still don't know what to do. It's possible that he'd disappoint her again, and I won't allow that to happen."

I pressed my lips together, shaking with anger. I looked out to sea, but could hardly make it out. I could only hear the rushing of the waves, but they couldn't wash away my anxiety. Christian stroked my arm a little awkwardly. Then he looked back at the rock.

"I saw you a few weeks ago. You were sitting a little farther seaward," he said, suddenly changing the subject. "At first I didn't know who you were, but then, after you gave me your address, I saw you again and I knew it was you. Stupidly, I never plucked up the courage to speak to you."

I remembered the encounter with the figure, his face concealed. I also remembered that I had believed the flowers to be for a past love, of whom I was jealous.

"Maybe I should have come after you," I said.

Christian shook his head. "It was a good thing you didn't at the time. I certainly wouldn't have told you the story connected with this rock back then."

"And now?" I asked. "Would you like to tell me now?" He didn't reply. That was answer enough for me.

"OK," I said. "You don't have to."

"Yes, I do. I want to. You've blown my cover. And, besides, the story's connected with the *Storm Rose*."

I looked at him in astonishment. "Really?"

Christian nodded. "Yes. I only wanted to have the *Storm Rose* because she's linked to an event from my childhood."

I thought back to the man in the photo who resembled Christian so closely.

"I was astonished when I saw her again in the harbor after such a long time. I couldn't do anything but go down there every day and look at her. As if she could tell me . . ."

He halted.

"No, I should begin at the beginning. I . . . I don't know if I can."

"Go back to the beginning?"

"No, talk about myself. You must have noticed!"

Oh, I certainly had! But I'd thought it was because he wanted to keep our relationship on purely businesslike terms. Now I sensed something else.

"I don't readily open up to other people. It's only when I know them well or like them that I reveal a little of myself."

"You think that moment has come?"

"The moment had arrived when we were in Hamburg and your father discovered the bullet holes. When we were out together that evening. But then the conversation somehow took a strange turn and my barriers shot back up. It happens sometimes, whether or not I want it to." He looked at me. "But now I'm sure."

I nodded and waited for him to tell me.

22

Christian

My father was called Jonas. He was a construction worker; a simple, honest man. He entered an apprenticeship when he was sixteen and became a mason, then worked in that trade day in, day out.

One day, he met my mother, Rosi Winterberg, at a club. The classic story. He wore flares and sideburns, she had a pleated skirt and one of those peasant blouses that were all the rage. They danced shyly together, talked, and agreed to meet again next time. It went on for a few weeks, until he finally plucked up courage to kiss her, and she asked him to walk her home.

At some stage during the summer, she became pregnant. When she told my father, he was over the moon, and proposed to her. Back then, in East Germany, too, it was frowned upon when an unmarried woman got pregnant.

They married three months later in her parents' yard, just in time— before her bump began to show. The marriage and their expected child took them to an apartment in a new development in the mountains. The future seemed secure.

I was born, and a few years later, my brother, Lukas. We were gradually molded by our parents and the education authorities into good Socialists, although in my case it was only partially successful. Western TV reception was good, and I liked the Rolling Stones, Alice Cooper, and David Bowie, not the homegrown pop stars with their thick shoulder pads. Like many of my classmates, I tried to look like our glam rock kindred spirits in the West. I dreamed of going to a concert by a Western artist, but back in 1983 that was nothing but a dream, particularly here on the coast. The best we could manage was to go to Rostock to see the Puhdys or Karat, but no one was really into them.

My parents constantly warned me to keep my opinions quiet at school—about things we talked about at home, the programs we watched, and the music I listened to. I tried to obey as much as I could, even though it was obvious that everyone watched Western TV.

My life went on like that of most other boys, until the day when my father forgot to pick me up from school. I had turned twelve a few days before, and was sitting on the crumbling steps outside school. My old leather schoolbag was beside me, and I was busy rolling little paper balls as ammunition for my catapult. Not that I had any adversaries. My classmates had long since left, on the bus, or those who were already fourteen on mopeds. But I was sure my father would be coming for me, so I waited.

I'd carelessly tossed my red Young Pioneers scarf to one side. I'd have worn it that Monday because, like every week, we were called to salute the flag, together with lots of talk about Socialism and school issues. I wasn't particularly interested in either, but you were expected to join the circle and listen.

I rarely paid much attention, but would stomp down and squeeze the water out from the soaked school-yard surface or draw shapes in the sand with the tip of my shoe. Afterward I'd have no memory of what had been said. I'd trot back to the classroom with the others and doodle in the margins of my schoolbooks.

"Hey, kid, are you taking root here or what?" a voice suddenly rasped behind me.

I looked up. The janitor was a tall, broad-shouldered man with a mustache, dressed in blue overalls. He always carried a packet of Juwel cigarettes and would often slip one to boys in the tenth grade as they sneaked into the smokers' corner. He never gave us younger ones any, but chased us off if we came too close to his flower beds or hovered around his workshop in the basement.

"I'm waiting for my father," I replied. "He's coming to pick me up."

Only then did I notice how empty the school yard had become. Even the after-school kids had long since gone, and there were only one or two cars left in the parking lot. A glance at my watch with the cracked face showed me that I'd been waiting for three hours. My stomach tightened as I realized that my father must have forgotten me.

"Perhaps your old man's working an extra shift. If I were you I'd go on home, or you'll be sitting here all night."

I wanted to contradict him, but something told me he was right. It would be better if I left. In any case, the janitor was about to lock the school gates, and there was no way I wanted to be climbing over the fence.

I grabbed my things and walked over to the bus stop, still on the lookout for our white Trabant. But there was no sign of it. After another half hour, the bus to the new housing development in the mountains finally arrived. During the whole journey I was close to tears. How could my father have just forgotten me like that? He'd promised he'd come.

Maybe something had happened. By the time the bus was close to our block, fear was raging inside me. I ran home as fast as I could. I had a key to the apartment, so I didn't need to wait for someone to let me in. Once inside the building I shooed Frau Hebbel's cat aside and ran up the stairs. I was completely out of breath by the time I reached our floor and opened the door.

As soon as I walked in, I knew my father was there. He wasn't supposed to smoke indoors, though he sometimes did when Mom was out. Inside, it smelled strongly of f6 cigarettes. I stomped angrily down the hallway and threw my schoolbag down by the coatrack. If he was home, why hadn't he kept his promise?

I found him sitting at the kitchen table, staring absently at the tablecloth. It was only then that I noticed how cold it was, or seemed to be, in the apartment. I didn't know if that was because of the April weather or something else. There was a strange atmosphere. My father seemed not to care about any of it.

I wanted to yell at him, reproach him for forgetting me, but the words stuck in my throat. I had never seen my old man like this. He seemed not to know I was there; his thoughts were miles away, his eyes fixed on a stain in the oilcloth. The ashtray beside him was full. Another cigarette hung, glowing, from his fingers, ash falling onto the table. If my mother saw it, she'd go mad because it had burned a small hole, and oilcloth was hard to come by.

"Dad?" I said.

I was afraid to see him like that. Something clenched inside me, and I had no idea why. My father remained motionless. I looked at the clock. The hands were inching their way toward 6:00 p.m.—the time my mother usually came home from work. If she were here, she'd know how to find out why he was acting so strangely.

The doorbell suddenly rang. I jumped and whirled around. Had my mother forgotten her key? My father still didn't move, so I went to the door. Frau Hebbel, our neighbor, was standing there. My heart skipped a beat. Had she noticed me scaring her cat away?

"Hello, Christian," she said in a kind voice. "I've just had a call from the nursery school. The lady was asking when someone's going to pick Lukas up. Are your parents home yet?"

The nursery school had called our neighbor? There was nothing new about that, as we had no phone ourselves—all our calls came through the neighbors, and they passed on any messages. But what was strange was that my little brother had also been forgotten that day.

"I'll tell them," I replied, avoiding my neighbor's worried eyes. I didn't want her to know that something wasn't right here.

I closed the door and paused a while before returning to the kitchen. Nothing had changed. My father was still sitting at the table, apparently unaware of the world around him. Carefully, I tugged at the sleeve of his jacket.

"Dad, what's wrong?" A sob rose in my throat. Something awful was happening, of that much I was sure. Maybe my father was sick. Only yesterday, Tim, a boy in my class, had told us about his grandfather, who'd suffered a stroke. Had my father also had a stroke? Were you paralyzed when you had a stroke?

"Dad, the nursery called," I told him fearfully. "They're asking when someone's going to pick up Lukas."

My father finally stirred. He breathed deeply, heavily, and looked at me. His eyes held so much sadness and despair—I'd never seen anything like it in a person before.

"Mom's had an accident," he said, his voice sluggish as though he'd been drinking. "She . . . she's dead."

I stared at him. I couldn't move and felt as though I was about to collapse. My mother was dead? It couldn't be true! What kind of an accident? My mother had taken the bus to work that morning, like she always did!

My father rose heavily, looking as though he'd aged twenty years.

"Come on, we'd better go and get Lukas," he said, squeezing my shoulder. He wasn't one for physical contact, and he wasn't particularly good at comforting people. But at that moment I didn't notice. I felt dreadful, my insides churning, but I couldn't cry. It all seemed so unreal. It couldn't be true that something had happened to Mom. It simply couldn't be true.

As we drove off in our worn-out Trabant, I stared at the sidewalks as though searching for my mother, as though hoping to see her. Perhaps it had all been a big mistake. Perhaps my father was taking me for a great big ride. It was one of his phrases. Whenever the news was on, he'd say that the newscaster was taking people for a great big ride when they spoke of the economy doing well. A state of affairs that clearly wasn't true, since people stood in long lines outside the shops whenever there were pineapples or bananas from Cuba. Even at twelve I understood that the successful economy they spoke of was spin, and that they didn't always tell the truth on the news. Perhaps the same thing was true when people spoke of accidents?

"They came to me at midday," my father began to tell me once we had left our building some ways behind. His voice still sounded sluggish. He probably really had been drinking. "Two of them, from the People's Police, brought along by my foreman. Neither of them had a clue how to tell me. And at first I didn't believe them. They told me about the accident, and that the driver had vanished. But a number of passersby noted the number—as if that was any consolation! Then they took me to the hospital. They'd clearly tried to save her, but she was already too far gone. The place where she . . ."

Tears choked his voice. Now he was crying freely and almost failed to stop at a red light. He saw it just in time and slammed on the brakes, throwing us both forward. I didn't care. Everything in me felt numb. As though my body didn't belong to me. I didn't make a sound as the brakes squealed and the Trabant skidded slightly to one side. If my mother was dead and if what the old people said about a Heaven was true, then she would surely be there, and if so, I no longer wanted to be here on Earth.

My father got the car back under control. Eventually we reached the nursery, where a lonely light was shining in a window.

"Do you want to come with me or stay here?" my father asked. His eyes looked at me dully as though they could see through me. I decided to go with him, as I didn't want to be alone in the car with my thoughts.

The nursery teacher looked exhausted. I could tell she felt like heaping reproach on my father, but his expression had the same effect on her as it had on me. Her mouth hung open, and from one moment to the next she seemed to have forgotten what she wanted to say. Lukas looked as though he'd been crying his eyes out. Like me, he'd obviously thought he'd been forgotten. Or, even worse, that he would simply be left in the nursery forever. When he saw us, he rushed over right away, although he didn't grab my father, but me.

"I'm sorry we haven't come until now," my father told the nursery teacher, who still hadn't said a word. "There . . . there's been an incident in the family. It won't happen again."

The teacher nodded, probably wondering what the incident was. But my father wasn't prepared to explain. She'd hear about it soon enough.

"So, I wish you a good evening, Frau Bauer," he said. He led us down the long corridor with its beige linoleum.

Not a word was said during the journey home. Lukas snuggled up to me. Could he have any idea what had happened? No, surely not. He was just upset with my father for abandoning him for so long.

I wondered how he'd react to the news that our mother would never be coming home again. Would he understand? Would something snap inside him? Suddenly I was extremely worried about my little brother. I felt like taking him and running away, but that wouldn't have changed anything.

Once home, my father parked the Trabant in the communal parking lot. The glow from the streetlights fell on the roofs of the other vehicles, some of which were already very old, although people somehow managed to keep them looking clean. Beyond the streetlights, the darkness seemed to swallow everything, including our apartment block, whose brightly lit windows seemed to float in the air like glowworms. I looked for our window in the vain hope that I'd see a light there. If there was, it could mean that our mother was back home. But I looked in vain. The window was dark. How could my mother be there when she was lying in the mortuary of a funeral parlor?

Our neighbor was waiting for us outside our front door. Had someone else called?

"Good evening, Herr Merten," she said to my father. "Say, isn't your wife home yet? I wanted to ask her if she could lend me a grater. But no one's answering."

How could they? I looked at Frau Hebbel angrily. Could she have been snooping around and already know what had happened? Was everyone in the building gossiping about what could have happened to my mother? My father glanced at Lukas, then at me. I understood now why he hadn't given the details to the nursery teacher. He hadn't wanted Lukas to find out that way.

"I'll bring you the grater, Frau Hebbel. Just give me a moment."

His hands shaking, my father unlocked the door then told me, "Help Lukas take off his coat, Christian."

I nodded and led my little brother down the darkened hallway. My father hurried into the kitchen, returned with the grater, and disappeared, pulling the door shut behind him.

"Where's Mom?" Lukas asked as I helped him out of his parka.

I pressed my lips together as I didn't want to be the bearer of such awful news.

"Isn't Mom here? Is she still at work?" Lukas insisted.

"Dad will tell you everything," I replied as I hung his jacket on the coatrack in the hall. Outside the front door, my father was still talking to Frau Hebbel. He kept his voice low so that I couldn't make out what he was saying. But that was fine, since it meant that Lukas wouldn't hear anything, either.

"Go and wash your hands," I told him. "Dad will be here soon, and then we'll have dinner."

The conversation with our neighbor dragged out endlessly. By then Lukas had finished splashing water on himself and was in the kitchen, bombarding me with questions as I set the table. When he realized he wasn't going to get anything out of me, he found his bag and got out a little box made of folded cardboard with a flower pasted on it.

"I'm going to give this to Mom," he announced with pride.

Tears leapt to my eyes. I turned away quickly so he wouldn't see, and emptied the ashtray into the garbage can. But I wasn't quick enough.

"What's the matter?" Lukas asked, bewildered. "Don't you like it?"

Fortunately, that was the moment my father came back in. The moment of truth had arrived. He had to tell Lukas. He looked like he had aged by many years as he sat down heavily on one of the kitchen chairs.

"Lukas, I have something to tell you . . ." he began.

I wanted to leave the room, but I stayed there as if rooted to the spot. Perhaps my little brother would need me. I couldn't simply make myself scarce.

***

My father cried in the night. It was the most dreadful sound I'd ever heard. I considered going in to him and trying to comfort him. But how could I have done that? Mom was dead, and I felt like weeping myself. I buried my head in my pillow and dared to hope, despite everything, that the world would be back as it should be in the morning.

The next day, the newspaper contained just a tiny piece on the accident. "Woman on the Way to Work Hit by Car." The report said that she'd stepped out from behind a bus, and the driver had been guilty of contravening the provisions of Section 1 of the Road Traffic Regulations: driving without due care and attention. He was also guilty of leaving the scene of an accident. Information had been received from members of the public that had led to the driver being arrested.

There was nothing else. They didn't report that my father had sunk into a black hole of despair. They didn't report that it almost tore me apart when it sank in that my mother wouldn't ever come through the door again and bring me something she'd bought while she was out. And no one heard about Lukas, either, how since the death of his mother he retreated into his own world, in which he would stare for hours at his building blocks without touching a single one.

The world continued to turn, but our corner of it had completely slipped its orbit. Dad got a sick note from his doctor and took time off from work. He was completely unable to leave the house, and it seemed as though he spent every day on his chair in the kitchen, waiting for my mother to return.

On the day of her funeral, the apartment was full of people, many of whom I hardly knew at all. Of course our relatives were there, but we didn't have many. And there were my mother's and father's coworkers. The apartment was thick with smoke, which my mother would have hated—but she wasn't there.

I sat on the sofa, letting it all wash over me, people tousling my hair and trying to speak words of comfort. In my mind I kept replaying the sight of my mother's coffin being lowered into the ground, and the noise of the sand being thrown onto the lid echoed through me. Lukas came and snuggled up to me. If I felt so utterly lousy, what must it be like for him? He stuck his thumb in his mouth like a baby. He hadn't done that for years. I put my arm around him, but had no idea how to comfort him. Everything I had once felt now seemed to have vanished. The apartment gradually emptied, and the clouds of cigarette smoke flowed out through the open windows.

The next day I was allowed to stay home, but I went to school all the same.

There, too, things were different. My teacher took me aside and told me how sorry he was that my mother had died. While I'd been absent, he must have told my classmates, as some of them approached me and awkwardly held out their hands to me. No one could have known what was going on inside me, but somehow I appreciated their concern. After a week or so, my school days seemed to settle back to normal, and I was glad of it. I didn't want to be the center of attention and constantly have to answer questions about how we were at home.

My father never again forgot to pick us up when he had promised to do so, but he very rarely came to get me. Taking the bus didn't bother me, though, because then I didn't have to see the downturned corners of his mouth or his sad eyes.

When I was at home, I made myself practically invisible, burying myself in my schoolwork or looking after Lukas. My brother looked as though everything was OK with him again, but it wasn't the case.

One day he asked me, "Do you think Mom can look down from Heaven and see what we're doing here?"

His question hit me like a fist in my stomach. It wasn't long since someone in my class had said there wasn't a Heaven and you became worm food when you died. He'd said it only to annoy me, but his words had left me with a deep doubt. What if there really was no Heaven? I couldn't talk about that with Lukas. He was still small, and I had to protect him.

"Of course Mom can see what we're doing," I said. "And she always will, even when we're old."

My brother was satisfied with that and leaned against me, sucking his thumb.

My father brooded for ages, staring into space and waiting for my mother, although he knew she wouldn't come. He hardly spoke. Then he would put on his work clothes and leave the house. He was still sad, he still cried at night, but he seemed to be back in control of himself.

At first I didn't notice that his sadness was turning into something else.

"They're going to prosecute the bastard," he said to me one evening after we'd sat in silence for hours at the kitchen table. I looked up in surprise from my homework. My father looked past me, his eyes glazed. I'd been concentrating so hard on my math exercises that I'd hardly noticed the bottle of schnapps appear on the table. Nor had I seen how many glasses my father had drunk. But it must have been a few, as he swayed around on his chair and mumbled again, "They're going to prosecute the bastard."

I secretly also hoped he'd be punished. I believed he deserved to spend the rest of his life behind bars. My school friend Ulli said he'd get no less than a life sentence, and added with a grin that if he were in America, he'd be put in the electric chair.

I doubted it, and Ulli saying such things was also dangerous, so I kept it to myself and held back from asking my father about this ominous-sounding electric chair.

That evening, like my father, I was convinced that the man would be brought before the court. Because of my mother and because he had fled the scene in such a cowardly way. I also had a secret wish that the guy would die. We still had no idea that the wheels of justice didn't always turn in the anticipated ways.

The weeks passed, and the summer break began. Life slowly got back on track. Lukas still missed our mother incredibly, and he cried a lot, especially in his sleep. I tried to comfort him as well as I could, although I frequently felt like crying myself. When I was at school, I could forget it all for the time being. School meant Ulli and the other guys, whom I got along with, and looking forward to going to summer camp together. Mom had organized it, and I was determined to enjoy myself at Lake Müritz.

My father didn't seem to care what he did. Apart from his work, he seemed only to be really interested in one thing. He visited my mother's grave daily, removed the old wreaths, and ensured that the grave was kept neat. Every weekend he took us with him and would sit brooding for hours on a bench near the grave while Lukas and I sat together, an incredible boredom washing over us.

With its dark trees, the cemetery swallowed up even the fiercest heat of summer, so that after a few minutes we felt as though we'd stepped inside a fridge. Lukas didn't understand why we were there and kept whining that he wanted to go home. I knew my father would continue his silent communion with my mother for at least an hour, so I tried to distract my brother by disappearing with him into the bushes and making up stories for him. I told him about cowboys and Indians, as I had recently been to the cinema with Ulli, where we'd seen *The Sons of Great Bear*. I thought Gojko Mitić was wonderful, better even than Pierre Brice as Winnetou. One day I wanted to be as big and muscular as he was, and fight for justice. In the Westerns the bad guys always got punished and the good guys were rewarded.

***

"Can the man who ran Mom down also be punished by the chief?" Lukas asked me one day. It struck me dumb for a moment. I knew my father was waiting for a case to be brought against the driver, but I hadn't expected Lukas to be concerned with the question, too.

"Of course he could," I replied after thinking about it for a while. "But he doesn't live in America. Here it'll be the police and the court who punish him."

That seemed to satisfy Lukas, but as I was lying in bed that evening, I wondered if a case really was going to be brought against the driver. They knew who he was by now—even my father knew, since some acquaintance or other had revealed it to him. I had no idea where this acquaintance got his information, but my father believed him. However, the man appeared not to have been summonsed. Day after day, my father waited to be called before the court, or at least to hear something. But nothing happened.

Then I went to the summer camp, and for the next three weeks all gloomy thoughts were driven from my head. During that time, during the boat launches, on night hikes, and around the campfire, I could occasionally forget that my mother had died. In a state of euphoria, I imagined writing to her about what I had been doing, and once I even began a postcard with *Dear Mom and Dad.*

But then I remembered, and as I didn't want to waste the card, especially because of the ten-pfennig postage preprinted on it, I simply scribbled something over the *Mom and.* Apart from that, those three weeks were completely carefree, since I didn't have to see my father's somber expression and was only very occasionally reminded of what had happened.

When I got home from the camp, my father had changed completely. His sadness had lifted, giving way to a strange anger that hung over him like a storm cloud. Even when he wasn't shouting at us, we felt as though we had to be careful around him, watching what we said and did. The only explanation I could think of was that while I was away something must have happened with the driver. Had my father had to make a statement in court? Was that what had upset him?

I didn't dare ask. Instead I took my little brother with me to my friends' houses when he didn't have to go to the nursery. Although my friends weren't thrilled about having him around and kept teasing him, it was better for him than hanging around in an apartment where my father muttered angry words to himself, or where he was left alone because my father simply wasn't there.

A few weeks later I was woken one evening by strange voices in the living room. We never had visitors that late. And the men's voices that reached me through the wall were completely unfamiliar. Although it would have been better to stay in bed—especially as I didn't want to make my father angry—I got up quietly and crept down the ladder of our bunk bed. Lukas, who slept on the bottom bunk because he was still too small for the ladder, didn't notice me slipping out of the bedroom on tiptoe and carefully opening the living room door.

"Are you sure you want to go through with it?" one of the men's voices asked. "It's a massive step and there'll be no turning back."

"Sure?" came my father's voice. "You're asking if I'm sure?" He laughed mirthlessly. "For four months I've been waiting for the man who has Rosi on his conscience to be brought to justice and finally punished. But nothing's happened! And now I know why it never will. Because the bastard's one of the Stasi. They can't lock up one of their own."

"Keep your voice down, Jonas. The walls have ears," another man, also unknown to me, warned.

"The whole world can hear it for all I care," my father replied. "It's the truth. They're not going to get the asshole because he's one of their eyes and ears. And what about us, huh? My boys have lost their mother just because the guy couldn't look where he was going and had only had his driving license for three days!"

He took a deep breath and went on, "The bastard's twenty-one! Twenty-one and he has a life on his conscience. And he gets nothing! No punishment whatsoever! I'd like to wring his neck!"

I was so frightened by the anger in my father's voice that I eased the door shut and crept back to bed. The bunk bed ladder creaked beneath my feet, but fortunately not enough to wake Lukas. The night stretched before me. My heart pounding, I stared at the ceiling and tried to work out what I'd heard.

The driver was twenty-one, and my father knew exactly who he was. And as I understood it, he wanted to kill him. Yes, that's what I thought, that my father was about to set out and kill this man. I knew the consequences of that only too well. If my father was sent to jail, we'd be put in a home. And then it would all be over.

I wanted to go downstairs and beg him not to do it. But I didn't dare. My father was bound to have been angry, and he certainly wouldn't have given in to me. I stayed where I was, listening for a while to the muffled, unintelligible voices, until I eventually heard a door closing and peace descending.

***

After that night something else changed for us. My father impressed on me more than ever that I shouldn't say anything about Western TV at school or at the neighbors' houses, and I shouldn't talk at all about what went on at home. Sometimes, when we were out and about in town, he would pull me into some building's entrance and look around with a hunted look. Sometimes he would stand for minutes at a time on the sidewalk, watching the people pass by. When I asked him why, he either didn't reply or gave an evasive answer.

I assumed it was because of fear. I still hadn't forgotten what I'd heard that night. Had my father really gone so far as to kill the man who had run Mom over? When I was alone, I would feverishly scan the newspaper, but I never found any report of a corpse being found. But hadn't Dad said himself that not every story found its way into the papers?

I was practically bursting with questions that I wanted to ask but dared not. In school I was incredibly careful not to tell anyone too much. My friends often asked me what was up with me, but I made the excuse that I was still grieving for Mom. I just wanted to be alone, to find out once and for all what had happened. I sometimes listened until deep in the night for the men to return, but they never did.

Then, one day, Dad woke me shortly after I'd gone to sleep.

"What's up?" I asked sleepily.

"Get up and get dressed. And then pack a few things you want to take with you in a suitcase. But for God's sake don't turn a light on!"

I suddenly began to tremble. What did my father mean? Packing a suitcase, keeping the light off—it all sounded like escape! Was he on the run from the police? I didn't move, simply stared at my father.

"Get a move on," he said and bent over Lukas to wake him, too.

What would he say if we had to run from the police? Would he understand what Dad had done? But—had he actually done anything?

"Dad," I managed to say, still shaking from head to toe.

"What?" he asked with annoyance, as Lukas mumbled that he didn't want to get up.

"Did you murder the man who killed Mom?"

My father froze, then straightened suddenly.

"No!" he burst out in shock. "I haven't killed anyone. What on earth gives you that idea?"

"I . . . I heard . . . You said you wanted to kill the man who ran Mom over."

Although the room was only dimly lit by moonlight, I could see my father turn pale.

"When did you hear that?"

"That evening when those men were here."

I grew even more afraid, but now it was my father I was frightened of. What if he punished me for eavesdropping? But his shoulders drooped with a heavy sigh, and all of a sudden his body seemed to have lost all its strength. He saw that his eldest son was too old to be put off with some story. And I saw that this was a situation that would change our lives completely.

"Those men are my friends," he said. "I got to know them when you were at summer camp. They want to help us cross the border."

"Cross the border? And go where?"

This kind of escape wasn't something my friends and I usually talked about.

"To the West," my father said. "We're going to the West, far away from all this."

"But that's dangerous!" I replied in shock, imagining all I'd heard in our civic studies lessons about West Germany. Stories of soldiers shot by Western spies, of the dreadful conditions there—all unemployment and deaths from drug addiction. And on top of everything else, I knew that people who tried to defect to the West were sometimes shot or arrested and then never let out of jail. What my father intended wasn't much better than murder.

"Yes, it's dangerous, but we've thought it all through, my friends and I. We'll escape over the Baltic so we don't have to worry about the Wall. There'll be a boat waiting for us out at sea that will bring us to shore in the West. You know, don't you, that the Baltic also has a coast-line in the West?"

Yes, I knew that, from the old tattered maps our geography teacher used to unroll for us at the beginning of our lessons. West Germany had never been mentioned, but I knew all of the Baltic coast in detail. My father gently took hold of me by my arms. He looked at me, his eyes clearer than they had been for a long time.

"Trust me, Christian," he said. "And please understand. I want to get away from here. I have to get away from here. I can't bear it any longer. I can't bear knowing that justice doesn't apply to those who spy on other people. I'll tell you all about it sometime, and when I do, I'll tell you who that man is who has your mother on his conscience. But now we have to go. We have to try. I want you to grow up in a country where the law applies to everyone, not only to some."

I didn't know exactly what he meant, but I trusted my father. And I was ashamed that I'd thought him a murderer.

"OK," I said and began to rummage in my dresser. Lukas was also awake by now, and although he didn't fully understand the meaning of this nocturnal journey, it was all a big adventure to him and he was eager to take part. I found it difficult to decide what I should take, but I knew I didn't have much time. I packed the sweater my mother had knit for me, along with two pairs of jeans, my tracksuit, some under-wear, and a few of my favorite cassettes. I had to leave most of my books behind in the apartment, but I was sure I'd be able to buy more in the West. My father said I should leave my school things at home, that I would be given other books in the West.

I could hardly believe I'd been doing my homework as usual that afternoon. If only I'd known. But there was no time to get upset about the wasted time. I quickly slipped into my sneakers and put on a khaki parka over my clothes. It was bound to be horribly cold when we were on the boat.

Lukas insisted on taking his plastic cowboys and Indians with him, and a few building blocks, the East German version of Legos. I also packed some picture books for him, because I knew my little brother would soon get bored. I could fit more clothes into his bag because he was smaller. As we left our room, we almost tripped over Dad's bag in the hallway.

"Come on, you two," Dad finally said. He shouldered his and Lukas's bags, while I carried my own backpack. "Be as quiet as you can. No one should hear us leaving the building."

He opened the door. Everything was dark and silent. A little moonlight fell into the corridor, enough to see the stairs by. I took Lukas's hand and followed my father down. Just as it had taken me a while to grasp that my mother was gone forever, now, too, I didn't want to think that I would never go up and down these stairs again. I didn't want to believe that I would never again shoo off Frau Hebbel's cat or get the mail from the dented mailbox.

We had no time to linger over good-byes. Once my father had made sure there was no one out on the street, we left the building. I'd assumed we'd be going in our old Trabant, but my father took us both by the hand and dragged us along the sidewalk, then into a side street where the streetlights were out. A car was waiting for us there, an old dark red Dacia whose motor rattled into life as we approached. Two doors were pushed open, but no one got out.

"Get in the back," my father told us, taking his own place in the passenger seat after putting our bags in the trunk. A man was already sitting in the back of the car. Like the driver, he was merely a dark silhouette.

"Go!" he said, and I recognized the voice of one of the men who had visited us at night.

We left the mountains behind and headed for the coast. It wasn't far, but the driver steered the Dacia over winding, sometimes very bumpy roads through forests and past lonely farms.

My brother huddled up to me. This journey was no longer an adventure to him; he was frightened. I also felt uneasy. If the police caught us, Dad would go to prison and we'd be sent to a home. That much, at least, I knew.

I kept turning and peering through the rear windshield to check whether we were being followed. Suddenly I caught sight of headlights.

"Who are they?" I asked, convinced that a blue light was about to start flashing, accompanied by a howling siren. Both my father and the driver looked in the rearview mirror.

"No one," the man behind the wheel said, but I could tell he was unsettled. At the next junction he put on his turn signal, slowed, and turned off. Now we would find out whether the driver behind us was actually after us. The man next to me tensed. We drove down the road for a while as though it was the way we intended to go. I turned around again.

"You'd better not do that, lad," the man next to me said. "Act as if everything's normal."

That unnerved me even more, but I did as I was told. I turned to face the front again, now watching the driver. He hardly moved his eyes from the rearview mirror. Finally he breathed deeply.

"They've gone past," he said, steering the car to a place where he could turn around.

Back on the right road, he was now driving a little faster since the brief detour had cost us valuable time. I wondered if the boat we were supposed to sail on would be anchored on the beach or whether we'd have to row out to it. Or maybe swim, even? I had never swum in my clothes, and I hadn't brought trunks. And what about Lukas? He couldn't swim at all!

We finally stopped in a thickly wooded spot. The wind was blowing strongly, and above the trees the moon regularly vanished behind thick clouds before reappearing. The Baltic, which now seemed really close, was roaring loudly.

"Come with me!" the driver said once we had taken our bags from the trunk.

We left the car behind and walked briskly through the trees. I still couldn't see the sea, but it sounded wild and formidable. On top of all my other fears, I now began to worry that our boat could sink. How big was it, anyway? I gripped Lukas's hand more tightly and wished my father had taken me into his confidence as his older son, and given me a little advance warning.

I had no time to get angry with him. We left the forest behind and came out onto the beach. Moonlight was now falling freely from a large gap in the clouds. Driftwood appeared before us, pale and ghostly. Long breakwaters and a small, crooked landing platform stretched out into the water, the churning waves breaking right over them in places. Surely we weren't going to be sent out to sea in weather like this? And where was the boat?

All I could make out was a small motorboat moored to a place on the landing platform where the water didn't wash right over. This was where the men were heading.

"Listen now. We're going out to the meeting point, where you'll transfer onto the main boat. It'll be a bit tricky, but you're all fit enough, so you should manage it."

"Isn't the sea a bit rough?" my father objected. He was obviously as afraid as I was.

"Oh, this is nothing!" The man waved him away. "We've had worse on other trips. And this time we don't have any women with us to kick up a fuss."

He must think Lukas and I were fearless. Little did he know.

"Anyway, this is the best time. We've studied the coastguards' schedules in detail. Honecker's in Rostock at the moment, so they're a little less alert right now. You'd best get a move on—you won't get an opportunity like this again. The captain will take you to Timmendorfer Strand, where you can go to the Western police. Is that all clear?"

My father nodded, and I copied him. And I realized that these two men weren't just some ordinary friends of my father's. They were escape helpers who had already sent many more people besides us over the border.

As we stepped out onto the rickety landing platform, I wasn't sure whether I really wanted to go. Of course I was disappointed that Mom's murderer hadn't been brought before the court, but I had Ulli and the other guys. And Lukas had his friends at the nursery, too. Had our father really thought about what he was doing here?

I couldn't say anything; fear kept my mouth shut as I climbed on board the boat. It swayed dangerously, and I clung to my father's jacket. The escape helpers waited until we were all seated, then one of them started up the motor. For a moment the clattering drowned out even the wind and the roaring of the waves. I held my hands over my ears, wondering if it would be heard by the border guards. There were watch-towers everywhere, and navy frigates were waiting out at sea. What if they caught us? But the men didn't seem to be concerned. It appeared to be a matter of routine as they steered the boat over the waves. My fear increased as I felt water spraying up into my face and onto the boat. We were rocked about wildly, and the farther away we got from the shore, the worse it became.

The sky finally closed in around us. I pressed up closer to my father and gripped Lukas's hand tightly.

"Who's going to look after Mom's grave?" I asked.

Strangely enough that was the only thing I could think of as we pitched and rolled across the water. My father put an arm around me.

"Your grandparents," he said. "They'll tend to it."

The way my father referred to my "grandparents" sounded strangely distant. His parents had died when I was still little, and we had hardly any contact with my mother's parents. They hadn't even come to her funeral. I had never found out why our relationship was so poor, and I hoped they really would take care of Mom's grave. Every now and then, when visiting her grave, I had noticed there were flowers that we hadn't put there. I tried to convince myself that they were from my grandparents and that everything would be OK.

***

The journey seemed endless. It was still pitch-black out at sea, since the boat had no lights on. The man who wasn't occupied with steering the boat was crouched behind a small radio unit he had pulled out from beneath a floorboard once we were a distance away from the shore. He put on a set of headphones and began to search for a frequency, clearly trying to contact the captain of the other boat. We couldn't be far from the meeting point.

We traveled on. The man with the radio only listened; he seemed to be getting no response. I looked at my watch. It was almost two in the morning by now. How long did we have to go? I looked at Lukas, who had managed to fall asleep despite the violent rocking. My father's face was deep in shadow. I would have loved to know what was going through his mind. Was he thinking of Mom? I was sure we wouldn't be sitting in that frail, pitching boat if she hadn't been run over. She definitely wouldn't have wanted to leave, and certainly not in a motorboat that gave the impression it was about to capsize at any moment.

My eyes eventually got so heavy that, despite my fear and the rocking motion, I couldn't keep them open any longer. But before I could drift into sleep, the radio came to life. I jumped and was immediately wide-awake. An almost incomprehensible voice was calling us. Our radio operator replied.

"Yes, Gardener, we're receiving you!"

The crackling voice stated the position at which the boat would be waiting. Our escape helper confirmed and called something to his partner. The boat slowed a little. I wondered how they'd see anything in that darkness, but then I saw a light. It only flared up briefly, but was clear enough.

"Over there!" I called out.

The men turned. After a while the signal flared up again.

"That way!" the radio operator called to the helmsman, who steered in a shallow arc.

The wind had grown stronger, but the sky had cleared a little. My eyes had gotten so used to the darkness that I could soon make out the boat. The men could, too, as they now made directly for it and came up alongside.

Our escape boat was a small fishing cutter with a passenger compartment. Its blue hull rocked on the water, the superstructure looming white against the pitch-black sky. The lettering *Storm Rose* could hardly be made out, but the name burned itself into my mind. *Storm Rose.* It sounded like a boat that would hold out well in bad weather.

The escape helpers hadn't underestimated the situation—the strong swell made it almost impossible to keep our boat in a position from which we could transfer safely.

"I'll take Lukas up first," my father said. "And then I'll come back for you and follow you up."

My father told my brother to climb on his back and hold on tight. By this time a small rope ladder had been lowered from the bigger boat. Tense and worried, I watched my father climb it.

The cutter was also pitching violently, despite its greater weight. I wondered if it wouldn't have been better for them to haul us up in a net, but I could see there were no nets on board this boat. After placing my little brother safely on deck, my father climbed back down. I would have liked to tell him he should stay up there, but at the same time I was extremely afraid to inch my way up that ladder alone. My father got back into the rocking boat, then it was my turn.

"Hold on tight," he told me, as he helped me to shoulder my backpack. "Don't be frightened; I'm right behind you and I'll catch you if you slip."

I wondered how on earth he intended to catch me when the boat beneath him was rocking much more violently than the cutter, but I put my foot on the first rung and heaved myself upward. My fingers gripped the soaked strands with difficulty, and I made slow progress because of the swaying. Once I really did slip, but as he'd promised, my father was behind me and caught me.

"You're doing well," he yelled against the roaring of the waves. "Keep going, you're almost there!"

It didn't look that way to me. When I peered up, the railing still seemed yards away. But I kept climbing, and suddenly found myself thinking about my friend Ulli. He'd have a thing or two to say if he could see me now! As soon as we were back on dry land, I'd write him!

After more words of encouragement from my father, I finally reached the top. My arms and legs were shaking, I was totally exhausted, and I had no idea how to scramble on board. A man reached out his hand to me. He had a gray-flecked beard, a stocky build, and was wearing a knit cap and thick woolen sweater. His hand felt coarse and calloused, and he was incredibly strong. He got ahold of me and tugged me up over the railing.

"There you are, boy. Welcome on board," he said.

I stared at him as though he were Santa Claus.

"Shit, they've seen us!" came a sudden cry from below deck. "They're sending a patrol to see what's happening. Get out of here fast!"

I started and looked at my father, who quickly climbed the ladder. The escape helpers quickly unlashed the boat, and the two of them were soon racing away. The captain, whose face I had only glimpsed, hurried to the wheel and sped off.

The boat jerked sharply, and the three of us were almost thrown to the floor. But our father picked us up and led us into the passenger compartment, where we were met with an incredible smell. It was like a school cafeteria, when the kids had gone back out to play and the dinner ladies were beginning to scrub the pans, but the smell of the meal just eaten still hung in the air. We crouched down on the floor next to one of the comfortably upholstered benches.

"It's better like this," my father said as if preempting our protests. "You never know, they may shoot if they see our boat."

That scared me, and I realized the huge risk the cutter's captain was taking by entering East German waters. Fear kept us silent for several long moments, then we heard a voice.

"Welcome on board the *Storm Rose*! We've just entered the territory of the Federal Republic of Germany. You're now free citizens!"

That should have been a moment for us to celebrate. The escapees before us had probably done so, but our father merely hugged us to him.

"We've done it," he said through tears. "We've done it!"

My father stood then, and we were able to sit on the benches. Lukas curled up on one of the seats; I tried to stay awake for a while. The boat continued to rock dangerously. I wondered where the sailors were. There were always sailors on a boat, weren't there? When I asked my father, he said they were at the front with the captain. But as this boat was no longer a fishing cutter, they didn't need a large crew.

"The engineer is in the engine room and there's bound to be someone to take the captain's place at the wheel if the journey goes on a while."

"So how much longer will it last?"

"A little bit."

My father ruffled my hair. Now he was back to the father he used to be before my mother died.

"Why don't you lie down for a while? I'll wake you both when we arrive."

I nodded and lay down along one of the bench seats. My legs dangled down, but it didn't bother me. My whole body felt heavy, and I was too exhausted to wonder about what would happen next. The main thing was that my father and Lukas were with me.

I don't know how long I slept, but at some stage I was woken by my father yelling out.

"Lukas!" he shouted in panic. "Lukas, where are you?"

It had grown light, and we couldn't be far from Timmendorfer Strand. I didn't realize at first why my father was so upset. But it soon dawned on me that my little brother was missing. I came to my senses with a shock.

"Dad?" I called, but he didn't hear me.

He rushed out of the cabin. I tried to follow him, but the boat lurched and I was knocked against one of the seats. I was briefly winded as the edge of a table dug into my ribs. I saw that the sea was steely gray and could hardly be distinguished from the cloudy sky. High waves towered over the boat and tossed it about furiously.

I cried out, grabbed the seat, and held on tight as the boat was flung around again. The storm I had feared in the night had arrived. And my father was standing out on deck. Where was Lukas? I was suddenly extremely afraid. What if something had happened to him? It surely wasn't sensible to go outside, but I had to know what was happening, where my brother was.

As soon as the boat's movement calmed slightly, I made my way to the door. There was no one to be seen outside. Had my father been washed overboard? My heart leapt to my throat as I skimmed the mountainous waves feverishly with my eyes. I couldn't see any sign of my father, or Lukas, so they must still be on the boat. I inched my way along the wall of the passenger cabin as well as I could until I finally reached the wheelhouse.

"You have to stop the engines!" my father yelled at that moment to the captain. "Please, stop the engines! My son's fallen overboard."

"Oh my God," the captain said and shut down the engines. "Are you sure? Perhaps he's hiding under one of the benches."

"No, no," my father cried in despair. "I've looked everywhere. He's not there!"

I spun around. It couldn't be true. Lukas couldn't have disappeared. He never went off on his own, especially not at night!

"Christian!" I heard my father call as I stormed outside.

At that moment the boat was tossed about again by a wave. I lost my footing, cried out, and hit my head against something hard. Stars exploded before my eyes, and I was sure I'd also fall into the water. But I didn't care, and I soon felt nothing more.

***

When I came to, I was lying in a room with a white ceiling. A spherical light hung above my head. The air was warm. At first I believed I was at home, but the noises were different. And the covers I was lying beneath also felt different.

I tried to sit up. Where the hell was I? Then I felt a sharp pain in my temple. I touched my head and felt a bandage. And then I remembered.

"Dad?"

My voice rasped in my throat, and I was overcome by panic. Where had they brought me? Was this a children's home? And where was Lukas? After a while I succeeded in sitting up. There was a fierce pounding in my head, but I managed to get out of bed and go to the window. My gaze fell on a wild-looking yard. Was that what a children's home looked like? Where was my father?

Suddenly, I heard voices and approaching footsteps. I staggered back to the bed and drew the blanket up to my chin. I hoped it wasn't the police! A moment later the door opened and my father appeared, accompanied by a stranger. The man was carrying a bag, which he set down on a chair by the bed.

"Well now, young man, are you awake?" the stranger asked, taking a stethoscope from the bag.

A doctor. The thought shot through my painful skull. *This man's only a doctor. You had a fall on board the boat,* I recalled. *That's why he's here.*

I let him examine me and change the bandage on my head.

All the while, my father stood by the window, his gaze fixed on the yard. I couldn't see his face, but something was missing. Lukas. Hadn't he found him?

"Dad, where's Lukas?" I asked.

My father didn't move. It was like the previous time, before he told me my mother had died. Suddenly I felt a sharp pain in my stomach.

"Dad?" I asked in panic.

The doctor turned.

"Herr Merten? You have to tell him. I'll leave the room if you like."

My father still didn't move. He seemed to be rooted to the spot by the window. The doctor looked at a loss. I was afraid. Afraid that my father was going to confirm the dreadful suspicion that was raging inside me.

After endless seconds, my father turned and came to me. He crouched down next to the bed but didn't look me in the eye. His gaze was fixed on the ceiling.

"Christian, your brother . . . we couldn't find him."

"Is he dead?"

My words boomed in my ears. First my mother. Then Lukas. It couldn't be true. It simply couldn't be true. My father lowered his head. The doctor laid his hand on my shoulder.

I fell into the abyss.

23

"My father never got over the death of my little brother," Christian said as he drew his story to a close. "In the months that followed they tried to reconstruct what had happened. While we were still in the transit center, police officers appeared and questioned my father about the night of our escape. And they also came to see me. I could only tell them that I'd slept deeply. And that I'd last seen Lukas when he curled up on the seat opposite me.

"By the time we were finally released, the experts had come to the conclusion that my brother must have woken in the night and walked around the boat. Perhaps he was sleepwalking. He'd never done so at home, but a pediatrician said that it could happen when children were under serious mental strain.

"My father reproached himself and sank back into the silence that had settled on him after Mom died. Only this time there was no one else to blame and he began to punish himself. He took to drink. It got so bad that he had to go to a rehab clinic so as not to lose custody of me.

"He was unemployed, but began to pull himself together and eventually got a new job. He didn't touch alcohol after that and I hoped things would all turn out well. I went to high school—I wanted to get good grades and go to college. But then, at the age of forty-six, my father was diagnosed with cancer of the liver. I was eighteen when I buried him and had to face life completely alone. I tried to make my own way, passed my exams, and got into college. When the Wall came down it didn't give me any pleasure, since all I could think was how happy my father would have been to see the all-powerful Stasi, and with them the man who had killed Mom, coming down with it."

As the wind carried off his final words, I felt horribly flat. At that moment I could have done with a schnapps. Christian had fled East Germany on the *Storm Rose*. That boat, the one he had bought, was the one from which his little brother had fallen and drowned.

I looked out to sea, my head full of the images that Christian's words had conjured up. An escape at sea, a father who couldn't come to terms with his loss and wanted to give his sons a better life—and paid for it in such a dreadful way. And our *Storm Rose*.

I wanted to say something, but couldn't. Christian seemed to sense it, and there was clearly more he wanted to say.

"When I saw the *Storm Rose* in Sassnitz harbor I couldn't believe my eyes. In my memory it was much bigger, almost the size of a cruise ship. But I knew it was the one. And I knew I had to have that boat. I had to."

"So you knew about it? From the start?"

My voice sounded strange in my ears.

"Yes, I knew the *Storm Rose* had been used to transport escapees."

"Why didn't you tell me?"

I couldn't believe what I was hearing. All that time he'd known the story of the *Storm Rose* and hadn't said a word? At any other time I might have been disappointed. But now I simply accepted his story and was only a little upset about his silence. Of course his story was a very private one, but he could at least have mentioned that the boat had something to do with his family history.

"I wanted to give you time to find out for yourself," he said. "You'd have come across it sooner or later—or I would have told you. I just didn't want . . ."

"You didn't want to tell the story of your family to some complete stranger, did you?"

"No," he replied. "I didn't. And if it's up to me, I'd rather this part of the boat's history stay between us. I don't want it to be made public, all that suffering in my family . . . It's for your ears only, OK?"

"Yes. I promise."

"Thank you."

I fell silent again. I still couldn't take in what I'd heard. My heart was thumping. It was all too much, far too much. I didn't know what to think or do; everything was churning wildly inside me. I looked out to sea, but the water had melted into the darkness. Only the sound of the waves indicated that it was still there.

We sat next to one another in silence for a few minutes. The joyful yelling of the people around the campfires and the music from the bars had fallen silent. The lights of the pier shone out into the empty night.

"He's the one you bring the flowers here for, isn't he? Lukas," I said at last.

"Yes," Christian replied. "Mainly for Lukas, since his body was never found. He has no grave. That's why I singled out this rock to be his memorial, so I have a place where I can come and grieve for him."

I suddenly thought of my mother. In all the years that had gone by, I had never wondered what her escape had been like. And never thought she might have paid for it. Goaded by the talk of the officials, I'd always believed that she'd sacrificed me. But now . . . What if I'd been the price? And what if she'd died for it? Was she still alive? An indescribable grief suddenly arose in me.

"I do also bring flowers here for my mother and father. Every now and then I visit their graves, but I tend to find that depressing. When I'm here I can remember how they were when they were alive."

It sounded beautiful to have a place where you could remember someone without the burden of death.

"What are you thinking about?" Christian asked, laying his hand on my back. His eyes were red, but otherwise he seemed more self-controlled than I was. Even though it was his brother whom the sea had swallowed.

"I'm thinking of my mother," I replied. "Of the price she must have paid for freedom."

"Did she go over too?"

I nodded. *Went over.* That's how it had been known back then. Such a harmless phrase, but it contained so much: preparations, fear, hope, racing heart, joy, disillusionment. We never said, "They crossed the border," as people did later. We said, "They went over." And depending on your political bias, you either admired people for it or were outraged.

"She disappeared one day, just like that. She'd put me to bed. When I awoke I was in a police car. My mother had gone. At first I thought something had happened to her, but the police officers told me she'd disappeared. I've never been so afraid in all my life. They brought me to a home where I was parked on a bed, surrounded by a number of other children. I was given no explanation. I lay there, terrified, and hoped that it was all only a dream, a misunderstanding.

"When I managed to sleep, toward morning, and then felt someone shaking my shoulder, at first I thought I was back home and it was my mother who was waking me. That it had all been a nightmare. But it wasn't. A Party official appeared and told me my mother had defected. For such a crime children were usually placed in the juvenile work-house, because it was assumed they'd helped their criminal parents. But at the age of six I was far too young to be accused of being an accessory. Of course I was asked what my mother had been doing during the days before she left, but I had no idea. If my mother had made any plans for her escape she had hidden them from me.

"Once they were sure I didn't actually know anything I was first taken to a home, then adopted by the people who are now my parents. My father was a faithful Party comrade, and as he and his wife were unable to have children of their own, he had long been on a waiting list for adopting. The Hansens took me in, and with me they accepted the price of being monitored by the Stasi—it was possible that my mother would repent and return to reclaim me. At least, that was the hope I clung to for years. But she didn't come. And I never found out whether she'd even looked for me. I still sometimes wonder whether she'd have been able to find me if she'd tried. As for me, I felt bombarded with so many opinions that I found it difficult to recognize the truth.

"After a few years I came to the conclusion that she simply hadn't wanted me. That she'd given me up for tights, coffee, and fashionable summer dresses. It was the simplest and best explanation. I didn't have the courage to seek another. And I certainly didn't want to go back to the children's home, didn't want to be abandoned, superfluous. I accepted my adoptive parents as my own. And to this day I can't say they were bad parents. I love them both, and that will always be the case."

My story was followed by silence. It was shorter than Christian's, but what else could I say? It was all I knew; I'd never questioned it.

Now fate seemed to be pursuing me—first the dream, then the boat, then Christian's story. Everything in my life that remained unresolved seemed somehow to be back.

"What about your mother?" Christian asked. "Has she never tried to find you? Or you her?"

I shook my head. "No. I'm sure she never tried and I . . . neither did I."

"So you believed what they told you about her?"

I jumped to my feet and folded my arms.

"Yes, I did."

"And now?"

I knew what he meant. Why had I accepted what others told me so uncritically? Convenience? Or because I really had believed it?

"I dreamed about her recently," I said. It wasn't really an answer, but to be honest I didn't know of a better one. Deep in my heart I still held the corrosive suspicion that she had simply left me in the lurch. German reunification had passed by me without triggering any deeper thoughts inside me. I hadn't even felt the slightest hope that my mother would one day appear before me and say hello. But now I was no longer sure.

Who could know what the officials would have told my mother had she tried to find me? Maybe somewhere there was a rock for me on which she came to lay flowers. Tears sprang to my eyes. I wasn't sure if they were for my mother or the story I'd heard.

I couldn't prevent a brief sob from escaping my throat. He was immediately next to me. His arms around me were warm and tender, his body strong enough to bear me up as I leaned against him. Now that I had no reason to try to be strong, I let myself go and wept with abandon.

Christian held me tight, gently pressed my head to his shoulder, and buried his fingers in my hair. I didn't feel the wind anymore, only him, and suddenly I felt something opening up inside me. The veil concealing a long-abandoned feeling burst open and released it into the open.

When I had calmed down a little, I turned to look at him. Not that I could see much in the darkness, but I sensed him getting closer. His lips touched my mouth tentatively, as though he were afraid of getting burned. Then we were kissing passionately, delving deep into one another. I nestled up to his body, which felt so shamelessly good, and felt him clinging tightly to me. We were two banners flying, flapping in the wind, which, once intertwined, had found the anchor they had long been seeking.

After a while we drew apart, but only briefly. I took him by the hand and led him over the pebbly beach to the steps that climbed to my house. I pushed the nagging doubt to one side. Leonie was asleep, she'd know nothing. And we'd be quiet.

Christian followed me willingly. We climbed the steps in silence, and at the top we kissed with renewed passion. As we walked past the shrubs, dew dampened our faces and our hair. I thought again of the dewdrop yard of my childhood, and a strange happiness flooded through me because now, at last, I'd found my prince. At least for now. Time would tell what came later.

We tiptoed through the house to the bedroom. On the way I cast a glance through the door to Leonie's bedroom, which stood ajar. She was sleeping deeply, as though she hadn't moved an inch. For a moment I wondered what I'd do if Leonie simply vanished from my life. Go mad—that was the only answer. Go mad with fear.

But she was here, and Christian was with me, and as we passed her bedroom, a surge of different feelings welled up in me, which had nothing to do with fear. It was as though, in telling me his story, Christian had opened up a door inside me. He had opened up himself, too, and now I had no need to fear coming out of my shell. All my body's desires came together in a single demand: to feel Christian on and inside me, and to experience with him what I'd gone without for so long.

We looked at one another and then, as though some invisible force was drawing us together, we fell into each other's arms. At first, Christian's kisses were hesitant but then, like mine, became more insistent. We undressed each other, kissing all the time as though we were both afraid of losing the other in a sea of desire.

As I pressed my breasts against his body and felt his skin that way for the first time, everything around me went hazy. There was only him, holding me, warming me. And as we sank down together on the bed,

I willingly took him inside me. At first he moved slowly, tentatively, pausing every now and then to look at me, to kiss me. Eventually I turned him on his back, positioned myself astride him, and began to move over his hips.

At first I was still worried that Leonie might burst in on us and tried to keep every sigh, every moan as quiet as possible. But then I no longer cared. I supported myself above his chest, his hands holding tight to my hips, and when we finally came, I sank down on him and enjoyed being torn apart by a maelstrom of fulfilled desire.

***

I awoke as the first light of morning fell through the window and the birds began to sing. For a moment I felt as though what had happened had been a dream. But then, to my huge relief, I realized it wasn't so. Christian was sleeping by my side, his head in the crook of my arm, his free arm resting on my hip.

With a smile I ran my hand over his chest, stopping at the spot where I could feel his heart beating. Gentle beats—if he was dreaming at all, it was of something restful. My touch drew no response for a moment, but then woke him.

He opened his eyes slowly, at first unaware where he was. At least, that's what I assumed. But then he remembered. The arm I had been lying on drew me to him.

"Good morning," I said, my hair falling over him like a protective cover.

"Good morning, mermaid," he replied and kissed me. "So you haven't jumped back into the water?"

"No, why would I? I've got my prince."

He raised his eyebrows in a question.

"Hans Christian Andersen," I said.

"I know," he said. "But am I your prince?"

"I think so. Don't you have your crown with you? Well, it's enough that you're a sailor."

Our lips found each other again, then I laid my chin on his breast-bone, which rose slightly beneath his skin.

"I'll just have to try and prove myself worthy of the title," he said as he stroked my hair.

24

It was crazy. I was intending to put in an ad asking a total stranger to contact me—a woman who had no reason at all to get in touch. A woman I wasn't even sure was living on the Baltic coast. And yet I hoped that Lea would read my request.

I went through the possibilities for hours. It would be too expensive to have an ad in all the major newspapers of the area. An Internet search produced a number of forums where people searched for missing persons. Sometimes they even brought results. I found one forum that seemed particularly promising, with exchanges between former East German defectors.

Since they were all free to use, I posted my request on all the busier forums, including the East German defectors' one.

I didn't reveal the content of the letter—that was Lea's private business—but I peppered the post with key dates that only she would recognize.

One afternoon, shortly after a meeting with Hartmann in which I presented him with my rough draft for the brochure, I met Christian. He had disappeared before Leonie awoke, since neither of us wanted her to be confronted with Uncle Christian in Mommy's bed just yet. Now he was trudging toward me along the Binz seafront, carrying a toolbox.

"Goodness, I didn't know you were bringing a friend," I said, indicating the huge box that looked as though it must once have been his father's.

"I promised you I'd help you assemble your furniture, didn't I?" he replied with an innocent expression. "I need my tools."

"Today?"

"Why not? Or are you expecting another gentleman caller this evening?"

He drew me to him and kissed me.

"No, but I hadn't expected you to be on the job this soon."

"Someone canceled an appointment this afternoon, so I thought I'd come and help a single mother in her hour of need."

I smiled. Since the night he'd told me his family history, he seemed to have changed—at least toward me.

"OK. You'd better come with me," I said, taking hold of his arm.

An older woman in a long copper-colored linen dress came toward us. She greeted Christian and smiled at me.

"Oh my God, that was Frau Rosenbohm," he said once she was out of earshot. "Now the whole town will know I've let myself be picked up by a woman."

"Is that such a bad thing?" I asked.

"No, but you know how I like to maintain an air of mystery. If people find out what's going on in my private life they'll never leave me in peace."

"You don't like the thought of your fan club camping out in front of your house?"

"You got it. And all those women throwing themselves off cliffs for me."

"Well, you'd better move to a new house, then—I intend to continue enjoying my life for a while longer."

Once back home I looked at the clock. A quarter past one. Plenty of time before I had to go and get Leonie—plenty of time for us to . . .

But I quickly dismissed such thoughts. Hartmann might phone, or one of Christian's clients. I'd have to keep my desires in check until that evening.

"So, where's the furniture?" he asked, looking around the living room.

"It's already upstairs. The delivery men were kind enough to save me from having to haul it up," I said, leading him over to my computer. I called up the forum post, which had already received five clicks.

"Read that and tell me what you think," I said, turning the laptop toward him.

I suddenly had a thought. Why didn't I also put out a search for my mother on these forums? The very idea triggered the old fear inside me. What if she read the ad but didn't want to get in touch? What if she really hadn't tried to find me, if she had in fact abandoned me?

If I was honest, I still held a glimmer of hope that she had wanted to find me, but the authorities had placed so many hurdles in her way that she had been unable to. What if the truth destroyed that hope? But on the other hand, what did I have to lose by initiating a search myself? If she didn't want to get in touch, it wouldn't change anything. And if she did . . .

"It looks good," Christian said. "Maybe you should spread your search more widely. There must be other similar forums? I could help you, if you like."

"That's very kind," I said. "I've already tried several, although we could look for more. But first, the furniture."

I led him upstairs to where the boxes were stacked. I'd already opened some of them to check that all the parts were there, but two of them were completely untouched.

"OK. I'm afraid this will probably mean me staying over tonight. It's at least half a day's work."

"I have absolutely nothing against it," I replied and threw my arms around his neck.

"What if your unexpected caller returns?"

"Then I'll introduce you to him as my new boyfriend and that's that."

We kissed, and then Christian turned thoughtful again.

"Have you heard from him again?"

I stepped back, a little surprised. I was amazed he was so concerned about it.

"He left me a message on the answering machine on Monday morning. He went to the hospital yesterday."

"Well, are you going to call him?"

"He's not my responsibility anymore!" My words came out more harshly than I'd intended. "Sorry. What I meant was, I don't actually know if he wants me to. He wants to be involved with Leonie, yes, but not necessarily with me. And I certainly don't want that."

"You're saying he really doesn't mean anything to you anymore?" Christian moved close to me and laid his hand on my back.

"No, it's over. But . . . Oh, I don't know—somehow he keeps managing to hurt me. I just want to be normal around him. That's all. But he hasn't made it easy so far."

"And now he's asked you for something."

"Yes. To be honest, I don't like it at all. I'm not at all inclined to grant him his wish. Not because I'm egotistical, but because I don't want him to hurt my daughter again if he changes his mind."

"But people can change," Christian pointed out.

"Maybe. And if he has changed, I've got nothing against him being involved with Leonie. I'm just worried that the change will only last for as long as he's ill. As soon as everything's all right again, he'll push her aside and I'll be back to thinking of excuses I can use to comfort my daughter when she cries."

Tears welled up in me again, but I managed to suppress them. It had all begun so well. I didn't want the afternoon to take a wrong turn. Christian stroked my back and brushed a lock of hair from my brow.

"I'm sorry," he said. "I didn't mean to spoil things."

"You haven't," I said. "It's good for us to talk about it. I hardly ever talked with Jan, and you can see where that led."

"That's true."

He drew me into his arms, gentle and affectionate. We kissed, and my desire flared up again, but this wasn't the time. He had said he'd be staying the night. We'd have plenty of time then to devote ourselves to passion.

"Shall we get to work with these cabinets, then?"

"I'll do it," Christian replied. "You get on with your work. I need something to keep me busy until tonight, don't I?"

"At least let me bring you some coffee."

"I never say no to coffee."

I went downstairs and switched the coffee machine on. On the laptop in the living room I saw that a few e-mails had arrived, including two new inquiries from potential clients. One was a hotel in Wismar, the other a woodworking company. Hartmann had obviously been doing a bit of word-of-mouth publicity for me.

Again I wondered if my mother could be looking for me. *Do it,* a small voice inside me said.

When the coffee was ready, I took Christian a cup and then called up the East German defectors' forum in which I'd posted my inquiry about Lea. After a little browsing, I found a thread where people tried to make contact with family members they'd lost because of separation through adoption or arrest.

At first I found it rather difficult to tell my story concisely. My hands suddenly felt clammy and ice-cold. But at last I had a passable text I could use. I posted it, my heart pounding, then stared at the screen for several long minutes. I was suddenly aware of a strange tension. What if she actually answered?

I started at the sound of the phone ringing. I jumped up, tripping over a cable and almost knocking my laptop off the table. Fortunately,

I managed to regain my balance, but it reminded me how much I was looking forward to being able to move into my office. I picked up, convinced it would be either my mother or my father. Maybe he was calling to tell me they'd found an engine for the *Storm Rose*!

But the voice on the other end of the line was completely unfamiliar.

"Frau Hansen?" The deep bass tones would have made Barry White jealous. "This is Palatin. My neighbor said you'd called to visit me a few days ago, wanting some information."

I was completely taken by surprise. The last few days had been such a whirlwind that I had hardly spared a thought for the sea captain from Timmendorfer Strand.

"Yes . . . um, I did. Thank you for getting in touch! Did you have a good vacation?"

"It was OK," Palatin replied. "When you've been around as much as I have, nothing surprises you anymore. But it was relaxing, and that's the most important thing, isn't it?"

"You're telling me," I replied, unsure whether to come right out with what I wanted.

"So you've bought the *Storm Rose*," he prompted.

"Yes, I have. Or should I say, *we*. I have a partner; you could say he has the stern. Or the bow, depending . . ." I laughed awkwardly, wishing I could swallow my words. "She's a wonderful boat. She's currently being overhauled in Hamburg, and then I hope we can put her out to sea again. I . . . I'm planning to turn her into an arts venue, where people can not only enjoy trips on the water, but can also get some culture. With coffee and cake, of course."

This was followed by a pause, which unsettled me. I had hoped for some reaction, but Palatin remained silent. Didn't he like our plans for his boat?

"What exactly did you want to know about the *Storm Rose*?" he asked eventually. I couldn't decipher his tone of voice. Was he annoyed or simply curious? Was he hoping I'd found something, or afraid of the idea?

"When I was cleaning it out, I found a letter hidden behind a wall panel. From someone called Lea. She indicated that she'd escaped to the West on the *Storm Rose*. I was so moved by the letter that I wanted to find out more about its writer and about the boat. I had the idea of going to see you. I'd really appreciate it if you could meet me sometime."

"Are you a journalist?" he asked, just like the man at the harbor had a few days ago.

"No. Actually, I'm an advertising executive."

"So you want to exploit this story for publicity purposes?"

Now his tone was clear to me; it was full of disapproval.

"No, but I want to bring the story of the boat to light," I replied, a little ashamed that I'd seen the letter as a good marketing opportunity. That had changed when I heard Christian's story, and now I really didn't know what I intended to do with the information. But I did want to know the history of my boat. "I'd like people to know that this boat brought people to freedom. But it certainly wouldn't be sensational. I had in mind a set of documents that people could look at if they want to."

There was another long pause.

"You know, for me it was never a matter of fame or becoming a hero. I did what I believed to be right. And to be honest, I had hoped that at some stage someone would find out what the *Storm Rose* had done. But there's no way I want her story to be exploited. Too many people's personal stories are involved."

"I know, and I promise I'll use anything I learn as sensitively as possible. I may even keep it all to myself."

"And you may be intending to turn the boat into one big theme park."

Did I really sound so unconvincing? I was a bit annoyed with myself for having said anything about bringing the story to light. But that was what I really wanted, and I didn't want to lie to the captain.

"I'd never do anything like that."

My pride was a little hurt, but I didn't want to tell him that my mother had also left East Germany.

"OK," Palatin said at last. I pricked up my ears. Did he really want to tell me something? "If it's convenient for you, come to our house on Sunday and bring me a bit of information about my old boat. Pictures, even. You must have taken some."

"More than enough," I replied, a grin spreading across my face. "I can also bring you the report we got from the shipyard. My father's a shipbuilder and he's thrilled with the *Storm Rose*. He discovered some bullet holes and he's dying to know what happened."

"Well, I'm not going to be able to tell you all the stories in one afternoon," Palatin said. "But I may remember the woman who wrote the letter. And perhaps you'll be interested in how I came to be helping to transport people across the border."

"I'd be very interested!" I replied, suppressing the image that leapt into my mind. Hundreds of faces—men, women, children—freezing out on the Baltic, in the hope that freedom and a good life would be waiting for them on the other side. Palatin probably had something to say about all his passengers.

"Good. Then get here around lunchtime. My wife's a wonderful cook!"

I thanked him and said good-bye. After hanging up, I stared at the telephone for a few moments. I hadn't imagined a meeting with the captain so soon.

I suddenly had an idea. I climbed the stairs to my office, where Christian was busy puttering around. He had assembled the desk and was hard at work on a cabinet. If he continued at this pace, we'd have plenty of time for other things that evening. Cardboard was scattered around everywhere.

"Christian?" I began.

My handyman let out a loud "Shit!" and threw the hammer to the floor. He had clearly scored a hit, but not on the wood. He held his finger, his face contorted in pain. I went over to him.

"Shall I blow on it?"

I couldn't help grinning.

"No, no. It's fine. I'll be OK."

He shook his hand. I took it and breathed cool air on it. A moment later he relaxed.

"There you are. It always helps with Leonie," I said, continuing to blow. "Sorry I made you jump."

"It wasn't your fault," he replied, kissing my brow. "It's that stupid desk. Are you sure you want it? I've cut myself once and hit my finger twice and I'm about ready to throw it out the window."

"I'll have to think about it—it cost me four hundred euros."

"OK, you've convinced me." Christian smiled. "What have you got to tell me that's important enough to interrupt my handiwork?"

"You won't believe who's just called."

"A magic fairy with a cheap diesel engine in good working order for our boat?"

I loved the fact that we were on the same wavelength.

"No, it was Georg Palatin. The captain."

"Oh, is he back from his vacation? Did he sound tanned?"

"What does 'tanned' sound like?"

"No idea. As you see, I tan like cheese." He held up an arm that was only slightly brown.

"Ah. Well, he doesn't sound like you, anyway," I replied. "He invited me to go see him this weekend, so he can tell me some of the boat's history. I wondered if you want to come with me."

Christian lowered his arm, his expression serious.

"Do you think that's a good idea?"

"I can understand if you're not too eager to meet the man again, when it was on his boat that your brother was lost. But maybe . . . maybe he can tell you a few things. In any case I'm sure he'd be pleased that the boat now belongs to you."

"Us," Christian corrected me, his expression now softened somewhat. "OK, I'm on board. It's fair to say that Palatin's in no way to blame for my brother's death—that night he was focusing on getting the boat safely over the Baltic. And if I'm honest I really would like to see the old sea dog again. I can hardly believe he's still around—to a thirteen-year-old he looked at least three hundred."

I laughed. "You're exaggerating!"

"No, seriously. He had a gray-flecked beard just like the guy on the fish sticks ads."

"The Gorton fisherman? You'd better not call him that, or he'll change his mind about telling us anything."

"Don't worry, I'll keep myself under control. But I do have a condition."

I raised my eyebrows. "A condition?"

"Yes. That I drive. In my car. I don't trust your old rattletrap."

"You're calling my trusty companion a rattletrap? It's a Volvo!"

"That may be, but it probably dates back to the year I was born. You shouldn't be making long drives in it."

"It's survived all the trips I've taken in it so far without breaking down."

"OK, but when it does break down—and believe me, it won't be long—I'll be glad to help you find a bargain used car I can be sure of you driving without anything happening to you."

I could have sat with him for hours, keeping him from his work, but my inner alarm clock told me it was time I went to the nursery school.

"I've got to go," I said, jumping up.

"Take care jumping into that rust bucket of a Volvo."

"I will. And don't you go letting strange men into the house," I warned him before hurrying downstairs.

25

The seats in Christian's car were quite a bit comfier than my car's, and I enjoyed not having to concentrate on the road. It was an unusual experience. For all the time I'd been married to Jan, he'd been the driver for all our weekend trips, and I drove only during the week. After the divorce I'd always been in the driver's seat. And now, at last, I had a man back in my life who could sometimes take the wheel. My mother would have gone crazy with joy. But I preferred not to tell her anything yet.

The cars in the other lane shot past us, but we had time. Christian drove as cautiously as if he had a load of nitroglycerin on board. Leonie was playing in her car seat after eating a chocolate muffin. A few crumbs still stuck to her chin. It looked funny on her face, so I didn't reach for a tissue right away, instead enjoying the views of the green landscape punctuated by thick drifts of fog that were gradually clearing. It all looked so calm and peaceful.

My cell phone suddenly buzzed in my bag. By the time I fished it out, it had already stopped. At first I thought it was my father trying to reach me, but the display showed Jan's number. I turned hot and cold in turn. He clearly wanted an answer. A whole week had now passed since he appeared, a week during which he had neither called nor made any other attempt to contact us. Did he want my decision now?

"You seem worried," Christian said as he pulled past a truck and then returned to the right-hand lane.

I shook my head. Yet he was right, I was worried.

"Is it about . . . ?"

I silenced him with a shake of my head.

"Later," I said, settling further down into the seat.

Having arrived in the district of Niendorf, Christian parked the car on a small lot. I brushed the muffin crumbs from Leonie's face and lifted her out of the car.

"So, how did you like the journey?" I asked.

"Great!" she replied happily. "Are we going to see the captain now?"

"Yes, we are."

"Then I can ask him, too, how you fill up a boat."

"Well, I don't know if the captain will be able to give you an answer to that one."

"If he doesn't know I'll ask the mermaids. There must be some here, too." She looked at Christian. "Isn't that right, Uncle Christian?"

"Of course there are mermaids here," he replied, giving me a wink. "We can go down to the beach this evening to see, if your mom agrees."

"Pleeease," Leonie begged, and I had no choice but to agree.

We walked down a narrow, grassy path to the captain's house. I was surprised by how well Christian knew his way around.

"How do you know that it's down here?" I asked.

"I told you that I woke up in a stranger's house after I was knocked out on the boat."

"Yes, I remember."

"It was Palatin's house. After all the trouble on board the boat, he took us in. He wanted me to get medical care before we registered with the police."

"How long did you stay here?"

"A few days. The investigation into my brother's disappearance was ongoing and the police questioned my father a few times. Then we had to move on, to the refugee transit camp in Uelzen. Palatin lent my father some money to help start his new life. It was a really sad journey, especially because my father was still weighed down by what had happened to Lukas. Since he hadn't been found, Dad still harbored a hope that another boat might have rescued him. He swung wildly between hope and despair."

Christian looked at Leonie, and I understood that he didn't want to say any more. I nodded and squeezed his hand briefly.

Once at the gate to the yard, I let Leonie ring the bell, which triggered furious barking.

"Rufus! Out of the way!" a woman's voice called out as a huge black dog leapt toward the gate. We stepped back in shock. The dog barked twice, looked at us, and then panted its warm breath over us.

"I'm sorry!" the woman called out as she came toward us down the path. She was wearing a short-sleeved sweater and a skirt, with support tights covering her legs. Her short hair gave her a youthful appearance. "Our Rufus is always eager to make his presence felt, but he'd never harm anyone."

I was surprised to hear that she had a slight Saxony accent. She called the dog to heel and stroked his head. Rufus, who must have accompanied the Palatins on their vacation, sat back on his hind legs, panting and stirring up small clouds of dust with his tail. I was nevertheless still fearful of crossing his path.

"I'm Irma Palatin," the woman said. "You must be the young woman who wants to talk to my husband."

"Annabel Hansen," I said, shaking her hand while watching the dog out of the corner of my eye. "This is my daughter, Leonie, and this is Christian Merten, who's bought the *Storm Rose* with me."

"I'm sure my husband will be pleased to see you," she replied. "Come in. And don't worry; Rufus won't do anything."

The dog looked eager enough for me to have my doubts. Christian must have sensed it, as he stepped fearlessly forward. When I saw that Rufus really did stay where he was, I followed him, all the time sensing the dog's eyes following me. I turned when I reached the door and saw him snuffling around the hedge that lined the fence. We were clearly of little interest to him.

"I was in the middle of getting ready for you; please excuse the mess in the kitchen," Frau Palatin said as she led us into the house.

The small hallway where we left our shoes led through to the kitchen. There was a smell of roast meat and potatoes, a pan was bubbling away merrily on the stove, and the air was full of steam.

The mess Frau Palatin had apologized for consisted of a bowl of potato peelings and a few sheets of newspaper. My kitchen would have looked quite a bit worse. Everything was in its place here, with not a trace of dust on the windowsill.

"Georg, your visitors are here!" the woman called, and gestured for us to follow her.

Georg Palatin was waiting in the living room. He sat in a wheelchair and at first glance looked rather frail, unlike his wife. He was wearing blue suit pants, a white shirt with fine red stripes, and a red patterned sweater. As soon as he saw us, the air of fragility seemed to drop away.

"Ah, here you are." His voice sounded even deeper than it had on the phone, with no trace of old age. On the phone he had sounded like a sprightly sixty-year-old, but in the flesh he was more like a sprightly eighty-year-old.

"Hello, Herr Palatin. Thank you for having us here."

The man shook my hand.

"I thank you, young lady, for wanting to talk to an old fogy like me. People of your age rarely do." An impish smile crossed his face before he turned to my daughter. "And I see you've come with your mommy, little miss."

"Yes, this is my daughter, Leonie," I replied for her, as the man in the wheelchair was filling her with awe.

"That's a lovely name. Leonie sounds like a lion. Are you one?"

Leonie shook her mop of curls, but she took the hand he offered and fortunately didn't ask why he was sitting in a wheelchair.

He turned to Christian, who offered his hand.

"I know your face from somewhere, young man," he said, gripping Christian's hand as though the touch could trigger something in his memory. "You resemble a man I once brought over."

Christian nodded. "That would have been my father. My name is Christian Merten."

The captain's mind worked for a moment, then he nodded as if he'd found the relevant information in his personal record of his life.

"You were only a child at the time, weren't you? You came over with your father." Palatin paused and released his hand. He also seemed to remember everything else connected with that particular escape. "I was really sorry that . . ."

"Thank you," Christian replied. "It was a long time ago."

"But wounds like that don't heal easily, do they?" Palatin continued, and I could see that he also blamed himself for Lukas's disappearance. "I remember every single person I brought over back then. But your fate has remained particularly clear in my memory."

"It's very kind of you," Christian said.

His voice was cracking a little. Had he or his father held Palatin partly to blame after all? Maybe the captain could have made his boat a little safer. But neither of the men seemed inclined to go into it any further.

"Take a seat, all of you," Palatin said, bringing the uneasy silence to an end, "and Irma will bring you something to drink."

He indicated a large comfortable-looking sofa, and we sat down.

"So, you've bought my old girl," Palatin said once his wife had set a large jug of homemade lemonade down before us. "I could hardly believe she still has the same name."

"*Storm Rose* is a beautiful name," I replied. "Anyway, isn't it supposed to be unlucky to change a boat's name?"

"No, I don't think so. A lot of boats have been renamed, especially after the war. No one wanted the name of some prominent Nazi on the bow of their boat, so many vessels were given new ones. The *Storm Rose* herself was called something else originally. A long, boring string of letters and numbers that no one would have noticed. I gave her the name *Storm Rose* because she was a pretty cutter—and because I hoped she would weather any storm. And she did."

He thought for a moment, then reached for his glass with an unsteady hand and drank.

"But tell me, you mentioned a letter you found. Have you brought it with you?"

I took the letter from my bag and handed it to him.

Recognition showed in his expression. He traced the writing with a shaky hand, as if tracing the lines, then put the page slightly to one side.

"I recognize this letter," he said. "Of course I do. She was a very pretty girl who came on board."

He paused, and I imagined the whole story playing out behind his eyes. It was a shame I couldn't follow the movie of his thoughts.

"But maybe I should tell you first how I came to be bringing people across from the East." He looked at his wife. "It'll be a while yet before lunch is ready, won't it, Irma?"

"A little while," she replied. "Anyway, make a start on your story. You can take a break for me to serve the roast if it's ready before you've finished."

Palatin gave her an affectionate smile, then turned to us.

26
Georg

My father thought I was mad when I told him I'd bought a boat.

"What do you want with a boat like that?" he asked when I showed him a photo of the little cutter. "It looks like a minesweeper; you can be sure the tub will have taken a few hits. It's likely to sink from underneath you."

I'd been going to sea for a few years and had just obtained my captain's license. And I believed a captain needed his own vessel.

The small wartime cutter, which had lain rusting at a mooring in the Hamburg harbor, was just right for me. It might not have been the most beautiful boat, but it was cheap. And I had a business idea.

"The cutter's in perfectly good working order, Father," I said. Not that I was accountable to him at thirty years of age. But in 1959, if you were unmarried, you were still expected to involve your parents in any important decision. My father was a seaman himself. He'd served in the navy and lost a leg in a battle. That had not only saved him from a watery grave, but had kept him out of jail, which had been the fate of many of my friends' fathers. He'd been brought back from the front a disabled veteran and put to work in a factory until Hamburg was razed to the ground. "I'll have it refitted, then it'll be as good as new."

"What do you intend to do with it? You'd be better off looking for a wife and making sure you start a family before you're too old. I want to live to see my grandchildren."

"You will, Father," I assured him, although at that time there was no woman I could imagine taking as my wife. I'd been in love with a few girls on and off, but it was never for life. "And I can assure you I've thought it all through. I'll earn money by taking people on trips up and down the Elbe. You wouldn't believe how many want to come and see the harbor now that everything's being rebuilt."

"You need a pilot boat or a tour boat for that, not a cutter! All you can do with that is catch fish!"

The discussion with my father went on for a long time that evening. Only once he'd put away a few glasses of schnapps did he finally fall asleep.

I was still convinced of my plan, so I set to work. Friends at Nikolai & Jensen helped me get the boat back into good shape, and convert it for use as a passenger carrier.

During the process I often felt as though my father had been right and I should have listened to him. The cutter had sustained a fair amount of damage in the war, which was why no one wanted it. But the heart of the vessel, her engine, was strong, and the damage to her hull was eventually repaired.

A year later, she was launched. Now she not only had an intact hull and a passenger cabin, but she stood out from the other tour boats. I just didn't like the name. However, I understood more about boats themselves than choosing names, and I was very picky. My friends' comical suggestions, *Mackerel Can*, *Ship's Rat*, or *Kobold*, were soon dismissed because I didn't want my cutter to be a laughingstock. I finally settled for leaving the numbers on the bow and postponing the launch party.

It was on a beautiful May day that I set sail. With my friends Hugo and Horst as crew, we carried my first load of passengers out of the harbor, something that smaller boats wouldn't dare to do. But business was slow to pick up. There were plenty of people who wanted to sail on her maiden voyage, but the numbers gradually fell. I didn't tell my father because I didn't want him to laugh or say *I told you so*.

On a summer's day in 1960, during a particularly bad patch, I was scrubbing the deck—an activity that was good for releasing my frustration. I was so short of cash by then that I worked at the harbor during the week and tried to get myself a place on a merchant ship. But that Sunday, when my luck had clearly deserted me, a woman appeared by my boat.

"Hello?" she called down, and waved.

I straightened up. I had blisters on my hands from all the scrubbing, and my back was badly sunburned.

"Yes?" I said.

I was stunned at the sight of her. She was very young, perhaps just turned twenty. And she was the prettiest girl I'd ever seen. Her hair was tied in a knot, with a few daisies twined in it. She was wearing a white cardigan over a pink dress, and carried a white bag. No model could have looked more beautiful to me.

"What can I do for you?" I asked.

The woman was looking me up and down from head to toe as though she'd been expecting something else, then she replied in a strange accent, "Do you take people out into the harbor? I've lost my tour group; they were on another boat. And now I'm alone here. All the boats have gone; yours is the only one still here. I've got to go home this evening and I'd love to see something of the harbor."

"Erm, well . . ." I said. Going out with only one passenger was sheer madness, an inexcusable waste of diesel. But the girl was so beautiful, and I'd probably gotten a touch of sunstroke. I heard myself saying, "Of course, we're setting off soon. Wait a moment!"

Whatever happened, I couldn't just set off as I was. Although it was fairly hot, I quickly donned my captain's uniform. Too late, I began to wonder if the girl was making a joke at my expense. Perhaps she'd vanished while I was down below and was now having a good laugh about the way she'd fooled me. As I came back on deck, I was already preparing myself for the disappointment of my life. But there she was, shading her eyes with her hand and waiting for me.

"Well, why don't you come on board, young lady," I said as I lowered the gangplank to the dock. She allowed me to help her on board, then peered in amazement into the passenger cabin.

"You're going out just for me?" she asked, a little surprised, as I got the boat ready to launch.

I was embarrassed by the way she figured out my lack of commercial success. But I'd never had a talent for making up stories, so I simply admitted it.

"As you can see, I'm hardly overrun with customers. But it's good for the engine to run every now and again. Make yourself at home; I'll just go and switch her on."

The diesel engine was indeed happy to be running again. When I came back up and headed for the wheelhouse, the young woman was already in the driver's position.

"Forgive me, I know I shouldn't be here, but there's no one else in the passenger compartment—perhaps I can sit with you?"

I saw no reason to refuse her, and it meant I could save myself the trouble of yelling down the bullhorn, so I agreed, and a few moments later we cast off.

I was a little uneasy about it, as being in control of a boat demanded my full attention, and the young woman was a real distraction. I could still hear my father's words about a wife and family, and despite the fact that I didn't even know her name, I had a gut feeling that she was the one. Or so she seemed. And since I had a girl like that on board my boat, I would have been crazy not to at least start a conversation with her. I didn't usually have any problem talking to women, but I was suddenly so nervous that my hands had gone clammy. What could I say that wouldn't sound awkward? How could I avoid alarming her?

"Where are you from?" I asked the young woman, who seemed to have more of an interest in my ear than the harbor buildings, as she stared sideways at me the whole time.

"From Rostock," she replied.

"Rostock?" I replied in surprise. She had a distinct Lower Saxony accent.

"Yes, I moved there a few years ago for an apprenticeship. And now I just don't want to leave."

Amazing. A girl from the Soviet zone on my boat. And such a pretty one at that. Of course people often came over to us in the West, usually to visit relatives. But I'd never met any of them. In general, we believed that in the Russian zone they had nothing to eat and only earned worthless money for their work—which was why they came to the West to look for work. But the girl next to me didn't look as though she was in need.

"So what do you do in Rostock?" I asked.

"I'm a nurse at the university clinic," she said.

"You must have a lot to do there."

"As much as in other hospitals," she replied with a shrug. "I enjoy the work; I couldn't imagine doing anything else."

"Yet you have time to come to Hamburg?"

The young woman laughed. "We do get the occasional day off, even under Socialism!"

Her words surprised me for the second time. I'd heard before how faithful they were to Communism and Socialism in the Russian zone. I wasn't particularly worried about Socialism, as Hamburg had always been fairly left-wing. My family had voted for the Social Democrats since 1946. It was just that we'd heard some awful stories about Socialism over there. It made the girl seem all the more attractive to me, as she didn't seem to take her Party leaders at their word.

"So what's it really like for you?" I asked.

I wasn't feeling any less nervous; my heart was still thumping in my throat. What did I think it was like over there? It was a stupid question, but she answered that one, too.

"Well, what can I say? Most of the time you do your work and you're grateful for what you have. But sometimes you'd like more. A few weeks ago two friends of mine defected. Their parents, farmers out in the country, were supposed to move to a collective farm. But they refused, so they had their land confiscated. They left."

That sounded dreadful! It seemed that there was some truth in the horror stories I'd heard from people who'd been there. And the Party bigwigs had shown several years ago what they were really made of when they suppressed the uprising.

"But as I said, I manage OK. And I still have my aunt here. As long as we're allowed to cross the border it's all bearable. Fortunately, my aunt's very generous. Take this dress—in Rostock I can wear it only on special occasions, or my colleagues would burst with envy."

The dress was pretty, but for special occasions? I'd seen more striking ones. Eventually we caught up with the boat on which the rest of her group had disappeared. They were young people, a mixture of men and women. I wondered if she was in a relationship with one of them, and felt a pang of jealousy.

"That must be them," I said, pointing ahead. "I'm sure your boyfriend will be pleased to see you again."

I tried to look unconcerned as I stared ahead, but I saw her smile out of the corner of my eye.

"I don't have a boyfriend," she said.

"I can't believe that a young woman like you isn't spoken for!" I said in amazement, although I was secretly relieved deep down. If her heart didn't belong to anyone else, maybe I had a chance. Even if she was from the East. That didn't matter if you'd fallen for someone, did it?

"Would you like me to make contact with the captain to say you want to board the other boat?"

The young woman shook her head.

"No, I'd rather stay with you. But if I may, I'd like to go to the railing and wave to them. It's not every day that I get a boat all to myself."

"Of course you can," I replied and watched her go.

She wanted to stay on board with me! Of course it was only for a moment, and because of the boat, but I wondered what she'd say to a different invitation. I couldn't imagine anything nicer. Once we were back in the harbor, she looked quite sad.

"It's a shame the trip's over already," she said, looking awkwardly at the toes of her white shoes. "What do I owe you?"

She opened her purse.

"No, there's no need," I said quickly and briefly laid my hand on her arm. "You don't owe me anything. It was a great pleasure to sail with you. I'd do it again anytime."

She looked at me curiously. At first I thought she was going to change her mind. But then she put her wallet back in her bag.

"Then I'm grateful to you, Captain. See you around."

And she left.

Alarm bells went off inside me. *Damn it, numskull, are you blind? Go after her, tell her not to go!*

"Excuse me, wait a moment!" I called after her. The girl turned. "I . . . I haven't even asked your name."

"Irma," she said. "Irma Neubert."

"Georg. I mean, I . . . My name's Georg Palatin." I took a deep breath. *Now or never,* I told myself. *She can only say no.* "And I'd like you to come for a coffee, if you don't mind me asking."

The most beautiful smile I'd ever seen on a woman lit up her face.

"I don't mind," she said.

From that afternoon onward, Irma came to Hamburg every now and then, and if she couldn't, because her shifts got in the way of her plans, she'd write. This went on for a year, and believe it or not, she brought me luck. My passenger numbers rose, and I was soon able to start paying my friends Hugo and Horst for their work again.

One evening, when Irma was visiting me, I took her out, and later that evening she kissed me. I could have swum a lap of the harbor! I cherished the hope that she'd accept my marriage proposal when I made it, and so I gradually prepared my parents for the idea that I'd soon be introducing them to a girl I wanted to spend my life with. My mother was delighted, and even my father had nothing against it when I showed him Irma's photo.

I persuaded my sweetheart to come to Hamburg the following Monday, August the fourteenth, so I could take her to meet my parents. She was free that Monday after a night shift and I hoped to rearrange my own shift. Nothing could stand in the way of our meeting.

I was probably more nervous than she was. I was hoping that my father wouldn't say anything about the Soviet zone. Neither he nor my mother knew that Irma was from the East. I wanted them to get to know her as the lovable person that she was.

My coworker Karl was a romantic soul at heart, and he'd agreed to swap shifts with me, so I went to work the Sunday before. My coworkers were sitting in the break room with the radio on. From all the noise they were making, I thought at first that they were listening to a soccer match. But so early in the day? It would have been unusual for a Sunday morning, too.

"Hey, what's up?" I asked as I stowed my bag in the locker.

"Shhh," one of them hissed. "The Russians are closing the border."

"What?" I couldn't believe what I was hearing. Why would the Russians close the border? At first I had no idea what it all meant.

"During the night they posted border guards in Berlin and they're building a wall. They're also preventing people from the East from going out."

My mouth hanging open, I listened to the reports on the radio. I tried to convince myself that the wall was being erected only in Berlin. My Irma lived in Rostock—she couldn't be blocked in there.

But I was forgetting that there was already a border fence between East and West. Every time Irma wanted to come and see me, she had to apply for an exit permit. Because she was a nurse, she'd always returned when she should, and she was also visiting a sick aunt, it had never been a problem before. But from what I was hearing now, no one would be allowed out of East Germany anymore.

I was seized with panic. Irma! She was supposed to be coming the very next day! And now the bigwigs over there were sealing the border, and shooting at anyone who tried to cross.

I began to pace up and down, rubbing my hands over my face, pulling at my hair with my fingers. What was I going to do? It was too late to go to Rostock.

The harbormaster finally arrived and broke up our little group.

"Hey, what's going on here, a cozy coffee klatch? Come on, get to work! Now!"

The men grumbled, but they weren't inclined to pick a fight with the harbormaster, whatever was going on with the border closures. We all got back to our work. However, my mind wasn't in it, and I was fortunate that it was all routine for me that morning. My thoughts were on Irma and what the radio announcer had said.

"What's bugging you?" my coworker Siegfried asked me over lunch.

"Leave me alone!" I muttered angrily.

"You know, don't you, that once you've married a girl the good times are over anyway."

I had naturally bragged about my Irma at work and had been fiercely proud when the others had made admiring or envious comments.

"There's not going to be a wedding," I snapped.

"Oh!" Siegfried was genuinely shocked. "Has she dumped you? Have you done something stupid?"

I shook my head. "No, I haven't done anything."

"So, what's up? Has she found someone else?"

"Not, it's not that either."

"I don't understand."

"I don't understand either," I replied, and looked at him. "I don't understand why they're closing the border."

Siegfried stared at me slightly stupidly, but then the penny dropped. "She's from over there?"

"Yes, genius." Unbounded rage surged up in me. Not against Siegfried, but against the whole crappy business that was called East Germany. "Because they're closing the border, I won't be able to get married."

I couldn't sleep all that night. I should have been dreaming of Irma and going to pick her up from the station, but that was over. Now my mind was plagued with the question of how I could get to her. Could you still cross the border? And if you did, once you were there would you be able to get back out? Would you be forced to settle there? What had happened to the West Berliners who, when the wall was built, happened to be in the Soviet sector?

After a few hours I couldn't bear to stay in my room. I got up, dressed, left the house, wandered through the dark streets for a while, and finally went down to the harbor. Thoughts were whirling wildly around my head. Should I give her up? No, there was no question of that. Would it be so bad to go to her and stay there? But I had my parents to think of.

What if I brought her over to me? But how? I found myself standing by my boat, for which I still hadn't thought of a better name. She rocked gently on the waves. I still had no answer to my silent question about what to do next.

I boarded my boat, as I still couldn't bear to be within the four walls of my apartment, which felt oppressive—and I wondered how Irma must be feeling right now. She was trapped in a cage of steel wire. And unlike me, who could simply leave my apartment, she would never be able to get out of her country. It broke my heart. I curled up on my bunk and wept bitter tears.

One day in September I received a letter from Hamburg, from an unknown sender. It must be a mistake. I opened it, anyway, and found a letter from one Frau Hastermann, who turned out to be Irma's aunt. Her niece had asked her to write me. At first I thought something had happened, but she was inviting me to Rostock and promised to arrange a permit for me at the border.

"You'll be able to see Irma again at last and she can explain everything," she wrote. But at that moment I didn't care about explanations. I hugged the letter to my chest, overjoyed. My Irma hadn't forgotten me! And she hadn't given up, even though I almost had.

It was a while before I could get an entry permit into East Germany. Every day I went to the mailbox and turned away in disappointment when there was no letter. But it came at last. This time it was from Irma herself, not through Frau Hastermann.

The permit was a rough piece of paper, but at that moment it was the most precious document I had. I kept it in a safe place. It was valid for thirty days. It would be impossible to get so many days' leave from work, so I arranged two weeks and decided to take it from there. If I decided to stay, I was bound to find work over there. And if not, I'd make my living with the excursions on my boat. In any case, I wanted to do something with my captain's license.

I didn't tell my parents anything about my visit. Deep down, I'd come to feel that if it couldn't be done any other way, I'd be prepared to stay in the East. Neither my father nor my mother would understand that, so it was better not to tell them until it was a done deal. It looked as though it was at least possible to send letters over the border.

With my heart pounding and a backpack on my shoulder, I made my way to the station one bright October morning. Doves were cooing from the rooftops and sparrows flitted across the station forecourt. The weather was still fine, but the approach of winter was in the air. If I did stay the full thirty days, snow might be lying on the ground by the time I returned. That is, if I returned. Although Irma had assured me I could go back across the border at any time—indeed I had to return if I was to avoid trouble with the authorities—I wasn't sure if I wanted to come back.

There was hardly anything I would miss. My parents would be angry, but they might come to understand. The only thing I would be sorry about was my boat. My beautiful, still nameless boat. Would it be possible to have her sent over if I had to stay in the East?

I wasn't sure if it would be possible to make money from pleasure trips in East Germany. But if necessary, I could have her converted back to her original purpose and catch fish. They still had to eat in the East, after all.

At the station I looked around for a final time. I was sure I'd never see my beloved Hamburg again. But if I had to choose between my city and Irma, I knew full well which was more important to me.

I entered the station, went to the counter, and bought a ticket to Lübeck. There was no direct connection between Hamburg and Rostock, so you had to change to the Cologne-Rostock express in Lübeck. There would be strict controls at the border, but I felt confident about my permit.

Several other people were waiting on the platform. None of them gave a second glance to the young man in his sailor's cap and blue peacoat, bag over his shoulder. I looked like a sailor on shore leave.

I whiled away the ten minutes' wait for the train to arrive by imagining what Irma was doing at that moment. She was probably still asleep. But it was also possible that she had lain awake all night in sheer anticipation. I hoped she was as excited as I was. When the train finally pulled in, I sat down behind a rather large man by the window, and huddled into my jacket. I wanted to try to get some sleep because a night spent awake and the early start had left my bones feeling leaden. Although I closed my eyes and my body was crying out for sleep, I couldn't relax. My skin was crawling. What would the next few hours bring? What was the border like? Would there be harassment from the guards, as others had reported? Would there be Russians with Kalashnikovs waiting on the platforms?

In Lübeck I transferred to the Cologne express that would take me to the border, and from there to Rostock. I was surprised to find the train quite full. I worked my way down the aisles of the carriages with my kit bag, looking for a free seat. A jumble of voices, all with Rhineland accents, swirled around me. Were these people really all heading for the Soviet zone?

As the train set off, I finally found a place in one of the carriages where there was a compartment with only three young men in it. One of them had removed his jacket and was sitting in his shirtsleeves despite the poor heating. His blond hair fell over his face in unruly bangs. The others were wearing coarse sweaters over their shirts. They looked like students to me. They didn't seem too happy about me joining them. As I appeared at the compartment door, their conversation ceased abruptly.

"Is there a free seat here?" I asked. The three of them stared at me mistrustfully.

"Depends where you're from," the shirt-sleeved guy replied.

The other two looked at him in incomprehension. They probably wanted to see the back of me. But why? I was going to the East like they were; there was nothing dishonorable in that.

"I'm from Hamburg," I replied. "If you don't like the city, I can easily find a seat somewhere else."

If they were behaving oddly, so could I. What did my city of origin have to do with whether I could sit there or not? The men stared at me for a while, then the shirt-sleeved guy nodded.

"OK, you can come in."

Something told me it might have been better to sit elsewhere. But the train was very full, and it was a long way to Rostock. I threw my kit bag and cap onto the luggage rack and slipped off my jacket.

"Looks like you're a sailor," the shirt-sleeved guy said. His voice sounded a bit more friendly now, but his eyes were still studying me. "Have you come back from a long voyage?"

I shook my head.

"No, I'm not a member of a ship's crew; I have my own boat. It's a small tour boat, but even so."

"We could use a boat," the man next to him said with a laugh. The third guy grinned. I decided not to go into it any further, but simply sat down. The others seemed to have lost interest, and I didn't feel like finding out where they were from and where they were going. I simply wanted to see my Irma.

Things were fine for a while. I let their conversation wash over me without listening, distracted by my excitement and anticipation. But the others decided to take an interest in me again.

"Why are you going to the Soviet zone?"

What business was it of theirs? They hadn't told me anything about themselves.

"I'm visiting someone."

"Family?"

"My girlfriend."

"Is she pretty?"

"No, she's got a horn growing out of her skull," I replied, a little irritated. What was my Irma's appearance to them? The others laughed—even the blond guy grinned. He reached into the breast pocket of his shirt. I thought he was about to bring out a packet of cigarettes, but he was holding two photographs.

"What do you think?" he asked, handing me the pictures. One showed the man sitting next to him and the other . . . resembled him very closely. There were small differences, but maybe the pictures had been taken at different times. "If you saw these two men, would you believe they were one and the same person?"

"Stefan . . ." warned the man from the picture, but Stefan ignored his unspoken reproach.

"We need an outside opinion," he said, looking at me. "His view isn't the Party line."

"If you didn't look too closely you could believe it, yes. It could be that one picture is a bit more recent than the other."

The shirt-sleeved guy nodded, then said, "Look more closely. Look as closely as you would if you were a border guard."

I didn't know exactly how closely a border guard would look, but I tried to detect the differences. After a while it struck me.

"One of them has a mole you don't have." I pointed to the man next to the blond guy, who darted me a piercing look. "And your hairline's different."

All of a sudden I was sure that these photos were definitely not of the same person. Superficially they could have been, but a closer inspection revealed the differences.

"They're two different men," I said, passing the pictures back to the man opposite. "Why are you asking me?"

"I'm afraid we can't tell you," the blond guy said seriously. "But you might realize sooner or later."

This would probably have been a good moment to vanish from the compartment. But my comfort won out, so I turned up the collar of my jacket and acted like I was asleep to prevent the others from asking me any more strange questions.

Once we'd reached the border, the train stopped and East German border guards boarded to check our passports. It was obviously routine, but I felt as though I were going to burst at any moment. First my fellow passengers asking me weird questions, and now soldiers. I felt as though I were in one of my mother's stories from when she'd been traveling to Holland and saw the Gestapo get on at the border to search for fleeing Jews. Sweat dampened the collar of my shirt, and although it made me look suspicious, I couldn't calm my nerves. The other three also looked tense, but not half as nervous as I was.

When two of the border guards appeared at the door to the compartment, my heart jumped to my throat.

"Passports and permits, please," one said gruffly. I looked at the others, who pulled out their documents matter-of-factly. I did the same and watched the guards compare our faces with the passport photos.

"Are you entering the German Democratic Republic for the first time?" a border guard asked me, holding my papers in his hand.

"Yes, I'm visiting my—" I almost slipped out that Irma was my girlfriend. "Cousin," I corrected myself quickly, since the entry permit was for a family member.

"Have you anything to declare?" the border guard continued, glancing around at the others in my compartment.

"No, I've only brought a few things with me. Clothes, soap, everyday things."

I indicated my bag on the luggage rack.

"Can we please look?"

I pulled the kit bag down from the shelf. As I knew there was a shortage of tights in the Soviet zone I would have liked to take some for Irma, but since I'd been unsure what would happen with customs, fortunately I'd decided against it. All there was in my backpack were a few items of clothing, socks, and underwear. But the border guards must have suspected me of carrying hidden weapons, because they began to rummage through it all.

I looked across at the other guys, but they acted as though they didn't have the slightest interest in me. The guards finally completed their search, handed me my papers, left me to pack my things away again, and turned away without a further word.

Now it was my companions' turn, but they had clearly made the journey to East Germany several times. Their bags contained nothing but socks, underwear, and a toothbrush. They obviously didn't intend to stay long—probably only as long as it took to complete the shady business with the photo.

The guards eventually withdrew, but it was quite a while before the train started moving again. When it did, a sigh of relief passed through the compartment.

"No need to worry—they do it to everyone who has a large bag," the blond guy said, color returning to his face. He grinned. "So you're going to see your cousin? Is that your girlfriend? Do horns on the head run in the family?"

If the situation had been different, I'd probably have grabbed him by his collar. But I could see the relief on his face, and I was also feeling as though I'd been fished out of the water after a shipwreck. We'd crossed the border. No one had been arrested.

"No, of course she's not my cousin," I replied, trying to calm my nerves. "It was just . . ." I hesitated. Could I tell them about Irma's little ruse? "That's just what my girlfriend said when she applied for the permit, because otherwise it would have taken longer to get one."

The man's face lit up as though he'd won the jackpot in the lottery. "You're OK, man," he said, nodding to the other two.

For the rest of the journey we had something like a conversation. I didn't find out much about my traveling companions, but the blond guy did say that he was also from Hamburg. We talked about soccer, and although I wasn't a great fan of St. Pauli I joined in the discussion about what position they'd reach in the league that year. From the teams the others supported, I concluded they were from the Rhineland, although that wasn't obvious from their accents.

We finally arrived in Rostock. It reminded me a little of Hamburg, and I thought again about how I might decide to stay there.

"Well, see you around," said the shirt-sleeved guy as I took my kit bag from the luggage rack. He pressed a packet of cigarettes into my hand. Inside was a piece of paper with a string of numbers.

"If ever you need any help in connection with your girlfriend, call this number."

He didn't tell me why I might need help, but I was sure I wouldn't be using the number. I said good-bye to the three of them and turned to leave the carriage. I was nervous again, but for a different reason this time.

I searched the crowd of waiting faces in the hope of seeing her. I didn't see her immediately and was seized by panic. Had she forgotten? Unlikely, but maybe she'd suddenly had to change her shift at the hospital.

"Georg!" I heard her voice from behind me, and all my doubts were swept away like clouds before a stiff breeze. Irma was standing there in a light-colored coat, beneath which she was wearing a flowery dress. As I turned, she ran toward me, hugged me feverishly, and kissed me.

It was wonderful to be with her again, even though I couldn't help noticing how frugal her apartment was in an old three-story building. The buildings were damp, and some of them still had signs of war damage. There was a long crack down the wall of Irma's kitchen, and the windows were drafty. At least there was a bathroom in the corridor. Things didn't look much better outside. But when I lay in her arms, none of it bothered me. I could have lived with her in a tree house—or a houseboat on the Baltic. I didn't care, as long as I had her.

She seemed to feel the same way. One evening I knelt before her and presented her with the ring I had actually intended to give her several weeks before. She put her hands up to her face.

"Will you marry me?" I asked, and although I had no doubt that she would accept my proposal, I was incredibly nervous.

"Yes," she said. "Yes, I want to marry you . . . but . . ."

The *but* shocked me a little. After all those lovely days, the *yes* was qualified with a *but*?

"But?" I asked. "But what?"

"But how will it work?" she asked, twisting the ring on her finger. "You belong in Hamburg and I can't come to live with you."

"I could move to live with you," I said lightly, although I knew it wouldn't be so simple.

"What would happen to your boat? What about your parents, when they get old and need your help? They only have one son."

She was right, but at that moment I wasn't thinking about what might happen later. I only wanted her.

"If we marry, won't you belong with me? Won't they have to let you leave?"

Irma pressed her lips together, and a tear ran down her cheek. It was the most painful moment of my life, when it should have been the happiest.

"I'm afraid it's not as simple as that," she said. "I have no idea if you're simply allowed to marry someone from West Germany. The enemy of the people."

"Enemy of the people?" I asked angrily. They couldn't call us something like that.

"That's what the Party officials say. They claim you intend to destroy our country. That's why they've closed the border. They say that you're going to bring back Fascism and that there'll be another war."

I jumped up. What madness! I couldn't believe it, and was almost regretting having proposed to her. Until then it had all been so lovely, and I would never in my life have dreamed that I'd be having a political discussion at that moment!

"Do you believe what they tell you?" My face was glowing. I felt like lashing out at something, but didn't want to demolish Irma's room. And I certainly didn't want to scare her.

"No, of course I don't believe it!" she replied. She sounded a little hurt and angry, and I immediately regretted my question. "If I did, would I have invited you here? You can't believe what a fuss I had with the authorities! The head of the hospital and the Party secretary called me in to explain why I wanted to invite a citizen from an enemy state into the country. I told them you were my cousin without knowing if they had any way of checking it. And you're asking me if I believe what they say? No, I don't. I believe you're a decent man, Georg Palatin!"

Irma was shaking all over. And I was the idiot who'd called her mental capacity into question. I went over to her and took her in my arms.

"Forgive me, my love; I didn't know any of it. I promise I'll never again believe that you approve of anything they say."

Her eyes still flashed defiantly as she looked at me for a moment longer, but then she softened and kissed me.

Over the next few days, I almost became an East German citizen myself. While Irma was at work on the wards, I took my place in the HO, as the state food stores were called, and tried to get the provisions on her list. I was amazed at how little there was and how soon the most popular items vanished. While our shops were bursting at the seams with goods, the shelves there were very scantily stocked. While our grocers had fruits from southern lands, here they sold cabbages, carrots, and celery.

After such a shopping expedition, I would think long and hard. Our shops were full. Sometimes an item would be out of stock, but the shopkeepers made every effort to order it in quickly. And people here were so stoic about it! They didn't complain if they couldn't get something, but went away with what they could and came back the next day to try their luck again.

One day, Irma's doorbell rang. At first I didn't know what to do, but eventually I opened up. It was a man in a mailman's uniform. One of his sleeves was empty and pinned up, and I guessed he'd lost an arm in the war. Under his healthy arm he was carrying a package wrapped in coarse paper. The sender's name looked very familiar.

"Oh, you're new here," he said when he saw me. "I hope Fräulein Irma hasn't moved out."

"No, don't worry," I replied. "I'm her fiancé. I'm visiting her for a few days."

"I see. Where are you from, if I may ask?"

"From Hamburg," I replied, surprised at the mailman's friendliness. I put it down to the fact that Irma had known him since she moved in here.

"Uh-huh."

The mailman thought for a moment, put the package down, and took out a piece of paper and pen, which he rested on the package. I was so surprised that I didn't realize what I was meant to do.

"Would you be so kind as to sign here?" the mailman asked with a smile.

At a loss, I did as he asked. The pen made a few blots, but he seemed satisfied. As I handed pen and paper back to him, he leaned toward me and whispered, "Watch out for the Stasi, young man. And tell your fiancée, too. They don't like people from the West, so it would be better if you don't tell anyone else where you're from. The Stasi have informers everywhere, even among people you wouldn't dream of suspecting."

His words scared me. At first I thought he wasn't all there, but then he moved even closer, looked around furtively, and continued even more softly, "Look at me! They took me for a saboteur and traitor. They locked me away in Bautzen and tortured me so badly that my arm had to be amputated. I was out after three years because they couldn't prove anything—they'd obviously mistaken me for someone else. And because they had guilty consciences they gave me this job. I don't normally tell this to anyone; they all think I lost my arm in the war. But young Irma is like a granddaughter to me. Take her away from here if you can, because if you stay with her here they'll never leave you alone—they'll always believe you want to upset their wonderful Socialism. And they'll find a reason to put you away, believe me."

He had scarcely finished when a door behind him opened, and an old woman in a colorful apron came out.

"Ah, Herr Meyer, my ears weren't deceiving me!"

The woman, whom I hadn't seen before, looked me up and down from head to toe, then smiled at the mailman. I felt weak at the knees.

"Frau Höfel, how lovely to see you again!" the mailman said to her. "Are your legs better?"

"It depends on the day and the weather," she replied, her eyes still taking me in curiously. "Have you anything for me today?"

The mailman reached into his bag, took out a folder, and held it against his chest. I was fascinated by the skill with which he held the folder and searched through the letters with only one hand. And I was even more fascinated by the fact that he hadn't been completely broken by the horrors he'd experienced.

"Oh, I have!" he said, separating out the letter with his thumb and offering it for the woman to take. "I hope it's something good!"

The woman looked at the letter and beamed. "From my granddaughter. Thank you!"

"See you tomorrow, I hope!" the mailman said.

He stowed his folder away.

"She's a lovely woman," he said as he prepared to leave. "Sadly, I don't come into the building very often; I usually leave the deliveries in the mailboxes downstairs. But some people really look forward to getting their mail. That's the nicest thing about my job."

I wondered if the old woman had heard what we'd been saying. She'd opened the door at just the right time. But he didn't seem to be afraid of her.

"Well, I'll be seeing you then!" he said and set off down the stairs. I returned his good-bye, then quickly took the package, which was from Irma's aunt, into the apartment.

I was preoccupied by the mailman's spine-chilling story all day. I didn't think he was feeding me a line. No one told lies like that about an amputated arm. The war veterans in Hamburg were all completely open about where they had lost fingers, hands, arms, or legs.

I thought again about the remarkable encounter on the train. The conversation that hadn't really made sense. The young man who'd thanked me for my help, when all I'd done was compare two photos. What was their business in East Germany? Could they have been Western agents? Were the photos intended for forged passports?

I remembered my mother's story. On her train, a man had been found to have a forged passport. The Gestapo had noticed that the picture in the passport wasn't of him. Were those young men planning something similar?

Irma arrived back soon after that and tore me from my whirling thoughts. I was very pleased to see her, and she was delighted with the package.

"Oh, how lovely—a parcel from the West," she cried out.

She clapped her hands and gave me a warm kiss. Her lips had a hint of disinfectant on them.

"I'm afraid they didn't have any coffee beans today," I said apologetically as I showed her the groceries I'd bought, which were laid out on the table since I didn't know where to put them.

"It doesn't matter," she replied happily, slitting open the parcel. "We can depend on my auntie!"

As she spoke, she took out a little pack of coffee beans. The apartment was filled with the rich aroma as Irma put the coffee on to brew.

The days went by very quickly, much too quickly for my liking. I could have stayed with Irma forever, but my visa was running out, and by the beginning of November it was time for her to take me to Rostock's main station.

Ignoring the other people who were waiting for the express train, I took her in my arms and kissed her. She buried her head in my shoulder with a sob, as neither of us knew when we would see each other again. I wanted every minute to last forever, but the train arrived and I had no choice but to board. Seeing Irma weeping on the platform broke my heart. I could hold back my own tears only with great difficulty.

As the train drew away and Irma slowly disappeared from view, I couldn't bear it any longer and bawled my eyes out. An old woman sitting opposite me handed me a carefully ironed handkerchief.

"You poor man. Young love is such a beautiful thing. Believe me, your girl's sure to wait for you. Men who allow themselves to cry have a good heart."

It was very kind of her, but at that moment I didn't really appreciate her words. I took her handkerchief gratefully and then gave myself up to my pain, even though my father had always tried to drum into me that men didn't cry.

Eventually we reached the border, and I got a grip on myself. This time the passport control went smoothly, possibly because I wasn't sharing a compartment with any dubious-looking characters. We'd no sooner left the border behind than I was hit by despair. Crossing the frontier seemed so final. When would I see my fiancée again?

I couldn't leave my poor Irma in that country. Not after what the mailman had told me and the conditions I'd seen. I couldn't stop thinking about how to get her out of Rostock. Then I remembered the cigarette packet. It was in the bottom of my bag, three cigarettes still in it. The piece of paper was still there.

I took it out and looked at it thoughtfully. Who were those guys? I'd heard on Irma's radio that there were occasional attempts to break through the "anti-Fascist protection wall"—especially in Berlin. I decided to call the number when I was back home.

As I arrived in Hamburg it was already dark, and I felt like an empty transport container. Without Irma it was as though someone had taken the essence of my life from my body.

On my way home I passed a pay phone. The paper in my pocket felt like it was glowing. What harm would it do to call the number? The man had offered me help in connection with my girlfriend. And now I needed help. I fed the change I had into the slot and dialed the number.

It took a while for me to be connected, then I heard a beeping. My heart leapt to my throat. How should I approach this? What if these men were criminals? How could they help me? Someone answered at last.

"Becker," a man's voice growled.

I recognized it as the voice of the man who had given me the number.

"I'm the man from the train. You gave me your number."

Silence at the other end. The man must have been trying to remember whom he'd met on the train.

"The captain," I said in an attempt to jog his memory.

"Oh yes, the sharp-eyed man from Hamburg," he replied with a laugh. "What can I do for you, my friend?"

"You . . . you said I could call if I needed help."

"Yes, I did, and I meant it."

"Well, I think I need help now," I replied. "I'd like to bring someone over from East Germany."

Silence. Maybe the man on the other end of the line was having a good laugh at my expense, but it was worth the risk.

"And you think I could arrange that?" he asked.

My face began to glow.

"Well, you had that picture . . . It must have been for a forged passport, am I right?"

He was silent again for a moment.

"It's a dangerous thing you're considering there," he said eventually. "I'll meet you outside St. Michael's Church tomorrow evening at five. We'll talk about it all then."

"OK, I . . ."

But he'd already hung up.

I looked at the receiver for a moment, then placed it in the cradle. I staggered on home, completely perplexed. My thoughts were on Irma. I recalled her arms and her body before I fell into a deep sleep.

***

The wind blew piercing wet gusts through my jacket. I looked for a place to shelter, in vain. There seemed to be nowhere; the stiff breeze caught me wherever I went.

Despite the dismal weather it was really busy at that time around St. Michael's. People hurried past, their collars turned high. I had my hands thrust deep in my jacket pockets as I kept a lookout for Becker. What direction would he come from? I looked at my watch. Nearly five. I leaned against the wall and let my gaze roam across the square. Above me, the bells began to chime the hour. There was still no sign of the man. Had he been delayed? Or had he changed his mind?

The echoes of the bells were dying away, when a figure approached. He was wearing a coarse medium-length jacket, and his hair came down over his ears. As he raised his face, I recognized the man from the train compartment. He appeared to be in a bad mood. Did that have something to do with me, or had something happened?

He offered his hand. "Pleased to see you again. I haven't even asked your name."

"Palatin," I replied, "Georg Palatin."

"Stefan Becker."

He took a packet of cigarettes from his pocket and offered me one. I rarely smoked, but it seemed impolite to refuse. Becker gave me a light and then lit his own. He blew a cloud of smoke into the damp November air before asking, "So you want to bring someone out of East Germany?"

I nodded. "My fiancée."

"Does she know how lucky she is?"

"That she's my fiancée or that I want to bring her out of East Germany?" I asked.

Becker laughed and clapped me on the shoulder.

"You seem like an OK kind of guy. Getting out of East Germany, of course. Have you talked to her about it?"

"No, I got the idea on the spur of the moment." The smoke burned in my lungs. "I found your telephone number again and thought about the photos you showed me. The ones I was to compare, to see if they looked similar."

"I remember. My friends almost lynched me for that. They thought you might have connections in the Stasi."

The word sent a shudder down my spine.

"No, where did you get that idea? I wouldn't have called you if I had, would I?"

"Yes. I'd say if you were working for the Stasi you'd definitely have called," he replied. "But I don't think you are. They'd have treated one of their own differently at the border; they wouldn't have searched through his things. And your passport's a West German one; I could see that a mile off."

"Tell me," I began, lowering my voice. People were passing us without taking the slightest notice, but you never knew whether someone might catch on to what we were saying. "Are you agents or something?"

"What? Agents?" Becker shook his head. "What makes you think that? No, we're students who occasionally have some business over there." He studied me for a moment, then looked me directly in the eyes for a few seconds.

"You bring people over, don't you?" I asked hopefully. "The photos had something to do with it."

"You'd better not say it so openly—not even to your girlfriend."

"Isn't it true, then?"

Becker glanced to the side as if he feared he was being watched.

"We bring people over, yes. We began with fellow students, but now we do it for others, too."

"Do you take payment for it?"

I couldn't imagine they'd put themselves in danger for nothing.

"No, we certainly don't. We just don't want our fellow countrymen to be caged in by the Russians."

My face was glowing with excitement.

"How do you do it? Bring them over?"

"We usually try and find someone who looks similar to the person who wants to leave and ask him if he'll be our front man. With this front man we cross the border, find our target and bring him back over with us. That's why it's important that he looks like the passport photo. The front man we've left behind then goes to the police and reports losing his papers. They usually send him back across after questioning him briefly."

"They don't notice?"

"It depends. After nearly losing our last man we're going to have to give this ruse a bit of a rest for a while."

"So how will you go about it now?"

"We're not exactly sure yet." He was looking at me the whole time. "But I think I can see a possibility."

"A possibility?"

What could he mean?

"You said you have a boat, right?"

"Yes, I did."

"And you've taken it out on the open sea before? I mean, you know how to handle it?"

"Of course, why else would I have a boat?"

Becker thought for a while, drawing on his cigarette.

"How's this for an idea? How about you go get your girl in your boat?"

I frowned. It sounded like a stupid idea, as the East German waters were bound to be as closely monitored as the land border.

"My boat's moored here in the harbor," I said. "And even if I went by the Kiel Canal and through to Rostock I couldn't simply pick up my girl, because I'm sure she wouldn't be allowed into the harbor. They watch it like hawks."

Becker thought some more. The cigarette between my fingers had burned out, although I hadn't taken another drag. I was trembling inside—from the cold, but also from excitement. The thought of picking up Irma with my boat appealed to me, but at the same time I was in no doubt that I knew far too little about the practices at harbors in the Soviet zone. If the border guards noticed that I intended to take off with her, they'd shoot us both, that much was certain.

"What if you don't pick your girl up from the harbor, but out on the open sea?" the escape helper asked then. "She could come out to meet you in a boat."

"That's too dangerous," I blurted out. "The Baltic's very rough. If she capsizes, she'll drown. Anyway, I'm sure she wouldn't dare row out."

"What if there are others with her? Others who perhaps have a small motorboat? Or a sailing dinghy? If several people were taken out? You wouldn't have to go near the shore; the escapees would come out to you." Becker's thoughts seemed to be racing. He threw his cigarette down and ground it out with his heel as he continued to ponder. "I've even heard of people swimming out into the Baltic in the hope of getting picked up by a Danish fishing vessel."

"Mine's a fishing cutter," I said.

The thought of Irma having to go out on the Baltic on some tiny boat still didn't fill me with confidence, but I didn't have a better suggestion.

"Excellent! That means it can handle the rough Baltic swells."

He fell back into deep thought.

"I'll think over the plan," he said at last. The look in his eyes was almost hunted. "Let's meet here again in a week's time. Maybe I'll be able to tell you more then."

We said good-bye. Becker vanished into the crowd. I watched him until I lost him from view.

***

The days until our next meeting dragged by, but Becker and I met again at last. This time his face glowed like the clear November evening.

"It's all dealt with," he announced. "Now all we have to do is ensure that the people are delivered to you. It looks as though you can take three additional escapees alongside your girl. Would you do that?"

I hesitated. Apart from my Irma I didn't really want to bring anyone over—but I knew that Stefan Becker wanted something in return for helping me. And I knew that I'd get nowhere without him.

"Yes, of course," I said. Becker shook my hand.

"Excellent. It's a deal. I'll give you more detailed instructions in the next few days. Do you want to tell your girl yourself, or should we?"

"How dangerous would it be for me to call her?" I asked doubtfully. I wasn't sure who might be listening in, especially since she didn't have her own telephone and had to go to her neighbor.

"Very dangerous," Becker replied. "The telephone she goes to might be bugged. It would be best if you gave us her address and a message for her, and we'll get in touch with her. We know our people over there and know who we have to watch out for. We'll get her to write you a reply and bring it with us when we come back."

"OK," I replied, although my heart still wasn't fully in it.

What if they were caught? And what if Irma didn't want to get involved? When I had been with her, we hadn't talked about escaping. What would I do if she didn't want to leave Rostock? And what if these men gave her the fright of her life and she believed they were from the Stasi? If only I could reach her and prepare her for what was coming!

Becker left without knowing the doubts that were plaguing me. And I left, too, aware that I had to use that evening to write a letter that would explain it all to her.

***

Days of uncertainty followed. I had managed to write a letter, but would Irma really believe it was from me? To be sure, I had mentioned a couple of things that only the two of us knew about, but would she even let the men get near her?

The more I thought about it, the more I became a mental wreck. I was jumpy, and my thoughts kept me awake at night, tossing and turning in my bed. I couldn't confide in my parents; they still weren't even happy about the fact that I'd traveled to East Germany. And as for my friends . . . would they understand what I was doing?

I still hadn't found a new job, so I spent the time puttering about on the boat. No one wanted to go on pleasure trips in winter, and I took the opportunity to work on all the repairs I could.

Then, one day shortly before Christmas, I met Becker again. He gave me a letter that looked as though it had been through a lot on its journey. He or one of his friends must have carried it against their body to prevent it from being opened by the Stasi. It was fairly thick, as though Irma had poured out her heart over several pages. I assumed that was out of fear. What if she didn't want to risk it, if she was breaking up with me? I felt the envelope, but couldn't find anything that suggested she was sending the engagement ring back.

Becker gave me time to open and read the letter. I pulled out the pages with trembling fingers. Most of them were blank, or sheets of newspaper. But among them I found two pages in Irma's handwriting.

She told me that what I was concocting was utter madness. I was about to despair, when I saw the sentence: "But because I love you I'll go along with this nonsense. And woe if you're not there to pick me up!"

I pressed the letter to my heart. That was my Irma! And I was even happier because she'd written that she loved me.

"Next week," Becker said and passed me a piece of paper containing the promised details. "Make sure your boat's good and ready."

The only people I opened up to were my two closest friends. I needed a small crew on the boat, since it was obvious that I couldn't control her at the same time as helping the escapees on the rope ladder.

Hugo was full of enthusiasm. "Of course I'll come with you. It'll be fun to be chased by the coastguards."

"Fun?"

"Well, you know. It's different. And you know they're not allowed to come over to our side, so once we're over we'll be safe. We can do this!"

Horst was a little more skeptical, but I could still count on his support.

A few days later we set out in the direction of Brunsbüttel, where we intended to enter the Kiel Canal. The weather wasn't on our side. It was foggy, and I soon realized how inexperienced I was at the controls of my boat. It was rather different cruising around Hamburg harbor from heading out the mouth of the Elbe. But I grew more confident all the time, and it was good to have my friends with me. They stopped me from brooding, and if there was nothing else to concentrate on, we talked about what lay ahead. That evening we reached Brunsbüttel and sailed into the canal. It was horribly foggy, but what could we expect with so much water below us?

Lying in my berth after my watch, I thought of Irma. How was she feeling with so little time before her escape? Was she afraid? It was such a dreadful shame that I couldn't be with her, to tell her it was all going to be OK. The old worries rose up inside me. Truth was, I didn't know that it would be OK. What if something happened to the boat, or the border guards got onto the trail of the escapees? I couldn't bear to think that Irma might have to suffer for my crackpot idea! Becker had promised to get in touch by radio on a frequency the border guards couldn't listen in to. We'd have to manage it one way or another!

A few hours later, as dawn was beginning to break, we sailed out onto the Baltic. We had passed numerous cargo ships. One Dutch freighter hooted in greeting even though they didn't know us.

We were too early. Much too early, as the operation wasn't to take place until the evening. We entered the port of Timmendorfer Strand, where we treated ourselves to a cup of tea and a hearty breakfast in a café. Although they were both delicious, they sat like a stone in my stomach. My thoughts strayed incessantly to Irma. She must be at the hospital now. I hoped they hadn't made her work a different shift. Was she calm or were her hands shaking? Would her colleagues notice anything when they looked at her? Had she been watched?

I looked at the café clock. Time dragged on slowly. *If only the evening would arrive,* I thought. We eventually left the café and began to walk aimlessly up and down the promenade. The wind was raw, and the sea cold and rough. Seagulls flapped over the surf-capped waves. I looked out to the hazy gray of the horizon. Somewhere beyond was my Irma. I hoped she wasn't changing her mind at the last minute.

The time came at last for us to get back on board the boat. Becker had said that he would radio us as soon as the escapees had come together. That night I wasn't bringing only Irma; I was also responsible for three other people, a woman and two men.

We sailed out onto the Baltic and tried to circle around the meeting point. I got increasingly worried as the height of the waves rose. I hoped that Becker's boat would be sufficiently robust and wouldn't capsize. Fishing someone out of the water in that kind of swell was almost impossible. The raging waves raised another question in my mind—how would we get them safely on board? When we'd planned the trip, we couldn't have foreseen the weather.

The hour grew near, and the sky turned dark. I'd never seen such a dark night in my life before. Not even the moon managed to send a little light through the thick clouds.

The radio signal finally came. We jumped as the white noise hissed through the ether, followed shortly afterward by a few words. Hugo immediately grabbed the headphones and sprang into action.

"They're nearby and waiting for you."

We were only a short distance out from the agreed-upon coordinates. As it turned out, Becker and his friends were not only fully aware of the implications surrounding smuggling people out, but they also knew a certain amount about nautical charts.

I turned the cutter carefully and made my way to the meeting point. Because of the black soup of the fog, we had to be careful not to hit the smaller boat.

"Look, over there!" called Horst, whom I'd appointed to keep watch. "A light!"

I cut the engine. Then I made it out, too—a small, bright point of light to our starboard. I stopped the boat and switched on a light on our deck. I had no idea whether or not I was in Soviet waters, but at that moment I couldn't have cared less. In that boat ahead of us was my Irma. And now I had to see to it that she and the others got safely on board.

I handed over the controls to Horst and ran out with Hugo. We rolled out the rope ladder. I could just make out the smaller boat when it came within range of our lights. It was an old motorboat with room for five people. I couldn't make out my Irma among the huddled figures, so I simply called out to them that they should climb up one by one.

A woman was the first to climb the ladder; I could tell from the way she climbed. She was wearing coarse trousers and a thick jacket, and her hair was tucked into a sailor's cap. As I pulled her on board, I saw immediately that it wasn't my Irma. She must be coming next, also wrapped up in thick clothes. And as soon as she touched my hand, I knew it was her. I practically dragged her up on deck, then drew her to me and kissed her. Her whole body was shaking, and she was crying.

"It's OK, it's OK, you're with me," I whispered into her hair.

I was close to tears myself, but there was no time for that right then. The two men climbed on board. They were also frozen through and at their wits' end. Hugo took all four of them into the passenger cabin, where they were sheltered from the wind. We'd brought flasks of coffee to warm them up.

"Do you want to come with us?" I called to Becker and his friend, but they shook their heads.

"No, we've got to leave East Germany the same way we came; anything else would arouse too much suspicion. See you in Hamburg! You'd better make yourselves scarce."

They turned away. I watched them go, then went back to the wheel-house. If we had strayed into enemy waters, we had to get out of there as quickly as possible. It wasn't until dawn, when I was sure we were within reach of Timmendorfer Strand, that I handed the controls back to Horst and went to see the passengers. My moment for welcoming Irma on board had been much too brief, but now I had time to catch up.

The escapees had shed some of their outer clothing—I couldn't bear to think what would have happened if they'd fallen into the water in all those layers. But I pushed the thoughts aside, as it hadn't happened.

"Here's our savior!" said one of the men, who introduced himself as Hans Grunau. He and his wife, Rosemarie, were doctors, and the other man, Peter Thoms, was a shipbuilder scarred by the war and subsequent captivity as a prisoner of war.

"There was no way I wanted to stay in a country populated with those bastards," he muttered darkly.

The doctors also had a good reason. They had been clubbed down and arrested during the protests in 1953. After a spell behind bars, they had been released but barred from practicing in the medical profession. Since then they had worked as agricultural laborers, but that wasn't the kind of life they wanted to live.

"The prospect of trying our luck at sea wasn't nearly as bad as the prospect of spending a lifetime unable to practice what we'd studied for," Rosemarie said with a smile of relief.

And my Irma had simply come for love. Although it was obvious that it had been a dreadful night for her, her eyes shone. And as she gripped my hand and gently pressed it, I not only knew that I had done the right thing, but I also knew that I would do it again.

Once we arrived in Hamburg, the other refugees set off for the transit camp in Uelzen, while I took the opportunity to introduce Irma to my parents. I was a little concerned, thinking that my father would now raise the same objections as he had when I told him about the boat. But when I told him how I'd brought my Irma from the Baltic, he took me aside and whispered to me, "You got yourself a good catch. Both the girl and the boat."

27

"Well, that's how it was," Palatin concluded. "I haven't regretted any of my decisions, not even when the Stasi were hovering over me like an angel of death. As you can see, they never caught me."

Silence followed his words. Even Irma Palatin, who was standing in the doorway, ready to tell us lunch was ready, said nothing. I glanced over and saw she was surreptitiously wiping tears from the corners of her eyes. What a story. And what a love! Would I ever have had the courage to risk all that to get Jan over the border?

No, that's not a fair comparison, I told myself, and looked at Christian, who also seemed really moved by the story.

"And isn't that a stroke of luck?" Irma Palatin said eventually. She went over to her husband and gave him a kiss. "Otherwise you wouldn't be around to eat the lovely roast I've prepared."

The story echoed in my mind for quite a while. When we had finished eating, Frau Palatin said to Leonie, "If you like, you can come with me and look at the yard. You all can too, of course."

"I'd be pleased to join you," Christian replied with a smile as he placed his napkin neatly next to his plate. "That was a real feast, Frau Palatin."

She waved him away. "Oh, it was nothing."

"She's too modest," her husband said. "But she knows full well that her food's been keeping me going for years. As she herself has. I don't know what I'd do without her."

I nodded, and once Christian had disappeared into the yard with Leonie and Frau Palatin, I said, "My father found bullet holes in the stern of the boat. Did you have any encounters with the border guards?"

"I certainly did! On one trip, which almost ended in disaster, they shot at us. But fortunately we had gotten too far and were back in West German waters. Sadly, one of the guys who'd transported the escapees out to the boat was caught. They tortured him until he couldn't help spilling who his friends were. My name was among them."

I stared at him, horrified. "What happened?"

"When I came home one evening, the woman from next door met me and took me aside. She told me that two strange men were in the area asking about me and my wife. They'd gone, but they'd hung around the building all morning. I drove straight to the hospital to see Irma, who was working in Eppendorf at the time. I went to the nurses' office on the ward and told her that we had to make ourselves scarce immediately because the Stasi were after us. Irma didn't question what I said. While she was finishing her shift, I got a few things together and arranged a car. I didn't want to take the boat because it would have been too risky. I picked Irma up from the hospital and we drove to Timmendorfer Strand, where my former coworker Siegfried was living by then. When he heard what was happening he let us stay with him. Irma phoned in sick, and I asked our neighbor not to let anyone into our apartment."

"How did things turn out?"

"I informed the police, and the Stasi snoopers eventually gave up. But I was too uneasy to stay in Hamburg. Deaths in such a large city were frequent, so two more murders could easily have gone unnoticed.

I decided to relocate my boat to Timmendorfer Strand and give her a new name."

"The *Storm Rose*," I said.

"That's it. The *Storm Rose*. Because of all the storms she'd weathered, and because in ancient Rome the rose is a symbol of discretion. Irma suggested it to me."

He smiled to himself, momentarily lost in thought.

"It turned out that the decision to move to Timmendorfer Strand was a good one. I found work at the little shipyard here, and Irma got a job in a nearby health spa. The business with the Stasi coming after us soon awoke my sense of defiance. Why not get even more people away from the clutches of those bastards? I'd read that the Soviets had begun to disguise their boats as Western vessels, and the escapees were running straight into their hands in the belief that they were heading for freedom. One time, the captain of an East German boat even tried to kill an escapee with the propeller. It all made me so angry that I returned to sailing over and getting people whom the escape helpers I knew had arranged to get out. They'd come out to meet me on a boat, I'd take the people on board and disappear with them."

"Do you remember the woman, Lea, who wrote the letter I found?" I asked. I was still itching to know about it.

Georg Palatin gave me a searching look. "Wouldn't it be better for her to tell you the story herself?"

"I'm sure you're right, but I'm worried that I won't be able to find her now."

"Why not? Have you tried?"

"Yes, on forums that discuss East German history. There are some contact threads for former defectors to exchange information. But I don't know if she's seen it. I haven't had any response so far, and apart from the letter I still have nothing. I don't even know where she lives, and to put an ad in all the local papers in Germany would swallow the budget I need for a new engine for the *Storm Rose*. That's why I was hoping you'd be able to tell me a little about her."

"Well, I took this Lea on board my boat in 1975. She set out from Ahrenshoop, but, as she told me, she originally came from Schwedt. Her name at the time was Paulsen. I never wanted to know the names of my passengers, but strangely enough they all got talkative as soon as we were over the border. And then I'd go around with a queasy feeling in my stomach until the next trip, because I didn't know if I could withstand the Stasi's torture if they caught me."

"But they never did."

"No, thank God. And I'm glad to say it's no longer a problem."

He took hold of my hand. His fingers felt cool and soft. I could hardly believe they'd once had the strength to grip the wheel of the boat.

"Use the boat well, give her a purpose. And as far as I'm concerned you can tell her story. But just think on this: I don't want to be a hero. I'm just an old man who did what he had to. I brought people over the border, no more, no less. The real heroes were those who tried to escape the system—who put their lives, and sometimes those of their families, on the line to reach my boat."

"Not forgetting the helpers on land."

"Yes, you certainly mustn't forget them. Without their support only very few would have made it. And there are some who helped others to freedom but stayed behind themselves to keep on getting others out." Palatin smiled at me. "The young man outside seems to have turned out to be a great guy. Despite all he lived through."

"Yes, I think so too," I replied and looked out the window. Christian was by the hedge, explaining something to Leonie.

"Maybe the two of us should go out for a spot of sunshine too, don't you think?" Palatin said, releasing the brake of his wheelchair.

As I jumped up to help him, he said, "No need. I'm fine. I don't let Irma help me, either, at least not while I can still manage myself. After the stroke I had to come to grips with the idea of these wheels, and I think I've succeeded quite well."

***

We took our leave of the Palatins that evening with the promise that we'd invite them to see us once the *Storm Rose* was back in the water.

Irma Palatin gave us so many leftovers from the lunch and the cake that we'd hardly need anything else to eat for the rest of the week. Full, satisfied, and with plenty of food for thought, I sat next to Christian as he capably negotiated the autobahn. I had enough clues now. Lea Paulsen. A bid for freedom that began in Ahrenshoop. A man called Bob. 1975. And a boat called the *Storm Rose*. There might be a few Lea Paulsens around, but only one who had a story like "my" Lea. I had a starting point.

There wasn't a lot of traffic on the autobahn. As we drove over the Rügen Causeway, all that remained of the day was a glowing red strip of sunlight over the towers of Stralsund. When we arrived in Binz, Christian steered the car up the lane to our house.

"Who's that?" he asked as he pulled up by the fence.

A man was sitting on the bench by the house. Jan. When he saw the car, he rose and walked to the gate.

Damn it, is he going to turn up here every weekend? I thought about his call, to which I hadn't replied. He'd probably intended to tell me he was planning to visit.

"That's my ex-husband," I replied. I looked behind me. Leonie was so tired that she hadn't even noticed we were home. "And I have no idea what he wants."

"I do," Christian replied, glancing at the backseat. "Should I leave?"

I'd been looking forward to ending this nice day snuggled up to him. And now Jan had slid between us. But why shouldn't I present Jan with the facts? Why not show him that there was a new man in my life? He certainly hadn't held back from letting me know who the women in his life were.

"No, why not come with me? There's no reason why I shouldn't introduce you."

Determined, I unfastened my seat belt and opened the door.

"Good evening!" he called out to me. "I hope I'm not disturbing you."

"What's up?" I said, getting straight to the point. I heard Christian closing the driver's door behind me.

Jan looked strange, somehow, as if he'd been drinking, and I was glad that Christian had stayed with me.

"Who's this, then? Your new man?"

Jan studied Christian from head to toe. There was no sign of his remorse from the previous week. Had the doctor perhaps told him that he wasn't ill after all?

"Yes, he is. Christian Merten. Christian, this is Jan Wegner, my ex-husband."

It felt strange to say out loud the surname that had once been mine. Christian offered his hand to shake, and I saw him tense up. I begged him with my eyes to stay calm. I also threw Jan a look of warning, which he seemed to understand.

The tension between him and Christian was now almost tangible. What was it all about? It was as though he was jealous of Christian. The last thing I needed now was for the two of them to come to blows—especially in front of my daughter!

"Jan, why are you here?" I asked coolly.

"I called you this morning," he replied. Not exactly an answer to my question. "I wanted to tell you I was coming to see Leonie. I didn't know you were out—and clearly so busy you couldn't even get to your cell phone."

He looked scornfully at Christian, who was obviously having a difficult time holding it together. It was hard to believe he'd almost spoken in Jan's defense when we were sitting on the rocks together.

"And what brings you here?" I asked again, promising myself I'd simply ignore him if he tried to beat about the bush again.

"I already told you, I want to see Leonie. Where is she?"

"In the car. She's asleep."

"Then wake her up. I can at least say hello."

Now I was certain that Jan was drunk. In this state, he was capable of anything. He had been in moods like this before, but he'd never touched me or Leonie. Still, I was still afraid of what might happen.

"Come back tomorrow morning," I replied. "You're welcome to say hello to her then."

Jan nodded, but a strange smile crossed his face. I had seen that smile plenty of times before, and it confirmed that he certainly wasn't sober.

"Yes, of course . . . you're perfectly entitled to say that—after all, you have custody of her . . . And I'm the idiot who pays."

"That's how you wanted it, don't forget!" I said.

"Yes, that's how I wanted it. And now I want something else. And I certainly don't want this guy having anything to do with Leonie! She's my daughter!"

Keep calm, I tried to tell myself. *He's drunk. He's trying to provoke you.* At the same time, I was wondering how quickly the police could get here if Jan did something completely unexpected.

"Yes, she's your daughter, and I said I'd think about what you asked. But now I really think it would be better if you go back to your hotel. We can talk about it in the morning."

Jan laughed scornfully. "I've been waiting here all day. And now you're just sending me away?"

"Please leave." Christian stepped in. He'd clearly had enough of Jan's little performance. Worried, I looked toward the car. Leonie was fortunately still asleep.

"Why should I? So you can finally fuck my ex?"

Christian fought to control himself.

"Just go!" he repeated quietly, but I could sense him seething inside.

Please don't do anything stupid, I begged him silently.

"Who are you to tell me what to do?" Jan lurched forward and made to grab hold of Christian, but he moved swiftly aside. Jan lost his balance and stumbled against the fence. "You bastard!" he cursed and aimed for Christian again. I moved between them.

"Jan!" I yelled at him. My voice echoed through the treetops.

Why don't you just hit me, instead! Then I most certainly won't have to share custody with you! The same thought must have penetrated the fog of his thoughts, as he stared at me, enraged, but didn't dare raise a hand against me.

"Go back to your hotel, Jan," I said as calmly as I could under the circumstances. I had a terrible cramp in my stomach, and my heart was racing. My skin was crawling in anticipation of a slap. Jan stared at me angrily, then stormed past me without even a glance at Leonie.

I closed my eyes and took a deep breath as he vanished between the trees.

A moment later I felt Christian's hands on my shoulders.

"Are you OK?"

I was shaking all over. I'd never experienced anything like it in all the time we'd been married.

"Yes, I'm fine," I replied, turning and throwing my arms around his neck. "Thank you for staying."

"Well, perhaps it's my fault that things got out of control."

"No, I'm glad you were here. At least he knows now."

I put my arm around his hips and looked in the direction in which Jan had disappeared. Once I was sure he wasn't coming back, I got

Leonie out of the car. Fortunately, my little princess hadn't been aware of any of the commotion. Half-asleep, she let me undress her and put her nightie on. Before I could sing her a lullaby, she was already in the land of dreams.

While I'd been getting her into bed, Christian had made coffee in the kitchen. I sank heavily down on a chair. I'd hoped to spend a lovely evening with him, but after Jan's appearance neither he nor I were in the mood. Christian handed me a cup of coffee and sat down opposite me.

"A nice way to end the day, hey?" I said, taking a careful sip. "I'm really sorry."

"No need to apologize." He smiled. "It'll all turn out right."

"You think so?"

"Definitely. Your ex will get his act together sooner or later. I'm sure of it."

I looked at him. Felt his hand around mine. And right then all I wanted was to be with him—despite my exhaustion, which even the coffee couldn't relieve. I wanted him.

I got up, took him by the hand, and led him into the bedroom. "Come with me," I said. "It's late and I don't want you to have to drive in the middle of the night."

28

The next morning, while Christian was still fast asleep, I slipped into my gray tracksuit and went down to the beach. I needed to move, to give myself time to think. Not about Jan—I pushed all considerations of him aside.

During the night I'd dreamed of my mother again. I saw her on board the *Storm Rose*, a woman who had placed all her hopes in a life beyond Socialism. Afterward, when I was awoken at sunrise by my inner alarm clock, she was all I could think about.

I'd hoped to be able to lay it all to rest when I came here, but I couldn't let go of my family history. And, to be honest, I didn't want to. For a long time, I'd avoided concerning myself with it, but now I was certain I had to do something. I had to leave behind the shadows that clouded my life, finally bring an end to this unfinished business. Whether I'd succeed in doing so was a different matter, but I'd made a start by coming to this decision.

I jogged toward the sandy beach, accompanied by the sound of the waves and the cries of the seagulls I scared into flight with my pounding feet. The idea of looking for my mother had occurred to me several times since the Wall came down, but the fear of discovering that she really had abandoned me had always prevented me from seeing my plan through. Until today. Now the missing person ad was out on the Internet. Even though no one had responded yet, I'd taken the first step. To a certain extent I had Christian to thank for that. And Lea.

Maybe the time had come to take another step? Palatin had made me see escape from East Germany with different eyes. And I now suspected that an online forum wouldn't be enough in my case. What if I requested to see the Stasi files on my mother? Or my own? There must have been a file on someone who defected. That might be a way of finding out whether she'd made any attempt to contact me.

I wasn't sure if I would be allowed to see my mother's file—unless she was no longer alive, but I didn't know that. However, I knew I'd gain access to my own file. It was possible that there were still some documents about me in the home where I'd lived. They might be easier to get ahold of than the Stasi files. If I then discovered that she'd abandoned me and hadn't tried to make contact, at least I'd have closure . . .

Having left the pier some way behind me, I turned to go back. My days of being able to jog for hours were over; I was wheezing like a walrus. But the run had done my mind good.

Back at the stony stretch of beach, I sat down next to the rose rock. The flowers there had wilted. Christian clearly hadn't had a chance to replace them for a while. I looked out to sea. How long did it take to be granted access to the Stasi files? I was sure they wouldn't be so much in demand as they had been after reunification. Or would they? Were there still numerous people like myself who had waited, wanting to forget what had happened, until the day came when some spark ignited the whole story again?

"So, here you are," said a voice behind me. He still sounded a little sleepy, but his voice sent a wave of warmth through my heart. "I was wondering where you went."

"I needed to think," I replied. "I do that best here."

"So I'd noticed." He kissed my temple. "Is it because of your ex?"

"No, my mother. I've decided to request the Stasi files. I need closure. One day, when Leonie asks me, I'd like to be able to tell her the story. And I'd like peace of mind for myself—since I've been here in Binz I've felt like my history has been pursuing me. That the old questions are demanding answers."

I leaned against him and allowed a few moments to pass, then said, "Did you ever find out who caused your mother's accident?"

Christian nodded. "Yes, I did. I requested the Stasi files on my father, and my own. Because my father was dead at the time, I was allowed to see them."

"Did your father never tell you who it was? He must have known."

"Yes, he knew. But he never told me. When things got really bad for him I didn't like to ask. I had other worries at the time."

"But it never left you in peace."

"No. And it probably won't for as long as I live. But it's part of who I am, just like the good things that have happened to me."

He kissed me and looked out at the water. He seemed to be seething inside, like water washing up against a dam.

"You don't have to tell me if you don't want to," I said. "I don't want to feel I'm forcing you, you know?"

"I appreciate that. But deep down, you do want to know, don't you?"

I nodded.

"It said in the documents that the man was an Informal Collaborator—IM (*Inoffizieller Mitarbeiter*)—for the Stasi. His code name was IM Seagull." He looked out to sea, a lock of hair blowing across his face. "Will you promise to keep the name to yourself?"

I nodded. Who would be interested in the identity of this IM Seagull? What was more important was that Christian was giving me something precious here. He was giving me his trust.

"Although his identity was uncovered, IM Seagull went on to have an incredible career—and has now become a hotel proprietor."

Christian looked at me, his eyes betraying a suppressed rage that would probably never fade. "His name's Joachim Hartmann."

I held my breath. Had he really said Hartmann? At that moment I was so shocked that I couldn't reply. Hartmann had run off after killing Christian's mother in a car accident? Sure, he seemed a bit slimy, but I would never have believed him capable of a hit-and-run offense.

"Breathe," Christian said, breaking me out of my spell with a kiss. "I don't want to have to practice mouth-to-mouth on you."

"Are you sure it was Hartmann?" I asked.

Christian nodded. "Yes, I asked for the code name to be disclosed." He stared at his hands. "At first the name meant nothing to me. There are plenty of men of that name in Germany. But after a little research and putting a few feelers out, I discovered where I could find this Hartmann."

"What did you do?"

"Nothing," he replied. "What could I have done? Gone up to him and taken him to task? Rearranged his face? I had no desire to do that. Anyway, what good would it have done? Nothing could undo what had happened. So I kept quiet—until now. You're the first person I've told."

I wasn't sure whether I should be pleased about that. The man whose business I was helping to succeed had destroyed the family of the man I loved . . .

"Why didn't you tell me before?" I said.

"Because I didn't want it to affect your work for him. Getting the Seaview Hotel contract is a good career move. And my father worked on the first phase of the renovations."

"Was Hartmann involved with the hotel at the time?"

"No. I've no idea what he was doing then. If the accident hadn't happened and if my father hadn't found out who was the guilty party, the name Hartmann would probably never have concerned us. But it shouldn't affect you. It would be a shame to pack it in, if only because it's a lovely hotel and it's created lots of employment. Hartmann did my

family a great wrong. If he hadn't killed my mother in that accident—
no, if he'd at least had the guts to answer for what he'd done—my father
would never have been moved to leave. Then Lukas would still be alive,
and probably my father, too. But you have nothing to do with his past
and you're entitled to be paid by him."

I sat there as though someone had given me a crippling poison. My
fingers were tingling, and my arms felt heavy; so heavy that I couldn't
have raised them. Hartmann was to blame for all that suffering. And
he'd been too cowardly to accept his punishment. Instead he'd had the
Stasi get him off the hook, or the Stasi had gotten him off the hook
because they needed his services.

"I really hope you'll keep your promise," Christian said, stroking
my hair. "Please don't tell anyone. And don't give Hartmann any indication that you know. It's a debt from another time. A debt between me
and him. I can't say to what extent it's still on his conscience. Maybe
sometimes he does still dream of my mother and the accident. He might
even have wanted to do something to put it right, but they didn't let
him. Only he knows what really happened. And I'll be damned if I'll
make myself known to him or bring a case against him. That would
mean I might have to forgive him, and I don't want that. I'll simply let
him live on and take his guilt to the grave."

His words continued to echo inside me as we climbed the steps
back up to my house. I'd promised Christian not to reveal any of it,
but I had no idea how I was going to act in Hartmann's presence now.
The job was extremely important to me, and the publicity campaign
had reached the stage where it was almost ready to be launched. All we
needed was a publicity video I'd requested from him, and then we'd
be ready to send the materials to all the relevant travel companies. The
filming date was set for the following Wednesday. Once the clip was
finished, I'd be out of the woods. Of course I'd continue to provide
support for the project, but it was up to Hartmann to build on it. I'd
have to meet with him only infrequently from that point.

Maybe Christian was right. I shouldn't make his business my own. But whatever happened, I'd see the hotel boss with different eyes from now on.

It won't be for long, I told myself. *Once this job's finished, you can go on your way and never look back.*

***

Once Christian had finished his breakfast and left, I got Leonie ready for nursery school.

"Mommy, why was Uncle Christian here this morning?" she asked as I helped her into her jacket. "Did he sleep here?"

I looked at her in surprise. And it occurred to me that I hadn't thought to tell her that Christian and I were a couple. Maybe this was the right moment. I may as well get it out in the open; I had no other choice now.

"Well, Uncle Christian . . . You like him, don't you?"

"Yes, very much!"

"And I'm fond of him, too. Very much."

I braced myself involuntarily, as though expecting a physical blow. What if she asked me if I loved him more than her daddy?

"Did he sleep in your bed?" she asked.

"Yes, he . . . People do, when they love each other."

"So does he love you, too?"

"Both of us, me and you."

"OK."

She said it lightly, but I knew she had more questions to ask. Not now, but later, when she'd inwardly digested this piece of news.

"Today I'm going to tell everyone I've met a sea captain," she announced with pride as we left the house. "And that he's got a big dog."

I was sure she'd delight her playmates, at least, with this. And I was also a tiny bit relieved that I'd told her about Christian. On the way to the nursery school, I was struck by the question of what my birth mother would have to say about her grandchild. If she'd deliberately abandoned me because I was a millstone around her neck, she wouldn't be interested in the slightest—but what if that wasn't the case?

"Mommy, you're not saying anything," Leonie complained, and I realized neither of us had spoken a word since we got in the car. "Are you sad?"

"No, Leonie, I'm just thinking."

"What about?"

"About your grandmother," I let slip. I regretted it immediately. To Leonie there was only one grandmother.

"What's the matter with her? Is she ill?"

"No, she's not ill."

I felt hot and cold as I wondered what my parents would say to the idea of me going out and looking for the woman who'd left me in the lurch more than twenty years ago and had never tried to find me. I could just see my mother's face darkening and my father's shoulders slumping. In the early days, when I'd caused them plenty of trouble, I'd often disappointed them.

"I was just thinking about her. Don't you think about me sometimes?"

"Yes!" Leonie cried out. "And about Grandma and Grandpa and Daddy."

Daddy. What would you think about him if you'd seen him yesterday?

We arrived at the nursery, and I was saved from any further questions. Another mother was outside the door, handing her child over to the care of the teacher. I waited a moment, since I wasn't in the mood for small talk, and then released Leonie from her car seat.

"Good morning." The teacher, Nicole, gave me a friendly smile. "I hope you had a good weekend."

"Yes, it was lovely. We went on a trip, didn't we, Leonie?"

"Yes, we met a real captain!" she said excitedly as she took off her jacket and hung it on the hook with her name label over it. "He was in a wheelchair and he was really old."

"Oh, you'll have to tell us about it later in our morning assembly," the teacher said. I saw a few children appear behind her, clearly waiting for Leonie. She looked up at me impatiently.

"Off you go, darling. Have a lovely day," I said and bent down to her.

"Bye, Mom!" she replied and gave me a kiss.

"How's she doing?" I asked Nicole as Leonie ran over to her playmates.

"Very well. She's settled in wonderfully."

"Does she still cry sometimes?"

"Only when she hurts herself. But that doesn't happen very often. She's a responsible little girl."

I felt proud of her. Before we could say any more, a few children came up to Nicole, wanting to know where the rubber frogs were.

"I'll see you this afternoon!" she said, and I made my way to my car.

***

At home I switched my computer on right away and called up the website of the department responsible for the state security service documents. I downloaded an application form and discovered that I had to have my identity confirmed at a residents' registration office. As my local office was only open on Tuesdays and Thursdays, I put it on my list of things to do the following day.

I got straight down to filling out the form. I hesitated over the item "Information about a missing or dead person." What if I tried to get ahold of my mother's file? But as I refused to believe that she was no longer alive, I checked only the request to view my own file, before working my way through the other sections of the form.

Then I came to the declarations. According to the notes I was entitled to view another file if it was relevant to me as a third party. That shed a whole new light on the case. What if I made two applications? One for myself and one as a third party for my mother's file? Without further thought I decided to print out a second application form.

I was so absorbed in my activities that I jumped when the phone rang. I left the printer to do its work and picked up without noting the number.

"Hello, darling, how are you?" My father's voice was so cheerful that I assumed he had good news for me. I heard a large noisy vehicle drive past behind him. "We haven't spoken since you came to see us."

"I'm fine," I replied. I was eager to hear his news. "I've just been doing a bit of research about the boat and I've had quite a lot on my plate, but I can't complain. How are things with you two?"

"Great! Have you got a moment?"

"Of course. What is it?"

Please, let him have found an engine, I begged silently.

"One of my coworkers has probably found an engine for you in Gedser."

My heart skipped a beat.

"Yes!" I cried out in delight.

"But there's a catch."

Oh no.

"And that is?" I narrowed my eyes. Did there have to be a problem? Couldn't luck be on our side for once?

"It's on a boat that's being put up for auction. It's to be scrapped and someone's had the bright idea of auctioning the parts off separately."

It sounded like it was going to cost a painful amount of money. I felt like a heavy boulder had been placed on my chest.

"What condition is the engine in?"

"If my coworker is to be believed, it's very good."

"That sounds like good news, at least."

"Yes, but it also means that there'll be other dealers and shipyards bidding for it. And scrap dealers, too, of course. So you'll have to make a real effort if you want it."

"Do you have any contacts there?"

"Sure, it's through a contact that we found out about the engine in the first place. But it doesn't affect the auction. You'll have to bid like everyone else."

And scrap dealers and shipyards had far more money than we did, I couldn't help reminding myself.

"OK, I'll discuss it with Christian," I said with a sigh. "Thank you for finding out for us."

"I'll e-mail you the contact details of the owner and you can look into it. And if you get the engine, let us know. We'll go and pick it up for you."

"That's really kind. Any other news? How's it going with the boat?"

"Terrific! Fortunately, there are some parts that we thought were worse than they actually are. The old girl never ceases to surprise us."

Just wait till I tell you about Palatin and how the boat got her current name, I thought, but that would have to be a story for another time, as my father said he had to go.

"Call me when you've decided. And any other time, of course."

"I will, Dad. Love you!"

"You too, honey. Give my little Leonie a kiss too."

I hung up. So close. We were so close to getting an engine. But would we have the money to win it at auction? I turned back to the computer. My father's e-mail was already there. The technical details would mean more to Christian than to me, so I forwarded it to him.

Then I tried to reach him on his cell phone, but it went straight to voice mail. I left him a message saying I had news about the boat, then returned to my forms. I'd just finished filling them out when my phone buzzed. It was Christian.

"What's new?" he asked. His voice sounded a little tired.

"One of my father's coworkers has located an engine for the *Storm Rose*."

"That's amazing!" he said.

"But there's a catch. We'll have to go to Gedser and bid for it."

"Bid for it?"

"Yes, they obviously have a nose for the value of old parts like that. My father's sent me a few documents. Should we get together this evening?"

"I'm sorry, I've got to go to Berlin for an appointment. But how about meeting this afternoon before I leave? There's a nice little café below my office."

"OK. What time would suit you?"

"Why don't you come around two—that would give us enough time before my train leaves and you have to pick up Leonie from the nursery. The address is on my card."

"I've got your card safe in my purse," I replied before saying good-bye.

29

Two hours later I had also contacted the youth welfare office in Leipzig and asked about the files of the children's home there. The woman had been friendly and promised me she'd look and see if there were any documents about me, to save me the trouble of having to go there in person. But at the same time she told me that I wouldn't be entitled to see the files myself—they would be read out to me by a caseworker. But that would be enough; all I needed was a reference to my mother.

Before finishing, I had another look at the online forums, but no one had responded in connection with either Lea or my mother. I switched the computer off, and went into the bedroom, where I stood in front of the closet. There was no question that I needed a shopping trip—my clothes all looked past their prime. I chose a green linen dress with lace and little rosebuds at the neck—my favorite dress, even if it was five years old—and changed.

Christian's office was in a two-story building that mirrored the style of the surrounding buildings, probably dictated by the building codes. It had a decorative gable, as my house did, and a pointed roof. The windows looked modern with their roller shades, and the door was a glassed-in, well-secured monstrosity, the likes of which certainly hadn't been known to the nineteenth-century spa architects.

I looked for the name *Merten* on the list of occupants' bells and found it in third place, below a lawyers' office and an insurance company. He was keeping good company.

"Yes," came a voice through the intercom.

"Room service," I said playfully.

"Oh, I don't remember ordering anything, but come up anyway."

The door buzzed. I pushed it open and entered. I was struck by the smell of polish. My steps rang out in the stairwell. There was also an elevator, a real luxury in a two-story building, but very considerate for any disabled clients.

I decided to take the stairs, as I felt overflowing with energy. I'd taken the first step toward finding out my mother's motivations. And we had the chance—albeit a small one—of getting a new heart for our boat. It was almost enough to make me forget the trouble with Jan.

Upstairs, Christian was waiting outside the door, a broad smile on his face.

"Oh, you've come empty-handed. What a shame," he said, feigning disappointment. I snuggled up to him and kissed him.

"You call that nothing?"

"Oh," he murmured. "It's more than I deserve."

"I beg to differ."

He kissed me again and led me into the office. It was as spartan inside as I'd imagined. The bright corridor was hung with framed black-and-white photos of boats and motorcycles. Christian's passions. Beyond a small lobby, with a waiting area for clients and a coffee table, was the office, which was dominated by a large desk. A bookshelf to one side was stuffed with everything anyone could want to read about business and finance. The only decoration was an abstract bronze sculpture near the window. And of course there were more black-and-white pictures—this time not of boats or motorcycles, but atmospheric landscapes.

"Don't you have a secretary?" I asked in surprise.

"Why would I need one?" he replied. "I take care of everything myself."

"You do all the paperwork yourself?"

"Just like you do, I presume. Or are you intending to employ a sexy secretary? In that case I'll ditch my job and get my application in."

We kissed again. His hands slid down my back to my behind. A pleasant shiver ran through my body, and it occurred to me that sex in the office wouldn't be such a bad idea. But I also saw that the windows of the building opposite had a first-class view into Christian's office. He seemed to be aware of it, too, because after kissing me once more, he drew away.

"Now then," he said, glancing regretfully at the window. "This is my kingdom."

"It looks . . . very businesslike." I smiled.

"The people who come to me aren't impressed by interior design. They want an air of competence, and that's best conveyed by straight lines and simplicity. I'm sure the advertising exec in you will agree."

"Totally. And I'm actually glad that's what I do, as it makes it perfectly legitimate for me to have a picture of a giant raspberry hanging on the wall of my office."

"Well, if you're doing a publicity campaign for one of these orchard-experience places that sprout up like mushrooms from the start of the asparagus season . . ."

"Don't tell me you don't like fruit?"

"Oh, I do, I'm one of their best customers. That's how I know how many of those places there are."

It was wonderful to wander off the subject with him like that. But a glance at the sober black-framed wall clock reminded me that we didn't have much time if we wanted to make ourselves comfortable somewhere. Christian followed my eyes and seemed to read my mind. He smiled, took me by the hand, and led me out of the office.

Outside, the sun was shining as brightly as my inner thoughts, because his invitation took us one step further. A step further into his heart.

We took our seats in a small café that offered a lovely view of the sea. The sky was cloudy despite the sun, making the Baltic look rather gray. The view was still wonderful.

Christian placed his cell phone on the table and called up the e-mail I'd forwarded to him.

"My father said the engine's in very good condition; it's the best part of the whole boat."

"That can happen," Christian said as he studied the data. "This boat's a complete wreck on the outside, but it had a good heart. And our *Storm Rose* needs a transplant."

"Well, it looks like we've gotten ourselves a suitable donor. But there are others after this engine. I have no idea what kind of money Polish or Danish scrap dealers can lay their hands on, but I doubt we stand a chance."

"Why not?" Christian asked. "Scrap dealers want the metal, not the engine. Shipyards present more dangerous competition. But this motor's a very specific kind—I doubt there are many boats of this construction around."

"So you think we might get it?"

"Of course! I can't give you precise odds, but we've got to try in any case." He leafed through the statistics. "When's the auction? Oh, here it is. We've got three weeks. I should familiarize myself with the best tactics for bidding on a ship's engine."

"It might be a good idea to be there in person."

"Definitely! It would also give us the opportunity to look around the town, and perhaps see a bit more of Denmark."

That sounded wonderful. And Leonie was bound to like it, too. I smiled to myself for a moment, then decided to tell him about the other thing I'd begun.

"I called the youth welfare office in Leipzig today."

Christian looked surprised by the change of subject, but I had to let it out.

"I asked about the files held by the children's home where I was sent after my mother disappeared. They may contain something about her."

Christian thought for a while, then nodded. "That's a good idea. I'd never have thought of it."

"It occurred to me, when I was looking for the Internet address of the authority responsible for the Stasi documents, that such files must exist and they might even have been kept—"

The ringing of my cell phone cut my explanation off midstream. I took it out and looked at the display. It was a landline number in Binz that looked vaguely familiar. I answered.

"Frau Hansen, this is Nicole Sander of the Starfish Nursery School." There was a catch in her voice. I pricked up my ears in alarm.

"What's happened?" I asked nervously.

Had Leonie fallen from the climbing frame or something?

"Your daughter . . . She didn't come back in after recess. I'm worried she might have run away."

"What?" It couldn't be true! She hadn't just said that, had she? "When?"

My heart was beating erratically, and I gasped for air. I jumped up from my seat in alarm.

"It must have just happened. We let the children out to play after their lunchtime rest and had them all in sight, but now she's no longer with them . . . We'll be calling the police right away, but if you could manage to get here . . ."

"I'll be right there," I said in a daze.

I felt as though I were falling. *Leonie.* Leonie had gone. How could it have happened? Didn't the teacher have eyes in her head?

"Annabel!" Christian's voice tore me from the maelstrom of my thoughts. He must have just asked me something, but I hadn't heard.

I stared at him.

30

"Leonie's gone!"

My body was still frozen. My heart raced and stumbled, my limbs were shaking, and I couldn't move.

"What?" Christian's voice yanked me back to reality.

"She's gone. That was the nursery on the phone. When they came in from recess she wasn't there."

"Oh my God!" Christian cried and dashed over to the counter to pay the bewildered waitress for the coffee and cancel the rest of the order. When he returned, he took me by the arm and dragged me out.

"Where's your car?"

"Somewhere in a side street near the hotels," I said, but couldn't remember exactly where I'd left it.

"Mine's nearer. Come on."

We ran to his parking space and jumped into the car. Christian started it up while I was still fastening my seat belt. Although his anxiety was plain to see, he didn't look flustered, but very focused.

"Has the nursery informed the police?"

"Yes; at least they were about to."

I was now shaking throughout my whole body.

"Good. You'd better call them anyway, just in case, and tell them you're the child's mother. You're the one they should keep informed, not the nursery."

I took my cell phone and dialed the emergency number. When someone finally answered, I told him what had happened. He knew nothing about the missing child, but promised to send someone to the nursery.

It was only a few minutes' journey, but those minutes seemed endless to me. My mind was racing and playing out a thousand horrific possibilities of where my little girl could have gone. The worst thing about it was that my ex-husband might have something to do with it.

"What if Jan . . ." I couldn't get the words past my lips. I felt like I was in a movie. "What if he's abducted her? From the nursery? He must still have been around today."

On the other hand, although there was little I'd put past him, I wouldn't expect him to have abducted his own child. But if not him, it could have been a complete stranger . . .

A lump blocked my throat. That was even worse than if Leonie was with her father.

"It can't be Jan who's taken her. Surely he isn't that stupid."

But Christian's jaws were working angrily as his gaze roamed the street. I was close to tears.

"We'll find her." Christian brought me back from the dreadful whirl of my thoughts. "I'm sure it'll all turn out OK. First of all, we should ask the teacher if there's anywhere she could have slipped away to."

We were quicker than the police, and the parking lot was as empty as the playground. I burst through the door. One of the teachers came to meet me.

"Where did you lose her? Have you seen anyone hanging around here?"

I was sure Leonie would go with her father without questioning him, especially if he promised to take her home.

"No, no one's been here. We let her out to play, and one of us was outside with the children, but there are some thick bushes down one side of the playground."

"Have you looked there?"

"Yes, but there was no sign of her. She could have slipped through, though. The other teachers are already searching. I called you as soon as we realized."

"What about the police?"

"They should be on their way, too. The man at the emergency service said you'd already called."

"That's right."

As I tried to stop my hands from shaking, I looked at Christian, who had his phone to his ear. I thanked the teacher and went out.

"OK, see you later," Christian said and hung up when he saw me. "Come on, let's go and look for her."

"What about your train?" I asked, confused, as my legs carried me without thinking into the playground. "You've got to get to Berlin!"

"I've rearranged the appointment. This is more important."

I ran past the jungle gym and the slide, to the hedge. There was a gap in the fence through which a five-year-old could easily squeeze. But had Leonie really run away? It wasn't like her. An adult couldn't fit through that hole, in any case. But he could have stood on the other side of it and called her through.

"Let's go around!" Christian suggested and ran on ahead.

"Do you think the teacher's asked the other children?" I panted as I caught up to him.

He was frowning as he ran out of the gate and around the nursery premises. Not far from there was a signpost pointing down to the beach. Surely Leonie wouldn't have run into the water? My stomach ached terribly, and my heart was still racing.

"If they have any sense they'd have done that before they went off searching."

If they had any sense . . . Did they have the sense? Maybe she was already dead . . .

No, she's not dead, I convinced myself. *I'd know it. Surely I'd know it.*

From the corner of my eye, I saw a police car pull up. Christian saw it, too.

"Go to the police officers and show them a picture of Leonie," he said. "I'll take a look down the beach path and then farther along. If you hear anything call me, OK?"

I wanted to go with him, but he was right—it was better for me to go to the police officers and give them all the information they needed. Then I'd go and start looking again. He ran off. I hurried over to the police car that had stopped outside the nursery. The two men who got out looked at me in amazement. I didn't hear the names and ranks they gave me.

"I'm the child's mother," I said.

I took my wallet from my purse. My hands were shaking so badly that I could hardly get a grip of Leonie's photo.

"Easy now, young lady," the older of the two advised.

How was I supposed to stay calm when my daughter's life might be in danger? I finally managed to grip the photo and handed it to the police officers.

"That's her. The teachers say she could have slipped through the fence."

"Does the little girl know her way around here?" the younger policeman said as he studied the photo. The question sounded strange to me. Did local children of that age know their way around the whole town?

"No, she doesn't know her way around. We moved here only a few weeks ago."

"OK. Well, you go and look down on the beach," the older police officer said. "I'll talk to the teachers and then we'll try the town."

He disappeared into the nursery while his colleague ran off to join the search. Should I have told them that I suspected she may have been abducted by her father? I had an idea. I grabbed my phone out of my bag and dialed Jan's number. If he had nothing to do with it, he would surely pick up or acknowledge my call. Of course he couldn't do that if he was on the run . . .

I dialed the number and listened tensely to the ringtone. I let it ring five times before the voice mail cut in. I hung up, enraged. Was he already on his way to Bremen? Somewhere else? I put my phone away, ran down the street, and called out my daughter's name, ignoring the puzzled looks I was attracting from passersby.

The hours that followed were hell. Wherever I went, Leonie wasn't there. I feverishly trawled my mind for clues about where she could have gone. She had a weakness for boats—had she perhaps gone to the pier?

In the end I began to stop random people on the street, showing them my daughter's photo. Judging from their reactions, they must have thought me crazy. In any case, they weren't much help, as each one said they hadn't seen a little red-haired girl. I finally sank down onto a bench in despair and cried.

Strangely, I found myself wondering how my birth mother would have reacted if I had disappeared. If it had been the other way around and I was the one who'd run away. Would she have searched for her child in panic as I was doing? I'd never had to ask myself that question, but now it was there, and my heart told me plainly that there was no doubt she would have searched for me.

At the same time, I could see now how difficult it was to find your daughter, even in a small town. It seemed that I had been doing her an injustice by presuming she no longer wanted me. My mother must have searched for me throughout Germany; in the times of the East, pursued by the Stasi, and after reunification, hampered by vanished files and silence. Maybe she'd sat down on a bench, like I was doing, and wept.

Then I received a call. I answered without looking to see who it was.

"Have you found her?" Christian sounded exhausted.

"No! I've even been asking people on the street, but no one's seen her."

"Where are you now?"

"On the promenade. Near one of those hotels."

"You'd best get back to the nursery. We'll try again, in the car this time."

Maybe we should head off on the autobahn toward Bremen, I thought bitterly, but I replied, "Yes, I'm on my way."

On the way back I searched every possible corner again. I walked along the beach in the hope of finding a clue. Perhaps she'd gone back to watch out for mermaids. I eventually staggered up to the nursery. Christian was waiting for me by the fence. Large sweat stains had formed under his arms.

"I walked the whole way along the beach as far as the rocks—but nothing. I even went to your house, but she wasn't there either."

"What about the police?"

"They're still not back."

My shoulders slumped, and I took a shaky breath. Where should we look now?

"Over there!" Christian shouted out suddenly, pointing over to the beach. A man in uniform was heading toward us from the direction I'd taken earlier. He was carrying something in his arms.

With a whimper I ran to meet him. *Please don't let anything have happened to my little girl,* I begged silently. I would give anything up, even the *Storm Rose,* but not my child. Then I saw that the girl in his arms was Leonie. She was gripping the police officer's shirt tightly.

"Leonie!" I called—no, screeched.

My legs went weak and scarcely obeyed me, but I forced myself onward. At last I reached the police officer. I almost tore my daughter from him, but then I noticed something wasn't right. Leonie was holding tight with her right arm, but her left looked strangely stiff. Her face was encrusted with dirt, and sand clung to her hair.

"What's the matter with her?" I yelled at the man.

"I'm afraid she's broken her arm. I found her near the woods. She tripped over a root and then fell down a dune."

Why had my little girl been lost in the woods? Why had she gone there?

"May I?" I asked and reached out my hands to her.

"Of course," the police officer said and handed her over to me.

"Leonie, my darling, what have you been up to?"

Tears sprang to my eyes.

Leonie looked at me a little foggily. Her injury and fear must have drained her of her strength, so much so that she couldn't even cry.

"Charlotte said she saw Daddy. So I ran off to look for him. But I couldn't find him anywhere, and then I fell down and couldn't get up again because my arm hurt so much."

Her words sent a shudder through me. Had Jan really been here? Had he stood outside the nursery like a stalker? How would Charlotte know what Leonie's father looked like?

"Thank you for your help," I said to the police officer before carrying Leonie over to Christian. He wrapped my little princess in his jacket and set her carefully down in the backseat. I could see that tears were running down his face, too.

"She's back!" I sobbed and hugged him. "She's broken her arm, and we've got to get her to the hospital, but she's back."

"You can't believe how happy I am," he said. "More than you could imagine."

By now we weren't alone. A few parents had come to pick up their children. But I didn't care about them. All that mattered was that Leonie wasn't lost forever. A girl came running up to us, too fast for her mother to hold her back.

"Leonie, have you hurt yourself?"

Was this that girl Charlotte? I felt anger rising inside me. I gave the woman she'd been with a malevolent look, but forced myself to be reasonable.

"I've broken my arm. But I'm sure I'll be back tomorrow."

"We were all really scared," the girl said, tugging at her flowery dress.

"Steffi, come back here!" came a cry in the background. A moment later the woman was at our side.

"I'm sorry," she said, reaching for her daughter's hand as though we might grab her and run off with her. "I heard what happened and I'm so relieved that you've got your daughter back in one piece."

"Leonie's my friend!" Steffi declared to her mother, who smiled and nodded at me.

"Yes, and that makes us doubly pleased that she's back."

"Frau Hansen!" one of the teachers called out, running up to us. "Thank God Leonie's back!"

Not that you had anything to do with it, I thought angrily. *If you'd kept your eye on her she wouldn't have rolled down the dune.*

"I'd urge you to block off the hole in the fence and to keep more of an eye out next time," I said coolly. "If it weren't for the fact that my daughter has found some lovely friends here, I regret I'd have to reconsider placing her back in your care."

With that I got into the car, and Christian drove off.

***

Half an hour later we reached the ER in Bergen.

I hoped we wouldn't have to wait too long—Leonie had gotten over her initial shock, and her arm was now hurting so much that tears were rolling constantly down her cheeks.

Christian carried my little princess to the reception desk, where the nurse was on the phone. I didn't hear what she was talking about, but she interrupted the call as soon as she saw us.

"My name is Hansen, and my daughter Leonie has just had an accident. She fell, and I think she's broken her arm. She may also have other injuries."

"Just a moment, I'll call our pediatrician on duty." She reached for the phone again.

"It's all OK," I said, trying to reassure Leonie, who was still crying quietly. "The doctor will examine you and make your arm better, I promise."

"It hurts, Mommy," she said between sobs. "I'll never believe anything Charlotte says again. And I won't ever run away again."

I wiped the tears from my own cheeks and tried not to weep out loud in front of her.

"It's all forgotten. Now what matters is for you to get better, OK?"

She nodded weakly and snuggled further into Christian's sleeve, which was dirty and soaked with tears.

"Dr. Bodenstein is on her way to see you," the nurse informed me. "Please take a seat for a moment."

Neither I nor Christian felt like doing that. I feared that once I sat down on the seat, I'd never get up again. My exhausted body felt like it was turning into a lump of lead. We sat down at the edge of the waiting room, and I tried to distract Leonie. She must be feeling intimidated by the hospital.

Only a few minutes later a middle-aged woman came through the door. She was wearing a white coat over her green surgical gown, and her blond hair was tied in a bun at her neck. She glanced at the nurse, who pointed in our direction, then came over to us.

"Hello, I'm Dr. Bodenstein. And I take it you're Leonie." My daughter nodded weakly. "Are you her parents?"

"I'm her mother," I said and looked at Christian.

"And I'm her mother's friend. Leonie isn't my daughter."

"OK. Will you come with me, please?"

She led us down a wide, brightly lit corridor into the examination room. It looked even more spartan than Christian's office. He laid her down on the bed and said, "I'll wait outside."

"Thanks," I replied, my concentration fully on Leonie.

"So she had an accident at the nursery school?"

"No, she ran away from the nursery, fell, and rolled down a slope. A police officer found her and said her arm's broken."

The doctor nodded and began her examination. She looked into Leonie's eyes, pressed various parts of her body, listened, tapped, examined her stomach and her back. My daughter let it all happen without complaint, but she whimpered as soon as the doctor touched her arm.

"Shhh, it's all right," the doctor said and immediately let go of it.

"At first glance it doesn't seem as though she's sustained any internal injuries, but her arm really does seem to be broken." She had hardly finished speaking, when a nurse came through the door.

"Tina, can you please tell the X-ray department that we have a patient for them?"

The nurse nodded and vanished again.

Dr. Bodenstein took a form from her filing tray and noted something down. A little later the nurse returned, this time accompanied by a young male nurse.

"How about if Tina takes Leonie to the X-ray department and you can tell me a little about the accident?" the doctor said.

I looked at Leonie. Would she want to leave without me? I wanted to be sure she wasn't afraid.

"Did you hear that?" I asked her. "They're going to take a special photo of your arm."

"Through the skin?"

"Yes, through the skin."

"How does that work?"

"They have a special kind of camera."

I smiled through my tears. If she was back to asking smart questions, we were heading in the right direction.

As I waited outside the X-ray room, my cell phone buzzed. I took it out and looked at the display. A message from Jan.

> I was at the doctor's and couldn't get to the phone. What's up?

The fact that he sounded so casual, as if the previous evening's altercation hadn't happened, made me so angry that at first I didn't even appreciate the fact that Jan was actually getting in touch. I pulled myself together. *He must simply have been drunk yesterday,* I told myself.

"You have to switch your cell phone off here," a nurse told me before I could type in a reply. I nodded and put the phone away. I'd send a message to Jan later, when I had my daughter back. First I had to get Leonie and go to find Christian, who had returned to the waiting room.

"Here you are, you can take your little girl with you now," the doctor told me after a quarter of an hour. She turned to Leonie again. "Make sure you don't knock anyone over with your arm."

"I won't," she promised. "Are we going home now, Mommy?"

"Yes, we're going home now."

"Is Uncle Christian coming with us?"

"Of course. He's driving."

"I'm glad."

She snuggled up to me, her injured arm in its plaster cast hanging stiffly in a sling. The doctor came to meet us as we left the area.

"Here are a few children's painkillers. Give her one when she needs it. And if you're worried about anything, come back here or call the duty doctor. Which pediatrician are you registered with?"

"We're not; we moved here only recently."

The doctor vanished into one of the rooms and returned with a business card in her hand.

"Here you are. I recommend this colleague of mine."

I tucked the card away and thanked her in the hope that it wouldn't be necessary to consult a doctor in the near future.

Christian was sitting out in the accident and emergency waiting area with a cup of coffee. He didn't seem to be enjoying the beverage, if his expression was anything to go by. When he saw us, he rose and dropped the cup in a nearby trash can.

"Well, here's our little mermaid hunter." He stroked her hair gently, then gave me a kiss. "Is everything OK?"

"Yes. She'll have her arm in a cast for three weeks. Otherwise she's unhurt, apart from a few bruises."

"Well, that's lucky, isn't it? Come on, then, I'll drive you home."

We followed him out to the parking lot. Darkness had fallen. An ambulance raced up, its blue light flashing spookily on the walls of the clinic building. I felt numb, and yet relieved. My little girl was alive; her broken arm would heal. It was almost funny, the way I'd watched her like a hawk to make sure she didn't go near the steps to the beach, and then she simply broke her arm falling down a dune.

In the car I got into the back with Leonie, who leaned back sleepily in her seat. I remembered the message.

"Jan sent a text," I said, getting out my cell phone.

"Oh yes? Is he apologizing for yesterday's idiocy?"

"No, I called him earlier. Wanted to see where he was, because I believed . . ." I looked at Leonie. No, I couldn't say out loud in front of her that I'd suspected him of abducting his own daughter. Christian understood.

"You didn't bawl him out, did you?"

"No, I let the phone go to voice mail and hung up. His text arrived while I was waiting for Leonie to be X-rayed. He said he'd been at the doctor's and asked what was up."

"Are you going to tell him?"

"I think it would be a good idea. If he turns up in the next few weeks to visit her he'll see that her arm's in a cast." I called up the text and typed in a reply. After all, he is her father. If he wants to take some responsibility, he'll have to cope with the difficult side too.

After sending the text, I put the phone back in my purse.

"What are you doing about your appointment?"

"I've postponed it until tomorrow. I'll go in the morning; that's soon enough."

"Did I ever thank you for being so generous?"

"No, but maybe you've got an idea about the best way to do that." I smiled. "Tonight?"

"Tonight I'm sure you'll be spending the whole time sitting with Leonie and watching over her. I'd have a bad deal there. In any case the two of you need to rest. I'll drop you both off and then go home, so I'm ready for action in the morning."

I could understand that.

"OK, but please give me another call before you head out."

Christian nodded with an affectionate smile. We sat in silence as we drove home. As we pulled into the driveway, my mind suddenly jumped back.

"Oh yes, where were we with the engine?" I asked after lifting Leonie out of the car.

"We'll get it!" Christian replied, blowing us a kiss and driving off.

***

I couldn't sleep even though I was weary to the bone. My head was full of all that might have happened. Thoughts of how my mother might have searched in despair and might still be searching. And Christian's story kept creeping in. I could understand now the panic he and his father must have felt when they realized Lukas was missing. I was so glad that our story had a happier ending. Would the search for my mother turn out similarly well? Or would it be more like little Lukas's fate?

I paced restlessly around the living room because I couldn't stay in the chair by Leonie's bed any longer; then I caught sight of the applications for the Stasi files. How long would they keep me waiting? Six months? A year? Several years? When could I have closure? Would there ever be closure?

I sat in the living room for a while, then went into my bedroom. It was getting light outside. I looked at my cell phone and realized that a text from Jan had arrived a few hours ago. He said that he couldn't visit Leonie in the near future, but would send her something in the meantime to make up for it. It was a side of him I hadn't seen before. It might be as materialistic as ever, but at least he was making some effort to show that he cared about his daughter. There was still no apology for his behavior on Sunday evening. We could talk about that the next time he showed up.

Eventually I took a shower and washed the night's leaden weariness from my body. I had an idea. In my tracksuit, armed with a pair of pruning clippers I'd found in a small cabinet in the hallway, I went into the yard and cut a few sprigs from the thickest rosebush. The blooms were heavy with dewdrops and gave off a wonderful scent.

I descended the steps with my little bouquet and went to Christian's rock. The dried-out roses must have been blown away, perhaps into the sea for the waves to carry off. I laid the fresh roses on the rock, sat down by them, and, looking out to sea, thought of Christian and his little brother.

Part 3
The Letter

31

With a sigh, I closed down the Internet forums. There had still been no response to my search requests. Not even a single comment. The threads were slipping remorselessly down the page. Frustrating.

Maybe Lea had left her past behind after her escape and didn't want to talk about it. But what about my mother? Did she have no idea about the forum—didn't she use the Internet, or did she simply not care?

Another dreadful possibility crossed my mind. Maybe she was no longer alive. Then all that remained to me would be to reconstruct what had happened from the files that I might be getting from the youth welfare service in Leipzig.

As I tried to suppress the sinister possibility of my mother being dead, I glanced at Leonie. Of course she hadn't been able to go back to the nursery the next day as she'd promised her friend. I'd simply taken her up to my office with me, placed her on a chair, and given her something to do. Her right arm was uninjured, so she could still draw. The pain had bothered her too much at first, but now the painkillers the pediatrician had given me began to work, and she was drawing. I'd called the nursery the morning after the accident. I had a long conversation with the remorseful teacher, who apologized most sincerely and promised that nothing like that would ever happen again.

I knew that such promises were hard to keep, but at least I would do all I could myself to make sure that Leonie never ran away again. The nursery teacher asked me to bring the accident record to her so she could give it to their insurance company. I promised to come by before the end of the week.

Christian was away until the weekend, but he called several times a day to ask how we both were. I looked forward to spending the weekend with him. I had quite a lot to think about. Especially about my mother. The woman from the youth welfare service had promised to get in touch soon, but I was tearing myself apart with impatience.

That afternoon I called my mom, since I'd failed to reach her the day before and hadn't wanted to worry her by leaving a message.

"My goodness, the things you get mixed up with," she said, clearly shaken.

"Well, apart from that, my life's very good at the moment," I sighed. "I thought everything was getting better, but then Jan suddenly appeared and chaos erupted."

"Jan?" said my mother. "Jan's back on the scene?"

I hadn't told her anything about it! Life had overtaken me somehow. And there was Christian. I realized that he was now the one I turned to first with my problems. I had an attack of conscience.

"I'm sorry I haven't told you anything about it," I replied. "Yes, Jan's back on the scene. He appeared suddenly and asked me to share the childcare responsibilities with him. He no longer wants to be just the man who pays child support—imagine that."

My mother sighed. "And I thought we'd put all that behind us."

"I thought so too. But that's life. One day you believe you've got everything under control, and the next it's all turned on its head."

"You know, you don't have to share the childcare with Jan. He let go of his rights of his own accord."

"Yes, but a lot's changed in his life since then."

I gave her a brief outline of his illness, his change of heart, and his second appearance at our house. My mother said nothing, a clear sign that she was extremely concerned.

"Is Leonie still going to the nursery?"

"No. As long as her arm's in a cast I'm keeping her at home. But I don't think Jan would try anything. He's simply frustrated, and given his diagnosis I can even understand him a little."

"You must be careful, you promise? And if it comes to having to share custody of Leonie with him, always listen to what your heart tells you. Whatever happens, you have our full support."

What was my heart telling me? That I preferred not to see Jan in the near future? That I didn't want Leonie to have to go to Bremen every weekend, or to spend every other week there . . . ?

"That's sweet of you, Mom, thanks."

"How is our little girl? Is she still in pain?"

"It's getting better gradually, but of course the cast's really getting in her way. And she's upset that she can't go to the nursery."

"The main thing is that she's not suffering too much."

"I've promised her I'll draw a flower on the cast every day. When the surgeon removes it he'll be amazed."

I realized I was smiling. It wasn't only Christian who could magically make me happy, but also my mother. It made me feel a little guilty that I didn't have the courage to tell her I'd requested my Stasi file and the documents from the home.

On Thursday the mailman rang my doorbell. I was sure it was only the usual stuff, maybe a delivery from the printers containing the proofs of the hotel brochure. I did get the expected thick package—but also a smaller envelope. My original Bremen address had been crossed out; it seemed my mail redirect was working fine.

When I saw the name of the sender, I caught my breath. It couldn't be true! The sender was one Silvia Thalheim from Hanover. I was shocked.

I looked at the envelope in my hand for several minutes, as though the writing had suddenly lit up. It wasn't possible! Was this my mother? And how did she get my address?

With shaking hands, I tore the envelope open and took out two folded sheets of paper. The letter was written in beautiful handwriting that looked slightly unsure of itself. I couldn't remember my mother's handwriting. Was it really her?

> *Dear Annabel,*
> *Please don't be alarmed by this letter, and please don't just throw it away. Give me the opportunity to explain.*
>
> *I don't expect you to be overjoyed; maybe I'd react like you if I were in your place. Your mother suddenly vanishes from your life and leaves you on your own for more than twenty years. What can I say?*
>
> *I'm terribly sorry that I've only now summoned up the courage to write to you.*
>
> *About nine months ago I was granted access to my Stasi file—after I'd waited more than six years for my case to be processed.*
>
> *You may ask why it took so long for me to get the idea to request my Stasi file. It's a very long story, one which I'd be pleased to tell you if you want me to.*
>
> *My long imprisonment left its mark on me. Even after I arrived in the West, my time in Bautzen weighed heavily on me. The things that were done to me there were like a brand burned onto my body. I was seriously ill as a result. At first that was what kept me from getting every-thing straight after reunification. And then there was the*

fear. Fear of confronting the past again, fear of finding out something that would shake me up again.

Eventually, in 2007, I finally found the strength to request my files. My health was stable by then and I was at last able to look to the future. I hadn't dreamed that it would take so long before I was able to see my documents. The fall of the Iron Curtain was already eighteen years in the past, and it would have been reasonable to believe that the rush to see the files was over. But for some reason it took that long for me.

In the meantime my health had taken a downward turn again, and all the fruitless deliberations, all the attempts to find you in other ways, sapped my strength. And where could I have begun? The Stasi had forced me to sign the adoption papers without telling me the names of the people who took you in and made you their daughter.

That was where I stood. I finally obtained consent to see the file. Unfortunately, I was unable to do so immediately, as hospital appointments got in the way. But I was given another opportunity and was finally able to see find out more of the facts behind the heartache that you and I suffered.

Thanks to your file I discovered who adopted you. I carried out some research—many doors open more readily to those who were victims of the Stasi's despotism—and I was at last given your address. I had all I needed.

But then my courage failed me.

I was suddenly terrified that you wouldn't want to hear from me.

I'm sure you have your own family by now, and it's possible that you forgot me a long time ago. I have no idea what you were told back then. They probably sold you a pack of lies. It may be that you even hate me for it and don't want to know me anymore.

All this was going through my head.

But then I found out that I don't have much time left, so I finally dared to take the plunge.

I'm leaving it to you to make contact with me. If I don't get a reply from you to this letter, I'll forget it and leave you in peace. But because I'd like you to know the real story, I'll make sure you receive something after I die that contains that truth. You can do with it what you will, but I hope you'll forgive me.

I wish you all the best and send you my love.

Your mother,

Silvia Thalheim

I sank down on the sofa. My head felt empty for several long minutes. I stared at the white kitchen wall and heard the clock softly ticking. The letter had hit me like a hammer. Maybe I should have opened it while Christian was with me. I read the words again, and this time felt as though I could hear my mother's voice.

After brooding for a while, I got up and began to pace restlessly through the house. Was this really happening? I'd applied to see the Stasi files only a week ago, and coincidentally she got in touch?

I picked up the envelope. The letter had gone to Bremen first. I looked at the postmark. Despite my mail-forwarding instructions, the letter had undergone a two-week detour. She'd probably given up waiting for a reply from me by now. It was only then that individual words seeped into my consciousness. Imprisonment? Bautzen?

They'd told me she'd defected. And she said herself that she'd come to the West.

"Mommy, can I have something to drink?"

Leonie's voice tore me from my thoughts. I spun around.

"Of course, darling," I said and hurried over to my daughter, who was standing in the doorway, clutching her furry rabbit with her uninjured arm. She usually had a nap at midday, but the cast on her arm made it impossible.

I brought her into the kitchen, sat her on the upholstered bench seat, and filled a glass with apple juice. I suddenly recalled how my mother used to do exactly the same for me—the mother who'd just written to me. Until I was six, apple juice had been the cure-all for every problem—for thirst, for broken toys and failed drawings. Until that moment I hadn't realized that I did exactly the same for Leonie.

"Here you are, sweetie," I said, putting a straw in the glass and setting it down in front of her. I poured myself some juice.

Leonie sucked greedily as I savored the taste of apples on my own tongue.

"You look so sad, Mommy," Leonie observed. "Aren't you feeling well?"

"I'm just a bit tired," I fibbed, as I could hardly tell her that her biological grandmother had written, stirring up all kinds of questions.

"Then you ought to have a nap too," she replied. "We could both get into your bed. I'm sure it would help me sleep better too."

Why not? I wasn't tired, but having her by my side would make all my thoughts easier to bear. We slipped into my bed, and with Leonie's back pressed to my stomach, I felt a little calmer. It seemed to be working for her, too, as within a few moments she had drifted off into sleep. I looked out the window, where the sun was lighting up one of the rosebushes in glorious pink. I thought of little Lukas, and Palatin's story. And then about my mother.

My thoughts moved back and forth for a while as I trawled my memories for explanations. I found none. I'd been six at the time, and it had all happened so fast. I hadn't been mature enough to question what I'd been told. And after a few years, it had been too late.

I eventually dropped off to sleep, exhausted both by the letter and the thoughts it triggered. I didn't dream, but when I awoke, my first thought was to wonder whether I should tell my adoptive parents about Silvia's letter. I'd found it difficult to broach the subject of my request for the Stasi file, but the waiting period made telling them easier to put off. Now Silvia Thalheim had entered my life for real.

I got up carefully and crept out of bed. The sleep had done me good, but I had work waiting for me. I was also hoping for a flash of inspiration.

As I left the bedroom, my cell phone rang.

"Hartmann here," my client's voice announced.

I froze. Hartmann. IM Seagull.

Make the switch, I told myself. *You're not Annabel, Christian's girl-friend, now. You're Annabel Hansen, advertising executive, who needs work to support yourself and your daughter.*

"It's good to hear from you, Herr Hartmann," I replied, although I didn't find it good at all. "What can I do for you? Did you receive the brochures?"

"Yes, they're wonderful!" he replied. "I wanted to ask if you'd like to come to our summer party. There'll be some important people there, and I've been singing your praises as a publicist to my business associates."

I wondered whether he'd also told his business associates about his Seagull code name. Surely not. How would they react if they knew?

"Hello?" Hartmann's voice brought me back to reality.

"Yes, I'm still here. I was just getting my calendar," I lied. "When's the party?"

"On June twenty-fifth. I'd be delighted if you could come."

I was torn in all directions. On the one hand, the party could be an opportunity to find new clients. Summer parties were an excellent opportunity for networking and making new contacts. But on the other hand, I had no desire to have anything to do with Hartmann beyond my work for him.

"I'll pencil it in and see whether I can get a babysitter for Leonie," I said, grateful for the plausible excuse.

"Oh, of course. Should I ask around for you?"

I'd rather have my arm chopped off, I thought, but replied in a friendly enough voice, "Thank you, but it won't be necessary. I have someone in mind, but it's just a question of whether they're free that evening."

"If not, let me know. I'm sure we can find a replacement."

"Yes, of course. When do you need a definite answer?"

"Ideally I'd like to have known today, but I understand if you want to leave it until everything's been arranged. Let's say by next week?"

"OK."

"Oh yes, before I forget. I heard you've bought an old boat down in the harbor?" His words hit me like a cold shower. How did he know that? Did he have some cronies from the old days around the place? Couldn't he lose the habit of snooping around? Despite the wave of anger that welled up inside me, I forced myself to stay calm.

"Yes, I have."

"I can't wait to see what you do with it. Maybe there'll be some opportunities to give one another mutual support."

Oh, that was just what I wanted! Should I tell him the boat had been used to smuggle people to the West, people who were fleeing from the system he'd worked for? The system that might also have torn my own mother from me? I almost threw it all back in his face, but fortunately I remembered in time the promise I'd made to Christian.

"We'll see what happens. Listen, I've got an appointment now. I'll be in touch by next week, OK?"

"Great, you do that. You can tell me all about your boat then."

After hanging up, I wondered whether I really should do that. It would certainly be interesting to see the expression on his face. But there was no way I wanted him to get that close to me or to the *Storm Rose*.

Once my anger against Hartmann had dissipated, my thoughts returned to my mother. I sat down at my computer and searched for information about the prison at Bautzen. It was only a vague name to me, one that people in my childhood had referred to in whispers but never spoken out loud. The pictures I found were shocking, as were the reports from people who had been detained there. I printed off a few articles and read through them.

By the evening I still hadn't summoned up the courage to phone my parents, although more and more questions were building up inside me. Had they known about my mother's fate? About the forced adoption? Had they taken me in to make a good East German citizen out of me? My thoughts were drifting in a direction I really hadn't wanted to take.

I reminded myself how the Hansens had been then and what they were like now. They had never tried to influence me ideologically. My father did have something against those who left the East and had also been a Party member, but no political disputes of any kind had ever colored our conversations. No one had ever had anything against me listening to music from the West. No one had forced me to go and watch the dreadful military parades on May 1 and the National Day in October. There was only the flag my parents had raised over our apartment building on the relevant occasions.

The fact that they had moved to Hamburg shortly after the Wall came down was evidence that they didn't particularly toe the Party line. But my doubts had grown so great that I felt almost unwell. I managed to get Leonie into bed that evening before my tears started to flow.

What if my parents had known everything? If it had been just a word from them that brought all the anger of the system down on my mother's head? Maybe I'd been escaping with her and remembered nothing of it. Perhaps I'd been sleeping so deeply . . .

But was that likely? Maybe she'd been caught while attempting to defect, having really intended to abandon me.

I was torn this way and that until I really had no idea what to do. I called Christian. I wondered if I'd be unlucky and catch him at a business dinner. But it was worth trying. He picked up on the second ring.

"Hello, my lovely. Are you missing me?"

At any other time his words would have made me smile, but now I was burning up so fiercely inside that I could only wish he was there, so I could look into his eyes and lean on him as I told him all that was worrying me.

"Christian?" I asked, brushing a tear from the corner of my eye.

"Yes, I'm here. What's the matter? Are you crying? Has something happened?"

"Yes, I mean no, nothing really bad. Leonie and I are fine, and everything else, but . . ." I took a deep breath. "I got a letter today."

"Bad news?" Christian sounded confused. No wonder, when his girlfriend called him in tears.

"My mother's written to me."

"Your mother? Doesn't she usually phone you?" he asked in surprise.

"Not my adoptive mother—my birth mother, Silvia Thalheim."

It sounded strange to speak the name out loud.

"But . . . where . . . where did she get your address?"

I could hear Christian sitting down.

"She must have been thinking along the same lines as I was—but seven years ago. Seven years! Can you imagine? It took six years for her to gain access to her Stasi file. I'm afraid it might take me just as long . . ."

"Not necessarily."

"I've no idea where she got my address. It was the Bremen address anyway. It was forwarded here. I keep imagining that she might have been in the city sometime and I walked past her without even recognizing her."

My thoughts were all over the place. Christian listened to it all patiently, then asked, "What did she say in her letter?"

"She apologized for having to abandon me. And a few other things. That she'd been imprisoned in Bautzen, for example."

"But . . . I thought she'd defected."

"That's what I thought, too, and she may have, but they caught her in the act. Maybe I was even with her and don't remember." I slapped my hand down on the letter that was lying beside me on the bedspread. "She says that they forced her to sign the adoption papers."

I sobbed out loud. Christian waited in silence.

"I don't know what to believe anymore. During the last few days I've been so eager to find out what happened back then. I really wanted to see the files. And now this letter arrives. I can't grasp it."

"Hm. Sometimes I think that our wishes are on the way to being granted before we've even thought about speaking them out loud. You wished to discover the truth about your mother. You've probably been doing so for longer than these last few weeks."

"Yes, but I always suppressed it."

"Deep down you wanted to find her; you probably have for a long time. You just lacked the impetus. Then you got the *Storm Rose*. And the boat revealed a fate that had been on its way to meet you for a long while. Things like that happen sometimes. If I'm right, you'd still have received that letter if you hadn't moved away from Bremen, but your attitude toward it would probably have been different from the way you feel now that you've found out a lot about those who fled East Germany."

He was right there. I probably wouldn't even have opened the letter. But now it had followed me.

"I . . . I don't know what to do about the letter now. Should I tell my parents about it? After all, they were involved in the adoption. I've always relied on the belief that what I was told was the truth. I trusted my parents. But what if the Hansens knew what really happened? If they even kept the truth from me when the system had been dismantled and I was grown up enough to understand?" I stared at the letter, felt my heart thumping with fear, and added, "What if everything I've always known falls apart?"

Christian said nothing for a long moment.

"I know it's your decision, and yours alone, but maybe you should ask your parents about what happened back then." He paused briefly then asked, "Do you really want to? Talk to them about it?"

"I think so," I replied and lifted my chin.

Christian's voice calmed the troubled waters inside me a little, even though I knew the storm would only truly die down when everything had been explained.

"I still want to know what really happened. In my head I've dreamed up so many possible scenarios . . . I don't want to wait any longer. And I can look at the youth welfare office files later in any case. Besides, she also said . . . that she doesn't have long to live. She must be really ill. Or she's just trying to get my attention."

"I don't think anyone would mislead you with a claim like that. I'm not asking you to read the letter to me, but maybe you can show it to me tomorrow."

"But tomorrow . . ."

". . . is Friday," he said, finishing my sentence for me. "I'll be done here early in the day. If you like, and if you don't have any other commitments, I'd love both of you to come and spend the weekend with me. What do you say to that?"

At first I didn't reply, but merely sniffed. I was almost choking with tears and snot.

"What I have to say is that you're simply amazing."

"You should hold back on that until you see my apartment." Christian laughed, but immediately turned serious again. "We'll find a solution for it all."

"I know. Thank you."

I wiped my eyes. My heart still felt heavy, and I was bewildered, but I knew I'd be with him soon. I just had to get through the night.

"Annabel?"

"Yes?"

"I love you. And I'm here for you."

"I love you too," I said.

32

"Your eyes are all red," Leonie said as we sat at the table for breakfast the next morning.

Although the conversation with Christian had brought me some relief, everything had risen to the surface again during the night. Questions, doubts, accusations, anger. A new phase of my life was opening up; I could feel it. And that was a good thing. Here was the new Annabel, who would try and understand what had happened. Who wanted to find out her true history. Who now knew what she had been looking for. I'd always felt I needed a purpose, to come to grips with that great unfinished business that had been lying dormant inside me, and to bring it to a conclusion.

"I didn't sleep well last night," I told her. "I've got a lot of things on my mind at the moment."

"Is something making you sad?"

My daughter clearly didn't believe the story about lack of sleep. She was growing up.

"Yes, there are a few things making me sad."

"Is it because of the boat? Because her engine's broken?"

She'd picked up on that, too. Great. Perhaps I really should be more careful in the future about what was said in front of her.

"Yes, that's why I'm sad," I agreed, since I really couldn't tell her about the letter and all it had unleashed inside me.

"Maybe we should go take a walk and look for those mermaids down by the water," I suggested to my little princess. "Uncle Christian said they can work magic. Maybe they also have a spell to make the boat's engine better."

I had to smile at my own words. How simple the world seemed to a child. For some things there were still fairies and mermaids who could make it all right. Leonie had no idea how much I wished the mermaids really could do something for me. But I had to deal with the business of my mother myself.

"Will you draw me another flower on my arm?" she asked after breakfast.

"Yes, of course, darling. Choose a color," I replied and watched her padding out of the kitchen to get a marker.

***

That afternoon Christian, my lifesaver, arrived. I'd already packed a few things for our stay, and Leonie was looking forward to it. Yet again I was amazed at the magical effect he had on her. Since he'd entered our lives, she had been less unhappy. She needed a father figure. And she probably sensed that he did me good.

"Here are my two favorite girls," he said as he got out of the car.

"No motorcycle today?" I asked as I locked the front door and shouldered our bags.

"It would have been a bit uncomfortable, unless Leonie was willing to sit on top of the tank."

He swung her up, causing her to shout out for joy, then set her back down on the ground. Seeing the two of them so close made me smile.

"I think it's best we stick with just one broken arm. If she breaks the other you'll have to spend hours telling her stories so she doesn't get bored."

I went up to him and kissed him.

"That wouldn't be a problem. I know enough stories," he said. "Nice blouse."

I was wearing a semitransparent white cotton tunic I'd bought on vacation in Morocco. I hadn't had Leonie yet then, but the blouse still fit me. It was one of the few things I'd brought with me from my old life in Bremen.

"It's quite old. I thought I'd rather wear something practical."

"I don't live in a ruin."

"I never said you did. But you live near the beach, and maybe we can go and sit for a while on the sand. That's a different matter from perching on the rocks."

"But the rocks are beautiful anyhow." He put his arm around me and whispered in my ear, "Thank you for the roses."

"You didn't have time to put out any new ones, and I didn't want your family to feel neglected."

He beamed at me and kissed me again.

We got into the car and slowly wound our way through the crowds of tourists spilling out onto the street. I didn't think it was warm enough for swimming, but there were a few intrepid people plunging into the waves, as evidenced by the beach bags and flip-flops left behind on the beach.

Christian's apartment was in a building that would have been considered a real gem by real estate agents—a picturesque villa called Sea Pearl. It housed six apartments, one of which had a lovely view of the marram-covered dunes and belonged to him.

"Don't be alarmed by the moose's head," he said with a laugh as he opened the door. "He only talks sometimes."

Leonie's eyes widened in astonishment. "You have a talking moose's head?"

"Yes, but he's not always home."

There was a panel hanging in the hallway that looked as though it could have held a moose's head. But instead it was hung with a small sign saying "I'll Be Back Soon."

"You see?" he said to Leonie. "He's not here."

"When will he be back?"

"It's hard to say. He may be on vacation in the mountains."

He said it so convincingly that Leonie clearly accepted it. He winked at her and murmured in my ear, "A silly gift for my thirtieth birthday. I just can't find it in myself to throw it away."

"And why should you?" I said. "Maybe you'll be a mighty hunter yourself one day."

"I think that's out of the question. I couldn't even swat a fly."

Christian's apartment was far cozier inside than his office. Warm brown tones were blended with gray and white, and there was a comfy sofa that looked perfect for snuggling up on.

"Here's Your Majesty's room."

He opened the door that led off the living room. My heart leapt as I saw a pink poster with unicorns and elves. He must have gotten it especially for Leonie. My daughter was similarly thrilled.

"OK, why don't you unpack your things," he told her, and I handed her little pink bag to her.

"Well, what do you think?" Christian asked as Leonie dragged her furry rabbit out, a little roughly, by the ears.

"It's wonderful. If I hadn't found my house, I'd have gone for this apartment."

"Could have been difficult. Apartments like this are pretty hard to find. There are plenty available as vacation rentals, but few to live in year-round. And the rents are astronomical for new tenants."

"How long have you been here?"

"Eleven years. The house looked totally different back then. But I was always determined to live by the sea, and fortunately my landlord realized that it pays to maintain it at least enough to ensure the four walls remain intact. It's been renovated, and a house that no one wanted to live in has been transformed into a desirable property. The owner's making a fortune from us."

He took my hand and led me to see the bedroom. It was decorated throughout in really elegant white, black, and silver. His bed was huge, and I felt a tingle of anticipation when I thought about lying with him on it.

"So, what do you think?" he asked, drawing me to him.

"It looks very promising," I replied and kissed him.

"Done!" Leonie called, reminding me that we weren't alone.

"Later," he said as though he'd read my mind. "We ought to have something to eat first. And since I'm a lousy cook, I'm inviting you out."

***

After the meal we sat on the sand and watched Leonie scaring the seagulls with her plaster cast. The waves broke onto the beach, washing shells and seaweed up from the depths of the ocean.

"Did you bring the letter?" Christian asked after we'd sat quietly for a while.

I nodded. I had it with me in my purse. I got the envelope out and handed it to Christian.

"The good old mail service—fast and reliable as ever," he said, after reading the date on the postmark.

"I'm just glad I've got a mail-redirect service set up," I replied. "Otherwise the letter might have ended up in Neverland."

"Or returned to sender. Despite all the upset it's caused, I'm glad it reached you. Everyone has a right to know the truth and their own history."

He studied the two pages carefully, probably reading them twice through, before lowering the letter.

"Your mother must have survived some dreadful experiences. She doesn't say whether she was in Bautzen I or II, but I assume it was the latter. Bautzen II was the Stasi jail where they put political prisoners. It doesn't really make a difference whether she was in there because she attempted to escape or because she was inconvenient to the authorities."

I brushed a strand of hair from my face. "I could have been with her when she left. I can't remember. I just have this image that comes to me in my dreams, where I wake up in a car and see a blue flashing light. It could mean they came to get me from the apartment, but maybe . . ."

". . . maybe they caught your mother and put you in the car as they took her away."

"Exactly."

"You ought to write to her," he said as he folded the pages. "Otherwise you'll spend your whole life wondering what happened."

"That's true. But I'm scared it could ruin everything. That I'll see my adoptive parents in a completely different light."

"You might," Christian replied. "But this letter is the ideal excuse for you to ask your parents now. Whatever you find out, make sure you don't lose sight of what they've been to you and what they still mean to you. I think they're both lovely, kind people who absolutely worship you. Without knowing the background, I'd say it wouldn't have been easy to have a child living with you whom the Stasi were monitoring. Have the two of them ever seen their files?"

I shook my head. He was touching on one of my deepest fears. What if my father had been an IM, an Informal Collaborator? What if he had not only been my father, but had also spied on me? The thought made my stomach clench, and I suppressed it. I didn't want to see my father in the same light as Joachim Hartmann, a man who hadn't had to take responsibility for his actions.

"If ever you get to see the file, you'll find everything out anyway. But as it is you've got the chance to talk to your mother. And it may be that all the doubts you have about the Hansens are cleared up. Not everyone who was favored by the system was bad."

I sighed heavily, but nodded. He laid his hand on my arm and squeezed it gently. We sat in silence for several long moments. Leonie was nearby, building something that looked a little like a sand castle. How suddenly everything you knew could turn into something completely different . . .

"There's a telephone number on the back of the first page," I said eventually, taking the letter from his hand and turning the page over. I'd noticed the number only that morning when I read through the letter one more time before tucking it into my purse. "It probably occurred to her that I could call her if I didn't want to write."

"Will you?"

I nodded. "Yes, it would be better if I did. I find it easier to talk than to write. And the letter was delayed. I don't want more time to go by, time she may not have."

"Why don't you call her later, when we're back in the apartment? I can play with Leonie to keep her occupied while you do."

"Thanks," I replied, snuggling up to him.

***

Three hours later I was looking at Christian's elegant white telephone as though it were a snake that could turn around and bite my hand at any moment. This call was going to change everything.

I tried to examine my feelings. Did I actually have any for my mother anymore? Until now they had been more negative than anything. Anger, rage, despair. It wasn't until the last few days that I'd begun to have a little understanding for her. What would I feel when I knew the whole story? I couldn't know until I'd heard what she had to say, so I gave myself a mental shake, picked up the receiver, and dialed the number on the letter.

"Sunnyfield Hospice, Sister Marion," a kindly woman's voice announced.

Hospice? At first I was so shocked that I couldn't say a word. My mother was living in a hospice. Didn't she have any family who could look after her? Was I the only person she had left?

"Hello?" the woman said.

"I . . . um . . . my name's Hansen. Annabel Hansen. I'd like to speak to Frau Thalheim."

Everything seized up inside me. Had she died since sending the letter? People only went into a hospice when they didn't have long left to live.

"One moment, please," the nurse said simply, and put me through.

A short time later a hoarse woman's voice came on the line. Had the nurse told her who it was?

"Thalheim."

My throat felt choked. What should I say? *Hello, this is your daughter?* That didn't feel right. And her voice . . . It didn't sound like the voice I remembered.

"This is Annabel," I began hesitantly. "Annabel Hansen."

Silence. At first Silvia Thalheim said nothing, but I could hear her heavy, slightly rattling breathing. She probably didn't recognize my voice, either. Why should she? I'd been six years old the last time she heard it.

"Annabel? My Annabel?" she asked.

"Yes," I replied, a little anxiously. "I . . . I got your letter. I've moved, so it had to be redirected and took a while to reach me; that's why I didn't call sooner."

Another moment's silence.

"How lovely that you're calling now," she said slowly. "I thought you must have torn my letter up."

"No, no, I didn't. I just didn't know . . ."

"Whether to get in touch with me? That's understandable, after all this time." Another pause. An intake of breath. "Let's be honest about this. I do realize that you'll hardly remember me. A bond that's worn tears easily. And who knows what they told you. But it's lovely to hear your voice. To hear I'll be leaving something behind in this world."

"I . . . I'd like to visit you, if I can," I said on impulse. Surely she wouldn't want to tell me her story on the phone. And I didn't expect her to, as it sounded as though a telephone call was a real effort for her.

"Of course you can," she replied, and I almost thought I could hear her smiling as she spoke. "But you shouldn't wait too long before you come. As you can probably hear, I'm not particularly well. Anything could happen at any time."

I knew she wasn't lying—and I felt something else: fear. I was afraid for her.

"What about next week? Tuesday or Wednesday?"

"I think I can hold out until then." The sound I thought at first was a rattle turned out to be a laugh. She still had her sense of humor despite everything. It made me warm to her. "You can come anytime as far as I'm concerned. I'm not going anywhere."

"OK, let's say Tuesday," I heard myself saying, although I had no idea how I was going to arrange everything. I could take Leonie to my parents' if necessary—even though that would mean having to tell them why.

"I'm looking forward to it!" She took a quick breath, then added, "One more question. Do you have any children yourself?"

"A little daughter."

"That's lovely. Will you bring me a picture of her? I'll spare the little girl the sight of me, but I'd love to see her."

"That's fine; I'll bring a photo with me."

***

After hanging up, I stared out the window for several minutes. The apartment suddenly seemed incredibly quiet. All I could hear was my own breathing, which was gradually growing calmer. Beneath my tunic I was soaked with sweat, as if I'd just sprinted a hundred yards. I'd arranged to meet my mother, a woman I hadn't seen for more than twenty years. I couldn't have dreamed of that a week ago.

That night Christian and I made love desperately. I wanted to forget it all for a moment and simply give myself up to my feelings. And I succeeded, if only briefly.

As we lay side by side, exhausted, he asked, "So you're sticking with your decision?"

"Yes. I'm going to see her. But I don't want to take Leonie with me. I don't want to shake the foundations of her world. She wouldn't understand what a biological grandmother is—she only knows one grandma."

"I think that's the right thing. In time she'll be old enough to grasp it all. She's still hurting from the split with her father."

Yes, that was something else. Jan, who wanted to be there for her more. Jan, who had behaved so incredibly stupidly. Jan, from whom I'd heard nothing since he promised to send Leonie something.

"So I'll have to take Leonie to her grandparents'. I can't expect a babysitter to take care of her for two days. I'm going to need a good excuse."

"So you don't want to tell them yet?"

"No, and I don't know if I ever will. It depends what emerges from the conversation. Maybe it will simply make me want to forget it all."

"You could just leave Leonie with me," Christian suggested. "Then you don't have to think of any excuses and no one will know a thing. Or even better, I can come and stay at your house."

"What about your clients?"

"Appointments can be rearranged. This is much more important."

"You're a real treasure," I said and kissed him. "We can do whatever's best for you."

"Then I'll come to your house. If I'm honest I like it much better than here."

"But I thought this was your dream apartment."

"It's nothing compared to your house."

"Well, it's your decision," I replied.

"I'll come to yours. And I can assure you that I won't let Leonie out of my sight for a second."

"Not even I can manage that."

I stroked his chest and laid my head down on it. I was so glad that I had him—the antidote to everything that had happened in the last week.

"She's in good hands, believe me."

He kissed the top of my head. And I believed him.

33

On Tuesday morning I woke with stomach cramps from sheer agitation. Once again I'd hardly slept. Fear and uncertainty penetrated deep into my bones and drove me out of bed.

After a cup of coffee, I succeeded in getting myself ready to leave. I pushed my bag, which I'd packed the night before, into the hallway, then looked out. Christian was still nowhere to be seen. I felt a little uneasy at the thought of leaving Leonie here. Not that I didn't trust Christian to look after my daughter, but I'd never been apart from my little princess for so long. And I didn't want her to experience anything like the feelings I had when I was little.

But this is completely different, I told myself. *You're only going to be away for two days and then you'll be back with the knowledge of what really happened on that night all those years ago.*

"Will you bring me something nice back with you?" Leonie asked.

She was standing in the hallway, also uneasy about the whole situation. I'd told her I had to go away for two days as I had some business to see to in Hanover. That satisfied her, as she knew her mommy worked for a living.

"Of course I'll bring you back something nice."

I'd been careful not to mention the present her father had said he'd send her, as I still didn't know if it would ever arrive.

"Will you draw me two flowers on my cast today? One for today and one for tomorrow?"

She handed me the markers.

"Of course," I replied and tried to still my cold, nervous hands so I didn't mess up the drawing. The leaves came out shaky despite my efforts. It didn't seem to bother Leonie. When I finished, she hopped away with her markers. As she did so, I heard the humming of Christian's car and went out to meet him.

"Good morning, you lovely lady. I hope I haven't woken you," he said as he got out.

"Very funny. As if I was able to sleep."

We hugged.

"Well, how are you? Apart from being stressed out?"

"I'm feeling really bad about leaving Leonie alone."

"You're not leaving her alone. I'm here."

"True, but I mean . . . It's because of the feelings I had when my mother went away."

"That's not the same at all." He kissed my brow. "You're coming back. Tomorrow. We'll manage fine for that long."

"I only hope that I manage."

I took a deep breath, but couldn't relieve the pressure inside.

"You will. And when you get back I'll be here and you can pour your heart out to me."

In the house I showed him all the important things and left him some phone numbers. The day before I'd made sure the fridge was well stocked and that Leonie's favorite clothes were clean. I'd also provided a new pad of paper since it was likely that she'd express her feelings by drawing.

"Are you expecting any calls?" Christian asked, indicating the answering machine. "From Hartmann, maybe?"

"No. If he wants anything he'll call my cell phone." I'd completely forgotten to tell Christian about the invitation to the summer party. It was unlikely that I'd be going, whatever contacts I might make there. "Only you and my parents have my private number, and if they call, tell them that . . . that I'm away on business."

"OK," he replied, although I could tell he was reluctant to lie to my parents. "And if they call, I'll take the opportunity to arrange the trip to the auction."

"Which I can't go to with a little girl whose arm's in a cast," I sighed. "She's got an appointment with the surgeon during the week to decide whether or not the cast should be removed yet."

"I think I can manage it on my own. You take care of the important things."

He took me in his arms and kissed me. I could have stayed there nestling up to him for hours, but trains didn't wait. Christian had advised me not to drive all that way on my own, and now I was really pleased he had, because I was sure I wouldn't be able to concentrate on the road.

"Be a good girl, darling. Mommy will text Uncle Christian during the journey and he'll read it out to you. And if you ever get scared you can have Uncle Christian call me on my phone." She nodded and fell around my neck. For a moment I was tempted to take her with me, but that wouldn't do. I had to face what was waiting for me in Hanover alone. With a heavy heart I said good-bye to her and to Christian and carried my bag to the Volvo. I'd be leaving it at the station parking lot—I was capable of driving that far, at least.

Binz station was full of vacationers on their way home—elderly couples, families with children, solo travelers like myself. As I carried my bag onto the platform, my cell phone suddenly rang. Was it Christian? Had I forgotten something? But when I looked at the display, I saw an unfamiliar number.

"Seeger from the Leipzig youth welfare service," a familiar woman's voice announced. "We spoke on the phone recently because you wanted to see the files."

Slightly taken aback, I paused for a moment to gather my thoughts. "Yes, I remember. Has my file turned up?"

"Yes, and if you like I can make an appointment for you for an initial reading in a couple of weeks."

"That . . . that would be great," I replied and made a mental note. I wasn't so sure about it now, as my mother could probably tell me what I wanted to know. Maybe it would be a good thing to find out what the East German authorities had recorded about me, however. After a brief conversation in which she told me again that I couldn't look at the files myself, but would be allowed to take notes, we said good-bye.

I put my cell phone in my pocket and looked across at the other platform. I remembered my dream. Of course my mother wasn't standing there, but I was on my way to see her.

After the train drew in, I took my luggage to my seat and put my large bag on the shelf. The sun pushed its way through the clouds; it was going to be a nice day. I didn't feel like talking to any of the other passengers, so I simply closed my eyes and felt the train pulling out. I was on my way—no going back now.

A few hours later, after changing in Berlin, we approached the main station in Hanover. I grabbed my bag and made my way to the carriage door. As the train came to a halt, I took out my cell phone and typed a brief text saying I'd arrived.

The sky hung gray and heavy over the roofs of the city. The weather had changed during the journey as if to match my mood. During the journey I'd tried to prepare myself for what awaited me. Again and again I'd looked at the picture I carried with me. The last picture I'd drawn at our kitchen table. The windmill and the girl. Maybe she remembered it?

Seeing the picture made me feel gloomy. All that time my opinion of my mother hadn't been particularly positive—but what if I'd been wrong? She had sounded very friendly on the phone. It was so unfair that she'd only found me now that her life would so soon be coming to an end.

Before I could think any more about it, the train stopped and I was swept out along with the throng of other passengers. In the station concourse there was a smell of croissants, but I wasn't hungry.

I had intended to go to the hotel first and from there to the hospice, but my nerves were shredded. When it was finally my turn at the taxi stand, I asked the driver to take me straight to the hospice. On the way we talked about the weather, and he wondered whether it would be a hot summer. I couldn't say, and the conversation soon dried up.

The hospice was on the edge of town, near a beautiful park. It looked like it had once been a villa; the former owner must have bequeathed the building. The driver stopped outside the main entrance, and I got out.

As he roared away, I shouldered my bag and looked ahead of me. Despite the colorful flower borders, there was something oppressive about the place. People who had no one left in their lives or who didn't want to be a burden to their loved ones spent their last days within its walls. It was as though an echo of their lives and suffering was lodged behind those windows.

I finally gave myself a shake and walked up to the glass entrance door, which opened with a quiet hiss. Inside there was a peaceful atmosphere. The walls were painted in a fresh yellow and hung with pictures of landscapes and flowers. There was a small group of chairs in the foyer, with a discreet reception desk nearby. A man and a woman were standing, talking, by one of the large glass windows. It all reminded me a little of a spa clinic. The oppressive impression I'd had outside was gone.

"Hello, my name is Annabel Hansen. I've arranged to see Frau Thalheim today."

The nurse smiled at me. "She's told us about it with great pride. She's really looking forward to your visit. Just go down the corridor to room seventeen."

I thanked her and set off down the corridor to the left of the desk. The smell of disinfectant wasn't particularly strong, but it was there.

I stopped outside the door to room 17. My mother was in there. My mother, whom I hadn't seen for more than twenty years. Who I'd believed had betrayed me, without even questioning it. Whose story I didn't know. I stood outside the door for a while, trying to summon the strength to press the handle. My mother was in a hospice; she didn't have long to live. Couldn't things have been different?

I felt a compulsion to call Christian or my mom. My stomach hurt, my hands were icy cold. I wanted to tell someone about how I was feeling, but knew I couldn't call anyone at that moment. The only person I could talk to about my feelings was on the other side of that door. I raised my hand and knocked.

"Come in," said a weak voice.

I took a deep breath to relieve the tension in my breast, then placed my hand on the handle and pressed it down. The figure on the bed was very thin and could almost have been missed if she hadn't been wearing a bright, colorful dress and a patterned scarf on her head. Her features were very pale, but nevertheless the face unmistakably resembled the one I looked at every morning in the mirror. I'd forgotten it, just as I'd forgotten that she and I had the same green eyes.

What should I call her? Mom?

"Bella," she said, and a smile lit up her face. "You're here!"

I nodded and shut the door behind me. As I went up to her, I looked at the room around us. Apart from the hospital bed, it looked like a perfectly normal hotel room. There was a TV on a brown chest of drawers, an armchair by the window with a coffee table by its side, a closet, and a table with two chairs.

And then I took in nothing more, because I was by her side. The illness had left its terrible mark. Her cheeks were furrowed, the wrinkles deeper than they should have been at her age. The scarf on her head only partially concealed the fact that she'd lost her beautiful red hair. I felt a lump in my throat. I was fighting tears.

For all those years my thoughts toward her had been a muddle of feelings: anger, lack of sympathy, longing, hope, and disappointment had followed one another in never-ending succession, leaving me help-less and afraid, then angry once again.

Those feelings and my inability to control them had compelled me to push all thoughts of her as far away from the front of my mind as possible. And now I felt a deep sadness.

"Mom."

Now I said it, and tears flowed down my cheeks.

There was no bond between us anymore; the Stasi had severed that. But there was still a thread, delicate and fragile. I felt it clearly.

"Come and have a hug, my little girl," she said, holding out her hands to me. Her right arm was connected by a tube to a drip above the bed. I gave myself up to her embrace, as it seemed the most obvi-ous thing in the world. My mother's body felt as fragile as a straw, and almost as light. I felt as though I could easily lift her up. Her dress smelled a little clinical, but mainly of roses. It was a scent I knew from my childhood.

"I'm so glad you're here," she whispered in my ear.

I couldn't respond at first as tears were blocking my throat. They dripped from the corners of my eyes onto her head scarf and the pillow. Embarrassed, I wiped my cheeks when she released me.

"You're wonderful," she said after taking a few deep breaths. "I always wondered what you look like. But I never imagined you'd be so pretty."

Her heart had clearly never forgotten me. What about me? What were my emotions telling me?

We looked at one another for a small eternity, then she said, "I wish it had all turned out differently."

"So do I."

She nodded.

"I want to tell you what happened back then. But first I want to know what they told you the night I disappeared."

"They told me you'd defected."

Silvia's features tightened. "That's what I suspected. But I can assure you that at the time they were taking you to the home I was still in the country—on the way to my interrogation, to be more precise. That evening they simply came to fetch me from the apartment, even though I hadn't done anything. They accused me of treason and conspiracy. They interrogated me for hours. And all because I hadn't gone along with what they wanted."

She fell silent to catch her breath. I could see how much talking sapped her strength.

"Have you ever thought of asking to see your Stasi file?"

I nodded. "I've submitted an application—shortly before I got your letter."

"So the story's been playing on your mind?"

"Yes, but if I'm honest, until recently I didn't have any interest in seeing you again. Because they'd led me to believe that you abandoned me."

"So what moved you to want to see the file in the end?"

"My boat," I replied. "I . . . I've bought a boat. Together with my new boyfriend."

"A boat?" What remained of my mother's eyebrows shot up.

"An old fishing cutter. I found a letter on board, from a woman who escaped to the West. That set the wheels in motion. I found out some of the stories about the boat and its passengers. Including how the captain came to be smuggling people across the Baltic. I put out a search for the woman who wrote the letter, because I wanted to know what had moved her to go over to the West."

I paused briefly as it occurred to me that I was now telling my mother enthusiastically all about things I had actually despised as a child because of what they'd drummed into me. But she couldn't know that.

"And so you realized that the time had come to take an interest in your mother's defection?"

I nodded awkwardly. "It never left me. Here." I took the drawing from my bag and handed it to her. "I've always kept it. It was the only memory they left me."

My mother took the drawing from me with trembling hands.

"That's the picture you drew that evening, isn't it? You took it to bed with you, and it looks like you didn't let go of it when they took you away."

I nodded. "I woke up in a police car. I had no idea what had happened. All I had was this picture. And what an official told me. They took me to a home, and a year later to the Hansens'."

I wanted to tell her that they were good people, but that was bound to hurt her. The picture brought tears to her eyes, and she let them fall. But she soon regained her composure.

"I'm sorry," she said, wiping the tears from her eyes. "I always try and use as little energy as possible. Crying's a waste of energy."

"Crying is also a relief."

I didn't know whether I felt relief right then, but I certainly felt different inside.

"For you, maybe, but I . . . I'm simply relieved that you're here. That I can finally put right what happened. That's been weighing more heavily than ever on me in the last few months."

She gripped my arm. Her hand felt soft and cool.

"I didn't want to abandon you. But they gave me no choice. They took me to Bautzen II, where I would probably have rotted away if the people from the West hadn't bought my freedom. In 1987 one of my guards came to me and said that I could choose whether to go over to the West. At first I thought it was a trap, but then I discovered that they wanted to buy my freedom. East Germany was broke, so they gladly accepted the offer. In the winter of '87 I was sent to the transit camp in Giessen. Like any escapee, but with the difference that I'd never intended to flee the country. I'd simply gotten mixed up with the wrong people."

She laughed bitterly and fell silent. Her chest rose and fell heavily. I looked at her and wondered whether she was telling the truth. But who, if not my mother, could know the truth? And what good would it have done her to lie to me? I sensed it really was the truth. My mother had been imprisoned by the Stasi and had only left the country once West Germany had paid.

"How did things get to that?" I asked eventually. My voice sounded hoarse, and there was a pounding in my temples. "Why were they after you? You never said anything."

"I couldn't. Just as I'm sure you couldn't explain it to your own daughter." She smiled at me, then asked, "Did you bring a picture of your little one? I'd really love to see her."

I rummaged clumsily in my bag and finally pulled out my wallet. I took out the photo and handed it to her. As I did so, I realized that Leonie had grown a little since it was taken.

"She broke her arm a little while ago. But apart from that she's a healthy, happy little girl."

Silvia looked at the picture, then stroked Leonie's laughing face. It was one of the loveliest pictures I had of my daughter.

"She looks like you."

"Like us," I replied.

"Maybe. But you also have a lot of your father in you. Does Leonie draw a lot?"

"Almost as much as I used to do," I replied with a small smile, amazed that my voice could get past the lump in my throat. "She paints boat filling stations and mermaids on rocks and lots of other things."

Silvia smiled. "Then she's just like you. It's a pity I won't get to meet her."

She sighed so heavily that I couldn't bring myself to promise I'd visit with Leonie. My heart told me that we wouldn't get the chance.

"I hope you don't mind, but I'd like to spend the time we have in finding out as much as possible about you," she said, then pointed to the chest of drawers. "When you leave I'd like you to take that cassette recorder with you, and the envelope that's with it. I've recorded my story on that cassette. The explanation of how I ended up in the mess I did. I recorded it shortly after I was admitted to the hospice. Even though I used it to fill up the time when I was afraid of looking for you, I always hoped that I'd see you again one day. Better late than never, huh?"

"Thank you," I said.

My mother smiled and took my hand.

"Thank you, my child," she said. "Thank you for forgiving me."

"What is there to forgive?" I replied. "That the State came between us and told us such a pack of lies that neither of us knew how to find each other?"

"You put it well. And I'm sure you're right. Then I thank you for doubting them and coming to see me. And now you must tell me all about yourself, your boat, and your life. We've got so much to catch up on."

I spent five hours with Silvia, during which I told her all about my life, including the adoption, our move, my studies, my marriage, Leonie's birth, and the divorce. I didn't hold back on telling her about Christian and the *Storm Rose*.

When a nurse came into the room to give my mother her medication, I realized it was time to say good-bye. My visit had obviously tired her, and after she took her medication, her mind seemed to wander a little. I still didn't know exactly what was wrong with her, but I could see it was eating her up. I imagined it was cancer, but didn't ask her.

We embraced each other for a long time in farewell.

"Give my love to your new man—and maybe you'll tell Leonie one day that she had another grandmother."

Although she spoke the words clearly and calmly, they brought tears to my eyes again. Would I ever see her again?

"I'll be back," I promised. Maybe next time I'd bring Christian and Leonie with me. She'd held out for so long; she must have more days and weeks left to her.

Silvia nodded and replied, "I look forward to it." But I could see in her eyes that she didn't believe it. "Look after yourself and your loved ones, won't you?"

***

Back in my hotel room, I felt leaden. My head was empty.

I opened my bag and took out my mother's cassette recorder. It was hard to believe that such things were still around. I looked at the cassette, which had a running time of one hour, and wondered what it held. I knew the most important thing about my mother now—I knew that she hadn't abandoned me. But I was a little afraid of the rest. What must she have experienced when she was imprisoned?

I couldn't bring myself to press the "Start" button, so I undressed and took a shower. Then I slipped into my nightshirt even though it was still light outside. I wanted to be comfortable if I was going to be listening for an hour. I came back into the room, sat down on the bed, placed the cassette recorder on my lap, and loaded the cassette. I tried to imagine her sitting in the armchair by the window and speaking the words I was about to hear. A tear ran down my face. I was overcome by regret. Why hadn't I taken the first step toward her long before this? Why hadn't I tried to find her?

Because I'd been blinded. Because I'd believed what I'd been told after she disappeared. Because I'd been afraid, just as she was. Who wanted the facades of their carefully constructed life torn down by the past? I knew now that it had been a mistake not to look for her sooner.

I wasn't sure I could stay calm if I ever discovered the name of the official who had lied to me so shamelessly. Maybe I'd react like Christian and do nothing. If the official didn't have the opportunity for atonement, it would be on his conscience forever. And if, as my mother believed, there was a Heaven, that guilt, together with all the other things he'd done, would earn him a place of honor in Hell.

But now it wasn't about revenge or my emotions. I wanted to hear Silvia's story, which was also mine. I pressed "Play" and waited through the initial white noise for her voice.

34

Silvia

My darling Annabel, this is for you. You should know that there's no way I abandoned you, as you may have been told. I was simply a victim of my thoughts, and the way I stupidly always voiced the truth without caring about the consequences.

I didn't do it with malicious intent or because I'd been incited to do so by the West, as was alleged. I simply didn't want to be guilty of letting down other people whose only intention was that our country should be a better one, a country in which you didn't live in a cage, in which you could say what you thought.

Sadly, that was my downfall. But more about that later; I don't want to get ahead of myself.

I have no idea where you are now, but they've assured me you were put in good hands. Of course that information didn't come from an official source. A Stasi employee merely took pity on me and told me that at least. She told me nothing more.

I don't know the family who adopted you, and I don't know the name you go by. I intend to look for you, but I don't know whether my search will meet with success. But I really hope that your life is a good one and that, despite everything, you've grown into a woman who speaks her mind freely. And I also harbor a slight hope that you won't forget me, regardless of whether or not you ever get this recording.

You were a child of the trade show, at least that's what I secretly always called you. In Leipzig, where I was living before you were born, there were jobs available as a trade show hostess in spring and autumn. Working there meant that you came into contact with people whom you'd most likely never have met otherwise.

Companies from all over the world exhibited there and brought the sparkle and scent of their countries with them. The halls were filled with the buzz of so many different languages, and even though we had the strictest orders not to make contact with the representatives of capitalist countries, of course we did talk to them and discovered that the propaganda that we'd been fed on TV was basically untrue.

Sure, there was fatal drug addiction and criminality, pollution and AIDS in the West, but they were normal people just like us. Nice or mean, friendly or grouchy, cheerful or miserable. They weren't the monsters portrayed by the propaganda.

As such contacts were forbidden, but couldn't actually be avoided, only the most reliable people were hired to work at the trade shows. Given my later history, it's hard to believe I was one of them, isn't it?

My parents were faithful Party members. My father worked at the newspaper, and my mother in the administration of a university clinic. I myself had from a very young age been involved in all the State activities—I was a Young Pioneer, a Thälmann Pioneer, and a Free German Youth (*Freie Deutsche Jugend*) member—do you remember the FDJ? I'd always worked hard at school and outside it, and almost every year I was elected a member of the Group Council. My dedication continued when I got to college. I got involved in fund-raising campaigns and organized FDJ events. I got a First in Marxism-Leninism, a compulsory subject that every student had to take, although I was far more interested in languages and literature. It was my ambition to work in one of the big East German publishing houses, and I was eager to join the Socialist Unity Party as soon as I'd finished my studies.

My life was a model East German career, which justified the trust placed in me when I was allowed to work at the booth of an Austrian company.

At that time Austria was considered a capitalist country, but since it had recognized the German Democratic Republic, it wasn't considered as evil as West Germany.

The people at the booth were very friendly, and although I had a few difficulties understanding their dialect on the first day, I felt at home there from the start. The company sold machine parts I didn't know about, but I was trained, and at the end of the day I was slipped a few tips in foreign currency.

I got to know him—your father—at one of their evening events. I hardly told you anything about him because I didn't want you to get into trouble; it was bad enough that I'd gotten involved with him at all. Everything that I could have become in the eyes of the Party was destroyed at that moment—the moment when he looked me in the eye.

I don't know if you remember me, but when I was young I had the same red hair and green eyes as you do. Sometimes I was a little sad that you didn't inherit more from your father, who had raven-black hair and brown eyes. Maybe now that you're grown up, you look a little more like him, with his angular features, perhaps, or his long hands.

He was ten years older than I was and didn't represent the company I was working for. He was the purchasing manager for a heavy engineering firm in Stuttgart—sophisticated, charming, and as I found out, extremely well-read. I'd never met a man like him. And presumably he'd never met a redhead like me, either.

Whenever I looked in his direction, he turned to me, as though he could feel my eyes on him. And I could sense whenever he looked at me. Eventually he came over to me and asked if I was from Austria. I was surprised, as I believed it would be obvious that I was East German—all the other women there were far more easygoing than I was. But he hadn't noticed any difference, and that made me warm to him.

He introduced himself as Thomas. Of course he also had a surname, but since I don't know whose hands this cassette might fall into, I'm keeping it to myself.

I know that kids don't want to know about their parents' sex lives, and especially not how they were conceived. But I'll tell you this much: that night I slept with him, and it was one of the most beautiful nights of my whole life. And more followed. We spent every night of the rest of the trade show in my little student apartment. My roommate, Karla, was openly jealous, but she was a good friend and discreet enough to stay out whenever I took him back. She went to stay with her boyfriend, Mirko, doing the same with him as I was doing with your father.

Once the trade show was over and I had to let him go, it was as though I'd sunk into a deep hole. He promised to write to me, and left me five hundred West German marks for emergencies. It was a fortune, and I hid it away immediately. Maybe I'd need it one day, and I certainly didn't want to squander it on frivolities.

It was a few weeks after the trade show that the men turned up. They were wearing badly fitting suits and sunglasses—they must have believed that made them more inconspicuous. They waited for me outside the university.

At first I didn't take any notice of them, as my head was full of literary theories and the Russian vocabulary I had to learn. I walked right past them to my bicycle and had a struggle to release the lock, which always refused to behave when you were in a hurry. If the lock hadn't been so stubborn, I would probably have simply ridden away from the men. But it gave them enough time to wait for their opportunity. They positioned themselves by me and asked, "Are you Fräulein Thalheim?"

Of course I was, as they knew full well.

"Yes?" I replied, astonished that two such weird-looking guys were hanging around the campus. One of them produced an ID card.

"Ministry of State Security," it proclaimed. The document vanished before I could make out the name. Hot fear whipped through my body. Had I been seen vanishing into my dormitory with Thomas? Had his clothes betrayed the fact that he was from the West?

A lot of women took men from the West back to their home during the trade shows, either because they'd fallen in love or to boost their incomes with a few German marks. The city was full of men in suits, which you could tell had not been bought in the VEB state menswear stores. I'd been careful not to be conspicuous with Thomas, but maybe one of the neighbors had seen something and blown the whistle on me. If that was the case, I certainly wouldn't be getting another job at the trade show.

"We'd like to talk to you for a moment. Is that OK?" asked the one who hadn't flashed me his ID.

"Yes, of course," I replied, trying to conceal my nerves. From the first moment I was a wreck inside. I felt really bad, and I shoved my hands into my pants pockets to hide the trembling.

The two men took me to a building that I'd always thought was a normal residential block. It turned out to be a meeting place for Stasi people. Informal Collaborators—IMs—came and went, and it was here that reports on people under surveillance were exchanged.

I was sure there was going to be trouble, serious trouble. What was I going to tell my father and mother? That the Stasi had taken me in because I'd gotten involved with a man from the West? Because my experiences at the trade show had led me to let go of the beliefs that had been so carefully drummed into us? That on that one occasion I'd broken the rules?

I was sitting in an armchair covered with rough mustard-yellow fabric, looking across not only at the two men who'd spoken to me, but at a third, whose lapel bore the Party badge.

"Young Comrade Thalheim," he said, opening a cardboard file.

Was that my file? I couldn't believe that State Security was keeping a file on me. I still felt ill, and sweat was running down onto the collar of my blouse, although it was a cool autumn day outside, and the room wasn't particularly well heated.

"Do you have any idea why we want to talk to you?" he asked.

I shook my head.

"You worked for a few weeks at the Leipzig Trade Show, didn't you?"

I nodded.

"For a company from a non-Socialist state. Austria?"

Again all I could do was nod, because that, too, was probably in my file.

"It's come to our attention that in addition to all that, you made contact with employees of West German companies. Is that true?"

Suddenly my face felt numb. So it *was* about Thomas.

"We . . . I mean, the company had an evening event, and representatives from West German companies were invited, too. I helped there."

The man folded his hands on the tabletop and leaned forward slightly.

"Did you hear anything? Anything that might be of interest to us?"

I raised my eyebrows. What kinds of things did he mean?

"Well, the conversation was mainly about business deals," I replied, as I was sure the State would be interested in that kind of thing.

"What about private matters?"

I felt faint. I couldn't tell them that I'd slept with Thomas! That was nothing to do with the State or the Party bosses.

"I don't know what you mean," I replied uncertainly, my mind racing to think of a possible way out.

The man before me sniffed. "Did you pick up on any private gossip, perhaps? Whether one of them is cheating on his wife, what hobbies they have, whether they've recently bought a yacht or the like? Or what schools their kids go to? Best of all, whether there are any skeletons in their closets. An affair or a bit on the side could be really helpful to us."

I stared at the man in horror. Had he really just said that? I was only a little trade show hostess. Did he really think the Austrians or their guests would have mentioned details of their private lives in front of me, including any juicy gossip?

"No, no, I didn't pick up on anything like that," I replied in bewilderment.

It was the truth. Thomas had told me he'd broken up with his girlfriend three months ago, but who would be interested in that? People break up with their partners here, too.

One thing was clear to me. The state security service was interested in dirty laundry. It shocked me to the core, since until then I'd believed that they were only concerned with making sure that hostile elements didn't threaten the well-being of our citizens. An interest in affairs and the like seemed to me to be more a matter of concern to the Western secret services.

"Is there anything else that may be useful for us to hear?"

I shook my head. "No. I . . . I didn't take much notice of what they were talking about. We were told to avoid having anything to do with non-Socialist trade show delegates."

I was proud of myself for coming up with that one! It was precisely what the people who prepared us for the trade show work had said. The man looked disappointed.

"Maybe you shouldn't have stuck to the letter of those instructions," he said suddenly.

And once again the image I had of the state security service took a battering. The unknown man before me was actually suggesting I should disobey instructions from the officials?

"Well, that's how it is. You could do better next time, huh?"

I had no idea what he meant. But he didn't keep me waiting long.

"Young Comrade Thalheim, in view of your exemplary activities at the university and in the FDJ, we'd like to offer you an opportunity to work for us."

The man leaned back and fixed his eyes on me. Although I was fully dressed, I felt as though I was naked in front of him. He was probably able to read my thoughts from the expression on my face, so I tried to clear my mind completely.

"The benefits you'd gain are obvious," he continued in a self-satisfied voice. "You'll be given a position at the trade show every six months, and we'll see to it that you'll be employed there permanently after you finish your studies. We could also get you State approval for travel. You'd be well paid for your work, and we'd make sure you were given everything you need."

I was stunned. There I was, terrified that I'd be arrested for my nights of passion with Thomas, and now I was being offered a position at the trade show and the chance to be approved for travel! What if I told them that I wanted to work for a publishing house later? It probably wouldn't be a problem.

"So what . . . what would I have to do in return?" I asked a little naively. What did I think people who worked for the Stasi did?

"We'd engage you in various different areas, but mainly at the trade shows. You'd keep your ears open and record all the conversations you heard. Of course the ban on private contact would be lifted. You'd bring us your observations for us to assess." He leaned forward again. His eyes were still fixed on me. "Of course you understand that it's of great importance to our country to stay one step ahead. That applies to both technological and private information. We need to know our enemies inside and out. You could be of great assistance to us."

I took a shaky breath. Travel approval, a job at the trade show, privileges—it all sounded good. If I hadn't met Thomas, I might have agreed to it. But at that moment I thought of the friendly Austrians, I thought of Thomas and his colleagues, and I knew that I'd never want to harm them—even if the Party considered them to be enemies of the state.

"I . . . I need to think about it," I said hesitantly. I didn't know what consequences that would have and what ace they had up their sleeves. But I couldn't just agree. Not right away. I probably never would.

The Stasi man sniffed in frustration and leaned back again. Had he really believed I'd jump at his offer? Minutes before I'd believed they were going to punish me for my contact with a man from the West!

"I understand," he said at last. "And you're perfectly entitled to ask for time to consider it. But let me tell you one thing: don't spoil your excellent prospects by hesitating unnecessarily. The sooner you decide to work for us, the better we can plan your future life. And you want a good life, don't you?"

I nodded. However, I couldn't accept the offer. I didn't want to spy on other people. I wasn't interested in their private lives, and although I'd been brought up to toe the Party line, I'd always believed in another world beyond the Wall, that I couldn't imagine was as evil as our propaganda painted it. My common sense told me that it would be wrong to stick my nose into things that didn't concern me.

"Very well. Let's say we talk again in a couple of week's time. I hope you agree. An employee will come to get your answer. If you say yes, you simply have to sign a formal obligation, and I'll instruct you personally on your duties. If you turn it down, then you'll be left to your own devices—provided you don't change your mind."

He held his hands up, as though my fate had nothing to do with him, and went to the door. Just before opening it, he turned back.

"Oh yes, I'm sure I don't need to tell you that this conversation is strictly confidential. Not a word to anyone, not even your friends or family, you understand?"

"Yes," I replied, instinctively holding my breath until he'd gone.

I left the building, shaken to the core. Darkness had fallen. My bicycle was still on the university campus, but at that moment I couldn't have found my way back there. The Stasi man's words were burning in my ears.

Don't spoil your excellent prospects by hesitating unnecessarily.

If I turned down the proposal, would they really make sure that I didn't get anywhere? That I didn't get the job I wanted? I would have liked to talk to my parents about it, but I'd been instructed not to tell anyone. I carried the secret around with me for days. I wanted to be a good citizen, but spying? I didn't want to do that.

Because I was afraid of meeting the Stasi people at the university, I called in sick and hid away in my apartment. It was only later that I realized they knew where I lived and could come to my home at any time.

As the day drew nearer when I had to give the comrades my answer drew nearer, I felt increasingly wretched. Whenever the doorbell rang—even if it was only the mailman—I jumped. Two weeks passed in that way, until I finally realized I couldn't hide away forever. I started going back to class again, but something had changed in the meantime. I felt hunted. There was no reason for it, and whenever I turned I saw no one suspicious-looking behind me. And yet I constantly felt eyes boring into my shoulder blades—the only relief was when the curtains of my room were closed.

A further week went by until one afternoon when I was leaving the university as usual and heading for the bicycle stands.

"Ah, Young Comrade Thalheim," said a voice behind me. I froze. I'd hoped it was over, that I'd be forgotten, but the Stasi never forgot. "Are you feeling better?"

So they'd obtained information about me. I was pleased I'd gotten an official doctor's note. It meant I could act as though I hadn't been deliberately avoiding a meeting with the men.

"Yes, I'm feeling better, Comrade," I replied. "Thank you for asking."

"Well, if that's the case, I'm sure you'll be happy to come with us for another talk. Our Comrade Section Leader is looking forward to your reply."

I froze. There was no way I was going back into that Stasi building!

"Now, Young Comrade, we can only hope that your attitude isn't going to spoil your prospects for the future. You can reconsider your decision at any time."

The undisguised threat left me speechless.

There was no way in the world I wanted to commit myself to spying on anyone, possibly even Thomas. Even if we heard from one another only occasionally, I still thought about him. I was still a little in love with him and hoped to see him again sometime. I thought of the friendliness of the people at the Austrian booth, and the fact that they weren't monsters, as the authorities tried to convince us.

I pushed my bike home in a rage and decided to drink that evening like I never had before. I might not be allowed to talk to anyone, but they couldn't stop me from drinking.

After the encounter, I saw the things going on around me in a completely different light. I'd believed that the slogans that surrounded me had some meaning that was worth fighting for. But now I could see they were made up of empty words. The Workers' and Peasants' State might care for its population superficially, but only provided they did what was demanded of them—and provided they didn't step out of line.

I had refused it—and would feel the consequences. But it was only much later that this entry in my file became my downfall. At that moment I had other worries, because I soon realized that I'd missed my period. When the morning sickness began, I had a really bad feeling, which was confirmed when I went to see a gynecologist.

"Congratulations, you're pregnant," she said, enthusiastically laying my record card down on the desk.

My world fell apart. Unmarried and pregnant. By a man from a capitalist state. I was sure the Stasi would have me behind bars when the news got out.

"If you don't want the baby I can give you an appointment for an abortion," the doctor suggested. She could clearly tell I wasn't at all pleased.

But I shook my head. "No, I want to keep it," I said resolutely.

The doctor accepted that with a nod. "All right. But if you change your mind, please let me know in good time."

I nodded, although I knew there was no going back.

I had to make some decisions, and fast, about how I wanted to live. My parents' world was also shaken when I confessed to them. My father wanted to know the name of the father, but I couldn't identify him. A man from the West—that would probably have driven him to a heart attack. I kept stubbornly silent, even when he threatened to disown me.

They finally accepted it somehow, even though I couldn't expect them to help me. My parents were away far too often to have been able to look after the child, and as an unmarried pregnancy was still a cause of shame, even for an enlightened East German citizen, there was no question of any other kind of help.

I was certain that I didn't want an abortion, since I still harbored a hope that Thomas would support me. One evening, I wrote him a long letter. It didn't contain any mention of the Stasi's recruitment attempts nor any state secrets—I didn't know any. I simply told him that there were consequences arising from our nights together and he was to become a father.

I sent the letter the next day in the hope that he would receive it and perhaps get in touch. I didn't ask him to marry me; that would have been impossible. I couldn't leave the country, and he certainly didn't want to come and live here. Nevertheless, I hoped that he would write me or even come to visit. People from the other side of the Wall were still allowed to come and visit at that time. Maybe he remembered me, maybe he'd even be pleased about the baby. And even if he wasn't, I still held out hope that I would hear from him.

No answer came. At first I was calm about it, since I knew that the mail between the two German states could take time. As I waited, I felt a creeping fear that the Stasi might have intercepted the letter. But after a few months went by and no one appeared to take me to task, I was sure that they couldn't have.

I wondered if it had gotten lost. I was sure that Thomas would have contacted me somehow. I hoped so desperately for an answer from him that I ran to the mailbox every day when I came home. But it was always in vain, and when six months had gone by, I gave up hoping and decided to take my fate into my own hands and raise my child alone.

I was heavily pregnant when I finished my studies, and you were born a little after that. I had no money, no job, but I had a baby and at least I'd be paid the child benefit. I lived with Karla for a while, but your nighttime crying soon began to get on her nerves. She didn't complain, but I could see she wasn't happy about it. She still had two semesters of cramming ahead of her, and it wasn't good for her to be awoken during the night because I had to feed or change you.

I applied for my own apartment, which wasn't easy for an unmarried woman, and was eventually told that I'd been allocated one. I'd hoped for somewhere in a new building, but I was housed in a dilapidated building in the old town. The bathroom and toilet were shared by everyone living on the floor. But I was pleased to have my own home at last. While you were asleep, I filled out job applications—to publishers, libraries, the theater. There must be a job for a Germanist somewhere! I received a flood of rejections. I gradually began to grasp what the Stasi man had meant.

There certainly wasn't a lack of jobs; everyone knew that too many people were employed rather than too few. Some people even had two jobs. But the good ones were given only to reliable people—people who had no problem with occasionally doing the State a little favor or two. And it looked like my way to these "good jobs" was barred.

I was at a loss. What was I going to do now? Officially there was no unemployment in East Germany, yet I still had no job. I had gone through the money Thomas had given me—I'd long since exchanged it on the black market so I could keep my head above water. In despair I wrote to him again. I asked him politely for help in supporting my daughter; after all, it would have been his duty to pay child support.

One afternoon our doorbell rang. I opened up, assuming it was the mailman. But the man standing there was completely unknown to me. I was afraid I was about to get another proposal from the Stasi, but the man was some official who, once I'd let him in, gave me a never-ending lecture on how wrong—antisocial, even—it was to be out of work. He gave me a list of factories where I could work.

I almost laughed when I saw what it contained. The list included textile collectives, state-owned stores, and production cooperatives. They were all looking for lowly assistants. I was a fully qualified Germanist with excellent grades, including in Marxism-Leninism.

When I pointed that out to him, I got a second lecture—one that detailed how not everyone could work in the profession they had trained for, and that it was no disgrace to make a different kind of contribution to Socialism.

I have no idea how I managed to control myself, but once he'd left, I flung a candlestick at the door in sheer rage. It was only your crying that brought me back to my senses, and I rushed to comfort you.

Because I needed a job and the Stasi had seen to it that I'd never work for a publishing house or a newspaper, I swallowed my pride and went to the employment office. They told me there were some positions for trainee sales staff. At least that was better than an unskilled assistant, so I applied. HO, the state-owned store, didn't want me, but the Konsum cooperative store gave me a chance. From that moment on, I found myself standing behind a counter, weighing out hamburger meat and cutlets and fending off people's disappointment when there were no Cuban bananas or pineapples.

I couldn't expect any help from my parents. When they found out I'd gotten pregnant and refused to name the father, they cut off all contact with me. They didn't even want to see their granddaughter. My mother came to visit me once, but only to reproach me. I asked her to leave, saying I never wanted to see her again.

In the evenings I did my homework for the vocational school or worked off my anger at the way we were supposed to put under-the-counter goods aside for certain people. The beneficiaries of these favors were Stasi members or people who had personal connections with the store manager. But I had you, so I decided to swallow it all and make sure I didn't "spoil my prospects" a second time. I passed my final exams as the best in my year and was taken on by the cooperative. That was a victory over the dark prophecy and the official with the list. Even if only a small victory.

I admit that there were moments when I considered going back to the Stasi building and telling them I'd changed my mind. I didn't know whether I was still worth anything at all to them—I certainly hadn't been hired at the trade show again.

They would probably have found some place for me where I could have kept my ears pricked. And then I might have been able to work for a publisher. But a glimpse behind the veil at the real face of this state had been enough to confirm my opinions. There might be drafts coming through the windows of my apartment, the stove might not work properly, the toilet might be notoriously blocked at regular intervals, but my common sense always kept me from any further contact with the Stasi. I simply wanted to live in peace, to raise my child, and live my life.

One day, when I had long since stopped hoping or believing, a letter arrived from Thomas. I hesitated for a long while before opening it. What would he say? That he wanted nothing more to do with me? That he wanted to marry me? I didn't know which I feared more. I still had a feeling that the Stasi were watching me. It was possible that they had read my letter and his and were now heartily amused by my situation.

I hoped that he'd at least found a few sympathetic words and would offer me a little help—even though after almost four years since our nights of passion, it was arriving rather late.

I was shocked to see that the letter wasn't from Thomas, but from his wife. She asked me not to contact her husband again and would I be kind enough to raise my "bastard" myself; her husband had paid for my sexual services and she wouldn't tolerate some "Russian whore" trying to seek advantage in that way.

Totally shaken, I sank down on the sofa that I'd bought with my first wages as a qualified sales assistant. You were playing with building blocks nearby and didn't notice how your mother was seething with anger.

Bastard, Russian whore—what the hell had Thomas told her? And why had it taken her so long to write me?

There was probably only one explanation: she must have found one of the letters that Thomas had kept hidden away. Maybe she'd then confronted him, and he'd admitted to sleeping with a prostitute, in order to save his own skin.

The fact that he hadn't gotten in touch himself over all that time spoke volumes. He'd never intended to see me again or to help me. Whatever his reasons for not destroying my letters, he was clearly such a coward that he was willing to lay all the blame on me when she questioned him, and to shift all the anger of his wife—whom he'd never once mentioned—onto me.

At first I was tempted to read this woman the riot act, but I realized it was better not to make any contact at all. Although my life was completely different from the one I'd dreamed of, it was at least back on track. My neighbors in the building were nice and sometimes gave me a helping hand if my money ran out at the end of the month. And they were particularly fond of you. As soon as I appeared anywhere holding your hand, old ladies whipped out coloring books and chocolate, sometimes even from the West, which I wasn't too fond of, thanks to Thomas and his stupid wife, but which I accepted gratefully. Despite its structural defects, I had my apartment and a new—as yet unacknowledged—application for a new home, which could all be put at risk if I wrote to an enemy of the state.

I tore the letter up in rage and threw the scraps on the fire. I swore never to get involved with a man again.

We spent two years in relative peace. I worked, rejected any advances from men, and devoted myself to you. You grew and began to draw. You translated everything I told you into pictures. I began to wonder if you might have inherited your love of drawing from your father.

One day, as I was leaving the cooperative with a shopping bag containing a few bananas that I'd managed to set aside for us, I saw a man standing on a street corner. He looked outlandish in a long coat, and it seemed as though he was waiting for me. Another Stasi comrade? After leaving me in peace for such a long time, did they now want to make another offer to me? What would happen if I refused again? Would they have me put behind bars this time? Take my child away from me? Tell me I wouldn't be able to work anymore? I kept my head down and tried to act as if I hadn't seen him.

"Silvia."

I froze. I knew that voice. Although I hadn't heard it for so many years, I knew immediately who he was. And I realized that it was the trade show season. I hadn't given it a second thought. Every now and then I'd heard someone mention it, but I hadn't heard much about it at the cooperative.

And now here was Thomas, standing before me. At first I couldn't believe it. Had I fainted behind the counter and was now dreaming? I looked at him angrily.

"What do you want?"

"To see you."

"And how . . . how do you know . . . ?" I couldn't finish my question.

"I called on my contacts. Your friend told me you were still in town and she'd seen you around here."

"My friend?"

Since my run-in with the Stasi and my pregnancy, I no longer had any friends. I didn't even have any parents who'd stand by me.

"The girl you used to live with."

I had no idea whether my former roommate remembered me or if she had become another set of eyes and ears for the Stasi. Was she working at the trade show, and he recognized her there?

"I wanted to . . . to explain to you."

"Explain what?" I snapped. My astonishment at his sudden appearance gave way to anger. "Why I haven't heard from you in six years? Why you told your wife you'd slept with a Russian whore in Leipzig and paid her well?"

I saw that he'd turned pale.

"What? But . . ."

"Your wife wrote to me saying I should bring up my bastard myself. Well, fine, that's what I've done! And I see no reason to continue this conversation."

"But, Silvia . . ."

His hand gripped my arm. I tore free.

"I've got nothing to say to you."

He pressed his lips together. His expression was stony. I was sure that he'd go off in a rage and disappear forever. But he stayed where he was.

"I'm sorry," he said. "I . . . I didn't intend for her to find the letter. But she did. I never said you were a whore; she inferred that herself. I didn't know she'd written to you."

"Well, she did. And, you know what, I'm glad! At least it means I don't have to deal with any more hassle than I've had since we met."

All the rage that had been building up pressed hard against my chest. I feared I'd burst at any moment if I didn't let it out. But I managed to control myself. If I'd yelled out there on the street what I'd experienced at the hands of the Stasi, I'd certainly have gotten myself put away.

"Come with me," he said then. "Come with me over to the West. I'll see to it that you and your child can get through. I can't leave you here."

It sounded like an attractive prospect, but he was still married. And there was no way out of East Germany. He clearly hadn't thought it through.

"There's nothing you can do," I argued. I didn't care who heard me. My voice grew shrill and began to crack. "There's no way out of here! Even you couldn't arrange that."

"Silvia," he said again, his voice so gentle that I found it difficult not to weaken. "Can't we go somewhere to talk?"

I looked at my watch. The nursery school would be closing soon. I had to go pick you up.

"I don't have time," I said. "I have to get my daughter."

I suddenly felt incredibly tired. My feet were hurting from hours of standing behind the counter, and I was hungry.

"Go home, Thomas," I said quietly, feeling a deep sense of disappointment. Not in him, but rather in myself—the fact that I didn't have the courage to believe him. "It was nice of you to come, but you can't help me. I wish you all the best."

With that I mounted my bicycle and pedaled off without giving him a second glance.

In the days that followed, I hoped Thomas would come back and try again to persuade me that he could do something for me after all. I followed the reports from the trade show, and even watched the news program on my black-and-white TV in the hope of catching a glimpse of him behind Erich Honecker and the other Party puppets. But I never saw him.

On the last evening of the trade show, you were sitting at the kitchen table, working on a picture of a windmill. Do you still have it? I don't know how much of your old life they let you keep. Maybe you still remember it. I tried to take the picture from you, but for some reason you wanted to take it to bed with you. Because I was tired and still hoped to see a report from the trade show, I let you.

You'd long been asleep when my doorbell rang. I tensed. Was it Thomas? Had he really come to try again? If he had, this time I wouldn't be able to resist him. My heart was thumping with anticipation as I went to the door. He rang the bell three times, clearly determined to get an answer. I feared he was about to shout to me and wake up everyone in the building. I smoothed my hair and my skirt, undid the chain, and opened up. I tried to look reproachful, even though I was secretly overjoyed.

It wasn't Thomas.

My face froze. I didn't recognize the men, but instinctively knew who they were even before one of them said in a hard, icy voice, "Ministry of State Security. Will you please come with us?"

They gave me no explanation, and I knew I couldn't expect one. They took me away, and I mistakenly thought they'd let me go soon— after all, I hadn't done anything wrong. I forced myself to stay calm, as I knew things could only get worse if I tried to resist. If I'd known what was to follow, I would have tried to scratch their eyes out.

They took me to the same building I'd entered a few years before when they made their first approach. The man who appeared after a while was the same as before, but this time he didn't make any attempt at oily friendliness.

They threw all kinds of accusations at me: spying, fraternization with an enemy of the state, treason. I couldn't breathe as they presented me with the "evidence."

That consisted of the letters—my two to Thomas and a copy of the reply from his wife. I hadn't forgotten the words, but seeing the handwriting again gave me a shock.

"You were observed meeting this man again three days ago and discussing leaving the German Democratic Republic."

I stared at him in shock. How did they know that? It was clear that my change of residence and new occupation hadn't gone unnoticed by the Stasi. I'd been naive to believe that I wouldn't be watched anymore. Thomas might also have been spied on. The appearance of my former roommate and "friend" seemed very suspicious to me, and I was annoyed with myself for not having been more wary.

"Frau Thalheim," the man concluded, his expression dark, "you should have cooperated with us years ago. And above all, you should have thought long and hard about getting involved with an enemy of the state. Now there's nothing more I can do for you and your daughter."

It was the meeting with Thomas that turned out to be my downfall. Although I'm sure his intentions were good, he'd finally brought disaster down on me. That was what I believed, anyway. I realize now that it had never been Thomas' fault—it was the State's. The State, which couldn't come to terms with the idea of one of its children refusing to become an informer.

The time that followed was sheer hell. I was interrogated again and again, shoved into a dark cell, kept awake, and once they even took my clothes away. I was humiliated, tortured with cold water, threatened. And they had a really good means of exerting pressure—you. At that time, I still believed I'd see you again sometime. I had no idea that they'd long since taken you away and handed you over to another family. I only discovered that when the West bought my freedom, and by then it was already too late.

But I don't want to waste the little time left to me in complaining. I prefer to think about your father, who, although he failed, intended to do good, and about you and the good fortune you meant to me for almost seven years, before I was sent to hell.

There's one thing you should know. It tore my heart out when they prevented me from waking you and saying good-bye to you.

Once that hellish period was over, I tried to find you, but the Stasi had been very thorough. My lawyer came up against brick walls at every turn.

When the real Wall fell, I still didn't get a chance to track you down. And there was the fear of what I might find out. I was afraid that you wouldn't remember me. Hopelessness had taken hold of me, and it was a long time before I had the strength to ask to see my Stasi file.

I tried to build a new life, but only managed to a limited extent. I got a job in a small publishing house, but my poor health prevented me from achieving much. Despite everything, I found friends who still stand by me to this day. You see, there were also more cheerful moments, but my imprisonment and the way my child was snatched from me left a shadow on my soul that never left me. It never will. All my relationships were overshadowed by it, and they all ultimately failed because of the mistrust of other people that I'd developed over the years and still can't shake off.

The tape's almost come to an end, so I'll use the remaining time to tell you that I love you more than anything and always will.

I hope you can forgive me and haven't forgotten me.

35

During the train journey home the next day, my mother's words echoed inside me. Her voice on the cassette was mixed up in my mind with my own memories, mistakes, emotions, and snippets of things I'd heard. It wasn't only her story, but mine.

Although I'd been away for only two days, I felt as though a whole year had gone by. I tried to get my thoughts in order. I would have liked to listen to the story again, but I had no headphones and didn't want to bombard my fellow passengers with words that weren't meant for them.

What should I do now? Carry on as before? Tell my adoptive parents of my visit? Would they be hurt by the fact that I'd gone to see my mother? Would I be hurt if I found out that they had known it all and deliberately kept it from me? I had to talk to Christian.

When I arrived in Binz, I found my old Volvo in the parking lot between two gleaming new cars that looked as though they'd only been there a few minutes. The roof of my car was covered in linden leaves and flowers. I placed my bag in the backseat, got in, and savored the familiar smell of the car's interior as I fastened my seat belt.

A rare feeling of peace descended over me. I knew now. My mother hadn't abandoned me. That was worth more than anything else.

I started up the engine and drove to my house. Christian's car was still there. It, too, had a light covering of pretty linden flowers. The house seemed peaceful. I looked at it for a moment and remembered how on my first day here I'd thought that when I came here I'd be free of the baggage of the years gone by. But I'd been wrong. You were never totally free of such things. But the baggage felt lighter if it was the truth you were carrying.

With a smile on my lips I got out, reached for my bag, and went to the door. I'd play the tape with my mother's story to Christian, as he ought to know who I was.

As I reached the front door, the cat, whose origin was still unknown, stuck its head around the corner. This time I didn't shoo it away, but called out, "Here, kitty!" I might as well not have bothered, since it vanished immediately. Strange animal. Maybe I should leave it some food. Leonie would be delighted, and if I could catch hold of it, I could take it to the vet and have it vaccinated.

I was about to unlock the door, when Christian opened it and stepped outside, his expression serious. I stared at him, my hand still hovering over the lock. Had something happened? Leonie, perhaps? The thought sent a shudder through me.

"What's the matter?" I asked fearfully.

Christian pursed his lips.

"Is something wrong with Leonie?" I almost screeched the words. He shook his head.

"The hospice called," he said. "Frau Thalheim . . . your mother died this morning."

I stood there, thunderstruck. It wasn't possible! I'd only just been talking to her. Sure, she'd seemed weak, but I'd been convinced that she had a few weeks left . . .

Christian took me in his arms. I lowered my hand, and the keys dropped from my fingers.

"I'm sorry."

I couldn't reply. The words I'd heard on the cassette whirled around my head. After several listens, I'd realized that her voice grew weaker toward the end, and she'd paused more frequently. I wondered how long it had taken her to tell the story, as she surely couldn't have recorded it in a single take. It was strange that I wondered about that only now.

Christian managed to maneuver me into the living room. Leonie rushed over to me, and I reacted mechanically, although I was still paralyzed with shock.

Silvia was dead. She'd held out for long enough to see me. Or conversely, if I'd gone only two days later, I wouldn't have found her alive. I'd only have had the recording and couldn't have spoken with her.

"Mommy, look! Uncle Christian has drawn me a great big blue whale on my cast!" Leonie cried out in delight. I shook myself from my thoughts and forced a smile.

My daughter—whom I'd never be able to introduce to Silvia—was waving her arm about in front of my face. The whale had a friendly smile and was blowing a fountain of water into the air. Waves formed rings around it like on an old sailor's tattoo.

"That's really beautiful," I said and tried in vain to hold back my tears.

"Why are you crying, Mommy?" Leonie asked.

I held her tight. "Because I'm so happy to be back with you." It wasn't a lie.

I had no idea how long we sat together on the sofa, simply looking out over my yard in the twilight.

***

"The nurse says she asked for her ashes to be scattered in a woodland cemetery," I said.

After supper I'd phoned the hospice, where they'd given me all the details. On the evening of my visit, the nurse had looked in on her once during the night, and the following morning they'd found her at rest.

"She'd been waiting for you," she said. "It's so good that you were there."

I wondered if she'd told her story to the people in the hospice.

"Do you want to go?" Christian asked, stroking my shoulder.

"I don't know."

"What about your parents? Will you tell them?"

During the journey I'd thought a lot about my adoptive parents. Should I tell them? Should I ask them any questions? It had been really difficult to come to a decision. But now, as I sat there in silence, things had crystallized.

I'd always considered honesty and trust to be of the utmost importance. I'd always expected people to tell me the truth, although they hadn't always done so. I needed to be certain about one thing now. I'd call them the very next day. I'd begin cautiously, gauging their reaction, and then ask the questions I needed to have answered. I knew I could forgive them if they'd kept anything from me. They were my family— even if the Stasi had made us what we became.

At last I rose and went into Leonie's bedroom. She lay asleep in her bed, totally unaware of all the things I knew. It was right that way, but it still made me sad. It was such a pity that she'd never meet her biological grandmother, but maybe she didn't need to. Her grandparents lived in Hamburg, and whatever they had told the system, they were good people.

After standing in the doorway for a few moments, I went back to Christian. Life was waiting for me.

**

The next morning I went down to the beach. I'd picked a few roses and replaced the bouquet on the rock. Walkers on the beach watched me.

They were probably asking themselves the same questions that I had a few weeks ago.

When I returned, both Leonie and Christian were still asleep. I looked at the clock. My parents would be up by now. I took the telephone into my office, where I wouldn't be disturbed. I sat by the window and made the call. Clouds had gathered over the water, and a yacht sailed by.

"Hansen," my mother said. My father would be on his way to work at that time, and I felt it was better to discuss what was on my mind with her first. I'd be far more likely to break my father's heart than that of my strong mother.

"Hello, Mom," I said, feeling the dichotomy inside myself. Silvia had also been my mom.

"What is it, darling?" my mother asked, her voice so carefree that I found it hard to begin. "Is everything all right with Leonie?"

"Yes, she's fine. I . . ." I hesitated. I could evade the issue with small talk. But I didn't want to do that. "I got a letter a few days ago."

"Who from?"

"From Silvia Thalheim. My birth mother."

Silence. My mother was rendered speechless. But what did I expect?

"Where did she get your address from?" she asked after she had gotten over her initial shock.

"I don't know. She gained access to her Stasi file and found out that you'd adopted me. She originally sent the letter to Bremen, and it was forwarded to me here."

My mother heaved a long, deep sigh.

"Please, will you tell me what you know from those days? I've never asked about it since I've been grown up, but . . . I need to know what you know. Otherwise I'll never stop wondering . . ."

"Whether we're partly to blame." My mother sounded hurt. That hadn't been my intention. "It's like this . . . We'd put in an application to adopt a long time before. I found out soon after we were married that I couldn't have children, but we'd always wanted one, so we tried the adoption route. Your father was an active Party member at the time, and considered a trustworthy comrade."

"Did the Stasi get in touch with him?" I burst out. As foreman in the shipyard, he would definitely have been of interest to them.

"No, not that I know of. We tried to keep out of those things. Anyway, someone must have liked him. We were informed that we could adopt a child. We were told that she was the daughter of someone who had defected, and we were being given the responsible task of bringing her up as a good Socialist. As I said, your father had a spotless record and I worked for the district council so was also considered reliable. We filled out a heap of forms and were called to an interview with an official. I have no idea if they had anything to do with the Stasi; no one showed us any ID. We were ordered not to talk to you about your birth mother until you were an adult. And we were instructed to keep you away from any potentially bad influence. We were pleased to agree to it, even though we didn't share the State's view about everything. Eventually we were allowed to go and get you. And I have to say that I fell in love with you on the spot. You were so pretty with your red hair and freckles. You had a bit of a Saxon accent back then, too—a pity you've lost it over time."

"And then I grew into a little devil," I replied with a giggle, a little relieved despite my continued nagging doubts.

"You had good memories of your mother—how were you supposed to react? You'd been taken to a family you didn't want to be in; it was natural that you wanted to go back to your mother. So you rebelled."

In retrospect, I was amazed at the equanimity with which my parents had accepted my behavior. If I went too far, they'd reprimand me, but I never had any other punishments. While my friends were grounded, I was never kept in. Eventually I came to understand that these people didn't wish me any harm. Nor was it they who had torn me away from my birth mother.

"Did you ever wonder whether you were being watched?" I asked. It seemed logical they'd be monitored if they'd adopted the child of an alleged defector.

"Of course we were watched; we knew that. But we also believed we were doing the right thing at all times."

"You let me watch Western TV."

"That wasn't wrong in our eyes. And it was only right that you could talk to the other kids at school about those things. In our opinion the officials who tried to prevent young people from having any contact with Western media were shortsighted, as a full education meant seeing all sides. But of course we had to be careful."

I thought back to how my parents had been when I was younger. Yes, they'd believed in the whole thing. Maybe they still did believe that something like Socialism could function. But it was true that they'd never cut me off from anything—apart from a few aspects of my own past, because they'd been forced to.

"Annabel . . . ?" my mother asked uncertainly. "May I ask what she said in her letter? Your mother . . ."

She had been open with me, so I had to be open with her.

"She said she hadn't tried to defect. That she was arrested because she had problems with the Stasi. She was forced to sign the adoption agreement."

"Oh my God!" my mother exclaimed. I knew her well enough to know that she was genuinely horrified. "We didn't know a thing about that. Do you believe she was telling the truth?"

"I can check it in the Stasi files. I've already applied to see them. But it could take a while before I'm granted access."

Now she would definitely be petrified if they'd been involved, because in that case their names would also appear in the files. I waited tensely for her reaction. My heart was pounding in my throat, and my stomach felt even more cramped than before.

"You could do that. And you should. You know, we've been wondering for a while whether we should apply ourselves, but decided against it. What point is there in knowing your neighbor spied on you? That reports were written about you? In our case the IMs must have fallen asleep with boredom."

We said nothing for a while. As I listened to my mother's breathing and she to mine, I realized how perfidious the Stasi had been. They hadn't given me to a Stasi couple, but to allegedly loyal comrades, so that I would effectively disappear from the face of the earth. That was their way of punishing my mother for her refusal to get involved with them.

"Mom?" I asked into the silence.

"Yes, darling?"

"Thank you. Thank you for talking about it."

My mother sighed. "No, thank *you*. You have no idea what a shadow's been lifted from my heart. I never had the courage to talk to you about it, and neither did your father. Somehow I always expected you to ask, but you never did, so I thought you'd forgotten all about it."

The Stasi had clearly also thought I'd forget. But that could never be. And similarly I'd never forget what my adoptive parents had done for me.

"I've been carrying all these questions around with me like a millstone around my neck, but now I can look to the future."

"Then we're both feeling much better, aren't we?"

I realized I was smiling. "Yes, it's been good to talk. Especially since Silvia . . . Mom . . . She died yesterday, you know. Shortly after I'd been to visit her."

I could have told her about the cassette, but I wanted to leave that until later.

"I'm sorry to hear it," she replied sincerely, and said nothing more for a while.

My mother now had quite a bit to mull over, so I merely asked her, "Please, could you look after Leonie this week? It's the auction for the engine, and I've still got something I need to sort out."

"Of course, my love, I'd be glad to."

My mother sounded relieved that I'd brought things back to normalcy. And so was I.

36

Since my visit to my mother, I had begun to experience bad feelings about hospitals. Those feelings were back with me now, as I imagined her emaciated figure in the bed before my eyes and the smell of disinfectant in my nose, although every effort had been made to dispel it in the hospice.

But this visit was as essential as my journey to see her had been. There was still one thing I had to clarify, even if it meant swallowing my pride and making myself face something that unsettled me deeply.

Leonie was staying with her grandparents, who were overjoyed to be looking after my little princess. She had proudly shown them her decorated plaster cast, and I knew I could rely on them to take good care of her while I resolved this last remaining uncertainty in my life.

I still didn't trust Jan, despite his expression of sympathy for Leonie's broken arm and the doll he'd sent her. But maybe a conversation with him would take me a step forward.

I'd driven to see him instead of going with Christian to the auction.

I took a deep breath and stepped through the door of the Paracelsus Clinic in Bremen, a bouquet of flowers in my hand. After his secretary had informed me that he'd undergone surgery and now only had to complete his course of chemotherapy, I'd decided to visit him. Without Leonie. She would have coped fine; her fracture was healing well, but I wanted to be alone with Jan. I wanted his full attention. Because unless he talked to me, unless I was able to be fully honest with him, there would be no sharing of the custody arrangements.

At the reception desk I was greeted with a friendly smile by a young woman in a flowery blouse.

"I'd like to see Herr Wegner," I said.

The receptionist gave me directions, and I took the elevator to the ward. Once there I found the room more quickly than I would have liked. But before I could hesitate, the door opened and a nurse came out, carrying a tray of medication.

"Who would you like to see?" she asked briskly.

"Herr Wegner," I replied. It would have been silly to be evasive and try and put it off.

"Oh, he'll be delighted!" She turned and called out cheerfully, "Herr Wegner, you have a visitor!"

Jan was sitting on his bed in a blue hospital gown. He was pale and had lost weight. No wonder, after everything he'd been through and still had to face. He had a cannula inserted into his hand, and a stand with a drip containing clear fluid was positioned by the bed. When he saw me, his eyes widened in surprise. He must have expected to see anyone but me.

"Annabel?"

I closed the door behind me, but found myself unable to go any closer.

"Yes, it's me," I said.

"You've come to visit me?"

"I'd like to talk to you." I did go up to the bed then, and handed him the flowers. "Here, these are for you. Get well soon."

"Thank you." His voice sounded a little awkward.

A long silence followed. I didn't know how to begin. It wasn't right to argue with a sick man—but would we be able to have a civilized conversation when it was about Leonie? About what Jan wanted and all the things he hadn't done?

"Bring up a chair and sit down," Jan said after watching me for a while.

I moved a chair from under the window to the foot of the bed.

"How are you?" I asked.

"As you see. The operation went well, but I've still got the post-op treatment to come. For a start I'll probably have to say good-bye to my hair. But the prognosis is good," he continued. "If I survive this I stand a good chance of living to a ripe old age."

"I'm glad to hear it," I replied, and we fell silent again. I sensed Jan's tension and couldn't say I felt any easier myself. My old scars hadn't fully healed.

"You don't want to share the custody with me, do you?" he said, looking down at the bed sheets in disappointment. "Well, I can't blame you after that business with your new boyfriend."

"Actually, I'm here to talk to you about how you'd want to go about the arrangements," I replied.

Jan stared at me incredulously. "You really want to . . ."

"Yes, but I'd like to know how you'd manage it all. Leonie's life should be as stable as possible despite our divorce."

"That's really important to me, too," Jan answered. "I know my behavior hasn't always been the best. I just want to set things right."

Could I trust him? I had to try, at least, if I was going to give him a chance.

"You'll have to rethink your life. I don't want Leonie to be torn from her familiar environment for long periods of time. She's gotten used to the house in Binz and it wouldn't be good for her to have to spend her time traveling between Binz and Bremen."

"And I suppose it would be out of the question for you to move?"

I shook my head. "I've made myself at home in Binz now and besides, I'm very happy with Christian. My new relationship's also doing Leonie good."

"Then you could easily replace me with him."

"It's not a matter of replacing you, Jan. It's the fact that he's there. That he cares about me. You'll always be Leonie's father, but in order to be a father you have to do more than transfer money, send a doll every now and then, and talk on the phone. You have to prove that you really care about her."

He thought for a while, then shifted his weight a little to one side, grimacing as he did so.

"Regarding the traveling around, in the past few days I've had plenty of time to think. When I was in Binz I saw a house for sale. It has two stories and it's reasonably central. I've been thinking about buying it."

"You want to move to Binz?"

I couldn't imagine it. Jan needed the bright lights of the city; not even Bremen was big enough for him. Hamburg was the smallest he'd go for, if not Paris or New York. And now he wanted to move to that small, pretty spa town? I thought about what Christian had said that time when we were sitting at the kitchen table. That maybe Jan wanted me back. But that wasn't going to happen.

"No, I won't be moving to Binz, at least not permanently. But maybe you'll want to go on vacation with your new boyfriend every now and then. Or enjoy a free weekend. Or you may have to travel on business. Then I could stay there and Leonie wouldn't be far from home."

"You'd really do that? Give up your free time for us?"

"I've got some good employees in my company and I can easily work from home."

"What about your girlfriend?"

"She'll have to get used to the fact that I've changed. Otherwise she's not the woman for me."

I looked at him searchingly. Had his illness really made a new man of him? I was inclined to doubt it, but sometimes life threw some positive surprises at you.

"Very well," I said. "If you stick to your plan, that could work. We don't need a court to confirm that for us. You can see your daughter whenever you like. And if you really do buy that house and want to look after her there, that's fine by me."

He took my hand. I looked into his eyes, trying to see something that might confirm my lingering doubts. But I found nothing.

***

An hour later I left the clinic. Rain clouds had gathered. Was that a good sign or a bad one? I was on my way to the parking lot, when my cell phone buzzed. I thought about Christian in Denmark. Was the auction over already? I looked at the clock. A quarter to five. We hadn't been given a precise time, but it was possible that a decision had been made by now.

I took out my phone and answered it.

"We've got it!" came an excited voice on the line. "The engine's ours!"

I took a deep breath and smiled broadly. "Well done! Now make sure you come home as quickly as you can. We've got something to celebrate."

I hung up and went over to my car. When I was in Hamburg, the first thing I was going to do was drink a toast with my parents and Leonie to the *Storm Rose*.

Part 4

Three Months Later

37

My heart was in my mouth with excitement. I looked out to sea, over which a beautiful October morning was rising, and knew she was on her way. In a few hours the *Storm Rose* would be arriving in Sassnitz, her new home port.

The preceding months hadn't been entirely easy. The costs of the restoration had veered wildly; sometimes they appeared to increase; then, through some lucky chance, they dropped a little. In any case, the new engine was worth every penny. My father thought we'd paid too much, but we had it, and the boat now had a strong heart.

Over the recent weeks I had been busy creating a publicity stir around the boat. The harbormaster had given me permission to organize a small party for around one hundred invited guests and visitors who had an interest in the boat. I had selected the guests very carefully. They included politicians, other people in public life, and the managers of hotels whom I wanted to win over to offer trips on the *Storm Rose* for their hotel guests. I had already concluded a few agreements to this effect, including with some businesspeople from Hamburg with my father's intervention on my behalf.

I had found it difficult to invite Joachim Hartmann. Of course, with his hotel he represented an excellent marketing opportunity, but I still hadn't forgotten that it was men like him who had caused Silvia Thalheim's suffering. For that reason, I hadn't attended his summer party, giving Leonie's broken arm as the official reason. It was Christian who'd made my decision for me.

"Go ahead and invite him—he has a lot of contacts and could be useful for you. This isn't the place for personal feelings; it's about our boat and our business. With the *Storm Rose* he can make up for things he's done wrong in the past."

I found the idea of a former IM supporting a boat that would tell people more about those who had escaped the East German regime to be a really attractive one.

"So you do want to give him a chance to atone for his mistakes?" I asked as I turned the invitation around and around in my hand.

"He'll never be able to make up for the death of my mother, but I believe my parents, especially my father, would have been pleased to see him helping us. Have you actually told him the boat was used to transport defectors to the West?"

"No, not yet. I'm looking forward to seeing his expression when he finds out."

"All the more reason to invite him."

I couldn't disagree, so I sent him an invitation along with the rest. He accepted immediately, probably because he relished the prospect of being seen in public.

I suppressed my thoughts and turned back into the house. Silvia came back into my mind. I often thought about my mother. A couple of weeks after I visited her, I'd gone to the office of the Leipzig youth welfare service to have my file from the home read out to me. Once again the arrangements had taken a lot of time and energy to plan, but thanks to Christian and my mother, I'd managed it.

The official had been very friendly, and led me into a bright and airy office where she began to read through the file. It mainly contained dry details, but there was also a note that my mother had been arrested—allegedly because she had intended to defect. There was no mention of her imprisonment, but the nice official read out reports on how I found it difficult to integrate into the group but that I was nevertheless making good progress.

Then came the adoption by the Hansens. The declaration of relinquishment my mother had told me she'd been forced to sign reduced me to tears.

"Would you like to come back another time?" the official asked, but I shook my head.

Once I'd gathered myself a little, I asked her to continue. But all that followed were reports on my progress. With her signature at the bottom of the adoption papers, my mother had vanished from my life. Anything else I wanted to know about her would be in the Stasi files, but it would be some time before I was given consent to see them.

I was hit again by regret—regret that I'd continued to believe what they'd told me after reunification. And regret that I had not followed my vague instincts and begun looking for her sooner. And I was also very sorry that I would probably never find out who my real father had been. What would he say if he ever saw me? Was he still alive? I would probably never find out.

I could have been angry with her for keeping it from me—but harboring a grudge would do no good. I preferred to think of how she'd embraced me and smiled at me with her last remaining strength. *Better late than never,* her voice echoed inside me. At least I'd found her, and that meant a lot to me.

Earlier, in August, I had gone to the forest cemetery where her ashes lay. I hadn't been the one who scattered them. Silvia had left precise instructions that three close friends should perform the ceremony. There had been a will, but after she had received her diagnosis and accepted it, she had given away all she possessed. I kept the cassette recorder and sometimes, when I was alone and wanted to hear her voice, I played the cassette again.

Leonie was waiting for me in the house, already dressed in her new frock. She had turned six in August and moved up to the preschool group at the nursery. She'd be going to school in a year—time really was flying.

Jan had kept to his promise and made an appearance every other weekend. He still hadn't completed his purchase of the house, but he took a room at the hotel and spent a lot of time with Leonie. Our relationship with each other gradually improved, too. My ex-husband's time in the hospital really did seem to have changed him a little.

However, he was unable to attend the maiden voyage of the *Storm Rose* because he had a business appointment. I forgave him, since he'd sent Christian and me a huge bouquet of flowers.

"Mommy, when's our boat coming?" Leonie asked excitedly.

Her broken arm was a distant memory by then, but it had ensured that she didn't run away from the nursery school again.

"It should be here around midday," I replied.

"You need to change into a dress, too," she said to me. "Uncle Christian's going to be on the boat, too, isn't he?"

"Yes, he's already on board. And he's coming with Grandpa and Captain Palatin and the new crew of the *Storm Rose*."

We had been surprised at how quickly we'd found people who were prepared to work for us even though we weren't able to pay much.

My father wouldn't have missed the first voyage of the *Storm Rose* for the world. Christian was also fired up about it and had come up with the idea of inviting Georg Palatin and his wife to accompany them on the maiden voyage. I would have loved to sail with them, but I had too many things to organize. There would be other trips as she sailed around the harbor of Sassnitz and a short ways out to sea.

I fixed Leonie's hair—these days she no longer wanted to wear it loose, but held in place with an array of colorful barrettes—then slipped into an elegant blue and white sheath dress I had found in a boutique in Stralsund. When we were ready, we left the house.

"Kitty!" Leonie called out. She didn't run after the cat but pointed to where it had settled down beside our car. The cat jumped up in alarm but then recognized us and relaxed a little. It still wasn't tame enough to let us touch it, but accepted the food I left out for it. I was optimistic that one day it would allow us to pick it up and take it to the vet.

Leonie and I got into the car, then drove to Sassnitz. As we arrived at the harbor, a few people had already begun to gather around the landing platform. It was much too early, but they probably wanted to make sure they got the best positions. I had organized a reception with a buffet to welcome the *Storm Rose*, and the catering firm was busy setting up. After a word with them, I rummaged nervously in my purse and drew out the speech I was intending to make.

I was extremely nervous. I had no problem with presenting proposals to my clients, but I had never delivered such a long speech. I went through the points one more time but found nothing that sounded clumsy.

A little later the first invited guests arrived. I greeted those I knew in person, and also spoke to a few who'd come in response to the newspaper report. I didn't see Hartmann yet. Maybe he had changed his mind.

The minutes drew out. I looked at the clock. A quarter to twelve. Enough of the personal greetings; I'd have to continue with those later. I took my place on the dock together with Leonie and gazed out to sea.

The *Storm Rose* appeared at the entrance to the harbor at 12:01 precisely. The chatter of the crowd behind me suddenly fell silent. Holding my daughter's hand tightly, I looked in fascination at our boat. Propelled by her new engine, she plowed her way through the blue-green Baltic, gradually growing larger as she approached. The blue-painted hull reflected the color of the water, and the white superstructure gleamed in the sunlight. The passenger cabin had new windows, which flashed in the sun. During the restoration works the last of the fishing tackle had been removed, so that the *Storm Rose* now looked completely like a passenger boat.

My only slight disappointment was that no one had responded to my search in the Internet forums—maybe Palatin would now tell me Lea's story so that I could add it to everything else I knew about the boat.

But at that moment my chest swelled with pride. We'd done it—the *Storm Rose* sailed again! And on board were all the people, apart from Leonie, who meant the most to me. What more could I want? A loud blast of the boat's horn sounded across the harbor. Applause broke out as the captain docked the boat safely. The passengers then disembarked: my parents, Christian, and finally Georg Palatin and his wife. They assembled in their allocated places of honor.

I looked across at Christian, who gave me a wonderful smile and a nod of encouragement. I was already looking forward to our private celebration that night. But first I had my duty to perform. I handed Leonie over to Christian, stepped behind the small lectern, and switched the microphone on. I looked out over the crowd for the first time. What a throng! The boat could obviously still cause a sensation, even among younger people. I took a deep breath, then began.

"Ladies and gentlemen, I'm delighted to welcome you here for the occasion of the maiden voyage of the *Storm Rose*. Not only is this boat going to be a new jewel in the crown of Sassnitz harbor, but she can also look back on an eventful history. Originally built as a fishing cutter, her wartime task was to clear mines. In 1959 Georg Palatin bought her and transformed her into a tour boat. It gives me great pleasure to welcome him here today."

I gave the people time to applaud and looked across at Palatin, who was holding his wife's hand and looking a little embarrassed. But he had given me his express permission to mention him, even though he still said he didn't want any fame or glory.

"At that time Georg Palatin had fallen in love with his wife, who is still here by his side, and thus began a new, adventure-filled episode in this boat's life. In order to be able to marry her, Georg Palatin took the huge risk of helping his wife and three other people to escape across the East German border."

My eyes scanned the crowd for Hartmann and found him near the bar. His face was as if made of stone. *Good,* I thought. *Now's your chance.*

"Between then and 1988 Georg Palatin sailed out several times to rescue escapees from the water or pick them up from unsafe boats. Once the *Storm Rose* even came under fire. It was a huge personal risk."

Thunderous applause broke out once again. I nodded at the captain, whose cheeks were burning red. He may not have wanted the acknowledgment, but he'd earned it.

"Georg Palatin is a very important part of the boat's history, but after the Iron Curtain came down he had to sell the *Storm Rose*. The boat lay unused for a long time, until Christian Merten and I discovered her here in the harbor. We immediately fell in love with her and decided to restore her to her former glory. At that time, we had no idea of her background.

"But one day I found a letter on board that gave us a crucial clue. It was written by a woman named Lea and told a small part of her own escape story. We tried to find this woman, but to date haven't succeeded. But nevertheless we want to thank her. Even though we don't know her true story, nor how badly she suffered, she was the one who set us on the right track. Now it's up to us to continue the *Storm Rose*'s story. That's what I want to celebrate with you today. Thank you for being here with us!"

Fresh applause broke out. I was simply relieved that the speech had gone well. I went over to Christian and kissed him, then greeted my parents with a kiss.

"You did very well, my girl," my father said and hugged me tight.

"No, you and your friends—you're the ones who've done well. Just look how magnificent she is! And how many people have come to see her."

During the next few minutes, crowds gathered. The first line was for the trip around the harbor, which was free of charge that day, and the other for the buffet. Christian and I went around, greeting more guests. While we were briefly separated, Hartmann came up to me.

"Congratulations, Frau Hansen. The boat's looking truly magnificent."

"Thank you; that's very kind of you. You must take a trip around the harbor."

"Thank you, I certainly will. And I stick by what I said before. I'll be happy to support you in any way I can."

At that moment Christian came up to us. I felt awkward, but we'd known he couldn't avoid meeting Hartmann eventually.

"Christian, this is Herr Hartmann. Herr Hartmann, this is my friend, Christian Merten."

I introduced them as dispassionately as I could. The men looked at one another. Did Hartmann remember him? Surely not. He and Jonas Merten had never met. Christian offered to shake his hand, poker-faced.

"I'm pleased to meet you."

"As I've just said to your partner, she's a wonderful boat. And I'll be happy to give you any support I can."

"That's very kind of you," Christian replied.

I could sense just how much effort it took to control his feelings. Hartmann noticed nothing. Fortunately, there were others behind him waiting their turn to talk to us.

"I'm delighted that you've come, Herr Hartmann. Enjoy the celebrations," I said, giving him a nod. I led Christian away.

"You did well," I whispered in his ear.

"What do you mean? I didn't do anything."

"Exactly!" I kissed him, full of pride.

We suddenly noticed a woman making her way toward us. She was around sixty, wearing a light-colored lacy summer dress and a white hat on her blond, medium-length hair.

"Frau Hansen, Herr Merten," she said and shook our hands. "I'm Lea. Lea Petrowski. Formerly Lea Paulsen."

I stared at her as if struck by lightning. Anyone could have claimed to be Lea, but I hadn't mentioned her surname in my speech.

"Really? You're . . . ?"

She didn't look like the delicate, elfin woman I'd imagined. This was a woman who could take any knocks life threw at her.

"I wrote the letter. And if you want proof, my letter was to my friend Bob, whom I was wanting to reach when I left the country. But things turned out rather differently . . ."

Christian and I exchanged glances. He was as unable to believe it as I was.

"But . . . why have you approached us only now?"

"Sometimes you just have to be ready to tell your story. I regularly visit forums in which former East German defectors talk to one another. Someone I know from one of the forums believed he recognized my details. When I saw your post I knew full well it was me you were looking for, but I still held back. When I heard that the *Storm Rose* was ready to sail, I decided that the time had come. So, are you still interested?"

***

Half an hour later the two of us were sitting in the café where Christian had taken me when we heard Leonie had run away. Everyone else was still celebrating. Leonie was with Christian and my parents, and

Captain Palatin was looking as though he wanted to set out on another long voyage. I'd return to them soon, but I wanted to hear the story of the woman who had instigated it all, and I had promised not to make it public.

I ordered two latte macchiatos and laid the letter before us on the table. She smiled and touched it cautiously.

"I haven't thought any more about it," she said. "But I clearly remember my reasons for writing it. Your advertisement brought it all back. I discussed it with my husband and he said I should tell you what happened."

The waitress brought us our coffee, and Lea began to talk.

"Bob was from America. His real name was Nolan, but because he looked like Bob Dylan I always called him Bob. We met during a summer vacation by Lake Balaton and I almost thought him crazy when he claimed to be from the US, because he spoke such excellent German. It turned out that he'd been a student in Hamburg. During the vacation I had enough time to get to know him better, and I was sure there was no nicer man. He spoiled me and sent me things I couldn't have dreamed of in East Germany."

She paused for a moment, smiling.

"I'm sure you can imagine what my parents would have said about an 'enemy of the state' like he was. Not only was he from the West, but from the USA, the embodiment of evil and the Soviet Union's major opponent in the Cold War."

"I certainly can imagine it," I replied, since even though I hadn't been given the full picture in our civic studies classes, I'd found out a lot in retrospect.

"In brief, it wasn't to be. When my father wanted to force me to go to the Soviet Union with the FDJ for the Druzhba Pipeline Project, the moment had come for me to make my decision. Do you know about the Druzhba Pipeline?"

I shook my head. East Germany had become history before I was old enough to join the FDJ.

"The Druzhba Pipeline was a project to lay a natural gas pipeline between East Germany and the Soviet Union. FDJ volunteers went to help with the construction in the Ukrainian Soviet Socialist Republic. My father, who worked at the Schwedt oil processing plant, wanted to force me to volunteer in order to improve my prospects of studying at Moscow University. I would have disappeared to work on the pipeline for months, if not years. That was the last thing I wanted. And the only person who was excited about me studying in Moscow was my father.

"When Bob came to visit me again, I told him my problem and we decided I would escape from East Germany. He had a friend who was a windsurfer and had the novel idea of windsurfing our way across the Baltic. This windsurfer friend in turn knew someone in Ahrenshoop who was willing to make the journey, so one dark, foggy night I ran off and made my way there, where I began to make a pair of surfboards with Manfred, as he was called. It was quite difficult because the materials were hard to come by. We tried to find as many windsurfing magazines and newspapers as we could. Manfred's grandma helped us a little when she went on trips to the West by bringing back the ones he wrote down for her. These magazines contained plenty of drawings and instructions of how to build a board yourself.

"An acquaintance of Manfred's was fortunate enough to obtain the materials we needed on the black market. All well and good— our project gradually began to take shape. But during the construction something happened—I lost my heart. It happened in Manfred's grandma's yard. She was a lovely old lady, who lived in a house like a witch's cottage with a fairytale yard. All kinds of fruit trees and bushes grew there alongside magnificent flowers. Maybe it was the magic spell of the gooseberries, but I fell in love with Manfred. Gradually. At first

I thought it was friendship. But I increasingly began to suspect that it was love. I was faced with a dilemma. I also loved Bob—who would I choose?"

She took a drink of her coffee before immersing herself in her past again.

"When the day came for me to leave, Manfred was determined to come with me. Our surfboards may have been a bit makeshift, but they would do the job. We floated out in the evening, in the hope that the coastguards wouldn't be able to see us. However, our greatest enemy wasn't the East German navy, but the sea itself. We got separated and I had no idea where Manfred was. I tried desperately to wait, but the weather didn't improve, and I knew I wouldn't be able to hold out for long in my cobbled-together wet suit. I had almost reached the end of my strength when a boat appeared and took me on board. It was the *Storm Rose*. At first I took her to be a fishing cutter, but then I realized she was a boat that transported escapees. That evening they took four more people on board. But I could think only of Manfred. I didn't want to be without him. Yes, I was sure then that I loved him. But where was he? Had he been caught by the coastguard? Or had he gone back? Was he looking for me, perhaps?

"I told the captain what had happened. He promised he'd search for Manfred provided he didn't have to enter East German waters. Full of fear, I kept a lookout for him, but we didn't find him. I was in complete despair. I was sure that Bob would be waiting for me in Hamburg, but did I still want him? Was my two-timing to blame for me losing Manfred?

"I wrote a letter to Bob telling him that we had to break up. I hoped that this action would give me Manfred back. And as if my writing contained a kind of magic, he was finally found. He was floating on the water, completely exhausted. Palatin, his crew, and the other escapees hauled him on board. I cried tears of joy, and shortly before going to the hospital with Manfred I gave Palatin the letter, asking him to destroy it. But he must have hidden it on board the boat."

"To leave a clue for those who came after."

"Probably. But maybe he just needed something as an emergency stopgap to fill a hole, who knows?"

Lost in thought, Lea gazed into her glass, which contained only a few dregs in the bottom. My glass was almost full, but the coffee had gone cold.

"In any case, I'm glad you found the letter. It was the happiest time of my life."

"What about Bob? Did you ever see him again?"

Lea nodded. "Yes, after reunification. I looked for him, actually, because I wouldn't have had any peace if I'd simply left him in the lurch. When I finally tracked him down, he was married with four children. And I'm glad to say he wasn't angry with me anymore."

She smiled to herself, and I could tell that she didn't want to say any more about him.

"In any case, I had Manfred. Nothing else mattered. I was so happy that he'd survived. We went to Uelzen and from there to Amrum, where we learned to surf properly. It wasn't until after reunification that we returned to Ahrenshoop. Now we live in his grandma's little house with the magical garden. Maybe you'll be able to visit us there one day?"

"I'd love to," I replied. I called the waitress over for the bill. "But first we have to take a trip on the *Storm Rose*."

She nodded, and a little later we left the café and headed back to the harbor. Christian and Leonie were waiting for me.

"So, all the secrets out in the open?" he asked with a playful wink. I looked at Lea. She nodded.

"Well, come on then. The *Storm Rose* has just come back in and she's ready for a new tour."

I took my daughter's hand, and we went on board together. As the cold sea breeze played on my face, I closed my eyes and knew that my new life had now begun. Of course, all the things I'd experienced over the last few months would still be on my mind, but I'd been given the chance to work through it all. And to pass it on to my daughter in good time.

As the *Storm Rose* set out, I nestled up to Christian and held Leonie tight. Now I had everything I needed.

About the Author

Photo © Hans Scherhaufer

Bestselling author Corina Bomann was born in Parchim, Germany. She originally trained as a dental nurse, but her love of stories compelled her to follow her passion for writing. Bomann now lives in Berlin. *The Moonlit Garden*, her English debut, was a #1 Kindle bestseller.

About the Translator

Photo © 2014 Sandra Dalton

Alison Layland is a novelist and translator from German, French, and Welsh into English. A member of the Institute of Translation and Interpreting and the Society of Authors, she has won a number of prizes for her fiction writing and translation. Her debut novel, the literary thriller *Someone Else's Conflict*, was published in 2014 by Honno Press. She has also translated a number of novels, including Corina Bomann's *The Moonlit Garden*. She is married with two children and lives in the beautiful and inspiring countryside of Wales, United Kingdom.